SLAYERS

SLAYERS

C.J. HILL

FEIWEL AND FRIENDS
New York

A FEIWEL AND FRIENDS BOOK
An Imprint of Macmillan

Library of Congress Cataloging-in-Publication Data Available

ISBN: 978-0-312-61414-0

Book design by Véronique Lefèvre Sweet

Feiwel and Friends logo designed by Filomena Tuosto

First Edition: 2011

1 3 5 7 9 10 8 6 4 2

macteenbooks.com

To my children, Asenath, Luke, James, Faith, and Arianna,
for the sacrifices they've made, and all the un-gourmet
meals they've eaten because their mom is a writer.

To my husband, Guy, who made many of those un-gourmet meals,
as well as helped me with car pool, scheduling, and everything else.

To my parents, for always supporting me. Thanks, Dad, for
trying to teach me grammar—even if it never stuck. (This is probably a good
place to also thank all the lovely copy editors who fix my grammar.)

Thanks to George Nicholson and Erica Silverman, who believed in my
dragons and, more importantly, believed in me. Also thanks to my ever-
tactful editor, Liz Szabla, for bearing with me through the rewrites.

SLAYERS

PROLOGUE

Mrs. Harriet Davis had never been afraid of dragons—until now. The
dragon in her dream hovered above Washington, D.C., watching traffic.
Against the fading light of the evening, its body seemed first brown,
then maroon, then the color of blood. The dragon turned its head side to
side, presenting a face that looked like a cross between a crocodile and
a cat, although with more disdain than a cat and less patience than a
crocodile. In size and wingspan it was comparable to a small commuter
plane, but the similarities ended there. It darted toward the street, its
batlike wings outstretched while it searched among fleeing pedestrians.
It was all beast: a primeval predator with golden eyes that showed more
than just hunger. Anger lurked there—purpose, something evil.

Harriet couldn't see the faces of the people who ran down the street,
ducking into building doorways or under parked cars. Their panic blurred
together in her mind. Her attention was riveted on the dragon.

It picked up a van with its claws the same way birds pluck fish from
the ocean. The dragon drew the vehicle to its face, viewed the screaming occupants, then with a growl of disappointment let the van fall. It

crashed into the street, the sound of glass and metal mingling with car horns. When the van finally stopped shuddering, it lay on its side, wheels spinning futilely in the darkening night.

The dragon dashed upward, turned, and surveyed the scene again. Dozens of cars clogged the intersections. The ones that hadn't already stalled were rolling to useless stops. Harriet didn't understand why this was, just as she didn't know why the traffic lights had gone out.

The dragon swooped down, picked up a screaming blonde woman, and examined her. It seemed dissatisfied by her thrashing and dropped her.

Harriet tried to open her eyes, tried to make the dream stop. She didn't want to see the woman fall, didn't want to hear the sound that came when she hit the ground.

It didn't work. The events unfolded in perfect clarity.

The dragon pushed upward again and soared toward the tidal basin.

And then the dream changed and Harriet was no longer just viewing the events, she was standing there underneath the cherry trees, a soft breeze pushing against her maternity nightgown and the feel of cold grass beneath her feet. The Jefferson Memorial was the closest structure, but it didn't offer much protection. It was an outdoor monument with a huge bronze statue of Jefferson surrounded by columns underneath a domed roof. She didn't have a lot of choices, though. The dragon was tearing through the sky in her direction.

She wasn't sure how she'd gotten here or why she was out during rush hour in her pajamas. Time didn't allow for those thoughts. She ran. She wasn't fast. The baby, due in two weeks, pressed into her ribs with every step she took. Her already crowded lungs strained to take in enough air. Tourists rushed past her; one nearly knocked her down.

The monument was still a couple of minutes away and the dragon was drawing nearer. Screams behind Harriet drew her attention and she looked over her shoulder. The dragon had stopped long enough to scoop up another blonde woman.

Was there a pattern? Harriet didn't know, but wished her own hair wasn't blonde.

Her terror made her run faster. She stumbled up the memorial steps, breathing hard, then staggered the rest of the way across the stone floor. Once there, she huddled with two dozen people at the feet of Thomas Jefferson.

They weren't protected. Not really. The memorial had no doors or walls, just the large, marble columns. But perhaps the dragon wouldn't notice them here, out of the way.

She didn't mind the press of people around her. They were warm, and the cold from the floor seeped through her thin nightgown. She shivered, shook really. Inside her, the baby kicked and pushed, seemingly as alarmed as she was. Could he feel her fear?

She peered through the columns into the night. Not much was visible. What had happened to the lights? It was late enough that they should have come on.

"Where did that thing come from?" a woman next to Harriet whispered.

"Shut up," someone said. "We've got to be perfectly still. Perfectly quiet."

No one else spoke, although how could the dragon not hear them when Harriet's breathing was so loud, so fast?

The screams in the distance stopped. The sound of beating wings filled the air, and then silence.

Silence.

Silence.

She caught the whiff of something she couldn't place. Something oily and unnatural. Did dragons have a scent?

Harriet wished she had her cell phone so she could at least text her husband, Allen. She desperately wanted to tell him where she was and that she loved him. Had she told him that today? She couldn't remember.

A brownish red tail dropped down the side of the building. It swished back and forth. The dragon was sitting on top of the roof.

Harriet swallowed hard. Her pulse hammered in her ears, and she pressed her back farther into the foot of the statue. She could hear the domed ceiling above her creak as the dragon shifted its weight. Would the roof hold, or would they be crushed?

She took hold of a man's hand who sat next to her, even though she had no idea who he was. He squeezed her hand back. She put her other hand on her stomach, shielding her baby the best she could. They had already picked out a name for him. Ryker. Last week she'd stenciled it onto the wall of the nursery in flowing silver letters. She'd poured love into those letters, hope, promise, and now she couldn't do anything to protect him. This hurt worse than losing her own life.

The baby kicked against her hand, agitated, as though he wanted to tell her something.

Then the dragon's tail moved upward and disappeared.

Let it have flown away, Harriet thought, but she didn't hear the beat of wings.

Seconds passed. The dragon stepped down onto the concrete outside the monument. Each step made the ground vibrate. Harriet had to clamp her lips together so she didn't cry out.

The dragon's head came into view and she noticed for the first time that he had a white patch on his forehead, diamond-shaped, that stood out like a glistening tattoo. She didn't consider it for long. The dragon turned two golden eyes on the crowd, searching, and then his gaze narrowed in on her. He let out a screech of triumph. It intermingled with the crowd's immediate and unanimous scream.

The dragon lunged forward, pushing its head through the columns. Harriet stumbled to her feet, a shriek tearing at her throat. She had to get away.

The columns held the rest of the dragon back, and it snapped its jaws in frustration. Its head reared back and breathed in a long, snarling breath. Harriet knew what would come next—fire. She, and everyone around her, scrambled to the other side of the monument. Some people ran out completely, but Harriet only made it to the far columns.

Then the fire came. Luckily Jefferson took the brunt of the attack. His bronze exterior blackened in the flames, his solemn expression erased in soot. The heat licked around Harriet, fluttering her nightgown against her leg and making her gasp. She raised her hand to protect her eyes.

Then the heat disappeared. And so did the dragon.

Where had it gone? More importantly, was it safer to run away or stay here? The night was growing darker, and she couldn't see a single light, not anywhere in the city.

A few days ago she had heard a professor of medieval history—Dr. Bartholemew—on a radio program. He'd claimed that dragons were real and would be unleashed on humanity again. She had laughed and told Allen, "Well, at least Bigfoot will have someone to keep him company."

But this Dr. Bartholemew was right. She wished she had listened to the rest of the program.

"Is it gone?" a man beside her asked.

Before she could answer, a searing hot claw grabbed her shoulder from behind.

Harriet gasped, let out a strangled scream, and found herself sitting up in bed.

Allen threw off his covers and turned on the lamp on their nightstand. His blue eyes were wide, but not quite awake as he jolted out of the bed. "What is it? Is the baby coming?"

She shook her head and drew her knees up, trembling, gasping. "A dragon grabbed me! Its claws burned into my back!"

Allen stared at her a moment, then laid back down with a thump and shut his eyes. "Okay, let me know when it's the baby."

Harriet clutched the blanket, her voice choked with emotion. "It flew through the city killing people, but it was looking for me. I know it was."

Allen flipped off the light. "It was a bad dream. The best thing to do—"

"It wasn't a dream." She reached around him and turned the lamp back on. "It was real. I can still smell it. Can't you?"

He took a deep breath. "Nope."

"My shoulder burns like crazy." She slid her nightgown away from her skin and gasped. Three long welts ran across her shoulder and down her back. "Look!" she cried. It was proof she would rather have not found. A wave of nausea swept over her.

Allen sat up, squinting at the welts. "How did you get those?"

Her voice spiraled upward. "I told you. It grabbed me."

"That isn't . . ." He was completely awake now and examining the place where she'd slept. "It must have been something else—something stung you and you had a bad dream."

She would have liked to believe him, but didn't. "What would leave marks this big? Do you think we have a colony of steroid-taking scorpions in our bed that just happen to sting in rows?" She pushed the covers off and swung her feet to the floor, then put one hand over her stomach, protecting the baby. She walked to the TV that sat on her dresser. Certainly the news would have something on about the dragon attack.

She clicked through the stations, flipping through infomercials and late-night movies—all regular programming.

"What are you doing?" Allen asked.

She turned back to her husband, puzzled. "Maybe the news stations don't know yet. I think there was some sort of power outage."

"Harriet . . ."

In the span of a sigh, her panic shifted to frustration and then to tears. "It was real and it was evil. It wanted to kill me."

He got up from the bed, walked over, and pulled her into a careful embrace so as not to touch her welts. "Harriet."

"You don't even believe me," she said, sobbing. Then she lay her head against his chest and repeated. "It wasn't just a dream."

The phone rang in Dr. Alastair Bartholemew's house. He rolled over and hit the alarm clock, then hit it again when the noise didn't stop. It took him a few more seconds to realize his alarm didn't play Beethoven's Fifth—that was the new phone. He blinked at the glowing numbers on the clock face: 2:11 a.m. If someone was calling him now, there must be an emergency. He clumsily grabbed the phone. "Hello."

"I'm sorry to call you so late, Dr. Bartholemew," a male voice said. "Especially since you don't know us, but we listened to you when you were on Coast to Coast, and, well, my wife wants to talk to you."

Alastair rubbed his eyes, and considered hanging up.

Alastair's wife, Shirley, opened one eye to check what the noise was. He waved for her to go back to sleep. "Radio fans," he whispered, his hand over the mouthpiece. Since the show last week, he'd heard from medieval buffs, people who thought they had been dragons in a past life, and people who thought they talked to invisible dragons.

Shirley groaned and turned over on her side, pulling a pillow over her head.

The man on the phone went on. "My wife thinks she saw a dragon. Or at least she dreamed of one, but she woke up with foot-long welts running down her back. She said that's where it grabbed her."

And then Alastair was completely awake. His glance fell on Shirley and the still healing slash that striped across her swollen belly. "Is your wife pregnant?"

"Yes," the man said, surprised. "How did you know that?"

"Do you live in D.C.?"

"Fairfax," the man said, his voice wary now.

It wasn't far away. "Give me your address," Alastair said, already out of bed and heading toward his closet. "I need to talk to your wife in person."

Alastair reached the Davises' home a little after 3:00 a.m. It was a small house but in an upscale neighborhood, the type where every bush and tree had been trimmed by a team of landscapers.

Alastair had thrown on some clothes but hadn't brushed his hair, and now he smoothed it down with one hand. His hair was prematurely graying and already more gray than brown at his bangs and temples, but he didn't mind. It counterbalanced a face that otherwise looked perpetually young. His university peers failed to take him seriously more often than not, and he wanted every appearance of age and experience he could get.

He knocked at the door, then stood impatiently, staring at the swirling woodgrain lines in front of him.

After a minute, Allen Davis opened the door. He was young, probably in his mid-twenties, with short black hair and rumpled clothes.

"Thanks for coming," Allen said, but his voice betrayed his doubt. He probably already regretted calling. He eyed Alastair uncertainly and motioned for him to come inside. "Harriet is looking at pictures on the Internet. She's trying to find a dragon like the one she saw."

They walked the short distance to the kitchen, where a blonde woman sat at the table, her laptop in front of her and a bottle of antacids opened next to it. She had a blanket wrapped around her even though it wasn't cold. From the size of her stomach, she was probably eight or nine months along.

Alastair smiled and shook her hand. "I'm glad you called. It's important that we talk." He pulled up the chair next to her and smiled again, keeping his voice casual. "My wife is pregnant, too. We're having a girl. How about you?"

She laid her hand across her belly. "A boy."

Allen sat down on a third chair. "So it's normal for women to have crazy dreams when they're pregnant, right? What I can't figure out is the claw marks. How did those get there?"

Harriet ignored her husband and clicked on an image on her laptop. "I haven't seen anything like the dragon I saw. The Chinese dragons are too skinny, but they have the whiskers right. It had wings like a bat." She closed one image and opened another: an elaborately colored dragon whose neck should have belonged to a swan instead of something that breathed fire.

Alastair nodded at Harriet. "Did the dragon you saw have golden eyes and a diamond on its forehead?"

She turned back to him. "Yes, how did you know?"

He noticed, as though he were a foreigner coming to America, all the electric appliances in the kitchen. The fridge, dishwasher, oven, stove, lights, cordless phone, ceiling fan, and computer. How dependant they were on it. What a long way civilization had come from the Dark Ages when monsters lived.

Alastair dragged his attention back to Harriet. "Because they're real. I've spent years studying them." He hesitated, wondering whether he should add that he'd seen some himself. Most people labeled him as crazy when he made that claim, and once somebody thought you were insane, it didn't matter what you said to them. But Harriet might believe the truth.

Allen let out a disbelieving grunt. "You studied them? How? By reading fairy tales? You can't be serious."

Which was the usual response. Just once Alastair wanted to say, "Look, I'm not an idiot. I wouldn't have spent half my life researching dragons if I didn't have proof." But now wasn't the time to snap. Patiently, he said, "Stories of dragons are found in nearly every culture—from Europe to China to South America to Hawaii. Even the Bible mentions dragons."

Allen's eyebrows dipped. "The Bible doesn't talk about dragons."

Alastair picked up Harriet's laptop and handed it to him. "Check. Run a search."

While he did, Alastair turned his attention back to Harriet. "I became a professor of medieval civilizations specifically so I would have access to early documents about dragons. Trust me when I say I'm an expert. The reason you dreamed of a dragon, the reason your body was so sure one wounded you that your skin blistered in response, is that your mind already knows dragons exist. It's genetic memory." Alastair tapped one finger against his temple. "Your subconscious is warning you that dragons are near, that you need to prepare for when they come back."

Harriet grew pale. She pulled the blanket tighter around her. "Come back from where? How?"

Alastair leaned forward, going automatically into professor mode. "Medieval records report that dragons can choose one of two gestation times for their eggs: a short span—which lasts between fifteen to twenty years, or a long span—approximately one hundred and fifty years. It's their way of escaping predators." He kept his eyes trained on hers. "Unfortunately, viable dragon eggs are somewhere in the D.C. area."

"You're sure?" Harriet's voice came out low, like a stone dropped into the silence of a pool. "Where do we go to escape from them? How do we get away?"

"We don't escape," Alastair said. "We fight."

Harriet gripped her blanket. "It picked up a van like it was a toy. It breathed fire. We can't fight it. You'd need missiles or military jets—"

He shook his head. "Dragons can outmaneuver planes and missiles. Their skin is radar absorbing, which means that they can't be tracked. They also have another advantage. When they roar, they send out an electromagnetic pulse that fries all electric components in the area." He went on shaking his head. "It's almost as if they were preparing, even back then, to fight us in the future."

Allen broke into the conversation. "This is what the Book of Revelations says about dragons: 'And she being with child cried, travailing in birth and pained to be delivered. And there appeared another wonder in heaven; and behold a great red dragon.'" He looked up at his wife and some of the color drained from his face. He skimmed the verses on the screen. "'And the dragon stood before the woman which was ready to be delivered, for to devour her child as soon as it was born. And she brought forth a man child . . .'"

Allen turned to Alastair, his eyes wide. "This isn't literally describing something that will happen, is it?"

"Those verses are probably symbolic of the Christ child. But the point is that even the Bible referenced dragons, so—"

Allen waved a hand at the computer. "I don't remember ever seeing a dragon at the Christmas nativity scene. One did show up in my wife's dream, though, and it tried to kill her and our baby son."

"Let me explain some more," Alastair said soothingly. "Do you remember back in the Middle Ages, how the alchemists tried to find a way to create gold? History got that wrong. They sought to create liquid gold—a substance that would give people the powers needed to conquer dragons. Luckily, they found it. Those superenhanced knights would have destroyed dragons altogether if some of the dragons hadn't used their long gestation periods to outlive them."

Allen wiped his palms on his jeans. "You know how to make this liquid gold stuff?"

Alastair realized he hadn't explained that part. "I don't need to. Once the knights drank the liquid gold, it changed their DNA. They passed that DNA down to future generations. When a dragon is close to hatching, its heartbeat emits a pulse that turns on the DNA of any of the dragon knights' descendants who are within a mile radius." He leaned over and put his hand on top of Harriet's arm. "You had the dream because you're a descendant of a dragon knight. At some point, you went near a dragon egg in the D.C. area."

She yanked her arm away and let out a half-strangled gasp. "That's why the dragon was searching for me? It knew I was a descendant?"

"Yes."

She stood up so quickly her blanket fell away and her chair toppled to the floor with a sharp crack. She didn't bother to right it. "I'm not fighting that thing. I don't have any special powers."

"You don't," Alastair agreed. "But your son does. The pulse can only turn on the DNA of babies." He gestured to her stomach. "Those who are still in the womb."

Allen stood up, joining his wife. "Our baby is not going anywhere near a dragon."

"Not when he's a baby," Alastair said. "We could have a decade or two before the eggs hatch—but not longer than that. Otherwise the dragon embryo wouldn't have been developed enough to trigger your son's DNA and your genetic awareness of it. But when your child is old enough, I'll need to train him to use his powers. The new generation of slayers are our only hope for defeating the dragons when they come."

Allen stepped in front of his wife, making a protective barrier between her and Alastair. "Wait. We're not agreeing to any of this." His hands clenched and unclenched at his side. "You can't walk in here and tell us you're taking our son."

This was the problem of getting ahead of yourself while trying to explain things. Alastair took a step back, to appear as nonthreatening as possible. "I'm not taking your son. He'll still live with you. I'll teach him when he's older—during the summers so he won't miss school. He won't be alone. There are other descendants. I'm not sure how many, but I know of one—my daughter. My wife had the dream, too."

Harriet's head shook so quickly she looked like she was having a standing seizure. "If there are other children, then you don't need our son."

"Of course he's needed." Especially since Alastair didn't know where any of the other children were. After Shirley's dream, he had gone on the radio show hoping for a flurry of calls from pregnant women who had dreamed of dragon attacks. So far, Harriet was the only one.

"No," Harriet said. "Absolutely not. We'll leave. We'll go someplace where it won't find us."

Allen's lips thinned into a tight line. "You can't seriously ask our son to fight—"

Alastair took a step toward Harriet. "You've seen a dragon. You understand what it will do to the city if we don't stop it."

She winced and took hold of her side. Pain, maybe labor pain, flashed across her face. Allen put his arm around her shoulder. "Go lie down," he told her. To Alastair, he said, "It's time for you to go."

Alastair opened his mouth to speak, but didn't know what to say. His own wife had been so much more understanding. But then, his wife had known dragons were real before she got pregnant. She'd realized having a slayer for a child was a possibility. "We're all tired," Alastair finally said. "You need time to process this."

Allen stared. Harriet pressed her hand to her lips while tears pooled in her eyes.

I'm asking a difficult thing of her, Alastair realized. She's just in shock. But now she knew lives were at stake. She would eventually do the right thing.

"You have my phone number," Alastair said. "Call me when you want to talk again."

Harriet didn't call. After two days, Alastair drove to their house. He would address their worries. He would appeal to their sense of duty. He would beg, if necessary.

A FOR SALE sign stood in the middle of their yard.

Well, that was a bit drastic, wasn't it?

He strode to the door, noticing a lock box already on the handle. He rang the doorbell. No one answered. He peered into the front window, his frustration growing. The furniture was gone. The whole place had been cleared out except for miscellaneous papers and books, things scattered on the floor that Harriet and Allen hadn't bothered packing.

The disappointment felt like a puncture wound in his chest. They were running away from the dragon instead of staying to help to fight it—instead of helping his daughter fight it.

I've failed, he thought. I knew where another child was, and now he's gone. How could Alastair possibly find this boy when it was time to train him? And what's more, how could he find any other children without producing the same results from their parents? Going on the radio again might turn up more pregnant women with dragon dreams. But when he told them the truth, what would keep the rest of them from bolting?

The children needed training; without it, they'd probably all end up dead, victims of their inexperience. Like Nathan. Alastair pushed the thought away. This wasn't the time to think about his brother.

Alastair trudged around the outside of the house, checking each window. Looking for . . . well, he wasn't sure what he was looking for. He just had to make sure they were really gone.

He came to a small room, which, judging from the Noah's Ark stencils, was the nursery.

All his years of research and piecing things together. They meant nothing if he couldn't train enough heirs of the dragon knights. And now he had nothing to help him find this one.

Except for the child's name. Because there it was, stenciled on the wall. His name would be Ryker. Ryker Davis.

Alastair leaned against the window, staring at the name. "I will find you," he whispered. "I'll think of a way to find and train all of you."

CHAPTER 1

From the passenger side of her sister's BMW, Tori surveyed the camp parking lot. It was dirt, with no white lines, so cars were parked at odd angles. True, the surrounding forest had a picture-perfect beauty to it. The oak and maple trees crowded together, their thick branches perfectly still in the early summer sun. But the buildings seemed shabby. The paint was faded in places on the main lodge, and even if it hadn't been, it still would have looked boxy and spare—rundown, really.

The sign read ST. GEORGE AND THE DRAGON, with the word CAMP tacked up underneath the other words like it was an afterthought.

Tori made sure she had her registration confirmation, then slid her purse onto her shoulder. Her mom was supposed to have driven her here, but ended up having to host a party for senators and their wives instead. The job had then fallen to Tori's older sister, Aprilynne.

Aprilynne lowered her sunglasses enough to consider the stream of people making their way through the parking lot. "It's just what I thought. Riffraff, gangster wannabes, and probable orphans."

Tori refused to be disappointed, at least yet. "They're normal kids," she said.

"Exactly my point."

"It will be fun." Tori opened the car door, stepped out, and swatted at some gnats. Two teenage boys with squirt guns darted past and chased each other into the forest.

Aprilynne wrinkled her nose. "They're not even clean now, and camp is just starting."

"They're campers, not doctors performing surgery on me."

Aprilynne pushed a button on the dashboard and the trunk popped open. Tori slid out of the BMW and went around to the back to get her luggage.

Through the open window, Aprilynne said, "Why come here for a month when you could be at a *good* camp? What about that one you went to in Cancún last summer? I thought you liked it there."

"That was a finishing school at a resort, not a camp."

"I bet the mattresses here aren't clean. You'll come home with lice or something even more disgusting."

Tori hefted one suitcase and then the other out of the trunk. Each weighed a ton. She had probably brought too many shoes and books. She had packed some romances in case camp turned out to be boring, and then had thrown in a few classics from her English reading list in case camp turned out to be really, really boring. She shut the trunk of the car with a thud. "Tell Mom I'll call her later."

It was probably better that her mom wasn't here to see the camp, Tori decided. She undoubtedly would have found several reasons why it wasn't suitable.

Aprilynne hung her head out the window. "You realize your friends have a bet going to see how long you'll last here. Now that I've seen the place, I think I'll wager a hundred dollars on three days."

Tori grabbed her matching shoulder bag from the backseat of the BMW. "I've got my stuff. You can go now."

Aprilynne started up the car, then glanced back again. "You know, there's no point in being rich if you act poor."

Tori ignored the comment. She should have never told Aprilynne that some kids came to Dragon Camp on need-based scholarships. Aprilynne wasn't impressed by that type of largesse. She had only rolled her eyes and said, "You mean, not only is dragon camp made up of Renaissance Faire rejects, but they're all broke, too?"

The BMW pulled out of the parking lot going too fast—Aprilynne's normal driving speed—and soon nothing was left of her sister but a trail of dust and designer perfume hanging in the air.

Tori walked slowly toward the main building and the hand-printed sign that read REGISTER HERE. She pulled her two suitcases, wishing too late that she hadn't brought the good luggage. The dust would probably ruin the canvas by the time she made it to her cabin. Still, she couldn't very well pick them up and haul them around; they were too heavy. Several kids streamed around her, jostling by with backpacks and duffle bags.

How had they managed to fit everything they needed for a month into a duffle bag? Tori's shoes alone took up that much space. Still, it had been a mistake to pack so much, or maybe just a mistake to come. Maybe Aprilynne was right. That occasionally happened. The beds would be hard, the food bad, and the stuff about dragon classes that had made her want to come in the first place—a bunch of hype to attract little kids.

Besides, she was too old for a camp like this. She was sixteen and a half, and most of these kids didn't look much older than the required entrance age of eleven.

Tori pulled her suitcases harder. They bumped along on the uneven ground, nearly falling over.

She thought about the cell phone tucked into her shoulder bag. Aprilynne probably hadn't even reached the main road yet. If Tori called her now, the car would be back here in minutes. They could be somewhere shopping by early afternoon.

Tori stared at the road leaving camp and wondered who would win the bet. Had anyone wagered she would only last five minutes?

As Tori pulled, her biggest suitcase gave a shudder and tipped over. A cloud of dust rose from the ground at the point of its demise. She bent to straighten it, and as she did, her shoulder bag slid down her arm, knocking into her other suitcase, which then joined the first one on the ground. She let out a huff of exasperation, set the shoulder bag down, then righted her suitcases.

Stupid dirt parking lot. Fine, it *was* a camp, but every camp Tori had ever attended had paved parking lots and sidewalks between the cabins. By the look of it, this one had neither. A worse thought came to her: What if this camp didn't have real toilets? What if it had outhouses?

She walked slower, searching for a restroom among the rustic log cabins that were scattered through the forest. The words from the brochure came to her mind: *Step into the world of dragon slayers. Campers will practice fencing, horseback riding, archery, and everything a young dragon slayer needs to save the world. Older campers can apply what they learn in medieval history class for college credit.*

The college credit part had been new this year and had finally sold her parents on the idea. She had wanted to go to St. George for the last four summers, but every time she'd asked, her parents had sent her to a camp they deemed better. One with a wider range of facilities. A higher camper-to-counselor ratio. More exclusive clientele. Ones for horseback riders, ice skaters, or debutantes.

But Tori had wanted knights, or answers, or perhaps magic. She had wanted a place where people understood her and her crazy dragon obsession, because then maybe she could understand herself.

Tori looked from the dirt parking lot to the huddled log cabins and gray trash cans. This place had nothing even remotely magical about it. Probably all she'd get out of the summer was a succession of sunburns, a few rashes, and a healthy appreciation of bug spray.

Did any decent restaurants even deliver out here?

And did any of these kids really have lice? None of the kids who poured past her seemed to be scratching, but if Aprilynne mentioned it, then it might be a real concern. After all, Tori had never even been to a public school.

The thunking of her suitcases suddenly stopped, and the next moment she felt them lifted away from her.

She turned to see two guys about her age hefting her suitcases off the ground. Both wore mirrored sunglasses, and both were tall, perhaps six two. One was blond, with muscular arms covered in a layer of dirt. The other guy had wavy dark brown hair, or perhaps it was just uncombed. His biceps were equally impressive, or at least they would have been if they weren't holding onto her luggage. With the sunglasses hiding their eyes, she probably wouldn't even be able to identify them once they made off with her possessions.

Tori held onto her luggage straps fiercely. "There's nothing of value in here—only my clothes—and if you don't let go, I'll scream."

The brunet set her suitcase down and turned to the other guy. "I don't want her on my team. You get her."

The blond shook his head. "No way. It's my turn to choose, and I've already got Lilly. You get this one, pal."

The brunet peered over the rim of his sunglasses at Tori. "We're not stealing your luggage. We're carrying them to your cabin—unless you want to drag these things across camp by yourself." He picked up her suitcase again, moving it from one hand to another. "What do you have in here anyway, your lead collection?"

Tori blushed and let go of the luggage straps. "Sorry. I didn't know the camp had bellhops."

The blond groaned and walked past her. The brunet forced a smile in her direction. "We're not bellhops. We're campers who happen to be doing you a favor."

"Oh, sorry. I didn't know . . ."

He walked past her shaking his head, which she supposed meant that tipping them was out of the question. She followed after him awkwardly. He picked up his pace. Not only were these guys strong, they weren't going to wait for her. She tried to keep up, but her platform sandals proved more decorative than useful, and pebbles and bits of twigs wedged into them as she walked. With every step, she fell farther behind.

This was off to a great start.

"Maybe she isn't—," the blond said to his friend in a voice low enough that most people wouldn't have heard it. Tori's hearing had always been exceptional.

"Dr. B thinks she is. Why else would she be here?"

If the blond had an answer to this question, he didn't give it, which was too bad. Tori was beginning to wonder herself.

The guys hauled her luggage into the lodge. Instead of setting her suitcases next to the front desk, where younger campers stood in noisy lines waiting to check in, the two went around the desk and down a hallway. The blond knocked on a door, only then glancing back to see if Tori had followed.

A voice called, "Come in," and the guys disappeared inside. Tori went in, too, taking off her sunglasses to let her eyes adjust to the light. The room looked like any small office: shelves lined the wall and a large metal desk was parked in the middle of the room. Books, pencils, and photos frames cluttered its surface. A middle-aged man with wire-rimmed glasses smiled as she walked over. He was tall, slightly overweight, and his thick gray hair had a sort of Einstein disarray to it. He had no wrinkles to match the gray hair, though, and it gave him the odd appearance of being both old and young.

His office window looked out on the parking lot. He had probably seen her struggling with her luggage and sent these guys out to help her. He'd undoubtedly also seen her reaction, and now before she'd even registered, she'd done something wrong.

Tori wished she was more like Aprilynne, who didn't care what she said, but Tori felt the weight of her father's job too keenly. Politicians stayed in office by making friends, not insulting people. Their daughters were supposed to do the same.

The man held his hand out to her. She'd been wrong about the wrinkles. His eyes crinkled when he smiled. "Welcome to Dragon Camp. You're Victoria Hampton?" He had the hint of an accent, but she couldn't place it. British maybe? Australian?

She shook his hand. "I go by Tori."

"Tori, then." He gave her another smile, which was good news. He probably wouldn't have kept smiling if he was going to yell at her for assuming everyone at camp was either a thief or a menial worker. She relaxed, but only slightly. Why was she here instead of out in the registration line?

"I'm the camp director, Dr. Bartholemew. Most everyone calls me Dr. B. It's easier."

She remembered reading about him in the camp literature. He was a professor of medieval studies at George Mason, which was why his class was good for college credit.

Tori cast a quick glance at the two guys. Both had taken off their sunglasses, and it didn't make her feel better to see they were both on the extremely warm side of hot—as in, way to make a fool of herself in front of what were likely to be the only cute guys her age here.

She turned back to Dr. B with an inward sigh.

"I've always admired your dad," he said.

"Thanks." She wasn't sure whether to be surprised that he knew her father was a senator. Hopefully her mother hadn't called and made a big deal about it. Sometimes her mom liked to throw the title around to drum up preferential treatment. Tori could imagine her phoning and saying things like, "You have adequate supervision, don't you? The boys and girls cabins are chaperoned? It would be such bad publicity for your camp if anything happened to a senator's daughter . . ."

"I'm glad you could join us at Dragon Camp," Dr. B went on. He glanced at the guys and some hidden meaning passed between them before Dr. B returned his attention to Tori. "I noticed from your application that you signed up for the advanced section of horseback riding and fencing. You've done those before?"

"Yes."

"And you didn't sign up for the tae kwon do class."

"I'm already a fourth-degree black belt."

"Ahh." He sent another meaningful look to the guys. "Any other lessons you've taken?"

"Ice skating." She had been competing since age twelve and had a shelf full of state and regional trophies to show for it. Her coach kept telling her she could go to nationals if she put in more practice time.

"Have you ever used a rifle?" Dr. B asked. "Gone hunting, perhaps?"

"I've done target practice." Her father had originally taken her shooting to impress his NRA supporters, but she'd liked it and had kept going. "Why do you ask?"

Dr. B clasped his hands behind his back and grinned. "I'm always curious to see what kind of people come to our camp. You'll find you have a lot in common with many of the other campers." He gestured in the direction of the guys. "Both Dirk and Jesse are black belts, as well. Jesse is the state champion for his age in fencing, and Dirk, well, one day I think we'll see him win a medal for archery."

If Dr. B thought this information would make them feel friendlier, it didn't work. Both guys regarded her with expressions that were at best guarded and at worst disapproving. She wondered which was Dirk and which was Jesse.

The blond was probably the one most girls would go for first. He was good-looking in a flashy, sensual sort of way, and he had a swagger in his walk that said he knew it. His hair was a little too long and scruffy, but when you had a square jaw and perfect features, you could get away with that sort of thing. Tori tended to avoid guys that were cocky, though. They always ended up being trouble.

The brunet was handsome in a serious, understated way that Tori liked best. She let her eyes linger on him for a moment. His eyes were dark and piercing, as though they knew secrets.

"I see you signed up for the dragon mythology class," Dr. B continued. "You have an interest in that topic?"

She had played an imaginary game of knights as a child, read every book she could find about dragons, and for the last few years perused websites on the subject. She probably knew more about dragons than Dr. B. "Yes," she said.

"Then I'll look forward to talking with you about them this afternoon in class." He gave a pronounced nod, signaling the interview had ended. "Dirk and Jesse will take you down to your cabin."

"Which cabin?" the brunet asked.

"Number twenty-seven," Dr. B said.

The guys glanced at each other and then back at Dr. B. "You're sure?" the blond asked.

"Quite," Dr. B said, then smiled at Tori. "You're in the same cabin as my daughter, Bess. She'll be here tomorrow. Right now she's busy with . . ." he hesitated, "something important."

He made it sound mysterious, but didn't elaborate. Instead, he picked up a sheet of paper from his desk and handed it to Tori. "I hope you'll fit in well here. I hope it very much."

Tori's name was printed across the top of the paper, with her schedule listed underneath. She noticed, without trying to, that hers had been the only schedule on his desk.

The brunet picked up her largest suitcase, swung it onto his shoulder, and headed out the door. The blond picked up her smaller suitcase and shoulder bag, then left, too. Tori had no choice but to go after them. As she shut the door behind her, Dr. B murmured, "Now if we could only find Ryker."

But she could have heard wrong. It was an odd phrase for a person to say as he stood alone in a room.

CHAPTER 2

Tori hurried after Dirk and Jesse. They weren't waiting around for her. It was clear they didn't want to help her, which made her feel worse about having them carry her luggage. She followed them out of the door and around the side of the building to where a row of dusty, golf cart–looking vehicles stood. The guys hefted her luggage onto a rack, then climbed in the front seat, leaving the backseat open for her. As she got in, she glanced upward and noticed a small black camera perched on the corner of the roof. It didn't seem that unusual until her gaze drifted to the trees behind the building. Another camera was nestled into the branches, half-hidden in the leaves. Was there enough crime at this camp that they needed that much surveillance?

The brunet started up the cart. It was the noisy, gas-powered kind. He drove around the building and toward the cabins, not slowing for any bumps or curves in the trail. As he drove, he pulled a cell phone out of his pocket and made a call. "She's on her way, so tell Lilly and Alyssa to move their junk off the extra bed." After a pause he said, "You'll see soon enough."

He was talking about her like she wasn't even there. Well, they had started out on the wrong foot, and apparently they were still there.

She tried to make amends by leaning forward across the back of the guys' seat and giving them her best politician smile. "What were your names again?"

"Dirk," the blond one said.

"Jesse," the brunet answered.

Jesse. She rolled the name around her tongue, nearly saying it out loud. It suddenly became a perfect name for ruggedly handsome guys. Then she made herself stop staring at him. She hadn't come here to meet guys. She had a sort-of boyfriend back home. Roland. He had been president of her sophomore class, spoke fluent French—his dad had worked at the embassy in Paris—and he was a straight-A student. He was only a sort-of boyfriend because they'd started dating at the end of the school year. By the time she got back from camp, he would be vacationing in Europe. Who knew how they'd feel about each other when school started again.

"Thanks for taking me to my cabin," Tori said.

Dirk stretched his legs. "Don't mention it. We're glad to do it since the bellhops have the day off."

Yeah. It was probably best not to comment on that subject. Tori scanned the map that had come with her registration information, then scanned it again. The cabin numbers only went up to twenty-five.

"Where exactly is cabin twenty-seven?"

Jesse momentarily slowed down to weave around some kids who walked across the trail. "Twenty-six and twenty-seven aren't part of the main camp. A group of us have come here for the last four or five years. Since we're older, Dr. B lets us have cabins that are off by themselves."

So that was why Dr. B had sent her to cabin 27 and why the guys resented it. She wasn't one of the regulars, but was too old to be with the rest of the campers.

And that meant she'd be seeing a lot of these guys during the month. She tried to think of some small talk that would help erase the awkwardness between them. "Five years. You must love this camp a lot." As soon as she said it, she wished she hadn't. They probably kept coming back because they were here on scholarship and couldn't afford to go anywhere else.

Really, all of her father's lessons on tact had deserted her.

"Oh yeah, I love it," Dirk said, with a tinge of sarcasm. "Mostly I love how we get to sleep in every day."

Tori checked the schedule in her hand to make sure she hadn't misread it. Nope. Breakfast was from 8:00 until 9:00. Her first class started at 9:30. That didn't seem too early. Maybe Dirk was one of those guys who liked to sleep until noon.

Jesse momentarily turned his head to appraise her. A flash of intrigue went through his brown eyes. "So what brings you here this summer?"

She didn't answer right away. It had been the lure of being with other people who spoke about dragons as if they existed. It had been, she thought dryly, her inner geekiness. Or worse, it was some broken part of her that didn't quite grasp reality the way it should. She hadn't been able to explain it to her own parents. She certainly couldn't talk about it to near strangers.

She shrugged. "It looked interesting."

Dirk cracked a smile, revealing perfect teeth. "Well, you're right about that, at least."

They left the groupings of cabins, then drove past some stables. The calls and noise of the other campers faded and then completely disappeared. They kept driving down an uneven trail until it finally became more of a suggestion than an actual path. Birds, squirrels, and rabbits bounded away from the clatter and buzz of the cart.

"Just how far away is cabin twenty-seven?" Tori asked.

"Two miles," Dirk said. "It takes about ten minutes in the cart, and then another five minutes of walking." He cast a look back at her sandals. "Well, it's five minutes if you're wearing normal shoes."

Two miles? Was he serious?

They breezed past a bright orange sign that read ENTERING PRIVATE PROPERTY. NO TRESPASSING.

This couldn't be right. The guys were playing some sort of practical joke on her. Perhaps they had been so insulted by the parking lot incident they'd decided to drop her off in the forest and leave her to find her own way.

Tori leaned forward again. "Um, are we going in the right direction? That sign said 'No Trespassing.'"

Jesse remained unconcerned. "Don't worry," he said, one hand casually draped over the steering wheel. "I know where I'm going."

Dirk shrugged. "And even if we did wander off camp property, it's still illegal to shoot trespassers." He leaned back in his seat nonchalantly. "Of course, that doesn't mean they can't set their dogs on us." He glanced over at Jesse. "You think this baby could outrun a pack of angry dogs?"

"Sure," Jesse said. "Unless they're big. Or fast."

Dirk turned back to Tori. "We'll be fine then. Most backwoodsmen only own poodles and Yorkies."

Tori looked back at the trail, trying to gage how far they'd come. "Um, yeah. Does Dr. B know you guys go joy riding in the woods in his cart?"

"Relax," Dirk said. "This is the way to our cabins. The sign is just there to keep the regular campers from wandering into the advanced camp. They're not allowed down here, so don't even tell them about it."

"Uh-huh." It was not only two miles away, it was a *secret* camp. Tori got out the map and looked over it again. There was no mention of an advanced camp, and both the cafeteria and her dragon mythology class were in the main area. Having cabins two miles away didn't make any sense. The advanced campers would have to carpool—or rather cart pool—back there every day. Why not just build cabins that were closer?

With every moment that passed, Tori was more sure this was some sort of prank or camp initiation. The guys were going to drop her and her luggage in the middle of nowhere and she would have to find her way back. She would be like Hansel and Gretel, but with designer luggage and no bread crumbs.

Then the cart went through an opening in the trees, and there it was: not just two log cabins but a completely different camp. It had another set of stables, a large grassy field, a good-size bathroom— that meant flush toilets—and three other buildings lined up around the field. One small, one large, and one that was long and flat.

"What are those?" she asked.

"Those are buildings," Dirk said.

"What *kind* of buildings?" she asked, annoyed by his evasiveness.

He considered them with mock contemplation. "Rectangular ones."

Very funny.

Jesse said, "The big one is the Dragon Hall, the long one is the in-door rifle range, and you don't have to worry about the small one."

She hadn't been worried, just curious, but she didn't ask any other questions. One of her father's axioms was: Sometimes the most tact-ful thing you can say is nothing at all. Apparently that was the case with these guys.

Jesse drove the cart across the field and to the back of the rifle range, where three other carts were already parked. Jesse and Dirk got out, hefted her luggage from the back, and headed toward the cabins. She was fine while she walked across the grassy field, but the dirt path from the field to the cabins was littered with twigs and pebbles, which kept getting lodged in her sandals. She had to stop more than once to pull things out.

Two teenage guys on horses came out of the forest and ambled in their direction. They both looked to be about Tori's age. The first—who seemed to be more shoulders and muscles than anything else—smiled cautiously as he rode up. His sandy blond hair was cropped short and he had easy, likeable features. With his tan plaid shirt, he reminded her of a lumberjack or a cowboy. "So you're the new girl?" he asked with a southern drawl.

Cowboy. Definitely.

"I'm Tori Hampton."

"Senator Hampton's daughter," Jesse added, and maybe only she noticed the contempt in his voice. He didn't stick around for further introductions. He and Dirk kept walking toward the cabins, hauling her luggage toward the one with a 27 painted above the doorway.

"I'm Kody," the broad shouldered guy said and motioned to the other rider. "This here is Shang."

Shang nodded. He was muscular, too; you just didn't notice it so much next to Kody. His shiny, black hair was neatly combed, his brown eyes thoughtful. He was the only one of the guys who looked entirely clean. No streaks of dirt smudged his clothes or skin, and his black riding boots shined. He was probably one of those meticulous people who never threw their clothes on their bed. He smiled at her briefly, then went back to studying her.

She realized how they must see her, standing there in pressed white cotton shorts, a linen blouse, and impractically fashionable sandals. She hadn't given a second thought to her manicured fingernails and toenails, to the blonde highlights her stylist had worked through her long, honey brown hair, or the gold rings on her fingers and topaz studs in her ears. Everyone at her school dressed this way.

She had always loved that people told her she could pass for a model, but standing here overdressed, she wasn't sure how she could escape the other stereotypes people had about models: that they were shallow, vain, stupid.

Shang gave her a half smile. "Glad to finally meet you."

"Finally?" she asked.

"Dr. B told us yesterday we would have an addition to cabin twenty-seven," Shang said.

Kody added, "We old-timers come out the day before camp starts to help Dr. B set things up."

Probably part of that whole scholarship deal.

She glanced over in time to see Jesse and Dirk disappear into cabin 27. "Well, it was nice to meet you. I'd better go unpack my things."

She headed down the trail to her cabin, barely managing to hear Kody and Shang's conversation behind her.

"She seems like an odd one," Shang said.

Odd? It wasn't what she expected in a first impression and the word stung. Odd, why? Because she obviously came from money?

"Lilly is either going to love her or hate her, that's for sure," Kody said.

"My guess is hate her."

Tori didn't slow her pace, but sometimes she wished her hearing wasn't quite so good.

When Tori opened her cabin's door, the conversation inside stopped. She hadn't heard what Dirk and Jesse had been saying, because music was blaring, masking the words. Still, she'd managed to catch her name, which meant they were talking about her, probably relating the whole parking lot story.

She stepped inside and let the door swing closed behind her. The cabin was sparse. Bunk beds were pushed up against three of the walls, making room for six girls. Four of the mattresses already had blankets and possessions scattered across them—magazines, bags of chips, half-emptied backpacks. Mismatched dressers stood between each of the bunk beds, and faded curtains hung at the side of the only window.

Dr. B obviously had a low decorating budget. Was it too much to hope that the bed would be comfortable? She should have taken that into consideration and brought an air mattress with her.

Her suitcases sat at the foot of the unoccupied bunk bed. Two girls stood by the far wall, talking to Jesse and Dirk. Both were toned and tanned, wearing cut-off shorts and tank tops that showed off their athletic bodies. Both girls also had shoulder-length, badly bleached-blonde hair. They looked like they were trying to be carbon copies of each other.

The shorter of the two appraised Tori in the way a girl sums up a rival. "I'm Lilly," the girl said and gestured at her copy. "This is Alyssa."

"I'm Tori." Tori sat down on the bed. The mattress hardly gave at all. She might as well be sleeping on the floor. She jiggled it and wondered if her parents could FedEx an air mattress to camp.

Lilly turned down the iPod on her bed. "So you're a senator's daughter? You live on Capitol Hill?"

Nobody actually *lived* on Capitol Hill. It was made up of office buildings, not subdivisions, but Tori didn't point that out. "No, my dad just works there."

"Hmm," Lilly said as though proving a point. "Do you get to hang out with the president?"

"I've met him," Tori said. "But he doesn't hang out much with high school kids."

Lilly tilted her head. "Meeting him isn't such a big deal. I bet he meets thousands of people each year."

Tori slid off the bed. "I never said it was a big deal."

Her answer made Dirk laugh, but Lilly's eyes narrowed.

Well, camp was getting better all the time. Now Tori was stuck with girls that hated her on sight. It was sort of like high school, but without her friends around to deflect any of the cattiness hurled in her direction. The only reason Tori didn't leave right then was that she didn't know how to get her suitcases back to the parking lot.

Tori cast a look at the guys, hoping to seem grateful. "Thanks again for helping with my luggage."

Jesse headed to the door. "As soon as you're ready, I'll show you around."

Tori glanced at her Rolex—another thing she shouldn't have brought, but had forgotten to take off beforehand. "I thought I was supposed to go to orientation."

"That's for people in the main camp. Dr. B asked me to get you familiar with the routine out here, to see what you can do."

See what I can do? There had been a note of challenge in his voice.

At that moment, she knew she would stay—at least long enough to show him and everyone else that she could kick his butt in tae kwon do, or archery, or whatever else he was good at. Because she was surprisingly talented at all of it.

She lifted one of her bags onto the bottom bunk. "Okay. Give me your number, and I'll text you when I'm done unpacking."

"I'm right next door. Just come get me." Jesse took hold of the doorknob, then turned back. "And change into some jeans and shoes. We'll be riding."

He and Dirk both left without saying anything else.

 **CHAPTER 3**

Inside their own cabin, Dirk leaned against the side of his bunk. "Well?" he prompted Jesse. "What do you think?"

Jesse let out a grunt. "I think we've unearthed Barbie's long-lost sister. She even comes complete with matching luggage."

Dirk laughed. One of the things he liked about Jesse was his ability to work vocabulary like "unearthed" into casual conversation. It probably came from having teachers for parents. "Yeah," Dirk said, "she doesn't seem like one of us." Her outfit, her makeup, her perfectly styled long, brown hair—that's how girls dressed to go to photo shoots, not summer camp. The rest of the girls in 27 hardly ever did their hair, let alone put on makeup.

Although, to be completely honest, that was probably Dirk's doing. Back when they were thirteen, he'd gotten so tired of waiting around for Lilly to beautify herself every morning, he stole her cosmetic case and refused to give it back until camp ended. Lilly had just borrowed Alyssa's stuff, but all the girls had cut down their morning routines after that.

Jesse walked over to the only window in the room. Through it, you could see the side of the girls' cabin. "I bet Tori has never done a day of real work in her life. She'll probably act like a spoiled princess the entire summer and refuse to do anything we ask."

"Which is why I'm glad she's on your team," Dirk said.

Jesse turned away from the window to glare at him.

Normally Dirk would rib him some more. After all, Dirk had put up with Lilly's prima donna behavior for years. Lilly could tackle you during a game, then chew you out for breaking one of her fingernails. It was about time Jesse had someone to drive him crazy. But Dirk couldn't help being suspicious of the latest arrival. "If she's one of us, why did it take her so long to come?"

Jesse shrugged. "Maybe she was too busy touring the world with Mumsy and Dadsy to be bothered."

"Maybe she's not really one of us."

Jesse walked to his bed and sat down. "You heard what Dr. B said about her. Do you think her age and athletic ability are a coincidence?"

Dirk shook his head. He didn't think it was a coincidence, but that didn't mean Tori was legit, either. Everyone at camp already had counterparts except for Jesse and him. Dirk had always figured Ryker Davis was Jesse's counterpart because Dirk couldn't imagine having a counterpart himself.

Counterparts had a link that let them sense things about each other. They understood one another in an unspoken, almost mystical way. Dirk didn't believe there was anyone like that for him. He didn't want it, either—somebody knowing him so well. And besides, even if he did have a counterpart, it wouldn't be some pampered socialite. Tori probably didn't know how to do her own laundry, let alone have the ability to sift through what was going on in his mind.

"It might not be a coincidence she's here," Dirk said. "She could be a plant, trained by someone who wants to know who we are and what we're doing." He sat down on his own bed with an irritated thud. "Dr. B is too trusting."

A frown creased Jesse's brow while he mulled over Dirk's words. "You could be right. We should be careful about what we say and do until we know for sure." He paused. "But we'd do that anyway."

Jesse lay down and stretched. Apparently, he thought the matter was closed. He picked up a book from the side of the bed and opened it. The Iliad. Only Jesse would bring ancient Greek literature to camp. Dirk was firmly ignoring his own reading list for next year's English lit class. What was the point of summer if you had to do homework?

He walked restlessly to the window and stared at the girls' cabin, even though he knew it wouldn't look any different than any other time he'd seen it. He couldn't help himself. Tori was inside, and he had no idea who or what she was.

CHAPTER 4

The camp brochure had said to bring either a sleeping bag or sheets. Tori had gone with sheets—five hundred thread count. She tucked them around the mattress, ignoring how forlorn their turquoise blue stripes looked against the blunt pinewood wall.

Lilly wandered over and peered into her open suitcase. "You brought an iron?"

"Yeah, in case they didn't have one here."

Lilly snorted. "Have you ever actually been to a camp before?"

Tori pulled out some jeans and put them into the nearest dresser. "Yes, just not one that was so . . ." She tried not to make the word sound like an insult. "Rustic."

Alyssa joined them, shaking her head at the contents of Tori's suitcase. "Gardenia-scented body spray? Okay, that's only going to be useful if it has insect repellant in it."

"She's not trying to repel insects," Lilly said. "She's trying to attract guys." Lilly leaned toward Tori, her blue eyes hard and unwavering. "Don't use any on Jesse. I have dibs on him."

Alyssa added, "And I have dibs on Dirk."

Dibs? Well, she had to hand it to Lilly and Alyssa for getting right to the point. None of that pretending to be your friend and spreading rumors behind your back that Tori typically got when girls thought she was competition. She was used to that reaction now, numb to it, actually.

Back in junior high when her braces and glasses had come off— back when Tori changed from being a tomboy who barely took time to comb her hair into an actual girl—the jealousy had been a painful shock. So many girls had turned on her; girls she thought were her friends. But now Tori shrugged off the barbs. It was just part of life. She only had a couple of real friends—the rest were just acquaintances to be wary of.

Tori put another pair of jeans into the dresser. "You've got to know by now; it doesn't do any good to call dibs on guys. They like whatever and whoever they want. They're like cats—but with less shedding." Tori smiled to soften her words.

Lilly didn't return the smile.

Great. Was it too much to hope that the other girls in the cabin would have steady boyfriends back home?

Tori glanced around the room, but saw only a few pegs to hang jackets on. Which meant it had been pointless to bring hangers. Could she even fit all her clothes into her half of the dresser?

Alyssa went back to her bed and a celebrity magazine she'd been reading, but Lilly kept watching Tori sort through her suitcase.

"You're not going to need an iron. Or hangers. And if you brought a bell to ring for the cabana boys to bring you drinks while you lounge by the lake—trust me, you can leave that in your suitcase, too. This is an extreme sports camp. We get dirty, and wrinkled, and some-times—" Lilly smirked, enjoying the next word, "injured." She turned and walked back to Alyssa's bed. "But you'll find that out soon enough."

Was that a warning or a threat? And what sorts of extreme sports was Lilly talking about? Body-slamming volleyball? Rowboat derby racing? Whatever. Tori wouldn't shy away from any of it. Lilly and her evil blonde sidekick could find out the hard way that they shouldn't underestimate her just because she dressed nicely.

Tori finished unpacking in silence. She pointedly put her iron on the top of her dresser where it would be easy to reach. Then she changed into riding clothes, refusing to feel awkward for disrobing in front of Lilly and Alyssa.

That's right, she wanted to say, I have designer underwear, too. Because nothing low class ever touches my rear end. When Tori finished dressing, she spritzed on some gardenia body spray, then left without saying good-bye.

"Good luck with your horse!" Lilly called after her, but she didn't sound like she meant it.

Tori tromped across the path to cabin 26 and went up its stairs. Jesse opened his cabin door before she knocked. As he stepped outside onto the wooden porch, his eyes ran over her, stopping on her riding boots. He still wore his dusty Nikes.

Her sneakers were for running; just like her hiking boots were for hiking, and her water shoes were for when she went to the lake. Half the point of any outfit was wearing the appropriate footwear.

"You're ready?" he asked, but it wasn't really a question. Jesse walked down the steps, and she followed after him. He moved down the trail with long, easy strides. He hadn't changed clothes, but she noted as though it were a new detail, the way his jeans—basic Levi's—had that worn, comfortable look to them . . . how they fit perfectly on his lean, muscular legs.

She forced her gaze to his face, to the strong lines of his jaw and his dark eyes.

"We're going to the archery targets first," he said, "then the shooting range, then the stables. The advanced fencing instructor won't get here for a few more days, so we'll skip that for now." He glanced at her boots. "You've ridden before?"

"I have my own horse." He was a palomino named Blitzer, which she boarded at their country club's stables.

Jesse nodded like he'd expected as much. "Mr. Reed takes care of the horses here. We call him Booker. He doesn't say much, and he comes off gruff, but he knows horses. He also knows everything there is to know about this camp, so don't get on his bad side."

They walked past the large building. A metal dome sat perched on its roof. "What's inside there?" she asked.

"You don't need to know that right now." He sounded like some government operative in a Hollywood movie.

"I thought you were showing me around."

"I am." He pointed to a trail that cut through the forest in the opposite direction. "That leads to the lake." His hand swept toward a log cabin with two entrances. "Those are the bathrooms. There's a limited supply of hot water, so we have a system: you get yourself wet, turn off the water, lather up, then rinse off. If you use more than your share of hot water, the rest of us carry you down to the lake and throw you in. That's not an idle threat, by the way. Lilly gets dunked every year."

"Okay," Tori said.

"We go running every morning at seven."

"How nice for the rest of you," she said. "I'm not a morning person."

He smiled at her firmly. "You will be starting tomorrow."

"I run in the evening," she insisted.

"Great, we do that, too. You can go with us tonight."

They went running twice a day? Talk about overzealous. She had no intention of running with them at either time. For her, running was a time to unwind, not some sort of social event. She would think of some tactful way to explain that later. Or better yet, she would just avoid the rest of them until after they'd gone on their nightly excursion.

A few minutes later, she and Jesse came to the archery range. A row of targets had been pinned onto the front of hay bales. Jesse took a compound bow and a quiver full of arrows out of a shed and handed them to her. "Let's see how many you can put into the bull's-eye at thirty meters."

She nocked an arrow into her bow, then sent it flying toward the target. It hit dead center. "One . . ." she said, and nocked another arrow, took aim, and released. It landed next to the first arrow. "Two . . ."

He watched her, unimpressed. "Can you do it faster?"

She sped up for her third and fourth arrows. They joined the first two. She turned to him in satisfaction, but he only nodded.

"Okay, let's move back to the seventy-meter line."

She had expected some surprise from him, some admiration. His expression registered neither. Which irked her.

Everyone in her PE class had been impressed when they'd done an archery unit and Tori effortlessly made the bull's-eye each time—and that was without ever practicing. Archery didn't seem that difficult to her. You aimed. You shot. The arrow did the rest of the work.

Her PE teacher, Ms. Wong, had told her she should join the archery club. Of course Ms. Wong had also told Tori she should join the basketball, track, and cross-country teams. She owed it to the school, in fact. But Tori had had enough of team sports back in junior high.

Her school's teams had been populated by the set of girls who'd turned against Tori. She was probably the only girl in junior high basketball history who was constantly fouled by her own players.

Besides, despite Tori's athletic ability, she had no intentions of ever becoming a jock. Athletes were just more muscled versions of actors, only there to entertain people.

She hadn't decided on a career yet, but she wanted a line of work that was refined, intelligent, and respected. Something along the lines of First Lady. Or maybe an ambassador to a country where guys had irresistible accents, like England, Ireland, or Australia.

Jesse walked to the seventy-meter line.

Tori followed, then turned and squinted at the hay bale. She nocked an arrow, took aim, and let it hiss across the distance to the target. It barely made it to the bull's-eye. She put in another arrow.

"Faster," Jesse said.

She lowered the bow. "Look, if you have somewhere to be, you don't have to do this. I don't mind if you don't show me around."

Patiently, as though it should have been obvious, he said, "I'm not telling you to go faster because I'm in a hurry. I want to see your accuracy under pressure."

She nocked another arrow into her bow, annoyed, and let it fly. It landed just outside the bull's-eye. She had missed because she'd rushed it, but she didn't slow down. Her third arrow missed the center altogether.

She shot three more arrows in quick succession, and only one reached the bull's-eye.

Jesse grunted his disapproval. "You need more practice."

She lowered her bow. "And maybe I would practice if there were any point to it. But when was the last time someone needed to defend themselves against a bunch of angry hay bales with a bow and arrow?"

He took the bow from her, nocked an arrow, then without taking his eyes off her, he shot at the target. His arrow, impossibly, hit dead center.

"It's not about defense. It's about eye-hand coordination, reflexes, and knowing where your target is at all times." Without waiting for a response, he walked the distance to the target and pulled out the arrows. After he'd finished putting the equipment back in the shed, he motioned for her to follow him again. "Let's go to the shooting range."

She trudged after him, glaring at his back, but not pushing herself to catch up with him. *Knowing where your target is at all times.* Boy, he took himself way too seriously.

She wondered how old he was. At first she had guessed seventeen, but the way he talked—so sternly—he was probably eighteen. When guys got that old, they thought they were adults. Real men. He would probably spend the entire month talking down to her.

She wanted to point out that she hadn't signed up for archery or any shooting classes, but she didn't. If he wanted to see her marksmanship, she'd show him. She could fire off a round at seventy-five yards and never miss the center of the target.

They went inside the shooting range. A chubby, middle-aged woman sat at the front desk, her curly black hair pulled back in a ponytail. She was reading a book, but looked up and smiled when they came in. "Well, aren't you a pretty thing! Victoria, right?"

Tori smiled back. "I go by Tori." Being a senator's daughter didn't usually make her such a celebrity, and it was a little discomforting that everyone knew who she was. A lot of students at her private school were kids of congressmen or ambassadors. It was no big deal. She blended in with them. Here, she stood out.

The woman leaned forward, keeping her finger tucked in her book to save her place. "Welcome to Dragon Camp, honey. You getting situated all right?"

Tori nodded politely. "Yes."

"I'm Shirley, resident range master and professional mom. Technically, I'm only Bess's mom, but I claim all the kids."

That made her Dr. B's wife. Apparently the camp was a family affair.

Shirley kept looking her over. "All of this can be overwhelming at first. You let me know if you need anything."

Jesse rested a hand on top of the counter. "Right now we need rifles, ammo—the whole shebang."

Shirley bent down behind the counter. "I have it waiting for you." She hefted out a long black case and a canvass bag, which she handed to Jesse. "Make sure you go over the safety precautions with Tori."

Jesse swung the strap of the canvass bag over his shoulder. "I will."

"And make sure she wears her helmet."

"I will."

Shirley took a key from a drawer and gave it to him. "None of that trick driving while you have Tori on the motorcycle."

Motorcycle?

"Don't worry," Jesse said. "I'll keep her in one piece."

Shirley beamed at him like she wanted to reach over and pinch his cheeks. "You have a fun time, now."

Instead of going back toward the shooting lanes, Jesse headed outside. Tori followed, blinking in the sunlight. "Where are we going?"

"I'm driving you to the outdoor range. It's by the mountain."

They walked to the side of the building and a garage that held over a dozen identical, sleek black motorcycles.

Funny, the camp brochure hadn't said anything about motorcycles. Which was probably for the best. Tori's mother thought they were unsafe. But just seeing them there, gleaming, made Tori's heart beat in anticipation. How fast did they go?

Jesse attached the gun case and canvass bag to the side of a bike, then went to a wall where rows of helmets hung. He tossed one to her, put one on himself, then climbed on the bike.

She put on her helmet and sat down behind him, awkwardly wondering how close she should be. And what was she supposed to do with her hands?

"Put your feet here," he said, pointing to the foot pegs, "and hang on to me."

Without further instructions, he turned the key and the motorcycle vibrated to life. It hummed softly—not like the rattling, chainsaw buzz that most motorcycles had.

She wrapped her arms loosely around Jesse's waist. "How come the bike is so quiet?"

He hesitated before answering. "We don't like to disturb the birds."

She wasn't sure whether he expected her to believe his answer. Before she had a chance to say anything else, the bike rocketed out of the garage and down a dirt trail. She held on to Jesse tighter, peering around his shoulder to let the wind rush against her. She liked both sensations: hanging on to Jesse and the feel of speed.

The trees whipped by them in a blur of glossy green, and the bumps on the uneven path made the ride more exciting. It was like jet skiing in the waves, but without the ocean mist.

The ten minutes it took them to get to the range didn't seem long enough, which meant maybe her mother was right about motorcycles. They could be dangerous. She wasn't the type of girl who should like holding on to biker guys. As Jesse climbed off the motorcycle, she forced her gaze away from him and tried to revive images of Roland, of guys who wore crisp khaki pants and expensive cologne. Guys who understood what stock portfolios were. After a few moments of this, she felt like herself again.

The range was a narrow strip of land that had been cleared of trees. So many clay remnants littered the ground, it looked like someone had put down a long, orange carpet. A ten-foot mound of dirt stood at the end. It had a target paper attached to it, but instead of the usual silhouette of a man, there was a picture of a dragon.

Jesse hung his helmet over one side of the handlebars and Tori put hers on the other. He unclamped the gun case and said, "We'll start with some targets, then move on to skeet shooting."

"You brought shotguns, too?" she asked.

He pulled a pair of goggles and earmuffs from the bag and gave them to her. "We use rifles."

There was no point in using rifles to shoot clay disks. Rifles were for big game, and very few deer or elk went gliding around the sky. "Why?" she asked.

He didn't answer. Instead, he took two automatic rifles from the case. Before handing her one, he went through a whole spiel about gun safety. *Always assume your gun is loaded. Keep the barrel pointed at the ground or down range at all times. Keep your finger off the trigger until you're ready to shoot.* She'd heard it before. While he spoke, Tori put on her goggles and earmuffs. When he started the lecture on how to use a rifle, she took the gun from him. "I think I can handle it from here."

Focusing through the scope, she aimed, then put a round into the paper target. The empty casing fell to her feet with a satisfied tinkle.

Jesse checked the mound through a pair of binoculars. "You completely missed the dragon."

"I wasn't aiming for the dragon. I decided to make him the outline of a cape instead. Now he can be Super Dragon."

Jesse lowered the binoculars. Only a hint of a smile at the corner of his mouth let her know he found her artwork amusing. "Okay, now I'll throw some clay for you. See how many you can hit."

He took three disks from the canvass bag and tossed them into the air in front of her. She hit the first on the way up, the second on the way down, and the third inches from the ground.

He didn't comment, just pulled out more clay. Four discs went up this time. She hit two; the other two broke on the ground. Not bad, really, but he scowled in disapproval.

"All right," he said, taking out another handful. "Now do it with your eyes closed."

She let the barrel of her gun fall to her side. "My eyes closed? What a great gun-safety tip. What could go wrong with that?"

"I'm standing beside you. You've got nothing to hit except trees or dirt."

"But what's the point?" She put one hand on her hip. "And what kind of camp orientation is this anyway?"

He held the disks up, ready to throw them. "Just do it."

She faced forward and shut her eyes. She heard the whiz of discs leaving his hand, then a slight noise above her in the sky. Was it possible to hear the discs spinning so far away? She shot toward the noise and a disc exploded. She shot again, lower this time; another crack. The next bullet hit only air, and the rest of the clay crashed onto the ground.

She lowered her gun and opened her eyes. "I got two?"

"Yes, but I threw up six."

"Still—two. That's pretty good for blind shooting."

"It's passable."

She raised an eyebrow. "Passable? How many people do you know who shoot as well as I do?"

"I know ten who shoot better."

"Oh, really? I'd like to meet them."

He sighed, took out four discs, and threw them in the air. He fired, holding the gun with only one hand. It didn't seem possible to aim holding the rifle that way, especially with the kickback, and yet every disc broke before it hit the ground. Then he threw up five disks, shut his eyes, and shattered three.

"You've already met Dirk, Kody, Shang, Lilly, Alyssa, and me," he said. "You'll meet the rest soon."

"I can hardly wait to see them shoot." She didn't believe him. He may have an uncanny ability with arrows and guns, but what were the chances that they all did? "When do the rest get here?"

At her question, a flash of something passed over his face, frustration or anger. She couldn't tell which. "Rosa and Bess will be here soon," he said. "I don't know about the others." And there it was again, an emotion that didn't match the calm tone of his words, but this time she identified it: pain.

"Come on," he said, already taking off his goggles. "Let's go to the stables."

 **CHAPTER 5**

They rode back to the indoor range and returned the equipment to Shirley. She gave them a cheery good-bye, which was a stark contrast to Jesse's brooding.

Honestly, what was with him?

At the stables, several horses were already saddled up, lazily nibbling grass in the corral. As Tori and Jesse got closer, a short, stocky man in baggy pants walked up to them, carrying riding helmets. A few days' growth of beard colored his chin gray, and he wore a baseball cap pulled down low. He eyed Tori the way everyone had done since she'd gotten here, but whatever conclusions he drew, they didn't show on his face.

"This is Booker," Jesse said, taking one of the helmets, "and this is Victoria Hampton."

"Tori," she said. She took her helmet from Booker and smiled at him, remembering Jesse's instructions not to get on his bad side. "Your horses are beautiful."

He didn't acknowledge her compliment, just turned to Jesse. "How did the shooting go?"

Jesse buckled his riding helmet. "She needs practice."

Tori put her helmet on and resisted gritting her teeth. "The only time I didn't hit most of the clay was when I closed my eyes."

Booker nodded, cataloging this information. "All right then, let's get you a horse. Bane has been waiting for a good rider."

"You should give her a gentler horse to start with," Jesse said. "Noche or Pepper."

Booker raised an eyebrow, so Jesse added, "At archery she missed the bull's-eye five times."

Tori buckled her helmet with more force than it needed. "What does that have to do with horseback riding?"

Jesse didn't answer. Neither did Booker. He walked to the corral.

"I've ridden horses since I was six years old," she said.

Jesse remained unimpressed. "You haven't ever ridden any of these horses."

She would have said more, but she noticed that Dirk, Kody, Shang, and the evil blonde twins, Lilly and Alyssa, had all come to watch her ride. They sat at the far side of the field as though waiting for a soccer game to start.

Booker took a black horse's reins in one hand and a brown horse's in the other. At a strolling pace, he led them toward Jesse and Tori.

Before Booker had gone very far, Jesse walked the last few feet to the brown horse. Booker gave him the reins, and Jesse smiled at the horse and stroked his neck. "Hey, General, are you ready for a ride?" The horse nickered and pushed his nose against Jesse's hand.

She hadn't seen Jesse smile before, and the sight of it made her breath stop in her throat. With a smile on his lips and gentleness in his eyes, he moved beyond good-looking. He was stunning.

She watched Jesse murmuring things to his horse for another moment. It was clear they had a bond. Tori forgave Jesse for some of his aloofness right then. A guy who loved horses had to have a good side.

Booker held out the black horse's lead. It was Noche and not Pepper, she guessed, because Noche meant "night" in Spanish. "You know your way around a horse?" Booker asked.

"Yes." To prove the point, Tori placed her foot in the stirrup and mounted without his help.

Booker stepped away from the horse and put his hands in his pockets. "Take him around the field easy-like for the first lap or two. After that, Jesse will take you down the trail to the Easter grounds. You holler for Jess if you have any problems."

If I have any problems? And this after they'd put her on the beginner horse. She tapped the horse's side to walk him over to General. Jesse had mounted already and was watching her—checking, she supposed, to see whether she knew how to hold the reins.

As she reached him, Booker called out, "Just stay mounted and you'll be fine!"

Always good advice when riding. His faith in her was touching.

Jesse said, "We'll walk to the field. On my lead, we'll go from walk, to canter, to gallop, okay?"

"Okay."

Jesse prodded his horse forward. Tori followed, and within a few steps, the stress of the day fell away. She couldn't be in a bad mood while horseback riding. There was something magical about riding a horse, a connectedness to nature that automatically happened. Sometimes when she rode Blitzer back home, she felt like she wasn't a person at all; she was part of the wind and the trees, and the horse's legs became her own.

The two horses sauntered over to the field. Tori glanced at the campers lined along the edge of the grass. Each set of eyes was trained on her. If they'd come to see her make a fool of herself, they'd be disappointed.

Jesse called out, "Canter," and General picked up speed. Tori urged Noche to go faster, and the horse immediately did.

Almost at once, Tori's body took on the rhythm of the horse's steps. Her leg muscles were used to this action. The two horses cantered around the field once, and when Jesse seemed satisfied that she wasn't about to slide off and be trampled to death, he called out, "Gallop!"

Galloping was always the most fun. "Come on, boy," Tori said. "Let's show him what we can do." The horse responded even before she tapped his sides. This wasn't a surprise. When one horse took off in a run, any others in the area were likely to follow. It was horses' instinctual fear of predators.

Tori leaned forward, enjoying the way her hair rippled around her shoulders.

A show-jumping course was set up on the side of the field. Some of the fences were pretty high, too. Good. She liked jumping, but her parents never let her go over anything higher than a couple feet. Camp must not have the same restrictions. She wouldn't mention this to her mother. Ditto for the motorcycle and shooting with her eyes closed.

Noche gained on General, and Tori decided not to hold him back. After all, Jesse had never said she had to stay behind him. If he wanted to be on the lead horse, he'd have to go faster.

They rounded the curve, and Noche sped up. For a few strides, he stayed neck and neck to General. Jesse stared at her, surprised and then worried, like he wasn't sure she had control.

"He's a great horse!" Tori called to him.

And then, Noche effortlessly took the lead. Nothing lay ahead of Tori but the open field and the startled faces of the campers on the sidelines. She rode like this for a couple of minutes until Jesse caught up and called out, "Rein him in!"

Well, it had been nice while it lasted. And hopefully Tori had proved that she was a competent rider. She pulled back on the reins, and Noche slowed to a walk, shaking his head. He seemed to resent the demotion.

Tori stroked his mane. "You're a marvelous boy. That'll show them to classify you as a beginner horse, now won't it?"

Jesse rode up beside her. She expected him to be angry, or at least disapproving that she'd gone so fast on a horse she wasn't used to. Instead, he looked pleased. "Apparently ten years of horseback riding leave their mark." He motioned with his head toward the forest. "I'll take you to the Easter grounds now."

Finally, approval. She shouldn't have cared, yet she smiled anyway.

Jesse's horse took off in a trot and she followed after him, thinking about the other sentence he'd just spoken: *ten years of horseback riding leave their mark*. So he knew she was sixteen. How much else did he know about her?

On the far side of the field, in the opposite direction as the cabins, a dirt road stretched through the woods. It was wide enough for both horses, so she prodded Noche to walk beside General. She had stopped resenting Booker for giving her the gentler horse. She loved the way Noche took direction so easily, as though he anticipated each of Tori's requests.

The air was getting warmer, the humidity blanketing the forest, but the horses clomped along, at ease on the trail. Jesse held General's reins in one hand with a relaxed stance. She wondered how many years he'd been riding.

He turned and saw her staring, so she said, "How far away are the Easter grounds?"

"About three miles."

"Why are they called the Easter grounds?"

He hesitated. "The advanced campers are split into two teams and we do competitions. We play a game up there that's like an Easter egg hunt."

"Oh, yeah. The teams." The memory of the parking lot—of Jesse and Dirk arguing because neither wanted her on their team—momentarily stung. "Did you ever decide which lucky team got me?"

He gave her a lazy smile. "That would be mine. Team Magnus."

"Named after St. Magnus, who defeated dragons in Switzerland?"

His eyebrows rose in surprise, and she allowed herself a second of gloating satisfaction. He hadn't expected her to know where the name came from.

"Right," he said. "I'm showing you around because I'm your captain. Dirk is the leader of Team Beowulf, but no one calls it that anymore. They're the A-team."

He waited to see if she could guess where that name came from. She sifted through her mental files on dragon lore, but couldn't make a connection. "Why?" she asked.

"There was an eighties show by that name. The star was a guy named Dirk Benedict. He's a dead ringer for our Dirk, so the name was a natural."

How was she supposed to have guessed that? "I see," she said. "This camp combines dragon lore and eighties trivia. The perfect blend of all that is geeky."

Jesse ignored the comment. "Shang, Bess, Rosa, and Leo are on our team," he said. "Dirk, Kody, Lilly, Alyssa, and Danielle are on the A-team."

It was going to take her a while to remember the names. Shang was the meticulous guy with black hair—and he'd called her odd. She wasn't likely to forget that. Kody looked like a cross between a bodybuilder and a cowboy. Lilly and Alyssa were the blonde clones. "When did you say the other girls will be here?"

His expression at once grew somber, and she wondered why the missing campers were such a painful subject. "Tomorrow," he said.

Perhaps he had dated one of them and it had turned out badly.

Or . . . she couldn't think of another explanation. It was love gone wrong or . . .

This went to prove what her mother had said about Tori all along. She was too much of a romantic. It was probably the other reason her parents had let her come to camp—they didn't want her getting too serious with Roland over the summer.

The first time Roland had asked Tori out, her father had grimaced and said, "You remind that boy I have friends in high places. If he so much as brings you home past your curfew, I will have state troopers trailing you on all subsequent dates."

What would her parents think if she started dating someone from Dragon Camp? After all, she'd met four guys so far, and each one had been handsome and buff and . . . she was staring at Jesse again and made herself stop. She gazed at the trees, at the cool, green branches held out like offerings.

Besides, Jesse was too uptight for her. Roland was outgoing, charismatic, and he smiled all the time. She would call him as soon as she had a free minute.

Jesse didn't say anything else as they rode, although she caught him stealing glances at her a few times. Then the pathway narrowed, and Jesse's horse took the lead. It would have been hard to talk at that point, so she didn't even try. She just enjoyed the sequestered feeling of the forest and the absence of city sounds: the crowds, passing cars, and airplanes. The fragrance of growing things swirled around her, filling her lungs with the warm scent of summer.

The last part of the trail narrowed even farther. It grew rutted and bumpy where rainfall had carved through it, then leveled out into a clearing. A ring of boulders surrounded a fire pit in the middle of the clearing, and a stack of cut wood sat next to it. Behind the circle of boulders, a large, gray shed stood guard over the clearing. Grass, bushes, and a few yellow and white wildflowers dotted the ground.

Several of the trees showed burned patches, evidence of some past fire.

"This is the Easter grounds," Jesse said, walking his horse around the stone circle. "It's a straight shot, so you can't get lost even in the dark."

She nodded, not sure why he'd given her this information.

"We come up here in the dark," he said, "when we go running at night."

"You don't use a lighted path?"

"There's enough light to see."

"Oh." She imagined everyone running with their flashlights jiggling out in front of them.

"Now you've seen it, so you'll have a mental picture of it when we run up here tonight."

Tori looked around the clearing and the uneven path that led to it. Yep, she had a mental picture. She had a mental picture of herself sitting on her bed going through text messages instead of running.

Jesse glanced at his watch. "I'd better take you back to camp now. Dr. B won't be happy if I make you late for your dragon mythology class."

So he knew her class schedule, too. Didn't these people have any sense of privacy?

Jesse rode his horse back down the trail, and Tori followed, enjoying the graceful lilt of Noche's gait and the way his black coat gleamed in the sunlight. She and Jesse didn't talk again until they got to the wide part. Then Tori, partially to be polite and partially because she was curious, said, "So do you live around here?"

"D.C.," he said.

"What do your parents do?"

He shot her a look as though she'd asked how much money they made. "My parents are teachers."

She pretended not to notice the edge in his voice. "That must be nice when you need help with your homework. What grade are you?"

"I'll be a senior."

So he wasn't much older. "What school do you go to?"

He tilted his head, his expression guarded. "Why do you ask?"

"Just making small talk."

He didn't answer. He was studying her, though she wasn't sure what he hoped to figure out.

She let out a sigh. "Look, I'm sorry for what I said in the parking lot. Really. But are you going to be this way the whole time?"

"What way?"

"Sullen. Moody." She would have added another adjective, but she couldn't quite put her finger on what else he was.

"You think I'm sullen and moody?" he asked with as much astonishment as offense.

"Yeah. This is a camp. It's supposed to be fun, but you're acting like a drill sergeant."

His eyes narrowed. "A drill sergeant? That would make this a military camp, I suppose?"

He was studying her again, waiting for her reaction. *Suspicious.* That was the other adjective that described him.

She forced a smile in his direction. "You know, you really need to work on your small-talk skills." And then, because she didn't want to try and resuscitate the conversation, she urged her horse to go faster. Noche happily galloped the rest of the way down the trail.

When Tori reached the field, it was empty. The rest of the campers must have found something more entertaining to do than wait for her return. Good. She rode Noche over to the stables, stroking his mane, and cooing words of thanks to him.

Booker, unsmiling, came out to meet her. "Where's Jesse?"

Before she could answer, Booker looked past her. "Oh, there he is."

She turned and saw Jesse riding across the field behind her. General's mane swished in the breeze, and he held his proudly, like he was returning victoriously from battle. She had hoped she'd left Jesse behind on the trail, though she'd never checked to see if he had sped up to follow her. She hadn't wanted to let him know she cared either way.

"Everything go okay?" Booker asked.

"Yep." Tori dismounted and walked the last few steps to Booker. "Noche is a great horse."

Booker grunted as he took the reins. "That's true enough, but you weren't riding Noche. This here is Bane." Booker reached up to stroke the horse's neck. The horse tossed his head and took a step backward, annoyed by Booker's hand. "Got named for Dragon's Bane, but it's more accurate to say he's the bane of my existence. Just plain ornery most of the time."

"Oh," Tori said, a little breathless at this information. Booker had given her the harder horse after all. "Well, he behaved himself for me."

"I imagine he did." Booker looked at Jesse as he said this.

"She's had ten years of riding lessons," Jesse said. "Of course she's learned a few things about handling horses."

"Of course," Booker said, but it didn't sound like agreement. "I'm sure that's why Bane's taken to her."

Jesse dismounted and turned to Tori. "Mythology class is back up at the main camp. It's in the building next to the cafeteria. You'll need to take one of the carts, follow the trail we used to come down here, and park at the office." His eyes didn't leave hers. "No one else is allowed to use the carts or come out here, so don't even mention this part of camp to anybody, okay?"

He waited for her to answer.

"Okay," she said.

Instead of giving General's reins to Booker, Jesse headed to the stable himself. "I'll see you later," he called.

Tori supposed this ended her orientation of Dragon Camp. Well, that was fine. It wasn't like she wanted to spend time with him and his friends anyway. In fact, she planned on doing as little of it as possible from now on.

# CHAPTER 6

Dr. B had told Jesse to text him after Tori's orientation. "Tell me what you think of her," he'd said.

Jesse fingered his phone, mulling over the question. Tori was either an excellently trained plant or a poorly trained Slayer. If she was a plant, then they had problems. If she was a Slayer, then she had problems. Tori would have to catch up on her training and do it fast. She'd have to learn strategies, skills, plans—and learn that the world held more dangers than she imagined. Right now she was just a babe in the woods.

The analogy made him grin. The woods surrounded camp and Tori was definitely a babe. The whole time she had shot targets, he'd found himself staring at her . . . at that Hollywood face, long legs, and smooth skin. Every time she'd flashed her green eyes at him, his concentration had fallen apart.

Yeah, that whole hot-girl thing was going to cause all sorts of trouble.

Beautiful girls were used to smiling and getting their way. Tori would probably question every order he gave and ditch the hard work.

On top of that, Lilly didn't like her, which could turn every practice into a cat fight. And if the guys liked Tori, they would start pulling stupid stunts to impress her. That was why Dr. B had always told them not to get involved with one another. For the most part, they'd done a decent job of following that rule. This year might be different.

Jesse texted: *She needs work.*

A minute later, Dr. B wrote back: *Then she's come to the right place.*

Maybe. Jesse slipped his phone into his pocket. If Tori wasn't legit, it would be evident soon enough. And then Jesse would make a point of finding out who had sent her.

CHAPTER 7

Instead of going straight to class, Tori made a detour to the showers. Her jeans were dusty from the horseback riding and she was afraid her shirt smelled sweaty. And, of course, a person's hair never looked good after being smashed into helmets most of the morning. Besides, who knew what the shower schedule would be like later? She took a brief shower—brief even by Jesse's Spartan rinse, lather, rinse standards—then threw on khaki shorts and a casual top. She French braided her hair, applied a touch of makeup, and walked to the back of the rifle range where the carts were parked.

As she slipped behind the wheel, she looked up at the roof. Just like at the main office, a small camera peeked out of its eaves.

Did the camp have a problem with vandals or something?

She turned on the cart, backed it up, and glanced at the tree branches, checking for more cameras. Yep, there was another one, not far away.

It was only because she was scanning the area for cameras that she saw it.

Something was in the forest, watching her. At first she thought it was a person. It was tall enough. But when she turned to get a better look, it leaped upward. One moment a form was there, the next moment a blur of blue and red disappeared into the canopy of leaves.

She didn't wait around to find out what it was. She took the cart out of reverse and pressed the gas pedal down, driving away from the spot as fast as she could.

Nothing pursued her. There was no sign, no noises from whatever had been in the woods. But her heart rate didn't settle down for several minutes.

Dragon mythology class turned out to be a disappointment. It wasn't that Dr. B was a bad teacher. He clearly knew a ton about history, and was good at asking questions that opened up discussions, but it was clear from the start of class that the rest of the students loved dragons; thought of them as flying hotrods or something.

Tori had come to camp in the hopes of understanding certain things about herself. Like why dragons always seemed to show up in her dreams, waiting outside her consciousness to pounce at her with gaping jaws. Sometimes when she went running through her subdivision at night, it wasn't her heartbeat she heard thudding in her ears. It was a dragon's. She could almost feel the deep inhale and exhale of its lungs, almost sense its presence hovering somewhere above her. If there was a way to vanquish these dragons, she wanted to know how.

Wasn't that the whole point of this camp—to slay dragons, not enshrine them?

One guy even said, "Man, it would be so cool if they were real."

It wouldn't have been cool. It would have been awful. Tori had known this from the time she was four years old and she'd smashed her father's glass dragon collection on the same day he'd brought it out of storage.

That was one of her earliest memories—her father yelling at her for destroying the figurines, while she'd stood there bewildered, wondering why he wasn't thanking her. He, inexplicably, liked dragons.

In fact, on her eleventh birthday, her father had bought her two crystal dragons so she could start her own collection. Really, he should have known better than to give her that sort of gift.

Granted, she had read every dragon book around, and when she and Aprilynne were younger, they used to pretend they rode dragons. The two of them would rush through the house, arms outstretched, soaring in their imaginary world. It felt exhilarating and a bit wicked.

But Tori didn't react well to the surprise theme of her eleventh birthday party. While the whole family sang "Happy Birthday," Tori's mother had brought in a cake frosted with fiery orange and pink flames. The crystal dragons stood in front of the glowing candles, peering at her with smug, treacherous eyes. Without thinking about it, Tori grabbed the dragons off the cake and threw them against the kitchen wall.

The crystal shattered with a chorus of cracks, then made popping sounds as the pieces hit the floor. She heard it perfectly because everyone stopped singing. They stared at her, open-mouthed, while pieces of glass skittered across the tile. She couldn't explain to her parents why she'd done it. She didn't know herself. She'd only said, "They looked mean."

Her parents made her talk to a counselor for several months after that incident. The counselor, a woman who wore loud, flashy colors and had so many gold bracelets they tinkled like wind chimes, told Tori's parents she was projecting her fears of failure, which she didn't know how to deal with, into the shape of the dragon—a creature she couldn't deal with. The counselor said Tori's parents put too much pressure on her to be a high achiever, and it had created a deep fear of not measuring up to their expectations.

The counseling sessions ended abruptly after that. Not because her parents were insulted, but because they knew they'd never pushed Tori to be a high achiever. Her parents didn't even insist she get straight As like so many of her friends' parents. They just told her to do her best in school. Which she did, if she happened to like the subject. If not, Bs were fine. After all, why overstudy when her dad could get her into any university she wanted?

Tori's father had decided she just had a vivid imagination and would probably grow up to be a writer. Tori's mother thought she had somehow transferred her own fear of dragons to her daughter. While Mrs. Hampton had been pregnant, she'd had a horrible nightmare about a dragon chasing her. For a solid year afterward, she couldn't look at any sort of dragon without shuddering and feeling the chill of dragon claws against her spine.

She figured she must have said something about dragons during Tori's formative years. Tori, in turn, internalized it and thought she needed to protect her family from this threat.

Tori liked that theory best, that her obsession with dragons meant she loved her family. Because she did. And that sounded so much better than being a writer or being unable to face failure.

Tori didn't say much in Dr. B's class. She even kept her mouth shut when he asked why dragon stories had shown up in so many societies.

Dragons had shown up everywhere, Tori thought, *because they really existed once.* If she had said that, her classmates would've spent the rest of the month asking about her position on fairies and alien abductions.

So she sat in her chair silently. It figured. Even here surrounded by a bunch of dragon nerds, she was the odd one.

The only good thing about class was that it was filled with people who were about her age, and who seemed decidedly nicer than Alyssa and Lilly. Which meant Tori could ask Dr. B to transfer her to another cabin, and camp would get much better.

After class while Dr. B erased the white board, she went up to talk to him about it. When he noticed her, he stopped erasing and smiled at her. "Did you get situated in cabin twenty-seven?"

She tapped her fingers against the edge of her notebook. "Um, I wanted to talk to you about that . . ." How could she put this without insulting the longtime campers who came early every year to help him set up? "I'm not sure I fit in with the girls in twenty-seven. Do any of the other cabins have openings?"

The smile dropped from his face, and she knew her efforts at diplomacy had failed. She had wounded him with the question. "What's the problem with cabin twenty-seven?" he asked.

"Well, they're such a tight-knit group already, and I understand that. They're comfortable with each other, and I'm new, and . . ." And Lilly and Alyssa were petty. "I think it would be better if I moved to a different cabin." As far away from cabin 26 as she could be, only she didn't add that part, either.

His eyebrows drew together in concern. "Perhaps you got off on the wrong foot with the advanced campers, and if that's the case, I apologize for them. They're a wonderful group of kids—and you haven't even met Bess and Rosa yet." He laid his hand on her shoulder. "Give it a chance. Lilly and Alyssa are coming to invite you to have dinner with them. I'm sure they're waiting right outside." He patted her shoulder. "We'll talk about this again in a day or two."

A day or two? She didn't even want to put up with Lilly and Alyssa for dinner. Only it seemed unreasonable to say so. Tori managed a weak smile, mumbled, "Okay," and walked out of the room.

Lilly and Alyssa were nowhere in sight, which shouldn't have surprised her. Dr. B didn't understand teenage girls as well as he thought he did.

Tori caught up with a group of kids from her class and walked toward the cafeteria with them. She was about to go through the cafeteria doors when Lilly and Alyssa strolled up to her. Instead of appearing friendly, the two girls seemed mildly put out. "Hey, we're here to get you for dinner," Lilly said.

"Thanks," Tori said, "but I'm going to eat with the people from my class."

Lilly and Alyssa blinked at her, apparently unwilling to believe she'd turned them down. "You're supposed to eat with the advanced campers," Alyssa said.

"Oh. Well, I'm not really an advanced camper, so I'm going to eat with the regular campers instead."

Lilly scowled. "Suit yourself, but Dr. B won't like it. You're part of Jesse's team." Then she spun on her heel, and both she and Alyssa stalked off, their blonde hair swishing angrily. They headed toward a cart, which made Tori wonder if they ate meals back at their secret camp. She didn't watch to find out.

Dinner consisted of hamburgers and fries, although the food had been given cutesy names. The potato wedges were now "dragon's teeth," which in Tori's mind made them less appetizing. She had to keep reassuring herself that they were fried potatoes and that putting them in her mouth wouldn't break her teeth into little shards.

Tori ate absentmindedly, letting the conversation flow past her like she was a boulder in a stream of words. That's what it always felt like when she was in a large crowd. The voices sounded like multiple sound tracks lying on top of one another, and she either had to concentrate and block out all but one conversation, or she relaxed and let them all wash around her.

Then she heard her name. Not called. Just spoken. Someone was talking about her. She glanced in that direction and saw Jesse, Dirk, Lilly, and Alyssa standing against the far wall by the door. They were staring at her and stopped talking when she looked up.

She forced a smile, which only Dirk returned. Even indoors his surfer-boy blond hair had gorgeous highlights. Probably all natural. He didn't look like the type that would set foot in a salon.

Tori wondered if the group had come here to reinvite her to eat dinner with them. She returned her attention to the people around her, but she tuned them out and strained to hear a few more words of the advanced campers' conversation. She shouldn't have been able to hear any of it. They stood too far away. And yet when they spoke again, she heard them.

Jesse said, "So much for your theory that Tori is a spy."

Dirk's voice held none of the friendliness his smile had. "Just because she's really here and not snooping around doesn't mean she's legit."

"I don't trust her," Lilly said. "Where has she been for the last five years?"

"She might have reasons," Jesse said.

"If the authorities wanted to snoop around," Dirk put in, "she's the type they'd send. We already know she has connections with the government. And she stunk at archery. You said so yourself."

Jesse's voice stayed even. "Dr. B trusts her. So does Bane."

Lilly let out a scoffing grunt. "Dr. B is an optimist, and Bane is a horse. Don't tell me you're going to trust a horse's judgment."

Jesse nearly conceded the point, but not quite. "The horse is impartial."

"And yet it's still a *horse*," Lilly said.

"Dr. B is just desperate," Alyssa added. "He's trying to make up for the fact that we've lost Leo and Danielle."

"We haven't lost them yet." The pain in Jesse's voice made Tori look up, as though his expression would explain everything. It didn't, and the group stopped talking again.

Tori forced her gaze back to the table and the people around her, not really seeing them as she tried to process what she'd heard. Why were they worried about anyone snooping around? What was there to find? And why the reference to her archery score—which hadn't stunk, but had been impressive—well, impressive until Jesse had shot a bull's-eye without facing the target.

"She heard us," Alyssa said.

"She couldn't have," Jesse said.

"Unless she's wired," Dirk said.

"Or we are," Lilly said. "Wouldn't we need to be the ones who are bugged for her to hear us?"

Then none of them said anything else.

When Tori looked over again, they had gone. Probably out checking their shoes and clothing to make sure no one had snuck electronic listening devices on them.

She inwardly laughed at the thought. It served them right for being so paranoid. But why were they? And if they were hiding something, was the camp staff involved, too? She thought of the people she'd met, letting each one drift through her memory. What was going on at this camp that made the advanced campers worry about spies? Drugs, maybe? Steroids?

Then another thought came to her mind. Dirk wore a red shirt and blue jeans. The thing she'd seen in the woods had been a blur of red and blue.

Had it been him? If it had been, how had he moved upward so fast?

She wasn't sure about anything except one thing. The sooner she transferred to the main camp, the better.

CHAPTER 8

After dinner, the campers had free time. Tori played volleyball with the kids at her table, then went to the camp library to write a paper for her dragon mythology class. Dr. B had assigned an essay and given them the choice of three topics: similarities found in dragon lore; dragon habits and abilities; or methods of defeat. She'd already read all the books on the reading list except for a book Dr. B had written. She decided to skim it to see what his philosophies were so she'd know how to slant—or defend—her viewpoints.

The library was a small cabin that housed several bookshelves, a few soft chairs, and a row of computers and printers. It didn't take Tori long to find Dr. B's book: *A Comprehensive Overview of Dragons and Their Ecology*. It was a thin hardback with a cover that looked boring enough to scare off the most avid dragon fan. She sat down with it anyway. He'd written an introduction about researching oral histories and medieval records. As Tori scanned the list of sources, she was impressed. She'd finally found a person who knew more about dragons than she did.

The book was divided into sections: similarities found in dragon lore; dragon habits and abilities; and methods of defeat. The same three topics they could choose for their papers. It was almost as if he wanted the class to skip the recommended reading list and just study his book.

She turned to dragon habits and abilities. That would make for an easy paper.

Although the size of dragon eggs and their natural nesting places remain unknown, it is clear that dragons lay their eggs in twos: One male and one female, thus ensuring the survival of the species.

Had she ever read that before? She couldn't remember, but it seemed right.

Dragons have no natural predators, so unlike other animals, they don't reproduce in large numbers. The female lays only one or two clutches of eggs in her lifetime and does not lay eggs until she is in her thirties, near the middle of her lifespan. The gestation period of the eggs is between fifteen and twenty years, thus assuring that her children will not compete with her for resources—or at least not for long. Various accounts and lack of fossil records indicate that dragons didn't usually die of old age, but were killed by younger, stronger dragons, perhaps even their own offspring. The victors not only got territorial rights, but also had a feast that could sustain them for some time.

Tori lowered the book to her lap. Dragons ate their parents? Creepy.

The key to dragons' long-term survival is their ability to choose their eggs' gestation period. If the mother is under

> stress from lack of food or other threats, she lays eggs
> which hibernate. These eggs won't hatch for one hundred
> and fifty years.

What? Tori knew she'd never read this before, and she gripped the book tighter. Where had Dr. B gotten that information from? She flipped through the pages, searching for footnotes, but didn't see any. She turned to the back, looking for an index. Nothing there, either.

It shouldn't bother her. Her heart shouldn't be pounding like this. It was a book about mythical creatures. Authors could say anything about them, because they didn't exist.

But her heart rate didn't slow down. Her mind was already doing the calculations. If dragons had gestation periods of one hundred and fifty years, then they could still exist. Back in the nineteenth century, the world still had enough wild places that a dragon might not be discovered.

She turned back to the book. The next sentence didn't make her feel better.

> This theory of dragons corroborates with several unex-
> plained sightings of flying creatures in southwest America
> in the 1800s, often called Thunderbirds by the Native
> Americans.

Tori's throat went dry. She'd noticed something about Dr. B's writing. He didn't talk about dragons in the past tense. The descriptions were written in the present tense, as though he expected a dragon to hatch any day now.

She tried to shake off the alarm spreading up her back. It was all hype. Most kids at camp probably got a kick out of a book that made you think you could see a dragon flying overhead when you walked out of the room.

She put the book down. Why had she thought coming to this camp was a good idea? It didn't make her feel understood. She wasn't really going to learn anything to help her defeat dragons or her stupid obsession with them. This camp would only give her nightmares.

Still, she picked up the book again.

Newly hatched dragons are the size of grown lions. Driven by hunger, they're capable of hunting and killing prey much larger than they are. For the first year, they eat voraciously, thus doubling their size in quick succession until their bodies alone are the size of busses. With wings, legs, neck, and tail added, some estimate that a mature dragon would weigh between twenty and forty tons, depending on whether dragons, like birds and some dinosaurs, have hollow bones. Once dragons near their maximum size, their appetites taper off, and like their reptilian cousins the snakes, they go weeks between eating and sustain themselves on smaller portions. Their diet includes large mammals, including humans.

Humans. Tori's stomach turned. This wasn't new information. All the old stories said dragons killed people. But seeing it written in present tense made it more gruesome.

Maybe she should write her report on methods of defeat. That was bound to make her feel better. After all, if knights could kill dragons using weapons from the Middle Ages, what did she have to worry about?

She flipped to that section.

Dragons are built as formidable killing machines. In addition to their claws and fire-breathing ability, their size, strength, thick armorlike skin, flight, speed, and maneuverability make them almost unstoppable. It is doubtful that weapons from the modern day would be successful in destroying a dragon.

Dr. B didn't explain why he doubted this, which annoyed Tori. She'd been happily thinking about combat helicopters.

So how did the medieval population deal with this threat? Some records indicate that people didn't try to defeat dragons. Rulers simply found ways to appease dragons with cattle or other sacrifices. Often these sacrifices were young maidens, as medieval society didn't place a high value on women. The fact that dragons ate humans accounts in part for the low population numbers during the Middle Ages.

Since dragons are solitary and territorial by nature, villagers were at least assured that they only had to feed one dragon. If another dragon tried to move in, the first would challenge it. Dragon fights must have been a fierce and spectacular sight for villagers to watch.

"Spectacular sight." Great. Where was the part about killing them? She skimmed farther down the page.

Kings offered huge bounties for slain dragons. People had little success in this endeavor until the alchemists invented gold. Not the precious metal, but an elixir which would change people's DNA, giving them the powers they needed to defeat the dragons. These powers included flight, the ability to douse fire, heal burns, and throw shields up.

With these skills in place, the dragon population dwindled. It was no doubt the work of these specially endowed knights which caused the few remaining dragons to choose a hibernation period for their eggs.

Tori stopped reading and flipped through the pages, scanning the headings. Where did it say how to make the elixir? That information had to be in the book. Dr. B wouldn't go to the trouble of studying the elixir and then not tell people how to make it.

She didn't see anything with a recipe or an ingredients list. No headings about the elixir. The frustration nearly made her rip out pages. She had to find it. She had to . . .

She put the book down in her lap and rubbed her forehead. It was only a story, a fairy tale. In all probability, one of the camp events would entail Dr. B making a big batch of root beer and calling it elixir. He'd have the entire camp drink it, and then proclaim them knights of the realm.

Tori let out a long sigh. Maybe that counselor with the jangly bracelets was right about her. Maybe she was transferring some deep-seated fear into the form of a dragon. This wasn't healthy, what she was doing to herself.

Tori stood up and put the book firmly back on the shelf. She would write her paper on the similarities of dragon lore from different countries. She could type that one right now, and it wouldn't get her worked up in the process.

She spent the next hour writing the paper, then drove a cart back to the advanced camp.

Cabin 27 was empty when Tori reached it. Which was fine. The day still had some sunlight left, so she changed into exercise clothes. She needed to unwind, and besides, if she ran now, she would have an excuse not to go with the advanced campers. A quick glance in the mirror satisfied her that in her Lycra shorts and slim-fitting shirt, she looked as toned and muscular as her cabinmates. Jesse couldn't fault her in that regard, even if he did think her archery score stunk.

She stretched, then set off in a casual run toward the biggest building, the one neither Jesse or Dirk would talk about. No one was in the field or anywhere that she could see on the trails that led to the different buildings.

The end of Tori's French braid slapped against her back as she ran. Bird calls sliced through the silence, sounding like shrill, ominous warnings. She drew closer to the large building. There weren't any windows. That was suspicious, wasn't it? As she came closer, she heard muffled noises from inside—shouting, but not shouts of fear or anger. Shouting like you heard during a football game. The advanced campers were probably inside doing some sort of activity.

She jogged over to the smallest building. It had large windows, but no glass. Some sort of thick mesh screen covered the openings. Perhaps that's why the sound coming out of them was so clear.

At first she thought it was a laundry facility. The noise coming from the building sounded like tennis shoes in a dryer—a loud and steady *tha-thump, tha-thump, tha-thump*. But after a few moments, she realized the sound was too regular. Tennis shoes in a dryer had some randomness to it. Things didn't always fall in the exact same place.

She slowed her stride. It must be some sort of equipment, a water pump maybe, or a generator. On second thought, she'd heard generators, and they hummed. A water pump then.

Something else about the sound bothered her. It was familiar somehow, like she ought to recognize it, but she had never heard a water pump before. She reached the front of the building. Instead of one door, two stood side by side.

Slowly, she walked to the doors. They might be open, and if not, she could peer into one of the windows and see what was inside. The noise would bother her until she figured out what it was.

But as she put her hand on the doorknob, she recognized the sound. It was a heartbeat—a large reverberating heartbeat.

She dropped her hand from the doorknob, afraid that at any instant something would burst through those doors and pounce on her. It was a ridiculous idea, and yet she couldn't shake it. Something in there was alive.

She took a step backward, ready to turn and sprint away. But she was no longer alone. A man had come up behind her. He stood so close that she plowed into him as she turned and ran. He grabbed hold of her arm to steady her, or maybe just to keep her from escaping.

It was only then that she realized it was Booker. He wore a gruff expression, although really, in the short time Tori had known him, his expression had always been gruff.

"What are you doing?" he asked.

She stepped away from him, putting a hand to her chest to regain her breath. "You startled me," she said, stalling while she composed herself. She was glad she wore running clothes. People expected joggers to be short on breath. "I was out for a run and thought I'd check out the laundry room." She motioned toward the building and tried to keep her voice light, unconcerned. "Then I decided to wait until I had some laundry." She watched his face to see if he bought the story.

His stance relaxed. He believed her. "It's not a laundry room. It's a storage space where we keep heavy machinery. It's off limits to campers."

"Oh, sorry." She forced a smile. He expected her to believe that? How many pieces of machinery had heartbeats? Then she realized what she should have known all along. Only *she* heard the heartbeat. Her and her oddly good hearing. He stood right next to her and didn't hear a thing.

"Where is the laundry room, then?" she asked, taking several steps away from the building.

"At the main camp."

"Maybe I'll just run to the lake, then." She didn't wait around for more conversation. She took off in that direction, going much faster than a normal jogger would have.

For the first ten minutes of her run, Tori planned on dashing as far away from Booker as possible, calling her parents, then heading to the main camp and waiting for them to pick her up. It would take them two and a half hours to drive here, and she debated whether it would be safer to wait in the parking lot or whether she should continue down the street to meet them along the road.

But what would she tell them when she called? That she had to leave camp right now because she'd heard the heartbeat of some living thing in one of their buildings?

Her parents would immediately take her back to Ms. Jingly Bracelets.

Tori sped along the path that led down to the lake. She needed to get rid of the energy that had built up inside. Her footsteps muffled the noises in the forest around her. Good. She didn't want to hear anything else.

When Tori reached the lake, the sun was setting, casting orange shadows into the blue-gray water. Waves carelessly lapped into an empty dock. Buoys bobbed up and down in the distance. It was the normal world again; she could think straight.

Monsters did not exist. Except for in her mind, where they ran rampant. But that wasn't such a big deal, really. A lot of people had phobias of silly things. Mice, heights, flying in airplanes. So she'd heard a strange noise and freaked out. Sometimes that sort of thing happened in life, even to brave people.

And it wasn't the main reason she wanted to leave camp anyway. The important thing was the advanced campers were hiding something. Something illegal, probably. For that reason alone, she shouldn't stay here. It had nothing to do with the heartbeat, so she didn't have to mention that part to her parents.

Tori slowed to a walk and took her cell phone out of her pocket. It searched for service, then kept searching. The light was fading now, but she kept walking along the lakeshore, slowing her breaths so she could talk without panting.

Her cell phone searched some more, then finally told her: No Service.

No service?

She stared at her phone as though it might change its mind. When it didn't, she shoved it in her pocket. Her phone would work back at the main camp. Jesse had used his cell phone while he brought her things to cabin 27. The problem was that the main camp was two miles away and she didn't want to go all the way back to the advanced camp to get a cart.

Tori stood by the lake for a few minutes, wondering how hard it would be to find the main camp from here. It couldn't be that far away. She set off in that direction, checking her phone every so often. She wished she'd driven her own car to camp, but her father hadn't wanted her to leave her new Lexus unattended in the parking lot for a month. *He should have known,* she thought wryly, *that the car wouldn't be there long at all.*

As the sun dropped lower in the sky, her walk turned into a run, fast again, because she suddenly felt cut off from the world. She usually ran in her gated subdivision. Here, running next to the shadowy forest, she was vulnerable. Something could pop out of the trees at any time. Finally, she came upon more docks, boats, and a path that had to lead to the main camp.

It was nearly dark when she came upon a couple of guys she recognized from her dragon class. Cole and David—two tall, thin guys who Tori would have thought were cute if she hadn't been bunking near four guys who could pass as Outback Gear models. Cole and David were walking to the main camp, flashlights in one hand, fishing poles in the other. Their flashlights cut arcs of light through the evening air.

Cole glanced at the phone in her hand and gave her a look like she should know better. "You can't get coverage up here. They told us that at orientation. The only phones that work are at the office and the nurse's station, but you're not supposed to bother the nurse unless you're gushing blood or have broken bones sticking out of your body."

Tori gripped her phone in frustration. "But Jesse's phone worked."

"Who's Jesse?" David asked.

"One of the advanced campers."

Cole raised an eyebrow. "Advanced campers?"

Tori didn't elaborate. Since she wasn't supposed to tell anyone where the advanced camp was, she probably wasn't supposed to say anything about the advanced campers, either. Which, now that she thought about it, was a bizarre rule. What was the point of hiding two cabins?

She glanced around to make sure no one else was near, then said, "Do you guys get the feeling something odd is going on at this camp?"

Cole shrugged. "Besides the fact that the food here is actually edible, not really."

Tori didn't laugh at his joke. She was already planning on how to use the phone in the nurse's office. And then Tori realized that it wouldn't matter anyway. Her parents were busy with their party. And even if Aprilynne could get away, she wouldn't want to drive on the back roads in the dark to get to camp.

Tori was trapped here for the night.

She shoved her phone back into her pocket, disappointed. She might as well go back to her cabin before it got completely dark. She hadn't brought a flashlight with her.

"I'll see you guys later," she told Cole and David and headed back, halfheartedly, in the direction she'd come.

"Where are you going?" David called after her. "Camp is the other direction."

She didn't answer or explain. She just broke into a run, racing the sunset.

The air was colder now. She took her hair out of the French braid so it offered some warmth to her neck. The forest around her had faded into gray shadows, and the sounds seemed amplified. She heard branches rustle. And other noises. Things she couldn't identify.

She ran along the lakeshore until she came to the dock by the advanced camp. From there, the trail was easy enough to find. It would take her back to cabin 27. And whatever was in that small building.

Dragons don't exist, she told herself. *And even if they do exist, they don't live in buildings in the middle of kids' camps. This is just my vivid imagination working overtime—the one that's going to doom me to be a writer.*

When the trail opened into the camp, she slowed to a walk, blinking at what she saw. Lights blazed from both cabins. The brightness spilled out into the night with such strength that the cabins nearly looked like they were on fire. She had to look away from them, letting her eyes adjust to the brilliance. What in the world were the advanced campers doing inside? Hiding spotlights?

Jesse stood outside, hands in his pockets, halfway between cabins 26 and 27. He reminded her of one of those long-ago knights she'd read about earlier. Rugged. Strong. He watched her walk up, and she wondered how long he'd been there, silently studying her.

As Tori got closer, she could see the disbelief on his face. "You curled your hair to go running?"

She touched her hair and the waves that had dried into it from being in a French braid all afternoon. She could have explained it, but instead shrugged. "A girl likes to look her best."

"Which I suppose is why you're in your fourth outfit for the day."

She had to count to make sure he was right. There was the one she arrived in, the one she wore horseback riding, the one she changed into after her shower, and this one. Yep, four. He still had on the same jeans and T-shirt he'd worn in the parking lot, although he'd added a jacket.

He looked her over again. "No wonder your suitcases were so heavy."

"I'm about to change into my fifth. My pajamas." She cast a glance at the bathrooms and wondered if the other campers would think it was excessive to take two showers today. She didn't want to get thrown in the lake, but she always showered after running. Besides, the water heater must have had a chance to reheat since her first one.

"Don't change yet," Jesse said. "We've still got to go up to the Easter grounds. We were waiting for you to show up so we could leave."

"Sorry, I already went running."

She tried to walk around him, but he shifted, standing in her way. "I told you that we go together every night. It's a team competition, and you're on my team."

"Yeah, about that . . ." She took a step sideways. "I'm not really into team camaraderie and camp spirit and all of that. Besides, it's stupid to run this late. I'd probably sprain an ankle."

He moved, blocking her way again. Even in the dark, his eyes looked deep and intense. His pupils were so large, his eyes seemed completely black. "You didn't have a flashlight on the way down, and you could still see fine."

"Yeah, but that's because it's not all the way dark yet . . ." She glanced at her watch. It was almost nine o'clock, well after sunset. She looked at the sky next, expecting the moon to be full and hanging in the sky like a giant night-light. Instead, only a curving sliver sliced through the sky. "Why is it so light still?"

"Your first night is an initiation into the group," he said. "You have to come."

Her gaze stayed on the moon, trying to understand. True, the stars blazed white and strong, unhindered by city lights, but they weren't bright enough to light up the forest this way.

So softly that he must have been speaking to himself, he said, "You *are* one of us."

She didn't pretend that she hadn't heard him like she usually would have done. Instead, she turned her attention to him. "And what are you, Jesse?"

He smiled at her, and the darkness left sinister shadows across his face. "You'll see up at the Easter grounds."

CHAPTER 9

The panic that Tori had felt during her run began to prickle up her spine again. Casually, she took her phone out of her pocket to see if it got service down here. It didn't. Why hadn't she gone to the main camp when she had the chance and insisted on sleeping there?

Dirk came out of his cabin, pulling on a sweatshirt. His gaze ran over Tori, studying her every bit as intently as Jesse had. "She's here," he called over his shoulder, and Kody and Shang followed him out.

Kody gave her a big smile as he came toward her. Even his walk reminded her of a cowboy. "You ready for a mess of fun?"

"I already went running, so I'm tired." She tried to sound apologetic. "I'll just have to go with you guys tomorrow night."

Jesse regarded her evenly. "You can make it up to the Easter grounds. It's only three miles."

As if three miles were nothing. And even though she wasn't that tired—all of her fear must have dumped a lot of adrenaline into her system—there was no way she was going to run three miles in the dark to a remote place with these people. No way. "I don't think Dr. B would approve of us running right now."

Jesse's eyes were still locked on hers. "Dr. B is up there waiting for us."

He was? Somehow the thought of him up there creeped her out even more. Maybe he was the one who fed random campers to the dragon. No, not random campers. In the medieval lore, they always fed a maiden to the dragons. A virgin.

Her.

It was a ridiculous thought, she knew, and yet she couldn't shake it, couldn't consign it to the realm of silly phobias. These people were dangerous. She felt it.

Tori's mouth went dry. She was so far away from the main camp. If she screamed now, no one would hear her.

She could try to fight. She knew martial arts. But they outnumbered her, and Jesse and Dirk were both black belts. In order to get away, she'd need the element of surprise and a good head start. She tried to keep her voice even. "Okay. I'll go, but don't expect me to be fast."

Jesse grunted. "Be as fast as you can." Over his shoulder, he yelled, "We're waiting, A-team!"

Lilly and Alyssa strolled out of cabin 27, both pulling on jackets.

"I should get a jacket, too," Tori said. If she could go to her cabin while the rest of them waited here, perhaps she could climb out the window, slip into the forest, and make her way to the main camp. Could she trust any of the staff to help her?

Before she turned to leave, Jesse took off his jacket and tossed it to her. "Here, use mine. We're already late." He motioned her to follow. Reluctantly, she did. The group headed down the trail that led to the field.

The colors of the forest had faded to shades of gray, but she could still see the outline of each tree. Their leaves made a jigsaw of silhouettes against the dark sky. As they went, Jesse stayed beside Tori. "The first competition is a race to the Easter grounds. The top four people score: forty points for first place, thirty for second, twenty for third, and ten for fourth. If you push someone down, your team gets negative ten points—but that doesn't mean it doesn't happen, so be careful. Rosa and Bess aren't here yet, so Team Magnus is at a disadvantage. We've only got Shang, you, and me. The A-team has Dirk, Kody, Lilly, and Alyssa. We need to get at least two scores for every game." He glanced at her shoes, then let his gaze drift to her legs. "How are you at running?"

"I can hold my own," Tori said, "when I haven't already been running."

He raised an eyebrow like he wasn't sure whether to believe her. "I guess we'll see. I'm one of the fastest, so I'll try for the forty points. If Shang can pull third or fourth, we'll be in good shape. Once we hit the trailhead, the race starts. Try to keep up with us. If you can't, we'll see you at the top."

Tori let out a breath of relief. They wouldn't be guarding her on the way up.

They walked past the first building, the larger one. When they went by the second building, she held her breath and listened, waiting to hear the *tha-thump* from inside. But nothing filtered through the night air except the sound of their footsteps and the crickets in the forest.

She could have imagined it earlier, but knew she hadn't. Whatever had been in the building was gone now. Or perhaps not gone, just waiting for them someplace else. Like the Easter grounds.

They reached the trailhead. Tori could make out the shapes of rocks, bushes, and individual tree limbs. What was it about this place that made everything glow with a dim light of its own?

Dirk yelled, "Go!" and the group took off. Jesse and Dirk sprinted ahead, shoulder to shoulder, all legs and muscle. Somehow, they made running look effortless. The others followed en masse, going too quickly for a three-mile run. Tori's pace was only a slow jog.

"Come on," Kody said, straggling behind to talk to her. "I know you're a mite faster than that. If you're last, Lilly's going to rub it in."

Tori didn't increase her speed. "I'll deal with the shame somehow."

Kody stayed beside her for probably a mile, encouraging her—telling her it wasn't that far, just a "hoot and a holler away." Any other time she would have appreciated his cheerfulness. Any other time she would have asked him exactly what a hoot and a holler was. But now she wondered about his motives. She remembered a dog catcher she'd seen once, coaxing a stray to come to him with a piece of bacon in one hand while he held a wire noose in the other. The dog catcher had spoken in that same lilting, cheerful voice.

So Tori spoke back to Kody in out-of-breath spurts, even though she wasn't breathless yet. She kept glancing at the forest, looking both for a place to hide and anything that might jump out. The trees seemed to be watching, standing guard along the path with arms that reached out for her.

At last Kody gave up his pep talks. He said Dirk and Jesse were probably already at the top wondering where he was, and he'd see her when she got there. Then he shortened the distance between him and the next slowest runners, Lilly and Alyssa. The two girls were barely visible on the trail up ahead, but every once in a while they looked over their shoulders to check on her.

As soon as Kody was a fair distance away, Tori turned and sprinted in the opposite direction. She had a surprising amount of energy, considering the running she'd already done. Still, she pushed herself to go faster. Every second that the others ran up the trail, and she ran down, put that much more space between them. And hopefully when Lilly or Alyssa checked on her next, they'd assume she'd fallen behind out of sight. With any luck, they wouldn't notice her absence until they reached the top. By then, it would be too late to catch her.

Unless Dr. B had a horse or a motorcycle up there.

She worried about that, then reminded herself that she'd hear a horse or a motorcycle before it overtook her. She could hide in the forest until it passed.

Her feet pounded along the trail. Her arms arced out in front of her as though trying to grab hold of the air and pull it toward her. *Faster,* she told herself, *faster.* The minutes passed. She was almost at the end of the trail, but she couldn't slow down until she'd reached the carts. Could she trust any of the adults here at camp? Maybe it was better to take the cart down the road and try to make it to the nearest town, someplace with a working phone.

Whenever she finally got a hold of her parents, they would think she had a nervous breakdown fleeing from camp this way, but she didn't care. She wanted to get away. Had to.

A breeze went through the trees, making the branches around them shudder. She could see the trailhead where the forest opened up into the field in front of the stables. Should she make a beeline to the carts, or try to follow the curve of the forest so Booker didn't see her?

Right before she reached the opening, it became a moot point. Jesse landed in front of her, blocking the path.

It was impossible that he stood there in front of her, his eyes flashing angrily. She had seen him sprint ahead of the group, fighting Dirk for the lead. The trail was straight, so he couldn't have doubled back and gotten ahead of her. Yet not only was he here, he apparently had time to climb up a tree in his search for her. How else could he have jumped down in front of her like he'd fallen from the sky?

"Where are you going?" Jesse asked. His voice had a hard edge. He walked a couple steps toward her, and she noticed in a detached way that he didn't even look like he'd broken a sweat running down here.

She fought back her fear and stood her ground, not taking her gaze off his too-dark eyes. "Get out of my way."

He didn't, but he didn't come closer. His voice was softer this time. "Where are you going, Tori?"

She put her hands on her hips, gulping in air as she tried to gage how to best get around him. "I'm leaving. Now, move."

He took a slow step toward her. "Why?"

She didn't have time to play games. If he had come back, the others might be here soon, too. She couldn't fight them all. "Look, I don't know what's going on at this camp, but I don't want to be a part of it. So you can go back to your competitions, your cult, whatever you are, but leave me alone."

He took another step toward her. "What do you think you know about us, Tori?"

She shook her head. "You're trying to stall until the others get here. It won't work. Move or I'll walk over you."

He held his hands out at his sides. "So walk over me. Let's see what you can do."

He was taller and stronger than her, but she didn't have a choice—in order to get away, she had to fight him.

She put her hands in front of her, fists clenched in guard position, then rushed toward him with a jump sidekick. He sidestepped her, avoiding the blow. She pivoted, turned, and thrust her leg out, kicking high.

He ducked, backing up. "Nice tornado kick."

It would have been nicer if she'd hit him. She swung her leg, this time landing a crescent kick in his chest. He took a step backward, but didn't go down. And she'd hit him hard.

He lifted an eyebrow, amused. "I'm glad to see you took martial arts more seriously than archery. You're not half bad at this."

She tried a roundhouse kick, but while her leg swung up, he stepped in and swept her other foot out from under her. She fell to the ground with a jarring thud.

He smiled down at her. "Of course, you're not as good as I am."

She rolled over and bounced back to her feet, her hands in guard position again. "Arrogance is the downfall of most men." She lunged into him with a reverse hook kick. This time he grabbed her foot and shoved her backward.

"Only the men who haven't practiced enough."

He was toying with her. Equal parts anger and alarm pumped through her. She had to get away before the others came, before he overpowered her. She pivoted in to strike Jesse's face. He blocked her hand with his own. She lunged one way, then spun the other, trying to get around him. She wasn't fast enough. He grabbed her and threw her over his hip to the ground. She knew the move. It was *hane goshi*, which meant he knew judo, too. Great.

He stood over her, breathing hard. "So what do you know about us? What are you running from?"

She did a backward somersault away from him, giving herself time and room to stand. "If anything happens to me, my father will level this camp. I was supposed to call him," she lied. "I'm sure by now he's getting worried. So unless you want this place crawling with police, you'd better let me go."

He didn't move. "What do you think we're doing here that would interest the police, Tori?"

It bothered her that he kept using her name. It implied a sort of intimacy she'd never given him. She pushed away the panic that pressed into her, that made her ears buzz. With a swift jump, she tried to land a reverse hook kick. All she needed was one good impact and she could run past him. She made solid contact to his chest, but he barely budged.

He was too strong. This was impossible. She wasn't going to be able to knock him down, and the last time she'd tried to go around him she'd ended up on the ground. Frustration welled inside her. "Just let me go!" She was surprised by the emotion that strangled her voice. She was nearly crying and hated herself for it. Black belts didn't cry.

She put her hands up in fighting stance, told herself to focus.

He relaxed his own stance. "I'm not the one you should worry about. I'm on your side."

"Really?" She didn't put her arms down. "Then explain what you keep in that building."

He didn't take his eyes off of her. His pupils were so large they looked like cat's eyes. "What building?"

"The one with the very large heartbeat inside."

Even in the dark she could see his confusion. "What are you talking about?"

"I heard it earlier and now it's gone. You moved it up to the Easter grounds, didn't you?"

"Oh." He let his hands drop to his sides as understanding dawned on him, and then in disbelief asked, "You *heard* that?"

"Yeah. Now get out of my way. I'm not staying here."

He took a step toward her. His manner was calm, but his stare didn't waver from her face. "What do you think it is?"

"Don't come nearer," she said.

"What do you think it is, Tori?"

She took a step backward, even though she knew she shouldn't let him force her to retreat. She had to put some space between them, though.

He watched her, still waiting.

She swallowed hard. "It's a dragon."

He smiled. Not a smile because her answer amused him, but because she'd gotten it right.

"Actually it's a dragon's *heartbeat*," he said. "Well, an electric pulse simulator of a dragon's heartbeat."

She took another step backward. "Right. That was my next guess."

"We have it at camp because the pulse turns on the part of our brain that gives us our powers." He held out a hand, palm up, as though showing her something. "It's the reason you can see in the dark. You have another power, too, something important, but we have to find out what. That's why the simulator is up at the Easter grounds."

He expected her to believe that? And yet, she could tell by his expression that *he* believed it. Tori finally lowered her hands from fighting stance. "You know, I thought I was going crazy beforehand, but I feel sane now."

"Because it makes sense?"

"No, because the rest of you are even crazier than I am." She dashed to get around him and made it, but in three long strides he'd caught up with her. He threw his arms out and tackled her. She tensed, waiting for the impact of the ground.

It never came. Instead, both of them rushed upward into the cool night air. The scream that had been building in her throat died in surprise.

Branches sped past her. The trees seemed to shrink into the ground as Jesse carried her higher and higher into the air. And then Tori's scream came back. It was short, startled, and when it lost steam, she turned and threw her arms around Jesse's neck, holding on to him tightly. "What's happening?" she sputtered.

He laughed and didn't answer. She looked over her shoulder. They were gliding through the treetops, making lazy turns to avoid the highest branches. Perhaps Jesse really had tackled her and she'd hit her head on the ground. Perhaps this was part of a concussion.

But every sense she had was working in overdrive: The wind pushing against her exposed skin, the smell of the forest, the feel of Jesse's arms around her, the sound of his breath near her ear.

This wasn't a dream.

The breeze fluttered Tori's hair into her face. She didn't dare let go of his neck to brush it away. His arms were wrapped around her waist, but it felt wrong not to be standing on anything. She couldn't find a foothold in the air. "How are you doing this?"

"Flight is my extra power. Isn't this great?"

She laughed. She knew it sounded hysterical. "Don't drop me. I'm sorry I called you crazy."

He smiled, an easy smile, like the one she'd seen when they'd gone horseback riding earlier. "I'm not going to drop you. Here, I'll turn you around so you can see better." He moved his hands onto her hips and twisted, but she wouldn't let go of his neck.

His face was so close, his lips brushed against her cheek. "If you don't let go of my neck, I can't turn you around."

"Just put me down. I believe you now."

"I'll put you down when we reach the Easter grounds." He tipped his head sideways to look into her eyes. "Don't you want to see where we're going? The other girls love this."

"Is this something you do frequently? You yank girls into the sky?"

He laughed, and his chest muscles moved up and down. "Only the girls from cabin twenty-seven."

He leaned forward so he tilted at a forty-five-degree angle and then sped up. The treetops skimmed by underneath them, a vast carpet of leaves and branches spreading out in every direction. Her fear, however, still outweighed her wonder. She clung to Jesse tighter. She should have taken his advice and let him turn her around. Of course, now that she was getting used to the speed and the feel of air gusting around her, she had to admit there was something comfortable about clinging to Jesse, something calming about his arms around her. She nestled her cheek into his neck and caught the faint smell of his shampoo.

No wonder the girls from cabin 27 loved this. Jesse was gorgeous, had rock-hard abs, and could fly. All he needed was a cape and he'd pass for Superman.

Finally, the Easter grounds clearing came into view. Jesse straightened, slowly descended into the trees, and landed inside the circle of stones. Tori didn't move away from Jesse. She kept her arms around his neck and shifted her weight, testing the ground for solidness in case it disappeared again.

The faint *tha-thump*ing sound came from over by the shed, and the rest of the campers stood nearby, a semicircle of people watching her intently. If Jesse could fly, what could the others do? He suddenly seemed like the only safe one around.

# CHAPTER 10

Jesse let go of her waist. When she didn't move, he put his lips next to her ear. "You can unhook yourself from my neck now. We're on the ground."

"Oh. Right." Tori reluctantly stepped away from him. The night air rushed in between them, chilling her where she used to be warm.

Dirk stood outside the stone circle, his hands on his hips as he regarded them. "Well, that was a subtle entrance. What happened to all that talk about being sure she was one of us before we did anything to give ourselves away?"

"She's one of us," Jesse said. "She can see at night."

Dirk's gaze flicked over her. His eyes were large and dark like Jesse's. "She could be wearing infrared contacts. She doesn't have our strength—she wasn't even running fast on the way up here."

"I saw her running down the trail. Trust me; she's fast." Jesse took a few steps toward Dirk. When Tori didn't move—her mind was still somewhere stunned and looping through the treetops—he came back, took hold of her hand, and pulled her with him out of the stone circle. None of the other advanced campers spoke. They seemed content to let the team captains discuss the matter.

Jesse let go of Tori's hand. She shouldn't have missed it, but did.

"She ran away because she heard the simulator and thought it was a dragon's heartbeat," Jesse said. "She figured we brought a dragon to the Easter grounds. Who would have thought that except one of us?"

"Someone who knew about us," Dirk said. "And besides, none of us can hear that well. If anything, that proves she's not one of us."

Jesse shook his head. "We can't afford to lose one of our own."

Dirk lowered his voice. "What we can't afford is to endanger the rest of us. Did you think of that?"

A man in a firefighter coat, helmet, and wearing what looked like binoculars strapped to his face joined the group. He had a cell phone up to his ear and it took Tori a moment to realize it was Dr. B. "Jesse found Miss Hampton," he said into the phone. "No need to hunt for her in camp, but thanks for your help." He snapped the phone shut and slipped it into his coat pocket as though all of this were perfectly normal. "I'm so glad you've joined us."

"He flew her in," Dirk said flatly.

"Ahh." Dr. B nodded. "Then no doubt you have some questions."

The goggles made him look insectlike and fierce somehow. Tori took a step away. "Why are you wearing those?"

Dr. B tapped one lens. "Infrared. I don't have your night vision. You can see in the dark because you are an heir of a dragon knight."

She wasn't sure she liked how that sounded. "A *what*?"

"An heir of a dragon knight. A Slayer." Dr. B's tone slipped into teacher mode. "You're a descendant of one of the knights who took the gold elixir and thus changed not only his DNA, but the DNA he passed down to his children, grandchildren, and so on. I'm assuming you read the information in my book about the history of dragons?"

"Most of it."

He gave her a knowing grin. "Slayers always do."

As he spoke, Lilly, Alyssa, Kody, and Shang walked a little ways off. Kody somehow lit a torch, then inexplicably threw it at Shang. The torch made a blazing arc upward, but the fire disappeared before it reached Shang. Tori couldn't tell what had put out the fire, but the torch fell harmlessly at his feet.

She turned her attention back to Dr. B, trying to process what he said next. "A small percentage of the population are descendants of the dragon knights, but the special genes lay dormant inside them, unused and inaccessible, until a pregnant woman goes near a dragon or a dragon egg. Something about the dragon's proximity triggers the unborn baby's DNA to turn him or her into a Slayer." He pointed a finger at Tori. "In this case, you. Perhaps you've already felt that you're different from those around you. There are things about you that your friends and family don't understand."

Tori was too stunned to reply, but he went on as though he didn't need her answer as proof. "The Slayers' powers don't fully manifest themselves unless a dragon is within five miles. I suppose that enables you to live normal lives when there's no immediate threat. But in order to give Slayers the opportunity to practice using their skills, I re-created a pulse wavelength simulator that mimics a dragon's heartbeat. That's what's enabling you to see in the dark right now."

Tori blinked and heard a roaring in her ears, the roar of every dragon she'd ever imagined, springing to life in her mind. They were real.

They were real.

They. Were. Real.

She took a step backward, gulping. "I can't fight dragons."

From beside her, Jesse let out a disappointed sigh.

She spun on him. "Are you kidding? Do you have any idea what dragons are like?"

"A better idea than you do," he said. "That's why we've got to fight them. No one else can do it."

Her lungs felt like they were constricting. Her voice came out too high. "What about the military? They have missiles—"

Jesse didn't wait for her to finish. "Even if the government could figure out a way to get planes or helicopters in the air, dragons will outmaneuver them. And dragon skin reflects radar, making it nearly impossible to hit them with missiles."

"Besides," Dirk added, "nobody is going to shoot missiles into a populated area anyway. Where would those missiles land once they missed the dragon?" He shook his head. "The military won't be able to do anything."

Tori took another step backward and put her hand to her throat. "I'm only in high school, and I have a full schedule, and I'm flammable."

Dr. B went and stood directly in front of her. "That's what this camp is for, to find and train Slayers." He took one of her hands. His fingers felt cold yet firm against her own. "I always thought one or two more of you would join our ranks. We waited every year, just hoping—and here you are."

Tori pulled her hand away from Dr. B's. She couldn't imagine herself, even for a minute, running around in armor and slashing at monsters. "Look, I appreciate what you're trying to do, but I didn't sign up for superhero classes. I'm not the type."

Although Lilly had moved away, Tori still heard her snort. "You can say that again."

"If the simulator can create Slayers," Tori said, gesturing to the clearing where the machine sat, "why don't you build some, and put them near pregnant women? You could create an army of Slayers to fight the dragons." She didn't add, but definitely thought, *And then I won't have to fight them.*

Dr. B shook his head. "The pulse wave isn't what triggers an heir's DNA to turn him into a Slayer. Unfortunately, it can only turn on powers that are already there, that were already created by contact with a dragon." His voice turned thoughtful, scientific. "I'm not sure what part of the dragon actually triggers an heir's DNA, but a few records suggest it has something to do with a diamond-shaped white crystal on the dragon's forehead. When one considers the myriad electric pulses in a dragon's system—" he stopped himself. "I'm getting technical, instead of alleviating your fears."

Dr. B drew in a breath and then smiled pointedly at Tori. He probably meant it to look comforting, but with the goggles and the darkness, it seemed menacing. "Don't worry. When the time comes, you'll be ready."

She ought to turn around and walk away. No, she ought to run. It was only her stupid curiosity that kept her here. "When what time comes? Where are the dragons now?"

"We're not sure," Dr. B said. "Overdrake has hidden them somewhere safe and will no doubt leave them there until right before he's ready to attack. They might even still be on St. Helena." He pronounced the word "He-lean-a."

She had never heard of it. "Where?"

Dr. B walked over and sat down on the nearest boulder, then motioned for her to sit down beside him. He rested his hands on his knees and leaned forward, preparing himself for a long explanation. Jesse and Dirk drifted off to join the others. Across the clearing, Kody hurled flaming balls through the night sky like they were footballs. Each snuffed out, midair.

"St. Helena is one of the most remote islands in the world. The Overdrake family owns most of it." Dr. B held up a hand as though rewinding his words. "But that isn't the right place to start. To understand the Overdrakes, you've got to go back to the Middle Ages when the kings promised fortunes to those who could solve the dragon problem. While some alchemists worked on creating the gold elixir, another group developed a different solution. They incorporated dragon DNA into their own bodies. This added DNA gave them the ability to control the dragons through a mind link. Instead of killing the dragons, these dragon lords used their power to influence the beasts to do things like fly away from a certain village or city. It was a skill the nobility were willing to pay quite a bit for. You wanted a dragon lord to live nearby.

"Later, when the knights came to power and hunted the dragons, some of the dragon lords spirited away eggs to remote spots to protect them. One of the Overdrakes' forefathers was a dragon lord who brought a pair to the island of St. Helena. Generations of Overdrake dragon lords cared for the dragons until civilization pressed in even on St. Helena. Then the dragon lord used his link to force the female dragon into choosing hibernation for her eggs. The last batch hatched somewhere between forty to forty-five years ago."

Tori shivered and pulled Jesse's jacket tighter around her. "How come no one knows about the dragons, then?"

"I know about them."

"They're just flying around the island?"

Dr. B adjusted his goggles, focusing them on Tori. "Overdrake kept them hidden on his plantation and only rarely let them out at night. But I've seen them. I grew up on St. Helena."

Which explained his accent, Tori realized.

"My father worked as the cattle boss for the Overdrake family. They own a large spread of land on the far side of the island and a few factories in Jamestown. Langston Overdrake ran the empire back when I lived on the island and he had one rule that he strictly enforced— except for his wife and a few handpicked servants, no women were allowed anywhere on the plantation. He had a fence and a guard posted to send away any vehicles with women in them. Most people just thought he was eccentric. When you're rich you can get away with all sorts of outrageous behavior."

Dr. B paused, apparently remembering that Tori's family had money. He cleared his throat and continued. "My mother was an accomplished seamstress and Mrs. Overdrake liked to design her own clothes and have them sewn. She used to come out to our house for her fittings. When Mrs. Overdrake was pregnant she felt too ill to make the trip to our home. She had one of her servants sneak my mother onto the plantation so she could have fittings for her maternity clothes." A note of tension crept into Dr. B's voice. "I suppose she wouldn't have done that if she'd known my mother was pregnant at the time."

Tori regarded Dr. B. "But I thought you said you weren't a descendant of a dragon knight?"

"I'm a descendant, but my mother wasn't pregnant with me. The dormant genes in my body were never triggered to give me powers." He said the words with a bit of stiffness, as though he resented this fact, or at least regretted it. "She was carrying my younger brother, Nathan. He was six years younger than me—a surprise."

Dr. B remained silent for a moment, staring off into the distance, and Tori could tell this story didn't have a happy ending. "Sometimes my dad would take Nathan or me to the plantation to help with the cattle. Around the time Nathan turned twelve, he developed powers whenever he went on the plantation—the night vision and extra strength."

Dr. B didn't raise his voice. His words were composed, but his tone had a bitter edge. "My father was in Overdrake's inner circle. He was the one who put the cattle into the enclosure to feed the dragons. He heard Overdrake talk with his son, Brant, about how they could use the dragons as weapons once they raised enough of them." Dr. B shook his head. "My dad never thought they'd go through with it. After all, the Overdrakes already ran the island, what else did they need? But my father underestimated their greed for power. One little island wouldn't have been enough for Alexander the Great, Napoleon, or William the Conqueror. It wasn't enough for any of the nations that colonized North or South America. The men who ran those countries took control because they could, not because they didn't already have empires of their own.

"My father never told anyone about the Overdrakes' plans. You pay a person well enough and it's amazing what he'll keep secret." Dr. B kept shaking his head. "My father knew what was happening to Nathan. Overdrake had warned him about Slayers, about the reason he kept pregnant women away from the plantation. So my father forbade Nathan to ever reveal his abilities or to go near the plantation again, but beyond that . . ." Dr. B let out a tired-sounding sigh. "My father was afraid that if Nathan knew about the dragons, he would want to kill them—that it would be in his nature because he was a Slayer."

Tori mulled that over. Back when she was four years old, she must have wanted to kill her father's glass dragon collection—she had turned the whole thing into worthless broken shards. And she had certainly killed the two miniature dragons on top of her birthday cake. But real dragons? She was pretty sure it was in her nature to avoid those.

She didn't bring up this point, since Dr. B was continuing with his story. "My father thought all he needed to do to protect Nathan was to tell him to keep away from the plantation." Dr. B rubbed the back of his neck wearily. "He should have known better. How can you keep a boy away once he knows a proximity will give him superpowers? By the time Nathan reached thirteen he'd not only gone back, he'd gone back enough times to realize he had another power besides the night vision and extra energy—the power to throw up shields. He used to tease the bulls, race them across the pasture, and then throw up shields when they got too close. One night Langston Overdrake caught him at it."

Dr. B paused for a long time. Tori nearly held her breath waiting for him to continue and wished he didn't have to. It was clear it pained him to tell the story.

"Langston Overdrake killed my brother. Oh, it was reported as an accidental drug overdose, but my father knew what really happened. Overdrake hardly made a secret of it. That's when my father told me everything. The dragons. The powers Nathan had inherited. And Overdrake's plans."

Dr. B's voice was still calm, but his hands lying against his knees were clenched. "I was so angry, I stole my father's keys, drove to the plantation, and broke into the dragon enclosure. I photographed both dragons, then turned the pictures over to the St. Helena police. They promptly destroyed everything—my camera, the pictures, our lives." Dr. B grimaced at the memory. "I should have known that Langston Overdrake ran the police, as well as everything else on the island. If I hadn't fled from the station, they would have probably thrown me in jail. I went home and told my parents what I had done. We had to leave right then, leave everything, in order to get off the island before Overdrake's men got a hold of us. My father bribed a ship's captain to smuggle us to England.

"We changed our names and got used to looking over our shoulders, checking to make sure Overdrake hadn't found us. When I finally managed to get a new ID, I went to college and majored in medieval history. I learned everything I could about dragons so that I could help stop them."

Tori's hands trembled in her lap. She looked at them, at her manicured pink-polished nails. They weren't the hands of a knight. "I'm sorry about your brother. Really, I am. But if the dragons stay on an island, why can't we just leave them alone?"

"Because they won't stay on the island." Dr. B leaned toward her, his face intent beneath his goggles. "Langston and his son, Brant, were never interested in protecting the dragons. They wanted power, the more of it, the better. Langston used his mind link to tell the she-dragon to choose the short gestation period for her eggs—fifteen to twenty years.

"Langston died nearly two decades ago, but Brant is still carrying out his plans. When the new dragons are grown, he'll use them to try and wrest control of the government. That's why D.C. is going to be the first target."

In the background, Kody and Dirk laughed about something. They looked like they were playing fire Frisbee instead of training to fight monsters.

Tori tried to concentrate on Dr. B's story and not the flames swishing by her. "But if you left St. Helena so long ago, how do you know that Brant is still planning on attacking D.C.?"

"Because Brant brought the eggs through the D.C. area seventeen years ago. All of the Slayers who've come to camp were born within eight months of each other. All of your mothers lived in the D.C. area when they were pregnant with you. The only reason Brant would have moved the eggs here is that it makes it easier for him to attack D.C.

"I'm sure he didn't mean to let the eggs go anywhere near pregnant women. He wouldn't have wanted to trigger powers in babies who could then grow up to fight his dragons. But through some mistake, piece of luck, or divine providence, it happened."

Dr. B. hadn't asked her if her mother had been living in D.C. when Tori was born, but then that information was easy enough to look up. Her father had become a senator the year before she was born. "If you know Brant Overdrake is in the United States you should tell the authorities, and they could—"

Dr. B waved away her words. "Brant wouldn't be so careless as to use his own name. I imagine he's even altered his appearance. Wherever he is, he has the resources to carry out a well-planned attack. And once the eggs hatch, we'll have less than a year before the dragons reach full maturity."

A noise like glass shattering came from the area where the advanced campers were goofing off. Tori turned in time to see pebbles falling to the ground.

Dr. B put his hand on Tori's arm, pulling her attention back to him. "Overdrake knows Slayers have been created. I fear it's only a matter of time before he finds our camp. In fact, an attack is probably long overdue. You'll need to be careful from now on. If anyone asks you suspicious questions here or after you go home, get away and alert the others. I have a special phone for you to use. I'll give it to you after practice."

His eyes trained in on her. At least, she thought they did; it was hard to tell through the goggles. "Make sure nobody sees you using your powers. No one can know about what goes on at this part of camp. Not your friends, not your parents. Letting the secret slip will not only risk your life and the other Slayers, but all the lives we won't be able to save. Do you understand the gravity of this?"

"Yes." The conversation she'd had with Cole and David earlier in the evening ran through her mind. She shouldn't have told him about Jesse or said she thought anything odd was going on, but she couldn't take it back now.

Jesse, Dirk, and the others had finished whatever game they'd been playing, and they strolled back toward the ring of boulders, talking and laughing. They were even stronger, more confident up here where they could exercise their powers.

"How many Slayers are there?" Tori asked.

"Ten came the first three years the camp opened. You're the only one to come since then. I know there's at least one more—somewhere—but his parents won't let me train him. I hope they'll change their minds, or that he'll find us. Beyond that, I doubt there are others. Their obsession with dragons would have led them to the camp. Like yours finally led you here."

Her obsession. It wasn't some deep-seated fear turned into psychosis. She was normal, after all. Well, normal in a really different sort of way.

Dr. B gestured toward the campers as he spoke. "So far the heirs' extra skills have come by twos. Two can douse dragon's fire, quenching it for several minutes. Two can throw up shields to protect themselves and bystanders, and two can send out both fireballs and freezing shocks. Two have the power to heal dragon-inflicted wounds. One can fly, and one can see what the dragon sees."

See what the dragon sees? What did that mean? And how did someone quench fire or send out freezing shocks? She wanted to ask him, but he didn't give her time.

"My guess is that your extra power will either be flight or sight, since those abilities don't already have doubles. But who knows? Perhaps our pairing of talents is random coincidence. You might repeat an ability that two slayers already have, or you might have something altogether different." He stood, then clapped his hands together in anticipation. "Let's get started. You've been in contact with the simulator since you checked in to cabin twenty-seven, and you're getting a strong dose now."

For the first time, Tori turned her attention to the machine sitting near the shed. Wheels attached to its cylindrical body, making it look more like a hot dog cart than a dragon.

"Along with your night vision, you should have extra strength. In fact, your legs will now allow you to leap better than an Olympic high jumper." Dr. B raised his voice, calling over to the group. "Who wants to show Tori a leap?"

Kody stepped forward. He bent his knees and swung his arms upward, launching into the air. It happened so fast, she didn't track where he went.

Tori scanned the clearing, trying to see where he landed. "Where did he go?"

Her question made everyone laugh. She searched even harder, but couldn't find him. Finally Kody called to her from a tree branch about eight feet up in the air. He waved and jumped down, landing on the ground as gracefully as a gymnast. He strutted back to the others, grinning.

Dr. B leaned toward her, and in an air of confidentiality said, "He makes it look easy, but I assure you, it took all of them several tries before they could land on the branches."

Several tries? She'd done leaps for years in ice skating and couldn't even imagine jumping straight up that high.

She remembered the blur of colors she'd seen earlier in the forest. Now it made sense. She'd seen Dirk jumping up into a tree. Had he been spying on her or simply practicing?

Dr. B headed toward the shed. "We'll have the other Slayers give you demonstrations of their powers and then see what you can do."

Tori took a deep breath, and then took another. Dragons. One of her ancestors had been a knight. With powers. Maybe flight. She tried to remember everything Dr. B had said, but the words slipped over the edges of her mind, like water over a glass filled too full. Two people could douse fire and two people could send out freezing shocks. What were the other powers?

She shook her head, trying to clear it. This sort of thing just didn't happen—dragons hatching and villains trying to take over the country. Yet Jesse had flown her up here. That had been real enough. And she could see in the dark. Was it possible that all along her genes had been forming her into some sort of a superhero and she had never known it?

CHAPTER 11

Dr. B took something out of the shed. At first she thought it was a fire extinguisher, but the nozzle wasn't right. He fiddled with it, and foot-long flames seared out of the opening. "If Bess or Leo were here," he said, gesturing with the blowtorch as though it had been a piece of chalk in one of his lessons, "we could demonstrate throwing up a shield. But as they're both gone, I'll simply tell you that if you have the power of shielding, you can put up an invisible forcefield that's about . . ." He turned toward Dirk, and the torch flame arced in that direction.

Tori winced. Really, was it a good idea to wave a blowtorch around so much kindling?

"How big would you say the forcefield is?" Dr. B asked Dirk.

Dirk hooked his thumbs through his belt loops. "About five yards by five yards."

Dr. B turned back to Tori, pointing the flame in her direction again. "It's a good size. If you throw it in front of yourself or anyone the dragon is trying to bake, you can save quite a few people." He held the blowtorch closer, and the heat from the flame shimmered near her face. "Do you have an urge to throw a forcefield up?"

Tori leaned away from the flame. "Mostly I have the urge to kick the blowtorch out of your hands, but I'm being polite."

Dr. B nodded, as though noting her reaction on a mental checklist, then he addressed Lilly and Shang. "Which one of you wants to show Tori how to douse fire?"

Lilly stepped forward, one hand smugly on her hip. She obviously liked doing something Tori couldn't. Without moving any closer to Dr. B, Lilly flicked her hand and the flame from the blowtorch blinked out.

"Well done!" Dr. B smiled at her proudly. "It's a handy skill to have around here, as cabin twenty-six tends to get rather rambunctious during cookouts. This way I don't have to worry about anyone accidentally burning down the camp."

Dr. B waved Kody over, then told Tori, "Watch."

Dr. B picked up a palm-size rock and threw it toward the trees. Before it could hit anything, Kody pushed his hand through the air in one quick motion. The rock made a sound like dropped china and splintered into pieces. They rained down on the ground with tiny thuds.

"Well done," Dr. B said approvingly. Then he told Tori, "Kody and Danielle can send freezing shocks great distances."

Kody put his fingers together and cracked his knuckles. "It won't kill a dragon, but it'll tick him off real bad."

"What *does* kill a dragon, then?" Tori asked.

Neither Dr. B nor Kody answered her question. Dr. B picked up a broken branch from the ground and held it up. "Here's another part of Kody's talent."

With a snap of Kody's fingers, one end of the stick caught on fire, making it look like a giant birthday candle.

Dr. B showed the burning branch to Tori so that she could see it was legitimate fire. "I suppose this gift is for those times when you need to fight fire with fire." He stepped toward Shang and called cheerily, "Extinguish this, please." Shang flicked a finger and the flame went out.

Next, Dr. B turned the blowtorch knob until a small flame protruded from the end. Kody walked back to the group, and Alyssa came forward, replacing him. Unlike Lilly, she didn't look smug. She ran a hand through her hair, then shook out her hands nervously.

"I don't like to do this," Dr. B told Tori. "But it's important for you to see the power of healing." Without further warning, he pulled back his sleeve and ran the flame across the back of his wrist.

He only flinched as his skin charred white and broke open, but his short, quick breaths revealed his pain. Alyssa immediately put her hand above the wound. She waved her fingers, plucking, pulling, making swirling motions. After a few seconds, Dr. B relaxed. "Well done." He patted her shoulder. "You get faster every year." He walked closer to Tori and held up his wrist for her to see. Only a faint white scar ran across his hand, as though a smaller wound had happened there years ago. "In an attack, make sure to protect Alyssa and Rosa so they can heal your battle wounds."

Battle wounds. Tori gulped at the words.

"You've already experienced the gift of flight. The last is the gift of sight. This ability isn't easy to demonstrate. I can only have Dirk tell you what it's like." Dr. B waved Dirk over, giving him the floor.

Dirk crossed his arms. "When I concentrate, a split screen opens up in my mind and I can see what the nearest dragon sees. Since they're still in eggs at this point, all I see is a faint red glow when it's daytime and black when it's night. And I can only catch snatches of it, like a TV with a bad cable signal. Hopefully when the dragons hatch and get closer, I'll be able to make a stable connection. Until then, it's not a real exciting skill."

He turned around and walked back to the rest of the group without waiting to see if she had questions. Which she did, but not for him.

"How do I know which skill I have?" she asked.

Dr. B regarded her with his binocularlike glasses. "When I showed you the others' powers, did you feel a sharp instinct to do something?"

"Not really." Although when he'd told her she would have to fight a dragon, she'd felt a clear and insistent need to run as far away from here as she could.

"When you flew with Jesse, did you want to try it on your own?"

No, mostly she'd wanted to cling to him. And if she was being completely honest, some of her thoughts strayed into the realm of noticing how built he was. But she wasn't about to tell Dr. B that.

"I didn't want Jesse to let me go." As soon as the words left Tori's mouth, she wondered if flying might be her gift after all. Her favorite dreams were the ones where she flew, drifting above unknown buildings and streets. It felt so natural to twist through the air. But everyone dreamed of flying. It didn't mean she could actually do it.

"Shut your eyes and concentrate," Dr. B told her. "Can you see the split screen Dirk spoke about?"

She shut her eyes. There was nothing but darkness and the feeling that everyone was staring at her. She shook her head and opened her eyes.

Dr. B looked upward for a moment, considering, then said, "Perhaps you have the gift of sight. All you would see right now is blackness. And it might be hard for you to tune in a real dragon anyway. You can't see what's in the simulator's mind because it doesn't have one." He shrugged. "Then again, perhaps the shock of the night is interfering with your instincts."

Or perhaps she just didn't have an extra ability. Was that possible?

"I'll have you practice with the others. Whatever your talent is, it's bound to manifest itself before long." Dr. B smiled and with his binocular eyes, it looked ominous. He motioned to Alyssa. "Why don't you work with Tori on her leaps? That's probably the easiest thing to teach."

Alyssa let out a sigh, clearly not thrilled by this assignment, but she took Tori across the clearing. When they got to the far side, she said, "The whole point of leaping is to avoid the dragon. You know, like if he happens to shoot flames at you or tries to swipe you with his tail or claws." She pointed toward the boulders. "See if you can leap to the fire pit."

The boulders were about fifteen feet away. There wasn't much of a chance Tori could reach them. "Um, aren't you supposed to give me some instruction? Isn't there a trick to it?"

"Yeah. Run a few feet, swing your arms, and jump."

The other campers had moved slowly to the edge of the forest. They were about to go somewhere, but apparently they wanted to see her attempt at leaping.

I might not be one of them, Tori thought. *It might all be a mistake—my night vision might be a fluke like my hearing.* She wasn't sure if this was a comforting thought. On one hand, it would be nice to have a pass on fighting a dragon. But if she wasn't one of them, what would they do? She knew their secrets.

She clenched her fists, took a few running steps, and jumped toward the boulders. She zoomed toward them too quickly. Her speed and height surprised her so much that when she landed, she nearly tripped. She only saved herself by taking stumbling steps into one of the boulders.

An assortment of laughter floated toward her from where the others stood. She wasn't sure whether to glare at them for laughing, or laugh herself because she'd done it. She had jumped a huge distance.

If she could have this extra strength with her when she ice skated she would blow the crowds away.

"A fine start," Dr. B called to her. Then to the others, he said, "Don't you have some eggs to find?"

"Oh, come on," Lilly called back. "We want to see her flatten a few trees."

"You'll never find them if you just stand there," Dr. B said. "Points are at stake."

At that, Lilly and the others faded into the forest. When they'd gone, Alyssa yelled over, "Now jump back here!"

Tori did. She thought it would be easier to control now that she knew what to expect. She ran and jumped, but when she landed, she pitched forward again, this time stumbling into a tree. The trunk shuddered and dropped a shower of leaves onto her. Tori's palms stung from where she'd hit the trunk. She shook them, trying to get rid of the pain, and was surprised she only had tiny scrapes on her skin.

This was cool.

"Next time try to avoid the trees," Alyssa said.

"Yeah, thanks for the tip."

Alyssa sat down on the ground, and waved a dismissive hand at Tori. "Okay, keep at it until you get the hang of it. Once you get the basics down, I'll teach you a few of the fancier moves."

Tori ran and leapt toward the ring of boulders and again slammed into one. A piece the size of a bread loaf broke off. She picked it up. It felt as light as a book. She really was stronger now.

"You're supposed to be *leaping*," Alyssa called.

So she did. Tori leapt back and forth, running into boulders one way, trees the other direction. Her landings always made her feel like she'd stepped out of a moving car. She couldn't keep her balance. Her only consolation at being so bad at this was knowing that everyone else must have struggled, too. Otherwise Lilly wouldn't have expected her to flatten trees.

Dr. B divided his time between watching the other campers in the forest, and shouting words of encouragement to Tori. Alyssa just said things like, "So, you understand that the point of this is to get *away* from the dragon, right? It won't do you much good if you leap away from his claws and then crash into his body."

Very helpful.

A few times she managed to avoid solid objects, and a few times she fell down when she landed. She always checked her hands, surprised they weren't bloody. Apparently her skin was stronger, too. Her landing powers, however, remained unchanged.

"Why don't you try straight up for a while?" Alyssa suggested.

The idea of launching straight up into the air frightened Tori. Well, not the jumping part—the falling straight down and dying part.

She tried a hop, went a couple feet into the air, and landed with a thud. Alyssa rolled her eyes. "Come on. You can go higher than that."

Tori jumped again, this time adding another foot to her height.

"Are you even trying?" Alyssa asked.

Tori jumped using all of her energy and went so high she screamed. On landing, she pitched forward and had to take several steps to steady herself.

"Well," Alyssa said with forced cheerfulness, "the dragon probably won't hatch for a while, so you have time to practice."

That was the most encouragement she'd gotten during her jumping lessons from Alyssa. Tori never tried to land gracefully on a tree limb like Kody had done. She was afraid she'd end up impaling herself.

After half an hour of this, the other campers came out of the forest, carrying an assortment of diving rings—the kind kids play with at pools. Tori couldn't see how they would help fight dragons. "What's the point of finding rings?" she asked.

"It's not finding them," Alyssa said. "It's retrieving them from the trees. You've either got to leap up there to get them or throw something to knock them out, and you've got to do it fast because the other team is gathering them, too."

Dr. B took the rings, and tallied the points in a notebook. "Tori," he said without looking up, "why don't you join the others for the next game?"

She wasn't sure if he wanted her to learn the next skill or whether he'd decided she was hopeless when it came to leaping. As though he could read her mind, he said, "With so many members gone, Team Magnus is undermanned. They need your help during hide-and-seek."

Hide-and-seek seemed tame enough, juvenile, actually. Well, at least until Kody explained the rules of the game. He sat out the first round and gave her a play by play. The game was actually tackle hide-and-seek. Two people—one from each team—were seekers while the others hid. When you were the seeker, you tried to find the members of the other team, but it wasn't enough to find them. You had to tag them before they could run around the stone circle and touch their original hiding place. If they made it without being touched, they got ten points for their team. If you managed to tag them, your team got ten points. As a seeker, you could help your teammates by interfering with the other seeker's ability to catch your teammate.

The game involved lots of very dramatic leaps where hiders tried to get around pursuing seekers. Seekers had no compunction about ramming into people, sometimes several feet in the air.

Tori watched it with her mouth ajar. She didn't want to play this game. She couldn't tell where any of them hid before they sprinted around trees or dropped from branches, and she was lousy at leaping. She was bound to lose every single time. Besides, the game looked a little savage. Wasn't it enough that she'd already slammed into trees and boulders? Did she need to get knocked to the ground repeatedly? Lilly and Alyssa were both on the A-team, and they would probably enjoy sending her face-first into the dirt.

When the players had either scored or been caught, Kody stood up and stretched. "Ready to play?"

"Can't I just give up my ten points and sit out again?"

Kody laughed and pulled her to her feet like she'd been joking. She hadn't been.

The first three rounds went like she thought they would. When Lilly was seeker, she pounced on Tori from five feet away. Tori had no idea how to avoid people smashing into her that fast. She tried to leap over Kody when he was seeker, but she couldn't regain her balance when she landed, and he scooped her up like a basketball on the re-bound. The only reason she didn't get tackled when Dirk was the seeker was that Jesse was the seeker, too. As Dirk bounded toward her, Jesse cut him off with a midair slam.

The next round, she and Alyssa were the seekers. Tori walked into the forest, searching, trying to keep track of where Alyssa went at the same time. Tori couldn't spot anyone. They would most likely wait until she passed by their hiding places to dart toward the boulders. She took cautious steps forward, staying on the balls of her feet. Dead leaves crackled beneath her shoes.

Every once in a while, branches waved. She couldn't tell if it was the wind or movement from someone hiding. She had just decided to go farther into the forest when Jesse dashed out from a nearby tree. Alyssa took off after him.

Was it better to block for Jesse or try to find one of the A-team hid-ers? Dirk didn't give her time to decide; he jumped out from behind a tree to her left. She tore after him, cutting off his way to the boulders. He tried to leap over her, but she jumped up, twisting in midair. She grabbed hold of his shirt and pushed him to the ground.

It should have hurt him, especially since she landed on top of his chest. Instead, he lay on the ground, surprised, and let out a satisfied laugh. "Hey, maybe you're one of us after all."

Kody whizzed by them. "Typical Dirk," he called over his shoulder. "Can't keep the girls off him."

Dirk smiled as though he agreed. Which is when Tori realized she should do something besides lie on top of him, exchanging pleasantries.

She stood up and bounded after Kody, dodging around the trees at high speed. She was almost to the clearing when a fireball the size of a dinner plate zipped past her shoulder. It smashed into a tree in front of her with an explosion of sparks. She spun around, her pulse hammering in her ears.

A whistling sound at her side told her another fireball was coming. An assault—Overdrake had found them. Her first thought was one of recrimination—she had said too much to Cole and David. Now they were being attacked, and it was her fault.

Tori didn't have time to dwell on her guilt. She leapt up, trying to dodge away from the fireball's path. It shot past her, so close that heat licked against her neck. Worse still, she crashed into a huge branch above her, slamming her head into the wood. The branch cracked apart, and both she and it fell to the ground. It landed squarely on top of her, a mass of leaves and bark splinters.

She lay there, stunned, wanting to breathe but finding her lungs uncooperative. Her back throbbed. The smell of acrid smoke surrounded her. If another fireball came at her now, she wouldn't be able to move away fast enough to escape from it.

CHAPTER 12

No other fireballs came. Instead, Jesse pulled the branch off her with one hand and held his other hand down to help her up. No fear flashed through his dark eyes, no worry, no frantic hunting for their attacker. It was over, then. They were safe. Tori didn't take Jesse's hand, didn't move, just let air refill her lungs.

Dr. B came from somewhere and stared down at her. She knew he would ask if she was okay and wondered if she was. She shouldn't be. Not after hitting her head, falling several feet, and having a huge branch land on her. She moved her fingers and wiggled her toes to make sure she could.

"When the fireball came at you," Dr. B said slowly, "what was your first instinct?"

The breath whooshed from her lungs for a second time. This hadn't been an attack. It had been a test to determine her power.

Just as slowly, Tori said, "My first instinct was to yell at someone for throwing fireballs at me."

"And after that?"

"I wanted to find out who threw the fireballs and hurt them."

Dr. B let out a huff of exasperation. "As a means of protecting yourself, what did you want to do?"

Tori pulled herself to a sitting position and wiped at bits of dried leaves that clung to her. "I thought I should duck, but I'd spent all of that time learning how to jump, so I did that instead. As you saw, that worked out real well."

She stood up and ran her hand over her hair. Part of it felt twiggy. And short. She held up her hair to check. A huge section by her face was now six inches shorter than the rest, and the ends curled together like melted plastic. She gasped at it, unbelieving. She would have to cut all of it now.

The thought stung worse than crashing into the tree branch had. Her long, beautiful hair was gone, sizzled, breaking off into ashy pieces in her hand. And it could have been much worse. It could have been her face.

She turned to Dr. B, still gasping. It was his fault she'd been scared out of her mind and hurt and had now lost six inches of her hair. "Look what you did! You don't hurl fireballs at people! What is *wrong* with you?"

She didn't wait for an answer. His shocked expression was answer enough. He wasn't sorry. Her anger seemed to surprise him. She spun on her heel and stormed off toward the trail.

As she walked away, each quick step carrying an exclamation mark, part of her realized that real superheroes didn't care about their hair. The rest of the campers were probably watching her with disdain. Well, she hadn't asked to be a dragon knight—or Slayer, or whatever ridiculously out-of-date name they called themselves. And if these were the people who were supposed to be on her side in the fight, they could forget about her help. She didn't want to be part of their competitions anyway. They were probably more likely to kill her than any dragon was.

Dr. B called her name. She didn't turn around, didn't slow down. She wasn't running, not yet. She wasn't about to let them see her run away. Still, she pounded down the trail, thinking about the places she could have gone this summer. Places with oceans and cable TV and sidewalks instead of dirt trails.

Besides, if dragons existed, it was the military's job to take charge. Who was Dr. B to say they couldn't do it? She would just have to figure out a way to explain the whole situation to her father and let him take care of it.

She didn't realize Jesse was behind her, floating off the ground, until he spoke. In a voice that he probably meant to sound consoling but that came out patronizing, he said, "If you aren't ready for an attack, you'll end up with a lot more than singed hair. It's part of your training. We've all gone through it. Being under attack is what usually gets your extra skill to manifest itself."

She didn't slow her pace. "What if one of those fireballs had hit me in the face?"

"Then Alyssa would have healed you, and Dr. B would have given you extra work for not being careful."

Tori shook her head. "Unbelievable."

"This isn't a game. People's lives are at stake."

"Yeah, tonight my life was at stake."

"It always has been," he said softly. "You're a Slayer."

"Not anymore. I quit."

He came around her side so he hovered in front of her. "Why don't I fly you back to camp, and we'll talk?"

She didn't answer. She wasn't giving in. She didn't want Jesse to think he could talk her into anything. Still, she did want to try flying again now that she wasn't so shocked by the whole idea. This time it might feel like the flying she did in her dreams.

"Carrying me doesn't make you tired?" she asked.

He swooped down and grabbed her around the waist. The next

moment, they soared upward as effortlessly as a plane lifting from a runway. "Nope. We've got increased strength. You could carry me if you tried."

She rested her arms over his, liking the security of his embrace. Facing forward was better. She no longer felt like she was about to slip. A breeze rushed against her face, bringing the rich scent of the outdoors with it.

"Scared?" he asked.

"No."

"Then we won't take the direct route." He dipped into the forest and slowly swerved around several trees. As they went past an especially tall oak, he turned on his side. They flew like this for a few moments, and then Jesse swerved around another group of trees and turned on his other side. If Tori had held out her hand, she could have run her fingers across the new growth at the branches' tips. She wanted to, but didn't dare let go of Jesse's arms.

He glided upward and out of the trees, then rolled on his back so she lay against his chest, facing the stars. Their studded light streamed down on her. It was like her own personal amusement ride, floating up here between the forest and the moon. She had to admit, it was incredible.

If she had the gift of flight, she would be out here every night, backstroking under the stars. But she probably didn't have that ability. Dr. B had said she most likely had the gift of sight, which even Dirk thought was boring. Who wanted to see what dragons saw, when dragons were such horrible, blood-thirsty creatures?

Besides, if Dirk could do it, why did they need her?

Jesse turned so they faced the forest again, and a calm sea of branches spread out beneath them. His arms held her snuggly, and everything seemed so tranquil. So intimate. He was sharing the stars and the trees with her; sharing spins and glides and lifts. It was like they were ice skating in the air. She felt close to Jesse in a way she couldn't explain—a connectedness. She let the feeling sink into her, saturate her.

"Okay, this is amazing," she finally said. "But it doesn't make up for the fireballs."

He lifted and took her straight up, speeding faster than he'd gone before. "Do you want me to let you go?"

She grabbed hold of his arms, panicked. The warm feelings she had for him evaporated. "Is that a threat? You'll drop me unless I stay?"

"No," he said slowly, "I was asking if you wanted to try it on your own." He let out a sigh of disappointment. "You don't seem to have the instincts to fly."

Well, she might have wanted to try it if he'd put the question differently. Why was everything these people did some sort of test? That ticked her off, too. Mostly because she'd failed the tests. Or at least, it felt like failure.

Jesse drifted downward again. "You can unclamp your hands from my arms now. I'm not going to drop you."

She made herself relax her hold. His arms had white spots where her fingers had gripped them. "Sorry."

"It's okay," he said. "I just really hoped you had the gift of flight."

"Why?"

He didn't answer for a few seconds, then said, "The original dragon knights had all the powers. Besides having night vision and extra strength, they could shield, shock, fly, heal, douse fire, and see into the dragon's mind. They must have been incredible to watch, to be . . ." He let the sentence, the wish fade into the air. "Chromosomes split when you pass them on to your children and most of the gifts split apart, too."

Jesse dipped down into the trees again, tilted on his side, and headed off in a new direction. "Do you remember back at the Easter grounds when Kody said his freezing shocks couldn't kill a dragon, and you asked what could?"

"Yes."

"No one answered because they didn't want to scare you if you were a flyer. When it comes down to it, the rest of the gifts are just support. The other Slayers contain the dragon to minimize damage so the flyers can get close enough to kill it." He said this unemotionally as though it didn't worry him. "I have to puncture the dragon's heart and make a big enough hole that it can't reseal itself. They used swords and spears in the Middle Ages. We're hoping that guns and arrows—if enough of them hit the target—will do the trick, too, but if not, I'm the only one who can go after a dragon in flight with a sword and reach the vulnerable part of its underbelly." He glanced down at her face. "You probably think I'm horrible for wishing you were a flyer, don't you?"

"No," she said, glad for the first time she wasn't one. What must it be like to know you not only had to face a dragon, but kill it? "Wow. By yourself. I'm sorry."

"I won't be by myself. I'll have the others with me. I'll have you, too." He said it like it was a statement, but she knew it was a question.

She didn't answer. He watched her, waiting for a response. She kept her gaze on the passing branches, all of them reaching for her. It felt like she was falling, falling into the darkness even though Jesse still held her close.

He flew higher up out of the trees again and increased his speed. Now that she could see the surroundings, she realized they were heading up the mountain, flying away from the camp.

"Where are we going?" she asked.

"I want to show you something."

They climbed the mountain quickly, hugging the tree line. The air was colder up here, and the wind chilled her cheeks, ears, and legs—everything that wasn't pressed next to Jesse. The rustle of leaves and branches sounded like the roar of the ocean.

They came to a rock outcropping, and he straightened, then landed. She let go of his arms and he walked over to the ledge and sat down. His legs dangled over the edge. She nearly told him to be careful, and then remembered he didn't have to. He could fly.

He turned and motioned for her. "Come look at this view."

She took small steps over to him, testing her weight with each footstep until she stood behind him. Underneath the ledge, way, way down, the tops of trees spread out beneath them in a lumpy silhouette. Off to the right, the lights from Hollings, the nearest town, glowed in protest to the darkness. She wasn't sure what Jesse wanted her to see. "It's a nice view," she said.

He patted the rock beside himself. "Sit down."

She didn't move. "I could fall."

"If you do, I'll go after you."

She wondered what speed people fell at, and if he could beat her to the ground. "It's okay. I'll stand. I can see the view from here."

He let out a sigh—probably of disappointment. How many times had she heard that sigh since she'd come to camp? Gritting her teeth, she walked to the ledge and sat down beside him. Her legs dangled down into nothingness.

She shifted her weight, moving back a little. "How long can you be away from the simulator signal before you lose your powers?"

"A half an hour. We've been out of range for about ten minutes. Don't worry, I know what I'm doing."

She sat stiffly on the ledge, her hands pressed against the rocky surface.

His lips twitched, fighting a smile. "If it helps, you can hold on to me."

She didn't want to. She didn't want to admit how frightening it was to sit on the edge of an abyss. Her hand didn't share the same pride, however. It grabbed hold of Jesse's hand and interlocked her fingers with his.

He gave her hand a gentle squeeze. "Look at the city lights."

She did. They glowed like facets of a jewel against a black canvass.

"Each one of those lights represents a life. A mom tucking her kids in. A dad up doing the dishes. You've seen D.C. at night. It's a blanket of lights for as far as you can see. More than half a million lives. Now imagine those lights extinguished."

She couldn't. It seemed impossible.

"When the dragons roar, they put out an electromagnetic pulse," he said. "Think of EMP as a radio wave that destroys anything nearby that runs on electricity. One blast from a dragon, and lights, phones, televisions, cars, computers—they're all ruined. Trucks won't be able to get groceries to stores. The water supply will be cut off because water pumps have electric parts. So imagine the city plunged into darkness, crippled, and with dragons swooping through the streets. The people won't stand a chance. How many cities will Overdrake have to destroy before the government buckles and surrenders to him?"

Tori stared out at the lights. "You said that enough bullets might kill a dragon. The one thing I know about D.C. is that it's well armed."

Jesse nodded even though she knew he wasn't conceding the point. "Let's say a few dozen bullets delivered at the same time to the heart will kill a dragon. Let's say Overdrake hasn't thought about that fact and hasn't given the dragon any bulletproof reinforcements on its underbelly. How many people will die before the dragon does? A hundred? A thousand?"

He was trying to guilt her into saying she would stay and train even if it meant risking her life and taking a few fireballs in the face and who knew what else—after all, tonight was only the beginning for her. "A dragon only needs to eat one person to feed on," she said. "Why would it kill a thousand?"

"Because that's what Overdrake wants. He wants bloodshed and confusion. He wants to threaten the leaders of the country. And he'll use his mind link with the dragons to get what he wants."

Tori looked at the forest and didn't answer.

Jesse pressed on. "But what if the dragon only did kill one person at a time? Would you walk away from the fight then? What if that one person was your father? He works in the capital, doesn't he?"

She let go of Jesse's hand and groaned, exasperated.

"If someone could help your father, but didn't, what would you think of that person?"

She still didn't answer. It was all too much. She didn't want to think about her father in danger, didn't want to admit Jesse was right.

"I know it feels overwhelming right now. We were all shocked when we first found out." He gestured toward the lights. "But those people need us. They're all somebody's father, mother—somebody's child."

Off in the distance, the city lights twinkled like a small constellation that had fallen to earth. Thousands of people must live there, and it was only a small town. "We should let the military know about the dragons—" she began, but he didn't let her finish.

"Telling people about our talents only puts us at risk. All it would take is one informant to sell us out. If Overdrake finds us, he'll kill us, and then . . ." Jesse gazed back at the lights again.

"I could tell my father," Tori said. "He wouldn't do anything to put the Slayers at risk—not when I'm part of the group."

"Exactly." Jesse fixed her with a gaze. "Your father wouldn't put you at risk, which is why you can't tell him any of this." Jesse leaned back, and then with a resentment she hadn't expected, told her the story about Ryker Davis, the boy whose parents had fled instead of letting their son be trained. "Dr. B keeps saying that one day Ryker will find us, but he hasn't shown up yet." Jesse shook his head as though to dismiss the subject. "None of our parents would let us fight dragons. They wouldn't believe it's the only way to defeat Overdrake. But right now it is." Jesse's dark eyes didn't waver from her face. "We need you, Tori."

She grasped the rock ledge so hard that tiny chunks of it crushed in her hand like sand. Her life wasn't supposed to be this way. She signed up for dragon camp, not saving the country. Still, it would be hard to walk away from all of this now. "Okay," she said, "but no more fireballs in my face."

"Practice only makes perfect, if it's the right kind of practice. Fire is involved when fighting dragons. If you get burned in the face it means you weren't paying attention . . . or sometimes that your team members weren't paying attention."

She tilted her chin down and gave him a disparaging grunt.

"It's not that big a deal. Everyone has been burned at one time or another." He stopped, correcting himself. "Well, everyone but Dirk. He says he can sense fireballs coming, but I think he's just lucky. And fast. It's the main reason Dr. B put him in charge of the A-team. You want a captain who's not going to be killed by the first fire blast."

Tori blinked at Jesse. "You're not making me feel better about being a Slayer."

"The scars aren't that bad." He pointed to his brow. "Look, I have one right here."

She leaned closer. A faint white line crossed his forehead above one eyebrow. "It's not that bad because you're a guy. It only makes you look tough. It wouldn't have the same effect on me."

He raised an eyebrow. "So you're saying your looks are more important than saving lives?"

Of course she wasn't. Because that sounded shallow. "Couldn't we wear welders' masks or something while we practice?"

"We wore helmets the first year," he said. "They just got in the way." He picked up her hand and held it up for her to see. "Now that you've been exposed to the simulator, your skin will be extraresilient.

Your hair will, too—eventually. Once the old growth is gone." He tilted his head, examining her. "I'm sure you'll look fine with short hair until then."

She pulled her hand away from him. She didn't feel comforted.

"You need to know about a few other things," he said. "Protecting your powers means taking care of your body. You can't do drugs. Not the illegal kind, but also not alcohol or tobacco. It interferes with the part of your brain that receives and implements the dragon's signal."

"Not an issue," Tori said. She'd never felt the urge, not even for a moment. Could her body have known all along what she was supposed to do?

"If you take enough drugs, or anything that's strong enough to make you pass out, you'll destroy the neuropathways in your brain that access your powers. They'll be gone, permanently." Jesse's voice dropped. "That's why Langston Overdrake drugged Dr. B's brother. He was trying to make Nathan lose his powers, but Overdrake gave Nathan too much and killed him."

The words settled in Tori's stomach like rocks. Nathan had been so young. He hadn't even known about the dragons.

Jesse took a thin phone out of his pocket and handed it to Tori. "Now that you're part of us, you'll need this. It's a satellite phone. Always keep it with you. That way your team can get ahold of you."

She fingered the sleek, black phone, flipped it open, and looked at the screen. It was expensive—just like the motorcycles and no doubt many of the other camp extras. "How is Dr. B financing all this? Who's giving him his funding?"

"He has a benefactor who helps out. Dr. B won't tell us anything about him except that his name is Sam. Or her name is Sam. He's vague about that point, too."

"Sam," Tori repeated with dissatisfaction. "That's it? And it doesn't bother you that you don't know more?"

"Dr. B is big on secrecy. The Slayers aren't listed anywhere on camp records. We're not allowed to tell one another where we live or to contact one another outside of camp unless it's an emergency. We won't tell you our real last names, and we'll do our best to forget yours." He gave her an apologetic smile. "It won't work, what with your father being Senator Hampton. Anyway, if your dad makes his bid for a presidential run, your picture will be splashed all over the media."

"He hasn't decided whether to try for a nomination yet," Tori said out of habit. It was the family's stock answer whenever anybody brought up the subject, even though her father was already interviewing staff for his campaign.

Jesse ignored her assertion. "Your government connection made us a little nervous at first. We were afraid the CIA had learned something about us and sent you to see what we were doing."

"Oh," she said, seeing that conversation in the cafeteria in a new light.

"The secrecy is for the group's protection," Jesse said. "If Overdrake caught one of us, it's better if we can't tell him much about anybody else."

She barely heard the last part of Jesse's explanation. Her mind was stuck on the *If Overdrake caught her* thought. Jesse was basically implying that she might be stalked, kidnapped, and tortured for information.

This was *so* not getting easier to handle.

"I guess it goes without saying," Jesse went on, "that you'll have to come back here every summer for training. You'll also need to go to college in the D.C. area so you're close by when the attack happens."

Tori gripped the phone, somehow unable to put it into her pocket. Putting it into her pocket meant she accepted all these rules. "I've been taking French since seventh grade so I could do a study abroad program there. You're saying I'll never be able to go?"

"Sure you can go. Right after we kill the dragons. I'll drive you to the airport myself if I'm still alive."

If he was still alive. He said it so casually, like he'd already resigned himself to the possibility he might not survive. It made her heart squeeze in her chest. What chances did any of them have? Jesse wasn't just asking her to stay, he was asking her to lay down her life.

Tori's throat felt tight. All of her choices, her freedom, was draining through her fingers.

Down below them, the city lights continued to glow steadily against the darkness. Each light represented a life. A happy, oblivious life that had no idea of the sacrifices she was being asked to make.

She didn't know if she could do it.

CHAPTER 13

Brant heard the beeping of his cell phone and put his other call on hold. He knew Ethington wouldn't like the interruption—considered himself too important to wait for anyone—but that was too bad. Brant had been expecting this text, and besides, it wouldn't hurt to remind Ethington that he was a supplier, not the buyer. Brant paid him well enough, so he could also make him wait. News from Dragon Camp took precedence, especially now that the eggs were so close to hatching. Brant would have put the devil himself on hold in order for an update on what his enemies were doing.

Brant, after all, was a careful man. His father had told him time and again never to underestimate the power of something that could kill you. His father had been referring to the dragons, but the advice applied to other aspects of life, too.

The Slayers, for example. They were an unexpected complication. Granted, they were only a group of teenagers with a few powers and a misguided sense of justice, but they were still dangerous. He wasn't about to forget that.

Brant flipped open his cell phone and scanned the message. No wonder the text had been late. There was important news. Leo and Danielle hadn't come back this year. Good. Any reduction in their forces was encouraging. Less bloodshed that way.

His gaze involuntarily went to the picture of his son and daughter that sat on his bookshelf. Brant didn't want unnecessary death. Especially not for teenagers, mere children, really. That was the difference between him and these knights-in-training; he would prefer not to hurt them, but they had no qualms about destroying him or the dragons.

Their whole purpose was to eradicate the masterpieces of the animal kingdom. Ironic. In their free time, they were probably all petitioning to save the spotted cheetah and humpback whale. But not the dragon. Humankind had always hated dragons because they couldn't beat them. People pitied only what they could easily slaughter. Perhaps that was why he pitied the kids at Dragon Camp. Their lives were in his hands, and they didn't even know it.

Brant stared at the picture of his children again, at the smiles that trusted him. He had promised he wouldn't hurt any of the Slayers if he didn't have to, and he was trying to keep that promise. At least for now. Promises were like laws; smart men knew when to break both.

Killing the Slayers now however, would be bad for a lot of reasons. He wouldn't want that sort of thing traced back to him. Not before the dragons were hatched and ready for their work. After that—well, then he would be at war with the government, and death was an unfortunate side effect of any revolution. Change always had a price tag. But once he took over, the people would realize he was a better ruler than the disorganized, self-interested mob that called themselves Congress—men who didn't know anything, being led by a president who knew even less.

Brant still remembered watching the U.S. president on television when he was a boy. Everywhere the U.S. president went—Europe, the Middle East—the media clamored around him. Cameras in hand, they waited for whatever words this leader would bestow on them, like eager seagulls waiting for falling food scraps.

"When will he come to St. Helena," Brant had asked his father, "so that he can meet with you?"

"He won't come here," his father answered, barely hiding his scorn. "The United States' presidents don't consider us important enough to visit. He probably couldn't find St. Helena on a map of the Atlantic."

The indignity of that slashed into Brant's pride, even back then. "You're more powerful than he is," Brant said. "You can control dragons. You could destroy entire cities if you wanted."

"Yes," his father said. "But nobody knows that."

That had been Brant's first lesson on power: It was impossible to wield power unless people knew you could destroy them. If leaders didn't have that knowledge, they never respected you.

That would change soon enough. Brant wasn't going to waste his power like so many of his ancestors had done. They should have ruled nations instead of hiding away on an island. But he would set that right. And Overdrake's children would finally have the legacy they deserved.

Brant scrolled down and read the rest of the message. Rosa and Bess had been sent to see if they could persuade Leo and Danielle to return to camp. This proved that not only were the Slayers woefully inexperienced, they were naive, as well. They should have realized as soon as Leo and Danielle didn't reenroll for camp that not only had their powers vanished, but their memories had fled, too. Surely Dr. B had discovered that piece of information in his studies. By some odd twist of the brain, when the neural pathway to a Slayer's powers withered, his mind twisted his memory of the powers, making excuses for what he could no longer understand.

Dr. B must have learned this; he just didn't want to accept it.

Brant scrolled down, reading the rest of the text, and then his thumb froze on the phone. So another Slayer had finally made her way to the camp. Victoria Hampton. No one knew her power yet. She seemed reluctant to be involved at all. He studied the snapshot his contact had forwarded to him. She was beautiful, the senator's daughter.

Brant leaned back in his chair and tapped his thumb against the phone. He knew Senator Hampton. The Republicans hoped he'd make a presidential bid next election.

Dr. B had always given the Slayers strict instructions not to tell anyone about their powers—not even their parents. As far as Brant knew, the children had kept this confidence. He'd never heard any whispers of rumors about dragon attacks from any of his sources in the government. But would Dr. B alter his tactics if he had the ear of such a powerful senator?

This could change everything.

Brant picked up his phone and texted a message back to his source. He ended it with two words. "Watch her."

 CHAPTER 14

When Jesse dropped Tori off at cabin 27's porch—literally dropped her, because he wanted her to practice landing from eight feet in the air—she was debating which was worse: that she had to risk her life fighting dragons, or that she had to rearrange her life until then. Spending every summer here would put a quick end to any plans she had for competitive skating, or, for that matter, vacationing. Her choice of colleges had just gotten a lot narrower—no Ivy League schools. No study abroad. And what if she had an appendix rupture or something? Was she supposed to tell the doctors to operate without anesthesia?

The cabin door was propped open. Even though Tori felt far too wound up to sleep she went inside to get ready for bed. Lilly and Alyssa were already showered, in their pajamas, and sitting on Alyssa's bed giving themselves pedicures. They regarded her coolly.

"I changed my mind about you bringing an iron to camp," Lilly said. "It turned out to be useful after all."

Tori glanced at the top of the dresser where she'd left her iron. It was gone. "Where did you . . . ?" she started, and then caught sight of the iron. It was sitting on the floor propping the door open. She grabbed it and returned it to her dresser with a thud. The door swung shut.

"There goes our cross breeze," Alyssa said.

Lilly calmly brushed red polish across a toenail. "That was great team support you showed up at the Easter grounds, Tori. If you storm off every time a fireball is launched your way, your team is doomed. Right now, you're down by ninety points. I'm sure Jesse just loves you."

Alyssa dabbed a piece of toilet paper across the side of a toe to wipe away a smudge. "Look on the bright side. You might start a new fashion trend at your prep school—the scorched-hair style."

Then both Lilly and Alyssa giggled.

These were the people who needed her, the ones she was supposed to risk her life for? Tori ignored them and pulled her pajamas out of her dresser. She slammed the drawer shut, then grabbed the caddy that carried her facial soap, shampoo, conditioner, washcloth, and moisturizer. Without saying good-bye, she headed to the shower.

One glimpse in the bathroom mirror confirmed that her hair was every bit as bad as she'd feared. The left side looked like someone had taken a machete to it.

She let out a groan and ran her hand over it, hoping this would somehow encourage it to grow. And then, even though it was stupid to cry over hair, tears pooled in her eyes.

She'd come to this camp with gorgeous, swishably long, cover girl hair. Now it was gone—a symbol of all the freedom she'd lost in one quick night. She was stuck at this camp with roommates who hated her, a camp director who might kill her before summer ended, and no real talent to help her fight the monsters that had suddenly become real.

The tears came harder, and she sat down on the floor, ignoring the gritty dirt that was there.

If only she could go back and change this day: rewind it, get back in the car with her sister, and drive away.

Because anything could happen now. Instead of having to worry about homework and dates and finding high heels that didn't cripple her when she wore them, she had to worry about fighting something that could roast her like a marshmallow.

How did Jesse do it? How did any of them? How did they manage to be Slayers and still live normal lives?

Tori took out the new phone and dialed her sister's number. She made herself take deep breaths, calming herself so her voice didn't crack. After three rings, Aprilynne said a questioning, "Hello?"

"It's me, Tori. I need you to drive to camp and pick me up."

Aprilynne let out a grunt. "It's eleven o'clock."

Tori stood up and checked the door to make sure no one was around to hear her. "You don't have to come right now, but can you please come tomorrow? Early. At quarter till seven."

"Do you realize what time I'd have to leave to make it there by six forty-five?" Before Tori could answer Aprilynne added, "Four fifteen."

"My new Jimmy Choo shoes—they're yours."

A muffled sound came from the end of the line, probably not Aprilynne setting her alarm for 4:15. "How about I pick you up at nine o'clock and you just let me borrow them when I want."

"It has to be six forty-five. I don't want anyone to know I'm leaving."

"Why? They're going to notice you've gone."

Tori moved back inside so anyone looking toward the bathroom wouldn't see her on the phone. "I don't want to tell anyone before I go. I'll throw in my Gucci handbag."

"That bad, huh?"

"You'll see when you get here."

Aprilynne let out a sigh. "Okay. The shoes *and* the handbag. I'll see you at quarter till seven."

"I'll meet you in the parking lot. Don't say anything to anyone about picking me up."

Aprilynne yawned. "You know, if you could have held out for two more days, I would have made a lot of money in the when-will-Tori-bail-out-of that-crappy-camp bet."

"Gambling is bad for you anyway."

"I'll be sure to mention that to Mom when I tell her she won."

That stung. Her own mother had given her less than twenty-four hours? "I'll see you tomorrow," Tori said and hung up. Then she leaned against the wall and shut her eyes. Even though she felt better now that she'd talked to Aprilynne, her hands hadn't stopped shaking.

Finally she showered, changed, gathered up her things, and stepped outside. She stopped short. No glow illuminated the forest. Darkness had spread through the trees, leaving everything black and hidden. The only light came from the bathroom porch light behind her and the faint porch lights from cabins 26 and 27 in the distance. She peered into the night, trying to make out the shapes that had been so easy to see on her way to the shower. What had happened?

Tori grasped her shower caddy to her chest and considered the possibility that she'd imagined everything and had gone insane. She reached up and ran her fingers through the left side of her hair. It was cold, wet, and still mournfully short.

She hadn't imagined the fireball.

But where had her abilities gone?

Taking tiny, cautious steps, she made her way toward cabin 27. She hadn't seen any rocks or tree roots sticking up in the path on the way over, so nothing should trip her on the way back. Still, it was hard to make herself walk when she couldn't see where to put her feet.

After several minutes, she made it to the cabin. The other girls lay on their bunks, unrecognizable lumps under the covers.

"I can't see in the dark anymore," Tori announced.

"That's because Dr. B turns off the simulator when we get back to camp," Lilly said from underneath her covers. "Otherwise we'd have too much energy to sleep."

Oh. So it had just been longer than half an hour since she'd been in contact with the signal.

Lilly rolled over with an exasperated tug of her covers. "The last one in every night locks the door."

Tori did, then made her way to where she remembered her bunk bed to be. She hadn't noticed her energy leave. In fact, she knew she wouldn't be able to sleep for quite a while.

She fiddled with the cell phone Jesse had given her until she found the alarm function.

"What time do you guys set your alarms to go running in the morning?"

Alyssa, her voice already going flat with sleep, said, "You don't need an alarm. When Dr. B turns on the simulator at seven, you'll bolt out of bed."

"Okay," Tori said. She set the alarm on her cell phone to vibrate at 6:00, crawled into bed, and slipped the phone under her back.

The forest sounds filtered into the cabins. Crickets. A bird of some sort, or maybe a bat. Branches rustling. And then the dragon's heartbeat.

Tori rolled onto her side. "I thought you said Dr. B turned off the simulator?"

"He did," Alyssa said.

"No, it's—" Tori didn't finish her sentence. The heartbeat had disappeared. She strained to pick it out again, but heard only the crickets and the wind.

She rolled onto her back again, kept listening, kept straining. Nothing.

Perhaps she'd fallen asleep for a second and dreamed the noise. That was probably it. Because even if the simulator was on, she was too far away to hear it. She shouldn't freak herself out about the noise. It wasn't like the dragon eggs were buried underneath her cabin.

But just in case, Tori got out of bed, felt her way to the dresser, and retrieved her iPod. She put it on the most soothing playlist she had, then went back to bed. She listened to song after song, concentrating on the music, trying to make herself relax. *I don't have to stay here*, she told herself. *Aprilynne is coming in the morning. I could tell my parents I want to go to that ice skating clinic in Denver. I could be on a plane by tomorrow evening.*

But every time she thought of leaving, she saw Jesse, his brown eyes somber, standing alone, in front of a dragon.

 **CHAPTER 15**

Jesse sat up before he opened his eyes. He stepped out of bed before he fully remembered where he was. He nearly bumped into Kody. Behind them, Dirk landed on the floor with a crash. Dirk swore, then stood up and brushed dirt off the front of his pajamas.

"That's it," Dirk said. "I'm not sleeping on a top bunk anymore. Only people who can fly should sleep on the top."

"No way," Jesse said. "I had the top bunk last year and never remembered I could fly until after I'd done a face plant."

Across the room, Shang pulled a crisp, white T-shirt over his head. "That's why I always set my alarm for five minutes before the simulator goes on."

Kody stretched and grabbed a T-shirt from a drawer. "It only takes a couple of days to get used to it. We'll be fine tomorrow." He put a hand against the bunk bed frame, then lifted the bed's legs from the ground and grinned. "Anybody up for a game of bed toss?"

"Save your energy for later," Jesse said. "You might need it."

After all, it had been two days since they'd come to camp, and Dr. B hadn't thrown any surprises at them. Not even a paintball ambush. Dr. B liked to point out, sometimes a little too cheerfully, that the Slayers had to watch out for gunfire. Dragons couldn't shoot guns, but Overdrake certainly could. They had to be alert and using their senses all the time.

Instead of putting the bed down, Kody pulled the thing into the middle of the room. It made a shuddering bang and undoubtedly added a new set of dents to the floor. "I sure wish I could have a simulator around when I play football." Kody flexed his muscles with satisfaction. "I love camp."

Dirk tossed his pajamas on his bed. "I bet Miss Socialite doesn't. How much do you want to wager she pulls a Ryker before the end of the month?"

"A Ryker's mother, you mean," Shang said. He combed through his sleek, black hair and checked his reflection in a small mirror that hung from a nail in the wall. He was the only one of the guys who cared how he looked before running. It wasn't that he was vain, just orderly. He had some philosophy about neatness being part of inner peace and was always trying to get the rest of them to pick up their stuff.

Shang put his comb back on the top of his dresser. "I bet Ryker still doesn't even know about the dragons. He's probably living on a houseboat with his parents in the middle of the Pacific Ocean."

During one of their many talks about dragons over the years, they decided that the ocean was the safest place to hide. If a dragon had nowhere to rest from a flight, he couldn't come after you.

"Tori's all right," Jesse said. "She just needs time to adjust." He slipped one foot into his shoe and pulled the laces tight. "It's a big shock for her to learn she has to spend the rest of her summers with Dirk. Anyone would freak out a little."

Jesse didn't have to look to see the shoe hurled in his direction. He felt it leave Dirk's hands, felt the air around him shift. It was part of being a Slayer that came after years of practice—an internal eye that told you where danger was. He caught the shoe with one hand and threw it back at Dirk just as fast.

Dirk caught the shoe effortlessly. "She'd better not walk out of the competitions again. And if she can't keep up on the run, we're not slowing down for her."

Jesse laced his second shoe. "Give her time to adjust." He smiled, then tried to hide it. If he smiled too much while talking about Tori, the guys would razz him. But despite his thoughts yesterday about her appearance being a problem, it wasn't really such a bad thing. It would just take some getting used to—that model-perfect face. He smiled again. He'd manage it somehow.

A knock sounded on the door, then from outside, Lilly said, "Jesse, I need you."

Kody snickered and Dirk said, "Does she ever." Which made Jesse wish he had something else to throw at him. Over the years, Lilly had rotated through the guys, crushing on them all in turn. He would be glad when she'd moved on to somebody else.

Shang glared at Dirk, and whispered, "Lay off. She'll hear you."

Shang, as Lilly's counterpart, was always the shoulder she cried on when she got too upset about anything. None of the guys ever hassled him for defending her, though. It was nice that someone had a built-in, genetically appointed patience for her.

"What is it?" Jesse called back.

"Tori's gone. When we woke up, we thought she was in the bath-room, but Alyssa checked and she's not there. Plus one of the carts is missing."

Jesse walked to the door and opened it. Both Lilly and Alyssa were there, already in their running clothes. Lilly had put on lip gloss. Probably for his benefit. "Did you call her?" he asked.

"She didn't pick up."

Jesse scanned the trees around them as though he might be able to spot her in the foliage.

Dirk walked up behind him. "Looks like she's not adjusting so well after all."

"Did she take her stuff?" Jesse asked.

Lilly shook her head. "Just her purse."

Alyssa said, "Someone with that much money—maybe she didn't care about leaving everything. If she had packed up her things, we would have heard her."

Shang joined the group. "Maybe she was kidnapped."

Lily tilted her head in disbelief. "Without waking up Alyssa or me? Someone picked the lock, carried her off, and then used one of our carts to get away?"

"Not really kidnapped," Shang said. "Dr. B could have arranged it as a test of our rescue skills. At this point, she's useless as a Slayer, so she makes a good victim. It would be hard to mess that up. She just has to sit there and wait for us to find her."

Alyssa scrunched her nose. "But she doesn't have a counterpart. How could we find her?"

Whenever Dr. B made them do rescue drills, it was almost always the counterparts who found each other first. Since Jesse didn't have a counterpart, he'd never really understood how it worked, but when counterparts were close to each other, they could sense things about each other's location.

Kody joined the group at last. "She might be up at the main camp trying to get something to eat."

Dirk grunted. "She did a Ryker."

They all looked at Jesse. As her team captain, he had the final say about what action to take. "I'll let Dr. B know she's missing. Dirk, take Lilly and Alyssa and search the main camp. Shang, take a motorcycle to the lake and see if she went that way. Kody, you try the *rifle range. I'll check the road out of camp. Report back to me in half an hour—sooner, if you find any clues."*

He didn't need to say more. The entire group dispersed into the forest, each going in the direction Jesse had told them to go. He dove off the patio, soaring upward until he hovered below the tree-tops. The cool morning air washed into him, pressing through his thin T-shirt as he weaved around branches. Squirrels chittered up and down tree trunks, eyeing him suspiciously. He hardly ever flew during the day, and never close to the main camp. Usually he would have enjoyed winging through the forest while the sunshine lit up the leaves like a million emeralds. Today he felt nothing but a tight ball of worry in his chest. Let it be one of Dr. B's games, he prayed *as he headed toward the director's cabin. But he knew that wasn't likely. Dr. B wouldn't have taken Tori's purse as part of one of his exercises.*

Tori was gone.

 **CHAPTER 16**

"Tori left?" Dr. B asked. His reaction told Jesse what he'd already suspected. This wasn't an exercise. "I thought she understood what was at stake."

"She does." Jesse stood in Dr. B's front room—a sort of combination living room and kitchen. "Maybe she doesn't think saving lives is that important."

Shirley, wearing an oversize white robe, stood at the stove cracking eggs into a frying pan. "Jesse, do you want some breakfast?"

"No, thanks," he said.

Dr. B let out a deep sigh. "Have a seat and I'll see where Miss Hampton has gone off to."

"How can you tell where she is?"

Dr. B didn't answer. He went to his bedroom and shut the door behind him.

Jesse didn't sit down. He paced around the room, listening to Shirley go on about how important a nutritious breakfast was. "Just because Tori has gone off somewhere, doesn't mean you should starve yourself," she said. "You need to take better care of yourself than that, hon."

Bess had told Jesse once that her mother had put him on the short list of people Bess was allowed to marry. Bess had thought it was funny, but Jesse wished she hadn't told him. He still wasn't sure whether to feel flattered or awkward when he was around Shirley now. He always wondered if she was moving him up or down on her list rankings.

"I'll eat breakfast if we have time," he said, then kept pacing around.

The cabin was a mixture of mismatched furniture, piles of clutter, and a few of Shirley's homey touches—floral pillows, family pictures, and a gun rack. A large map of the United States hung on the wall. Dr. B had written notations around the edges of the map that none of them could decipher. He'd also placed different colored pins on cities where he'd searched for Ryker Davis. Hawaii looked like it had caught a multicolored rash.

Jesse wondered if there would be a new set of pins for Tori now.

He'd been wrong about her—thinking she belonged here. She was a coward who had run away and left the danger to the rest of them.

Jesse turned away from the map, refusing to stare at its many colored pins of loss and longing.

Dr. B came back to the room, carrying a small laptop and a jacket. He put the jacket on as he walked toward the front door. "I've located her. She's in Hollings. Cypress Street, to be exact."

"What's she doing there?"

"I have no idea, but let's find out. As far as I can tell, she's staying put." Dr. B tucked his laptop under his arm, and he and Jesse walked toward the door.

Shirley came at them with a plate of toast. "You can at least eat something on the way."

Jesse and Dr. B each obediently took a piece of toast and went outside.

Dr. B munched unhappily as he walked toward the ATV he used to get between the two camps. "My wife has gone on a multigrain kick. Now there are seeds and oats in my toast. It's like eating compressed bird food."

Dr. B was right about that, and Jesse wished Shirley had given them something to wash the toast down with. While he was still chewing, Dr. B called Dirk and told him to lead the teams in their normal schedule until he and Jesse got back.

It was too noisy to talk on the ATV, but once they reached Dr. B's car in the camp parking lot, Jesse again asked the question that had been on his mind. "How do you know where Tori is?"

Dr. B unlocked his car door and slid behind the steering wheel. He pursed his lips as though debating whether to answer Jesse's question. It wasn't until Jesse was buckling his seat belt that Dr. B spoke again. "Each of your phones has built-in GPS. I can track them using a program on my laptop."

Jesse's gaze swung around to Dr. B's face. "Why didn't you tell us?"

"That information in the wrong hands could pose a danger to you. What if Overdrake learned you could be traced?" Dr. B cast a glance at his laptop, which lay on the seat between them. "What would he do to get hold of this computer and my passwords?"

Which was the point. Jesse had carried around a tracking device for years without knowing it.

Dr. B turned on the ignition and drove the car toward the street. Even though he wasn't going fast, the car bumped along the uneven surface.

"I understand why you didn't let the staff know," Jesse said. "But you should have told us. We wouldn't endanger ourselves."

Dr. B spoke evenly, as if he was delivering one of his lectures. "Are you sure about that? Two Slayers didn't come back this year, and we don't know why. It's better if you don't let the others know about this."

Jesse nodded, but he wasn't sure he agreed. The Slayers always carried the phones with them. It only seemed fair they should know the phones could be a liability. After all, Overdrake knew the Slayers existed. He had come looking for them once already.

It had been the first year of camp, back when they were eleven-years-old. Only four of the Slayers had found camp at that point: Bess, Rosa, Shang, and Jesse. They'd been discovering their talents and finding ways to use them. Rosa had healed a dozen minor burns on Dr. B, and he wanted to see if she could heal larger ones. He loaded the simulator in a U-Haul and took the group to a burn unit in a D.C. hospital.

Dr. B had dressed up as a priest and told the hospital staff they were delivering care packages from his congregation. He asked if the kids could spend a few minutes chatting with the patients. No one would have suspected Rosa of doing anything out of the ordinary, especially back then when her petite size had made her look closer to nine than eleven. She'd worn her long black hair in pigtails, blinked her big brown eyes, and adults had had no choice but to trust her.

They'd gone into each room, delivered the gifts, then Dr. B asked the patients if he could say a prayer with them. They all agreed, even though some looked uncomfortable with the idea. Dr. B had stood by their heads, blocking their view of Rosa as much as he could, then he'd instructed the patients to shut their eyes. While Dr. B prayed, Rosa held her hands over the patient, turning the seeping wounds underneath their bandages into new skin.

Before Dr. B had quit speaking, each patient gasped and opened their eyes, reaching for wherever their wound had been. "It feels tingly now. What happened?"

"Hallelujah," Dr. B always said, managing to make the word sound stilted and suspicious. "Give praise to God, but don't take off your bandages until the nurses give you permission."

The last patient they visited was a six-year-old with burns over her entire face. Bandages covered her head, so that only her eyes, nose, and blistered mouth poked out from the gauze. And worse yet, the way the bandages lay against her head made it clear that one ear was damaged, perhaps missing.

Rosa gasped when she walked into the room. "I don't know if I can do this," she whispered. "Her ear . . ."

Dr. B patted her on the shoulder. "Anything you can do to help is fine."

The girl's mother sat in a chair by the hospital bed and regarded them wearily. She didn't look like the type who liked visitors or pity.

"We're from St. Teresa's down the road," Dr. B said. There was a church by that name, and no one ever asked Dr. B for any sort of proof that he was actually a priest. "We've brought some things for your daughter." Dr. B motioned to Rosa, and she handed the mother a decorated box full of books and stuffed animals.

Dr. B smiled graciously. "Might we say a prayer for your daughter?"

The mother gripped the box awkwardly. "We don't go to church."

"That's all right," Dr. B said. "We pray for all in need."

The mother's lips twitched uncertainly. Jesse knew she didn't like the idea. That's why they brought the gifts. It was hard to be rude to someone who'd given you presents. "Okay, then . . ." the mother said, dragging out the words as though somewhere in the sentence she might change her mind.

"Let's close our eyes and pray." Dr. B stood directly between the mother and the bed so she couldn't see Rosa's hand motions. "Our Father in heaven," Dr. B began, but Jesse didn't pay attention to the prayers. He let his eyes squint open to watch Rosa. She held both hands over the girl's face; pulling her fingers together, moving them to some unheard rhythm, caressing the air. Her gestures were quicker than usual, more frantic. She didn't even slow down or lessen the motions when the girl opened her eyes and looked like she would speak. Rosa just held one finger to her mouth to indicate she needed silence.

It had to be working; the girl touched her face like she could feel a difference. Rosa didn't stop, though. Her forehead grew moist with perspiration.

Dr. B came to his usual stopping place in the prayer—the part where he said, "And let us remember that all good things in life come from heaven," but he peeked at Rosa and continued, "And let us remember everything else we need to remember. And let us remember to do good works quickly. Very quickly . . ."

He was stalling, but Rosa didn't notice.

She made one last flourish over the girl's ear, then reached for the bandages. Rosa had never touched any of the patients' dressings before. She carefully unwrapped the bandages, but the rustling from the bed made the mother open her eyes. She stood up. Dr. B stepped in her way. "We're still praying over here."

The mother barely looked at him. "What are you doing?" Then she saw the bandages on the bed. "Are you crazy!" she yelled, and pushed Dr. B out of the way with more strength than Jesse expected.

The woman stopped and stared mutely when she saw her daughter. Rosa had taken off the last of the bandages, revealing the girl's pale, new skin. Rosa turned the girl's head, and sighed with relief. The ear was there—a crisp C of skin resting against the side of her face.

"We should go now." Dr. B took hold of Rosa's arm and led her toward the door. Bess and Kody followed. Jesse glanced back before he left. The mother sat on the bed holding her daughter's hand, crying. She was also pushing the nurse-call button.

"Hurry," Dr. B said, and he didn't have to say more. It wouldn't take long before the hospital staff decided to detain them. They walked quickly down the halls and out the lobby doors.

Once they were back in the truck and pulling out of the parking lot, Dr. B nodded philosophically. "Well, I think St. Teresa's will be a bit more crowded next Sunday."

A doctor dressed in scrubs came out of the building, blinking against the sun as he scanned the parking lot. He didn't see them. He probably didn't expect a priest to be driving a truck and towing a U-Haul.

Rosa saw the doctor and shrunk down in her seat. "I'm sorry I messed that up. But I had to know whether I'd gotten the ear right. I wasn't sure it worked."

"You did marvelously," Dr. B said.

"I want to go to another hospital," she said. "I should heal all the burn patients. Maybe we could even work something out with the doctors. Maybe we could explain a little to them about why I have this ability."

Dr. B didn't answer for a moment. "We'll think about it and discuss it later."

They did discuss it later, after the miracle healings made the news, after the patients gave complete descriptions of their angelic visitors to reporters.

Dr. B's voice had turned uncharacteristically grave then. "Overdrake will know what the healings mean," he said. "He'll know someone is teaching at least four children to be Slayers and that one of them has the power to heal burns. I should have made you wear disguises. I should have only taken Rosa with me."

But Jesse knew without asking why Dr. B had taken all of them. When Rosa had healed the people, when she'd unwrapped the girl's bandages and they'd seen her unscarred face, something had cracked open inside him. He couldn't describe it. He only knew he'd never felt anything quite so powerful before. He wanted to help people the same way. He had to.

After that, whenever he trained he thought about empty hospital beds. In his mind's eye, he saw rows of beds that wouldn't be filled if only he could destroy the dragons.

The day after the national news ran the story about the miracle healings, the hospital's surveillance tapes were stolen. The footage hadn't been shared with the media and Dr. B and the Slayers waited for it to show up on some tabloid program. When it didn't, they knew Overdrake had the tapes.

Now as Jesse and Dr. B drove toward Hollings, Jesse fingered the satellite phone in his pocket. For the first time, it didn't make him feel more secure to have it.

Twenty minutes later, they reached the town. Dr. B parked at a McDonald's and turned on his laptop. He had to wait an annoyingly long time for the GPS function to boot up before he typed his passwords. Then he held the laptop at an angle so Jesse couldn't see what he typed, which irked Jesse. Shouldn't the team captains know the passwords? What if something happened to Dr. B? He and Dirk might need that information.

"She's still in the same place," Dr. B said.

"Or at least her phone is." Jesse was suddenly certain she'd ditched her phone in a trash bin. Why would she keep it if she ran away?

"You may be right," Dr. B said. "In which case, we'll need to retrieve the phone anyway. But not to worry. Tori's father isn't likely to disappear the way Ryker's parents did. We'll be able to help her overcome her fears."

Jesse didn't want to help her overcome her fears. He wanted to tell her off.

Dr. B shut his laptop, started the car again, and they drove to Cypress Street. As soon as they turned onto the street, Jesse recognized Tori's car. It was the same blue BMW that had dropped her off at camp. Dr. B parked behind it, immediately making his Ford Taurus look old and cheap by comparison.

A huge pink cursive sign on the nearest shop read BRANDI STEWART'S BEAUTY SALON. Inside the glass windows, an entirely pink waiting area was visible. A teenage girl sat lazily flipping through magazines in one of the chairs. She was an older, blonder version of Tori and almost as pretty. Behind her, Jesse could make out a couple of women working on someone's hair.

They'd found their missing dragon slayer. At a beauty salon.

The absurdity made Jesse laugh. "No way," he said. "She got up early and ran away to get her hair done? Who does that?"

Dr. B's eyebrows drew together. "Well, part of her hair did get singed last night. Perhaps she wanted to even it out."

"That's not it. She wants to look good before she goes home to her high-society friends." Jesse reached for the car's door handle, but Dr. B didn't turn the car off.

"Let her finish. They have to come out front to get into their car. We'll talk to her then." Dr. B backed up into the next parking space so Tori and her sister wouldn't see them sitting in the car waiting.

Once they were out of view, Dr. B called Dirk and gave him an update. Then Dr. B opened his laptop and typed notes for his next class lecture. Jesse got out of the car and leaned against the hood.

Maybe he couldn't do anything to stop Tori from leaving, but she was at least going to face him and explain herself before she did.

The minutes ticked by. What could Tori possibly be doing that took this long? And what sort of haircut took two people? It's not like anyone had to take extreme measures to make Tori look beautiful.

From his angle, Jesse could see the sister's legs. They were nice legs, granted, but lacked the muscular definition Tori's had. Tori had great legs. Not that he'd been checking them out yesterday. At least, not much. He'd only examined them as evidence she could be one of them. All the Slayers were muscular.

Finally, the sister stood up.

Jesse knocked on the car window, motioning to Dr. B. A few seconds later, Tori and her sister breezed out of the salon.

Tori did a double take when she saw Jesse leaning against Dr. B's car, and her green eyes widened. "What are you doing here?"

"I should ask you the same. Why did—" The accusation died on his lips. He realized she didn't look any different than she had when she first came to camp. Her hair was long, all of it. Impossibly, it flowed down her shoulders to her back. "What happened to your hair?"

She ran a hand over it. "Extensions. It was the only thing I could do besides a bob, and I had a bob when I was nine. I can't revisit that hairstyle for a while." Dr. B had come around the car to join them, and Tori gave him a severe look. "Extensions are a hassle to put in, and I had to pay Brandi and her assistant extra to come in early, so I hope cabin twenty-six doesn't fling any more flaming marshmallows around the campfire."

Dr. B's gaze darted to the sister, then back at Tori. "I'm sure everyone will be more careful."

The anger that had encompassed Jesse all morning thinned and popped like a bubble. "You're not leaving?"

"No," Tori said.

The sister looked Jesse up and down. "And suddenly it's become clear why she's not."

Tori blushed, but didn't laugh or agree with the comment the way Lilly would have done. "This is my sister, Aprilynne. Aprilynne, this is Jesse and Dr. B from camp."

"Did you come all this way looking for Tori?" Aprilynne asked. "I told her she should have said something before she left."

Dr. B gave Tori a forced smile. "Yes, it's against camp rules to leave the premises."

"Which is why I didn't tell you I was leaving," Tori said, and then added, "Sorry. I figured I'd be back before anyone worried about me." She glanced at her watch. "Breakfast hasn't even ended yet."

Jesse's old anger had vanished, but a new type took its place. She'd broken the rules and worried them to death just to fix her hair. "I told you we went running in the morning," he said.

Tori met his eyes. "And I told you I didn't run in the morning."

"We spent half an hour searching for you," he said. "We didn't know—"

She ignored him and turned to Dr. B. "Are you kicking me

out of camp for breaking the rules?" Her voice almost sounded hopeful.

Dr. B shook his head. "Of course not. But I must emphasize that you can't leave camp again. If we hadn't found you, we would have had to call the police and report you missing—you see how bad that would be for the camp?"

"Yes," she said, and finally sounded sorry.

Her change in tone didn't lessen Jesse's anger. He waved a hand at her. "And you didn't pick up your phone. Why?"

Tori shrugged. "I left it in the car. I don't usually talk on the phone while I'm getting my hair done."

Dr. B said, "Well, we've found you now, so everything is all right. You can ride back to camp with us and spare your sister the trip."

"I have another errand to run." Tori gazed down the street and she edged toward the BMW. "I need to buy a welder's mask."

"Why?" Aprilynne asked.

Tori hesitated. "I'm taking a welding class at camp."

"Doesn't the camp have welder's masks then?" Aprilynne asked.

"We can see to that," Dr. B said. "You'll be fine."

Tori regarded him with suspicion. "I'll need two. One for the back of my head. I'm not buying more extensions."

"We'll take care of it," Dr. B said.

Aprilynne tilted her head. "Are you sure you don't want to come home?" She lowered her voice to a whisper and leaned into Tori. "One day at camp and you're strapping welder's masks to the back of your head?"

Tori let out a martyred sigh, but nodded. "I'm staying."

Aprilynne leaned in and gave Tori a parting hug. "Okay. But if you change your mind, give me a call. I've got my eye on your blue Dior skirt."

Tori didn't laugh, and Aprilynne looked her over more closely. "I'm just kidding. You don't even have to give me your Gucci handbag for today. The shoes are enough."

Tori stepped away from her sister reluctantly. "It's all right. I want you to have it." She sounded as though she were preparing her will.

Aprilynne didn't seem to notice. "If you insist." She opened her purse, took out her keychain, and clicked the unlock button. The car chirped happily at her. "Well, I'd better go. I have some things to put in my new purse. Have fun at camp." She sashayed to her BMW, slid inside, and handed Tori her phone through the window. With a good-bye wave, she started the car and drove down the street.

Tori stood, her shoulders held stiff, watching the retreating car.

Dr. B regarded her. His voice was soft, understanding. "You didn't tell us where you went this morning because you weren't sure you were coming back."

Tori nodded, still watching the BMW make its way down the street.

"What made you decide to stay?" Dr. B asked.

"My father has devoted his life to serving this country. How could I do less?"

Dr. B smiled, clearly happy with this answer. "Let's go. We have a full day of training ahead of us."

Jesse didn't smile. He couldn't muster the type of understanding Dr. B was so good at. Or maybe it was just that Jesse was more doubtful of Tori's commitment. She had probably agreed to return with them because she was too embarrassed to tell Dr. B face-to-face that she wouldn't be a Slayer. Odds were, the next time Tori had a chance, she would ditch camp. Then she'd ease her guilt by having her father make a large donation to Dr. B. Rich people thought you could buy anything, even a clean conscience.

Jesse didn't look at Tori as he climbed into the front seat of the car. Dr. B had said they had a full day of training. Jesse was going to give Tori a full day and then some.

 CHAPTER 17

Tori made up for missing breakfast by grabbing an apple from the main camp's cafeteria, then she and Jesse took a cart and headed to the Slayer camp. She ate slowly because it gave her an excuse not to talk to Jesse. She didn't want to talk to him; not when he was still steaming.

She did feel bad about worrying everyone, but what did they expect after they'd hurled fireballs at her head and told her she'd have to alter her entire life so she'd be around to help them fight off the huge, flying carnivores?

Really, all she'd wanted was a nice summer camp.

So let him be mad about it. She hadn't told him the truth about why she'd decided to stay anyway. It wasn't just because of her loyalty to the country. She came back because she couldn't stand the thought of Jesse fighting the dragon without all the help he could get. If she walked away from this place and he died, she'd always blame herself.

There. That was it.

She was obviously some sort of romantic fool for developing

feelings for him, but she couldn't help it. She remembered what it felt like to fly through the forest with his arms around her, the way his dark brown eyes had looked into hers while they'd spoken on the outlook. He had said he needed her. How could she turn her back on him?

All in all, it was probably better he was mad at her. She knew practically nothing about him. Odds were, he wasn't the right type of guy for her to develop a crush on. It would help her keep her head if he kept his distance.

"Dr. B may have let you off the hook with only a reprimand," Jesse said, gripping the steering wheel harder than he needed, "but I'm not. As your team captain, I'm letting you know that you've lost your lunch break. You have fifteen minutes to eat and then you'll use the rest of the hour to help Booker clean out the horse stalls. You'll also need to find time to make up the run you missed this morning, but when you do it, you'll run with twenty-pound weights on your arms and legs. We keep those in the archery shed."

See, her plan was working. She already felt less romantic about him.

He glanced over at her, looked as though he was going to say something else, but then shook his head and returned his attention to the trail.

"What?" she asked. The word came out with a sharp ring of defiance she hadn't intended.

Jesse answered slowly, the anger simmering in his voice. "Overdrake had a motto he used to say a lot when Dr. B lived in St. Helena: *Homines suas vitas magis quam bonum publicum aestimant.* It means: People care more about their own lives than the common good. That's what Overdrake is depending on—that most people would rather accept him as a ruler than risk their lives fighting him.

"I've never thought the saying was true. But I just noticed something." He glanced at her again. Even though his eyes were only on her for a moment, she didn't miss their disdain. "None of the rest of the Slayers are from wealthy families. Why do you think that is?"

She smiled, shrugged, and gave an answer she knew would needle him. "Overdrake must have taken the eggs through some slummy part of D.C. After all, my parents went everywhere campaigning."

"I think," Jesse said, ignoring her barb, "that Slayers were born to wealthy families, but rich kids don't care about anything but themselves, so they didn't bother coming to camp. It's why Ryker isn't here and why you'll take off the next time things get hard."

Tori breathed in sharply. Maybe she deserved an insult after her slummy part of D.C. comment, but Jesse's words still made her bristle. He hadn't said them to get a rise out of her—the way she'd said her comment—he actually meant them.

She wanted to say, "Why would anyone want to stay here and train with the rest of you?" then get out of the cart and call Aprilynne to pick her up.

But that would just be proving Jesse's point.

And maybe, Tori realized with a sort of horrible twisting in her stomach, he was right. Her own friends and family had a bet on how long she would stay at camp, and they didn't even know about the Slayer stuff.

She wasn't the type who ran away from hard things, was she? She didn't care more about herself than the common good. This morning when she'd gone to Hollings, well, she'd just reacted like any normal teenage girl would react when faced with fireballs, dragons, and impending doom.

She was normal.

Maybe that was the problem, though. Maybe Overdrake was right and normal people were self-centered to the point of cowardice or at least inaction.

Tori didn't like any of these thoughts. Worst of all, she didn't like doubting how she would react when things got dangerous.

Could she lay down her life for this cause?

Her stomach twisted again.

Death was such a big commitment to make.

Finally, they reached the Slayer camp. Jesse parked the cart behind the rifle range and then the two of them walked to the large field. Shang and Lilly were riding nearly identically chestnut quarter horses, effortlessly jumping over four-foot fences. Alyssa and a girl Tori didn't recognize shot arrows into Styrofoam disks that a machine spat into the air. The new girl had tan skin and lush black hair that poured over her shoulders. Tori didn't see Kody or Dirk anywhere. Perhaps they were at the rifle range.

Tori waited for Jesse to tell her where to practice, but a glance at his profile told her he'd completely forgotten about her. His gaze trained in on the girl with the long black hair. He picked up his pace, heading straight to her and ignoring everything else. Tori followed after him slowly.

When he got close to the archery range, the new girl looked over at them. She barely took in Tori. The girl's gaze stopped on Jesse and tears welled in her brown eyes. Her expression fell, and she let out a sob. Jesse jogged the last few steps to her.

"Leo isn't coming back," she said and another sob choked off her words.

Jesse let out a punctured breath, shook his head as though he didn't know what to say, then pulled her into a hug. Her bow fell to the ground, unnoticed, while she buried her head into his chest.

They stood that way for several seconds, the girl crying, Jesse ashen and pained. Tori stayed far enough away that they had some privacy. It wasn't polite to stare, yet she couldn't drag her gaze away.

"It was awful," the girl said, her words tumbling out between sobs. "He drinks now, and his memories of us are all twisted. He thought dragon camp was childish, and he said you were a jerk for bossing everyone around. Even Bess couldn't reach him. The part of him that was her counterpart is gone. He's not one of us anymore. And he doesn't even care."

Jesse didn't speak, just let her cry into his shoulder. He shut his eyes and leaned his cheek onto her dark hair. They stayed that way until the girl pulled away. "Dr. B says there isn't anything we can do, but there must be something. If we can prove to him that we have powers, he'll know we're telling the truth."

"And then what?" Jesse's jaw tightened. "He made a choice not to follow the rules. We can't make him undo it. We can't give him back his powers."

It wasn't until then that Jesse seemed to remember Tori. He waved her over for introductions. "Rosa, this is Tori. She got here yesterday."

"Hi," Tori said.

"Hi." Rosa wiped her cheeks. "Sorry. I'm a mess."

Tori smiled sympathetically. "It's okay." She already liked Rosa more than Lilly and Alyssa. Rosa was so soft-hearted. Tori also noted, although she didn't want to, that Jesse and Rosa had been pretty quick to hug each other.

Apparently, Rosa hadn't gotten Lilly's memo on that whole dibs issue.

Jesse looked around the field, squinting against the sunshine. "Where's Bess?"

Rosa picked up her bow from the ground and brushed off some dry grass. "She's still talking to Danielle. Danielle didn't register for camp because she didn't want to leave her boyfriend. Bess thinks she can convince her to come, that she might not be as far gone as Leo." Rosa swallowed hard and lifted a hand in frustration. "I started crying on the way over to her house, so I wasn't a lot of help. Bess told me she'd handle it herself." Rosa's lips trembled again. "Why did Dr. B send me to talk to them? He should have sent you or Dirk. Dirk could have brought them back. He can talk anybody into anything."

Jesse put his hands on Rosa's shoulders, gently massaging the tension in her back. "That's not true."

"Remember the summer Dirk taught cabin twenty-six how to play poker?" She said the words like they proved her point. "He insisted that the losers had to shave their heads, and every single one of you ended up looking like marine recruits."

Jesse kept massaging her shoulders. "Remember last year when we had a contest to see who could get the best tan?"

"Yeah," she said glumly. "You disqualified me for being Latina."

He went on as though she hadn't spoken. "And you kept trying to make us wear sunscreen because you were afraid we'd get skin cancer? Dr. B sent you to talk to Leo and Danielle because you care about everybody."

"I failed," she whispered.

"You didn't." He dropped his hands from her shoulders, then turned to Tori. His expression was strained, but when he spoke his voice was brisk again, professional. "We do rotations in the morning. Start with the indoor firing range, then move on to archery and horseback riding. If you have time after that, I'll take you to the motorcycle range to practice there."

He headed toward the indoor range, and she followed after him. "If we can ride motorcycles to fight the dragon, why do we need horses?"

"Motorcycles won't work against the dragon's electromagnetic pulse. Besides, knights have always had a special connection with their horses. Pretty soon Bane will obey your commands nearly before you give them."

"Really?" she asked, but she already believed him. She'd felt it the first time she'd ridden Bane. "So why do we practice on motorcycles?"

"The motorcycles are for now—if Overdrake attacks the camp, we'll need a way to escape fast. Motorcycles are the best way to get around the back roads."

And on that happy thought, Tori did her rotations.

She spent an hour shooting impossibly small moving circles in the rifle range, then spent an hour shooting spinning Styrofoam disks at the archery range. Perhaps the continued pulse from the simulator helped her aim. Her score improved each time she went through a round.

Horseback riding was her favorite. When she'd gone to the stables, Booker had Bane saddled up. "He's been antsy all morning," Booker said, leading the horse over to Tori. "Just waiting for you to come get him, I suppose." Bane tossed his head, nearly slapping Booker's face with his mane, and whinnied impatiently.

"Ah, get on with you," Booker said. "No one wants your dramatics around here." But the horse calmed down once Tori took the reins.

She raced Bane through the show-jumping course, complete with four-foot fences, without any problems. It didn't earn her any respect among the other Slayers, though. With the exception of Rosa, who was preoccupied with being miserable, all the Slayers were angry at her. Dirk smiled and joked with everyone but her. He wouldn't even look at her. Every time Tori finished an exercise, Lilly pointedly asked her how her hair was holding up. Jesse was the worst, not because of anything he said, but because every time she saw him, his words from the morning came back. *You'll take off the next time things get hard.*

CHAPTER 18

At lunchtime, Tori wished she could go back to the main camp and eat with the regular campers, but due to Jesse's punishment, she only had fifteen minutes. Besides, the Slayers were supposed to eat together in the Dragon Hall. As they assembled to walk there, Dirk got a phone call from Bess. As he listened, the smile dropped from his lips and his expression grew hard. Finally, he snapped the phone shut. "Danielle's memory is gone, too. She's not coming back."

Rosa teared up again and her lips pressed together with silent emotion. Jesse rubbed her shoulder consolingly. Lilly had the opposite reaction. She let out a stream of swear words, picked up a dead branch from the trail, and hit it into a tree trunk so hard it shattered. Bits of wood flew toward the group like confetti.

Kody sent out a freezing shock, which hit the falling pieces and pushed them back toward the tree.

No one made note of this. Apparently such displays were commonplace.

Shang stared grimly off into the distance. "That's two we've lost."

"Isn't there something we can do?" Alyssa crossed her arms determinedly. "If we kidnapped them and brought them back to the camp, maybe they'd get their powers back."

Dirk plunged his phone into his pocket and scowled. "If their memories are gone, so are their powers."

"We don't know their powers are gone," Alyssa said. "We're just assuming they're gone because of the stuff Dr. B's read. Those records could be wrong."

Dirk blew out a huff of exasperation. "And what will we do when the FBI comes here searching for the kidnapping victims? A lot of good we'll be to D.C. if we're in prison." He headed down the path to the Dragon Hall and the rest of the Slayers followed.

Alyssa kicked a rock on the trail. It arced upward, then spun and shattered.

Kody watched as his handiwork rained pebbles down on the ground. "Danielle could send out shocks—well, so can I. Leo could throw up a shield—well, so can Bess. We ain't nowhere close to being beat yet."

"We've trained as two teams," Dirk said, "Now both are short-handed."

"Then we'll just have to work that much harder," Kody said.

Rosa was still crying. She let out stifled gulps as the tears ran down her cheeks. Jesse put his arm around her. "What it means is this battle will be won or lost in the decisions we make back home when we're by ourselves. None of us is indispensible."

Kody said, "We're only down by one anyhow. Tori's here. We still don't know what she can do."

Every pair of eyes turned to Tori, appraising her.

"She can do her hair," Lilly said.

Jesse shot Lilly a sharp look. "Stop it. We can't afford to fight with each other."

"Sorry," Lilly said. She didn't sound like she meant it.

When Jesse turned to Tori, his eyes were softer than they'd been all day. "Have you tried to see a split screen in your mind lately?"

"Yes," she said stiffly. "Nothing happened."

Dirk studied her, but didn't say anything. She could feel his eyes on her as they walked.

She hoped she had an amazing gift, something that none of the rest of them had—like laser vision that could be used to blow up large, flying reptiles.

The Slayers filed inside the big building. It was the first time Tori had been in the Dragon Hall. A sunken floor gave the two-story roof even more height. The dome she'd seen earlier made sense now. A mechanical dragon that was the size of a school bus hung from wires that connected to a motor in the dome. Someone had painted a red X on the dragon's belly, and several large canisters were attached to its mouth. She knew without asking that fire came from those canisters.

Even though the dragon hung there gray and lifeless, it made Tori feel on edge. She didn't want to turn her back on it.

In the front of the room, a picnic table, white board, and TV were set up. "What's the TV for?" Tori asked Shang. She knew it wasn't for something fun, like watching the Style Network.

"We record our dragon fights and then analyze our tactics."

Nope, nothing fun.

Shirley stood at the picnic table arranging condiments by a stack of sandwiches. "Sub sandwiches and carrot sticks," she called. "The lunch of champions." The group went over, still talking about Leo and Danielle, and picked up their food. Tori was last through the line. Shirley smiled and gave her arm a squeeze as she went by. "You'll be fine."

The sympathy made Tori feel worse. She'd pushed her emotions away all morning, pretended she didn't care what anybody thought about her. With that one sentence, her feelings surfaced again, fresh and stinging. Still, Tori smiled back at Shirley, then went to the end of the table, sat down, and forced herself to take a bite. She hadn't had much breakfast. She needed to eat something before her fifteen minutes were up.

Shang, probably for lack of room, sat across from her. No one sat next to her. Shirley picked up her tray, told them to practice hard, then left.

Lilly broke her carrot stick in two and let the pieces fall back onto her plate. "Did either Danielle or Leo think about the fact that they put our lives in danger by their stupid decisions?"

No one answered.

"It must be nice to forget your responsibilities that way," she said. "Poof. No worries."

Dirk opened a packet of mustard and spread it on his sandwich. "We're wasting our time complaining about Leo and Danielle. It won't bring them back."

This didn't, however, curb the conversation. Everyone had an opinion or a memory, some bit of pain to share. They were so immersed in their loss, no one noticed Tori anymore, let alone spoke to her. She ate and watched the metal dragon hanging from the middle of the ceiling. She tried to concentrate, to feel something, to lift herself off the bench by flight. Nothing happened.

When her fifteen minutes were almost up, Tori leaned over the table toward Shang. "How long did it take the rest of you to discover your extra talents?"

He pushed a stray piece of lettuce back between his bread. "The rest of us knew during our first trip to the Easter grounds, but it's different for you. You're older. When you're eleven or twelve there's a part of you that believes in the supernatural. The instincts to accept magic are still there. At sixteen, you've told yourself for a long time that superpowers don't exist. It makes sense that it will take you longer to find your gift."

"Thanks," she said, because she knew he was trying to make her feel better. Even if she didn't. Was it possible that she didn't inherit any extra abilities? Maybe her night vision and her extra strength were all she would ever have.

She stood up, dropped her trash in a can by the door, and walked outside. Jesse followed her.

"Tori," he called.

She stopped and waited for him to walk over.

He took a deep breath before he spoke. "Look, I'm sorry I got so upset this morning. I know we're asking a lot, and you're not used to any of this. So you don't have to clean the stables or do the run. Just don't leave without permission again, okay?"

She wasn't used to any of this? He could have meant the idea of fighting dragons, and yet somehow she was sure he meant work, rules, and discipline.

"Do you still think I'm going to take off the next time things get hard?" she asked.

His gaze ran over her, then lingered on her hair. "I'm hoping you won't."

"I'll do the stables and the run," she said. "I don't want special treatment."

One of Jesse's eyebrows rose in surprise, but he didn't try to talk her out of it. "Okay, after you're done with that, work on your shooting until dinner. The rest of us are going to fight fire in the Dragon Hall."

"I thought you had welder's masks so I could practice with you."

"Until we know your talent, you'll just get in the way. It's better for you to spend the time working on your aim."

"Oh. Okay."

"See you later." He turned and strode back into the Dragon Hall.

She watched him disappear behind the door and felt completely alone. It was stupid. She hadn't wanted to practice with fire in the first place, but it still made her feel worthless to hear she would only get in the way. Especially from Jesse. He was the guy who had made her feel romantic and swoony when he'd flown her around. The guy she'd come back to camp for. The guy who had decided that rich people were cowards. And the guy who Rosa had been draped over every time Tori turned around.

That will teach you, she told herself sternly, *not to fall for guys just because they're gorgeous and have superpowers. It never ends well.*

As she walked to the stalls, she tried to channel her frustration into laser vision so she could incinerate things with her eyes. That didn't work, either.

Despite Tori's extra strength, it didn't take long until she grew tired—tired of horse stalls, tired of running, tired of shooting. Tired of camp. And this was only her second day here.

At six o'clock, she left the rifle range and walked toward the Dragon Hall for dinner. Most likely, no one would talk to her during this meal, either. Yep, it was going to be such a long month.

She'd only gone a few steps down the trail when she hit something hard. One moment everything was fine, the next it felt like she'd run into a sliding glass door. "Ow!"she yelped, and staggered backward. Nothing stood in front of her, and yet her hand, foot, and face stung from the impact. She shook out the pain from her hand and looked around, trying to figure out what had happened.

A tall girl with chin-length curly brown hair appeared from around one of the trees. She was tan, athletic, and also laughing. "Having a problem?"

Tori put one hand out in front of her and felt a wall of resistance against her fingertips. It was like pushing the wrong ends of magnets together. There was no way through. She let out a sigh. "I really don't need this right now, okay?"

The girl sauntered over. "Hi, I'm Bess."

"The one who can throw shields up."

"Yeah, I used to be able to do it and then blame it on Leo. Man, I'm going to miss him." She said the words lightly, but a flash of sorrow shot through her eyes. She wasn't joking.

Tori put her hand up to see if the shield still blocked her way. It did. "Are you going to move this thing so I can get through?"

"My dad asked me to show you my talent."

Her dad. Tori had forgotten that Dr. B and Shirley were Bess's parents. Bess had her mother's curly dark hair and her father's height and eyes—but in Dr. B the gray-blue eyes seemed gentle, calm. In Bess, they shined mischievously. Beyond that, Tori didn't see any resemblance between Bess and either of her parents. She was elflike somehow, as though she'd popped into the forest to play a few tricks and then would disappear into another realm.

Bess stepped closer and flicked the forcefield with a finger. It shivered for a second, distorting the forest like a funhouse mirror, then turned invisible again. "So do you have any desire to throw a shield up in retaliation? I could run if you want. Leo knocked me out cold the first time he put a shield in front of me."

"Knocked out as in *unconscious?* Doesn't your dad worry about that sort of thing?"

"Nah, we're a resilient bunch."

Tori smiled. "All right, then. Go ahead and run. I'll see what I can do."

Bess jogged down the path a little ways. Tori focused on her retreating figure, trying to feel something, trying to conjure up some sort of wall in front of her. Nothing happened.

Bess stopped, turned around, and jogged back. "Well?"

"I can't do it."

"Ah. Sadly, not everybody can be as cool as me."

Tori checked to see if the forcefield was still there. It was. She put her hand on her hip and let out a frustrated groan. Perhaps it came out too loud and lasted too long.

Bess pursed her lips and considered Tori. "So I take it you're having a tough time here at camp."

"Pretty much everyone hates me. So yeah, I guess you could say that."

Bess blinked, surprised. "Wow, the Slayers all agree on something? How did you manage that?"

"Your dad singed half my hair off last night, and I left camp without permission this morning to get extensions put in."

Bess waved a hand, and the resistance from the forcefield faded away.

"I guess I'll have to break ranks with the rest of the Slayers on this one," Bess said. "I'm just not feeling the hatred. So much for solidarity."

Tori walked toward the Dragon Hall, and Bess fell into step beside her. "Besides, I don't believe for an instant that Rosa hates you. She likes everybody."

"Rosa only got here at lunch, but I'm sure everyone has filled her in on my failings."

A hornet buzzed along the trail coming toward them. Bess lifted her hand. The bug smacked into a forcefield and fell to the ground, stunned. Another wave of Bess's hand erased the forcefield, and the girls continued down the path. "Trust me—Rosa is too busy feeling sorry for herself right now to pay attention to anyone else. She was totally in love with Leo."

"Oh." Tori shouldn't have been happy about this fact, but she suddenly saw Jesse's attentions to Rosa in a new light. A better light. Jesse was compassionate. He was a supportive friend. How sweet.

They'd almost reached the building. Bess slowed down and lowered her voice. "And the next time you want to sneak out of camp, ask me for help. Danielle and I used to do it all the time, and we never got caught." She gave a small laugh. "Well, Jesse caught us once, but we bought his silence with an Oreo shake. Hollings has an ice cream shop that's to die for."

As quickly as the smile had come to Bess's face, it fell away again. "I'm going to miss Danielle, too."

Bess pulled open the door to the building and they walked inside. Shirley stood at the head of the picnic table with a basketful of garlic bread and a sheet of lasagne in front of her. She scooped out pieces and slid each onto dinner plates. "Now don't make me come back to get these dishes," she told them, "or you'll be eating nothing but gruel for the rest of the week. After you finish, send someone up to the kitchen to drop them off."

Lilly called out, "Low score gets the job," and looked pointedly at Tori.

Great. Not only would she be beaten at every competition, she'd have to haul dishes around every day, too. She wondered what other jobs low score had to do.

Bess slid into the table. "I guess that means Rosa and I will do it. We haven't scored at all." Bess looked at Tori and gestured toward the bench beside her. "Come sit by me."

Tori did, and for the first time thought she might make it through the month.

CHAPTER 19

After dinner, Dirk walked over to the stables to bring his horse, Montpellier, an apple. Dr. B walked up beside him, his brows drawn together in earnest intent. He had obviously sought Dirk out to talk to him about something. "Can I join you for a bit?" he asked.

"Sure."

Dr. B inclined his head so he could better study Dirk. They had talked privately a hundred times over the years: easy, casual conversations. This time Dr. B's gaze made him stiffen. It always took Dirk a few days to get into the rhythm of camp, and each year it was harder to step into his Slayer persona. Did Dr. B realize that about him?

"Dirk, are you all right?" Dr. B's voice came out in its usual tranquil cadence. It was like the tick of the clock or the waves brushing against the shore. So quietly dependable.

Dirk only hesitated for a moment. "Yeah, I'm fine."

"You've been tense since Tori arrived."

Dirk relaxed a bit. That's all this was about. Dr. B was about to give the everyone-needs-to-get-along speech. He saw the Slayers as brothers and sisters with himself as their father—a father incapable of thinking badly about any of them. At that moment, Dirk wished Dr. B was his father and that they could all stay at camp forever. Dirk wanted to settle down under a canopy of bright green leaves and never leave. "A new person at camp changes everything," Dirk said, "makes things more complicated." Which was not even stretching the truth in the case of Tori's arrival.

Dr. B slowed his pace. The wind rippled across the ferns by the side of the path, making the leaves shiver. "You're worried about the alterations Tori's arrival might mean to the teams' structure, aren't you?"

Dirk shrugged. It was as good an excuse as any for his tension.

Dr. B's expression softened. "The world wants us to believe that we're not important unless we're in charge of things. It isn't true, though. Whatever part we play, whatever position we have on the team, it's valuable. Even old men with no powers, like myself, are important. You understand that?"

Dirk didn't answer.

"Tori will not only need Jesse's help, she'll need your help, too, in order to find her way. You'll help her no matter what her extra ability turns out to be?"

Dirk nodded. "Sure."

"You won't let your team play practical jokes on her? No stringing her clothes on the tops of the trees or freezing her belongings?"

Dirk's lips twitched, but he suppressed his smile. "Not unless she gets on my nerves."

"Dirk . . ."

Dirk held up one hand. "Okay, we'll be good."

Dr. B smiled, his mood lightening. "Wonderful. That will help me sleep easier." He put his hand on Dirk's shoulder, giving it a brief squeeze. "You know, you can always come to me if something is bothering you. I consider you boys the sons I never had."

"And we consider you the medieval studies professor we never had."

Dr. B laughed, and the sound of it flowed around the trees as though it belonged to the forest. "I try not to play favorites—Bess would argue that I try too hard. She thinks I ought to throw some favoritism in her direction once in a while. But I will tell you this. You remind me of my brother—your humor and self-confidence. I want you to know that I admire you for doing what's right."

The compliment pinched Dirk like shoes that were too small. It didn't fit and he couldn't wear it. "It's Jesse who believes in always doing the right thing."

"I know," Dr. B said. "You don't entirely believe it, but here you are doing it anyway."

Dirk half grunted to show he didn't consider himself so admirable, but for the few minutes it took to get to the stables, he believed the compliment and glowed inside. Dr. B admired him. Dirk would do the right thing.

Later when they parted ways, Dirk only wished he hadn't been so flippant by answering, "We consider you the medieval studies professor we never had." He could have said, "And I consider you the father I never had." It would have been partially true. Because his father was nothing like Dr. B.

# CHAPTER 20

It turned out Jesse was right; the welder's helmet was a hassle. Tori had done her hair in a tight French braid before they left for the Easter grounds, tucking the end of her braid under the back of the helmet, but every time she landed from a leap, the helmet jostled on her face and she had to right it again. Plus, it cut into her peripheral vision, which meant she kept getting tackled from the side.

Finally, she said to Dr. B, "How about we make a deal. You promise not to throw any fireballs at me tonight, and I'll take off the helmet so I can play the game right."

Dr. B smiled, the curve of his cheeks pushing up into his infrared goggles. "Certainly."

But Jesse, who stood nearby, took her hand as she reached for her helmet. "Don't do it. One of the first lessons he likes to teach Slayers is that you can't trust anyone. If you take off the helmet, you're asking for a fireball to the face."

Tori turned back to Dr. B, who was still smiling. "Jesse has a point," he said. "You should never put your safety in someone else's hands. They may not take care of it as well as you'd like."

Tori's mouth dropped open. "You're our leader. You're not supposed to lie to us."

"You're a Slayer. You're supposed to take care of yourself. Which of us will suffer more for our negligence?"

She didn't answer. You should be able to trust some people. You should at least be able to trust the people who were training you. She tugged the helmet back down onto her face and went back to the game.

Tori always chose hiding places close to the boulders. Her only hope of making it around the ring of the boulders was to do it while the A-team's seeker chased someone else. Tori's leaps had improved from the day before, but she couldn't leap from branch to branch like the others.

When Lilly was the A-team's seeker, she barreled after Tori right off. Tori tried to jump over her, but Lilly effortlessly leapt up and tackled her in midair. Tori slammed down into one of the boulders, its sharp edges stabbing into her back. She rolled limply to the ground and lay there, hoping the air would eventually return to her lungs. How long could she retain consciousness without oxygen?

The other campers didn't even stop the game to see if she was okay. Somewhere in the forest Jesse called out, "Get up and walk it off. You'll be fine!"

It was touching how he looked out for her like that.

Luckily, not much later, Dr. B ended the games for the night. He tallied up the score—Team Magnus was still down fifty points. Then he ended the evening by giving the Slayers a pep talk about concentrating on the task at hand, even if they were grieving for their missing teammates. "In battle, you might see one of your friends killed in front of you. You'll have to go on, no matter how hard it is, just as you have to go on now."

When his lecture ended and everyone moved toward the trail, Tori took off the welder's helmet. Even though she knew her hair hadn't gone anywhere in the last few hours, she ran her hand over the braid, glad for its length.

Dr. B came up behind Tori. "I saw a marked improvement in your abilities tonight. You'll give the rest of the Slayers a run for their money soon enough."

It wasn't heavy praise, but it did make her feel better. "Thanks," she said, and joined Bess and Rosa heading down the trail. Before they'd gone far, Jesse's voice came from above them. "Rosa, do you need a lift?"

Rosa smiled up at him. "Sure." She held her arms out and Jesse flew down, picked her up around the waist, and the two of them soared upward. Tori watched them disappear into the treetops.

So, Jesse was compassionate, but only toward Rosa. If Rosa had smashed into the boulders he probably wouldn't have told *her* to walk it off.

Tori thought about this as she kept pace alongside Bess. She knew she had no reason to resent Jesse for picking Rosa. He'd told her yesterday that he flew all the girls around. They would undoubtedly all have a turn in his arms before he thought of Tori again.

Yet it did bother her. Last night when Jesse had taken her in his arms and they'd flown lazily through the trees, the stars glowing wild and fierce above them, it had seemed so personal. But apparently it hadn't been. She'd just been another passenger to him—well, probably not even that. She'd been a problem to solve. And he had. He'd convinced her to stay.

Jesse hadn't even looked at her tonight when he'd scooped Rosa up. He certainly wasn't thinking about her now, with Rosa in his arms.

Tori felt used, though she couldn't say why. It was flying, not kissing.

Bess was talking about how it always took her a day to get the feel of everything again, but after that, using your powers was like riding a bike—you didn't forget. Tori nodded, but was only half listening. Mostly she was reprimanding herself for feeling things she shouldn't.

And then a familiar whooshing sound came up behind Tori. Familiar and frightening. The sound of a fireball heading toward her.

It took her a split second to make the decision. Last time she'd tried to jump away from the danger. It hadn't worked, so this time she dived for the ground. As she fell, a searing ball slammed into the back of her shoulder. The fire took hold of the material on her jacket; animallike, clinging to her, ready to sink its teeth into her flesh. Almost before she could process what happened, she rolled onto her back, smothering the flames so they couldn't spread. She waited for the pain. She could feel the heat of the scalding material against her skin. But the throbbing sting didn't come. She vaguely remembered hearing that if burned badly enough, a person didn't feel the pain because their nerve endings were destroyed. It must be bad then.

She sat up and ripped her jacket off. It now had a hole in the back, and when she twisted her head to see her shoulder, she saw a matching hole in her shirt. Melted pieces of fabric stuck to her skin, along with dirt and dried leaves. But there wasn't a wound. Only a red, irritated patch.

"Alyssa!" Dr. B called running up to Tori with the flame gun still in his hand, "Hurry!"

Tori gingerly ran her hand across her shoulder. It should have been oozing and bloody. She should be writhing in pain. Thank goodness her skin had extra strength now. Still, she glared at Dr. B as he knelt beside her. "Why did you do that?" she demanded. "The games were over."

"The games are never over. Not here, and not when you're at home." Dr. B bent down to examine her shoulder. "Now you've learned two things tonight. Don't trust others with your safety, and always be prepared for an attack." He examined her shoulder, gently moving the hole in the shirt to find the wound.

Alyssa trotted over and dropped to her knees beside Tori. "How bad is it?"

"Amazing," Dr. B said, and moved away for Alyssa to see.

Alyssa ran her fingers across Tori's skin. "How did you manage not to get burned? Your shirt's destroyed."

"Slayers have extra strong skin," Tori said, but her gaze bounced between Alyssa and Dr. B, trying to figure out their surprise.

Alyssa examined the ruined edges of Tori's shirt. "Not this strong. You should at least have a huge blister."

She'd been lucky somehow, then—probably because she'd dropped to the ground and rolled right away. The thought didn't bring her a lot of comfort. Tomorrow she might not be so lucky. Tori stood up and wiped the dirt from her hands. The cold night air brushed up against her bare shoulder, making her shiver.

Alyssa and Dr. B stood up, as well. "Is your shirt flame retardant?" he asked.

"It's Versace. I don't think those come in flame retardant."

By this time Lilly, Shang, and Kody had joined them. "Perhaps your skin is more resistant to fire than the other Slayers," Dr. B said. "The only way to tell for sure—"

"No," Tori said. "You're not burning me again to experiment."

"—is to wait until the next time you're caught unaware by the flamethrower." Dr. B pulled out the clipboard where he kept the team tallies. "Which reminds me, minus ten points to Team Magnus, because I caught Tori in a surprise attack."

It wasn't fair, and Tori hated the smug look that Lilly sent to Alyssa.

Her eyes narrowed at Dr. B. He had told her that she'd learned two things tonight. Actually, she'd learned three. She'd learned that her camp director was a sneaky, sadistic—well, she was too well-mannered to say it all out loud. She couldn't even complain to Bess about it. Dr. B was her father. Without another word, Tori picked up her jacket, tied it around her waist, and jogged down the trail.

When she reached cabin 27, Rosa and Jesse were sitting on the porch steps, talking in low voices. Rosa's eyes were red and swollen, a sign she'd been crying again. Tori felt guilty then for ever being angry that Jesse had flown with Rosa. She obviously needed the comfort. Tori walked past them, loosening her jacket and contemplating how many more pieces of clothing would be torched before the month was over. When she reached the door, Jesse asked, "What happened to your shirt?"

She waved her scrunched jacket in the direction of the trail. "After the games ended, Dr. B launched a fireball at my back."

Jesse let out an aggravated breath. "How many points did it cost the team?" he asked.

Tori let her jacket drop and grabbed hold of the doorknob. Jesse hadn't been worried about her—only the team's tally. "I don't care about the stupid points."

"You'll care when we have to clean the bathrooms and the stables."

She wondered, but didn't ask, how many points it would cost her if she hurled objects at her team captain. Instead, she walked inside and slammed the door behind her. She snatched up her pajamas, towel, and caddy.

As she did, she heard Rosa softly say, "You're being too hard on her. You don't have to be a team captain all of the time. Sometimes you can just be a friend."

Jesse lowered his voice. He probably thought Tori couldn't hear him. "We can't baby her. If anything, we need to be harder on her than Dr. B is. She has one summer to learn things that took us years to learn."

"Jesse . . ." Rosa laced the word with meaning.

"This isn't a game she can quit when she doesn't like the rules," Jesse said. "If she's not prepared she'll get hurt, maybe killed." His voice dropped even lower. "I don't want that."

That made two of them. Tori pushed open the door and pounded down the stairs without speaking to Jesse or Rosa.

CHAPTER 21

After Jesse finished talking to Rosa, he went to find Dirk. "You want to raid the kitchen?" he asked. That was their code for talking privately. Back during Dirk's first year at camp, they actually had raided the kitchen one night while everyone else slept. Dirk knew how to pick locks—had practiced it the same way he'd practiced martial arts. They'd broken into the kitchen, taken a couple ice cream sandwiches from the freezer's stash, and sat on the floor talking for half an hour.

It had become a tradition after that. Once every summer, they broke in, and despite the ice cream sandwiches that went missing, they'd never been caught.

Dirk said, "Sure," but instead of walking toward the main camp, they went into the forest behind their cabins. These days, they broke into the kitchen only near the end of the month. After a few minutes, the two found a sturdy tree and went up it. Jesse flew and Dirk half climbed, half jumped up the branches.

Jesse always felt more relaxed, more in control, when he was up high. He could see the world spread out beneath him, like a chess player looking down at the board.

After they were both situated on branches, Dirk asked, "What's up, besides us?" Then he leaned back against the trunk while raising his eyebrows. "Let me guess. You want to talk about Tori."

Jesse did want to talk about Tori, but that's not why he asked for this meeting. Besides, he wouldn't have known what to say about her. In the short time she'd been here, she'd mostly managed to frustrate him. Although if he was being honest, she also made him feel guilty because he knew he was being hard on her; and he felt worried because he was afraid her training would be too little too late. And he had other feelings, ones he shouldn't have because he was a fellow Slayer. And her captain.

"It's not about Tori," Jesse said. "I found out something you should know." He gazed down at the ferns that grew like miniature fountains over the forest floor.

"What?" Dirk asked.

It was hard for Jesse to betray Dr. B's confidence. Two years earlier, he wouldn't have done it, but now, well, Dr. B always told them to think for themselves. All last summer Dr. B had emphasized that the Slayers—especially the team captains—had to make decisions on their own. Dr. B couldn't be in the thick of things, fighting the dragons with them. They had to take charge.

So Jesse had been mulling over the matter all day. "Dr. B can trace our phones from his laptop. If Overdrake got hold of it and broke through the passwords, he could find any of us. Dr. B doesn't want the other Slayers to know. He's afraid if they do a Leo and Danielle, they could inadvertently leak the information. But I thought you should know. At some point, the phones could be a liability."

Dirk nodded, his expression growing serious. He didn't speak for a few moments, but Jesse hadn't expected him to. Neither of them were the type to work through things by talking a lot.

"It probably won't ever come to that," Jesse said.

"But you never know," Dirk answered.

That was one of the main problems of second-guessing Overdrake—they didn't know nearly enough. After a few more minutes, Jesse and Dirk slipped down from the trees and walked silently back to cabin 26.

CHAPTER 22

Tori took a short shower, so short that the other girls were just making their way to the bathroom when she finished. Her sight hadn't faded yet, and she made her way back to the cabin without a flashlight, which was a good thing, since she'd forgotten to bring one again.

Jesse no longer sat on her steps. She glanced over at cabin 26, then told herself to stop it. There was no point in having any sort of feelings for him. He didn't see her that way. He hardly even saw her as a girl. She was just a team member he had to bring up to speed.

Tori lifted her chin and straightened her shoulders. She would show Jesse how quickly she could catch up to the rest of them. If it meant hard work, fine. And fireballs? Well, at least she could hear them coming.

She walked inside her cabin, picking up her iron from the floor where it was propping the door open again. She set it back on her dresser, braided her hair so the extensions wouldn't tangle while she slept, then read one of her books until the other girls came in. Lilly and

Alyssa's blow-dried hair flowed down their backs in straight blonde curtains. Rosa had a towel wrapped around her head and chided Bess for leaving her wet hair uncovered. "You'll catch a cold," she said sternly.

Bess flipped her hand through her short curls. "I never get sick. I laugh in the face of germs."

"I've had colds before." Rosa turned to Lilly and Alyssa for support.

"I'm as healthy as a horse," Lilly said.

Bess nodded with an air of seriousness, which made her look like her professor father. "And that's just one character trait she shares with our equine friends."

Lilly narrowed her eyes. "Like you would know, Elspeth."

"Elspeth?" Tori asked.

Bess flopped down on her bed with an exaggerated sigh. "Yeah, medieval scholars really shouldn't be allowed to name children." She put her feet up so they rested against the footboard. "Technically, my first name is Elspeth, but no one calls me that as I tend to rip the limbs from the people who do. I'm only making an exception in Lilly's case until we kill the dragons. Then she's going to be completely limbless."

"Oh, grow up," Lilly said.

Bess stretched and shut her eyes. "I laugh in the face of growing up."

Tori smiled. She'd been expecting the camp director's daughter to either be a prima donna or some sort of informer and was glad Bess hadn't turned out to be either. It made Lilly and Alyssa seem bearable.

The next moment, a wave of exhaustion washed over Tori, and she put her book on the floor under her bed.

Rosa climbed on top of her bunk. "You can always tell when the simulator has been off for half an hour. It feels like you're hit with a bag full of tired."

Alyssa grumbled an agreement, turned off the light, and the room went black.

After seeing so clearly, the dark seemed unnatural, and Tori blinked as though she could refocus if she tried hard enough. When she couldn't, she shut her eyes and forced herself to relax. She heard the sound of the other girls rustling into comfortable positions. Then the crickets outside. The smooth hush of branches moving in the wind. An owl calling in the distance. And the heartbeat. Just like last night.

Tori propped herself up on one elbow, listening more intently. She wasn't dreaming; it was a real sound.

"If the simulator is off, where is that noise coming from?" Tori asked.

Lilly grunted in annoyance. "What noise?

"The noise that's going *tha-thump, tha-thump, tha-thump.*"

"I don't hear anything," Bess said.

Tori gripped her blanket in annoyance. "Well, I'm not making it up. It's there, and it sounds like the simulator."

"How come no one else hears anything?" Alyssa asked.

"I've always had exceptional hearing. I can hear things other people can't."

Lilly snorted. "You mean like voices in your head?" She and Alyssa both snickered.

Rosa said, "Alyssa, turn on the light."

Alyssa gave a moan of protest, but Tori heard her slide out of bed and feel along the wall until she found the switch. Light washed through the room and Tori squinted, adjusting her eyes. As she did, the sound stopped.

The other girls sat up in bed and stared at Tori, waiting for her to say more. She cleared her throat uncomfortably. "It's gone now."

Lilly lay back on her bed with a *thump*. "Along with five minutes we could have been sleeping."

But Tori wasn't about to let it go. She thrust her covers off and got out of bed. "Is this some sort of prank?" She strode to the window and pushed the curtains aside. "The guys are out there making that noise, aren't they? That's why they stopped when the lights came on."

Rosa gave the other girls pointed looks. "Is it a prank?"

"Not one of mine," Alyssa said.

Bess held up her hands, palms forward. "Don't look at me. I had nothing to do with it."

Lilly put her arm over her eyes to block out the light. "There's nothing there. Now, will you guys please be quiet so we can go to sleep?"

Alyssa turned off the light, and the other girls settled back into their beds. Tori stayed by the window. She took her flashlight from the dresser, but didn't turn it on. If she waited long enough, she'd be able to catch whoever was hiding outside the window.

She waited. The sounds of the night surfaced again. The crickets. The wind.

The heartbeat.

The noise had to be right outside. She flipped on the flashlight and pointed it out of the window. She expected to see someone crouching by the cabin, or at the very least, running away. She only saw a scraggly bush and a couple of small boulders.

Alyssa let out a groan. "What are you doing?"

Tori didn't answer. Alyssa's words had drowned out the sound of the heartbeat, and she needed to focus to find it.

There it was again.

She made her way to the door, then stepped outside. The sound of her own footsteps nearly covered the noise, but she walked across the patio and down the steps, still able to keep hold of it.

She swung the flashlight around, searching.

Nothing.

Fine. She'd find whoever was drumming the heartbeat by sound alone. She walked into the space that separated the cabins and shut her eyes. The heartbeat grew louder.

Tori drew in a sharp breath and opened her eyes. It had been a mistake to come outside. Here, alone in the darkness, the sound took on a more sinister tone. The shadows drew closer. Things in the forest rustled.

"Stop it!" she yelled. "It's not funny!"

She tried again to tell where the sound came from, but couldn't. She jerked her head in one direction, then another. The heartbeat seemed to be everywhere—coming from the boys' cabin, coming from her own. It was above her, beside her, growing louder. Now she wanted it to stop, but it wouldn't.

A loud, creaking noise sounded at her side. She swept the flashlight in that direction.

Cabin 26's door had opened. Dirk peered outside, with Jesse standing behind him. Dirk put his hand up to block the flashlight beam, then turned his face away. "You want to point that thing somewhere else?"

Jesse stepped around Dirk onto the patio. "What are you doing out here?"

"Is this some sort of practical joke?" she asked. "Because I've had a long day, and I want to get some sleep now. So just turn that thing off!"

Kody and Shang joined Dirk and Jesse on the patio, staring at her cautiously. All of them wore pajama bottoms and sweatshirts. "What are you talking about?" Dirk said.

"What's going on?" Kody asked.

Behind her, the door to cabin 27 opened. Lilly called, "The new girl is having a nervous breakdown. She must have got slammed into the ground one too many times."

They were all coming down the stairs now, filing out to look at her. Tori felt breathless under the weight of their gazes.

She pointed the flashlight down so it wouldn't blind anyone, even though she wanted to keep hunting for the source of the heartbeat. It couldn't really be the heartbeat of a dragon. She would notice a dragon hanging about, and besides, if one came near, everyone would have their powers again. She wouldn't need a flashlight to see in the dark.

But what was it?

Dirk ran a hand across his forehead. "Did Dr. B put you up to this? Are we supposed to assume Overdrake is attacking? Because if that's what this is, you need to be more specific about what's going on."

The heartbeat was so loud now that it reverberated in her ears. She looked from face to face. Their expressions were half-hidden in shadow, questioning. "I can't be the only one hearing it." Her grip tightened around the flashlight. "It sounds like the simulator. Why are the rest of you pretending it doesn't exist?"

Jesse took a step closer, a sudden understanding in his eyes. "You hear something that sounds like the simulator?"

"Yes."

Jesse held his hand out for her flashlight. She wasn't sure why he wanted it, but gave it to him anyway. He handed it to Bess. "Run and get your dad. I think we found Tori's talent."

Tori looked at him questioningly. "And that would be what?"

Jesse smiled, but it had an air of sadness to it. "You're Dirk's counterpart. You can hear what the dragons hear. And right now, all they hear is the sound of their own heartbeats."

CHAPTER 23

When Bess came back with Dr. B, everyone else was sitting in cabin 27, peppering Tori with questions. "You can *hear* what the dragons hear?" Dirk repeated as though he still didn't believe it. For the first time since she'd met him, he didn't look on the verge of smirking. His blue eyes widened as he studied her, but he didn't look pleased, just surprised. Tori could only think of one reason why: he didn't want to be her counterpart.

Earlier that night as they jogged up to the Easter grounds, Bess had told Tori how the counterpart thing worked. "Counterparts have a connection," she had said. "It's like you can understand how your counterpart thinks. It helps when we're fighting, because a lot of times you can anticipate what they're going to do. And if they've been away from the simulator for more than half an hour and their power is drained but yours isn't, you can touch them and some of your power will flow into them. It's like jump-starting a battery."

Tori had immediately thought about the time she'd flown with Jesse. "You feel a closeness to them?" she asked. "An intimacy?"

"Like you'd feel toward a brother or sister," Bess said, and her voice had gone soft, sad. "Leo isn't here anymore, and it feels like I lost a brother."

Tori didn't think of Jesse as a brother, which perhaps should have been her first clue that he wasn't her counterpart.

But she didn't feel sisterly toward Dirk, either.

Dirk's eyes fixed on Tori's. They seemed to look through her, into her, making her vulnerable in a way she hadn't expected.

"You can't *see* anything?" he asked. "There's no split screen in your mind?"

"No, but my hearing is split. When I'm listening to you, the sound gets fainter. It's like background noise. But when I tried to sleep, or when I went outside and shut my eyes—when I wasn't concentrating on something else—the heartbeat grew louder."

Alyssa leaned forward on her bed. "Do you hear one heartbeat or two?"

"One," Tori said, glad she could break Dirk's gaze and look at someone else.

Rosa turned to Dr. B, who had just stepped inside. "Does that mean there's only one dragon egg?"

Dr. B clicked off his flashlight and slipped it into the pocket of his worn bathrobe. "It could mean several things. Perhaps she can hear only one dragon at a time, or perhaps her mind connects with one dragon, and Dirk's mind connects with the other. Or perhaps the dragons' heartbeats are in sync with each other. Legend has it they hatch at exactly the same time. It prevents one from being bigger and stronger, and thus more likely to eat the other." He smiled at Tori. "This is quite interesting, really. You have Dirk's gift, but you don't. It's an odd double, isn't it?"

She'd been so excited to have found her talent, it wasn't until Dr. B said this that she realized how useless her gift was. Dirk would be able to locate where the dragons were headed before they attacked by seeing the landscape through their eyes, but what good was hearing what the dragons heard?

She leaned against the wall by her bed. "It's a pointless talent. I already know what the dragons will hear when they attack. A lot of screaming people. How will that help us fight them?"

The other Slayers looked at her, but no one said anything. Apparently, they had come to the same conclusion.

"Maybe one of the dragons is blind," Rosa said, "so you can't see what it sees, and your hearing developed instead of your sight."

Lilly let out a cough of disbelief. "Yeah, that's it. One of the dragons will be feeling his way across the streets of D.C. with a cane clutched in its wing, terrorizing anyone who can't shuffle out of its way in time."

Rosa's brown eyes flashed at Lilly. "Bats hunt by sound, and they manage well enough."

Dr. B held up his hand to stop the fighting. "We shouldn't disparage any gift. Every talent is valuable."

Lilly said, "Except that one," but she said it softly enough that Dr. B didn't hear her.

Tori did and couldn't even disagree. Compared to the others, her fighting skills were woefully undeveloped, and her genes had given her a nearly useless skill. Would she even be able to tell when the dragons hatched like Dirk would?

Though she continued to look at Dr. B, she felt Dirk's gaze on her again, heavy with thought.

"How do I disconnect myself from the dragon's heartbeat?" she asked, already feeling suffocated by its constant presence. "I don't want to hear it all the time."

Dr. B held a hand out to Dirk, giving him the floor.

He hesitated, choosing his words carefully. "When I don't want the dragon sight, I concentrate on it, like I'm peering through an open doorway at it. Then I minimize the door. It doesn't go away, but it shrinks to the point that I can ignore it."

"You minimize the door?" Tori repeated. How could she do that?

Dr. B smiled at Tori encouragingly. "I'm sure once you experiment with it, you'll get the hang of it."

She shut her eyes, concentrating on the heartbeat. Immediately, the sound grew louder. She tried to see a door around it, but couldn't. How did you see a door around a sound? After a moment, she opened her eyes and concentrated on the people and sounds of the room. The heartbeat faded into background noise again.

"Any better?" Dirk asked.

"A little." She was unwilling to tell him she couldn't even control her own talent. She fiddled with the blanket on her bed, tracing the stitching with her finger. "My hearing has always been unusually good. Is that why? Because it's part of my dragon skill?"

Dr. B inclined his head upward as he considered the idea. "An interesting theory. Do dragon talents carry over into normal life? Or perhaps Tori's talent became hearing because she was gifted at it to begin with? Perhaps gifts follow the neuropathways that are already there." His gaze traveled around the room. "Do the rest of you see any overlap of your skills in your normal life?"

"I douse fire," Lilly said. "How would that carry over in my normal life?"

Bess blinked innocently. "Well, in your normal life, you're not that hot."

Lilly picked up her pillow and threw it at Bess. Bess caught it one-handed, put the pillow behind her back, then settled into it. "Comfy."

Jesse was leaning against the wall by the door. "As a kid, I used to jump out of swings when they were at their highest point because it felt like flying. I also used to leap from our balcony onto our trampoline."

Rosa stared at him and shook her head. "I'm surprised you're still alive."

"And in Rosa's real life," Bess said, making her voice sound like an announcer, "she tries to keep everyone from getting hurt or having fun. It's sort of like healing people, but more irritating."

"I'm a healer, too," Alyssa said. "And I don't try to keep people from getting hurt."

Bess shrugged. "That's because long ago you gave over your will and identity in order to become Lilly's evil twin."

Alyssa picked up her pillow and threw it at Bess—which wasn't the best way to demonstrate her independence from Lilly. Bess caught the pillow, added it to Lilly's, and leaned back again. "Supercomfy."

Dr. B shot Bess a stern look. "Enough, or I'll have to deduct team points. Remember, no house divided against itself can stand." His bathrobe belt had loosened and he pulled it tight with a flourish.

Bess watched him and rolled her eyes. "Honestly, Dad, can't you get a better bathrobe? That one's embarrassing."

Dr. B smoothed down the sides of his robe. "I've had this one since college."

"Yeah. That's one of the reasons it's embarrassing."

Ignoring his daughter, he pulled his flashlight from his pocket. "Well, it's good to know what Tori's gift is. Now I can plan how best to employ her abilities."

Lilly leaned over to Alyssa and whispered, "She can hold our stuff while we kill the dragon."

Tori shouldn't have been able to hear it, but did.

Dr. B moved toward the door. "It's late, and you need your rest. Big day tomorrow."

This brought forth moans from several campers. Dr. B held up one hand to fend off their complaints. "If you are prepared, you shall not fear. And as you ponder those wise words from the Bible, I will wish you a good night." He waved a good-bye to them, flipped on his flashlight, and walked out the door.

Alyssa watched him go. "Do you think that quote is really from the Bible, or does he just make up stuff because he knows we don't know the difference?"

Lilly leaned back nonchalantly. "I'm not reading the Bible to find out."

"Trust me," Bess said, "if it's an ancient text, he's studied it, highlighted passages, and discussed parts of it with guys who came to pick me up for dates."

Which, Tori supposed, was another disadvantage of having a father who was a medieval scholar. It sort of made senator look like a normal profession.

The guys got up and sauntered out the door, talking to one another about what sort of thing Dr. B might have planned for them tomorrow. Before they left, Kody called back to them, "Good night, y'all," and the door thunked shut behind them.

Tori didn't move from her sitting position. She had thought of another question. "How come no one else's gift works when the simulator is turned off, but I can still hear the dragon's heartbeat?"

Bess climbed into her bed. "It's the same for Dirk. The simulator tricks your body into thinking a dragon is around so your night vision and strength turn on. You can't connect with the mind of the simulator, though, because it doesn't have one. You, girlfriend, get to listen to the actual dragons."

"But aren't they somewhere far away?" Tori asked. "I thought the dragons had to be within five miles before they triggered our abilities."

"Not for the mind connection you and Dirk have." Bess pulled back her covers and lay down. "You have a wider range. We don't know how wide, because we don't know where the eggs are. It could be a hundred miles. It could be ten."

A hundred miles. Tori felt insulated by that number until she remembered that dragons could fly fast. How long would it take them to travel a hundred miles? An hour? Two? Not long enough.

"If I can be far away from the dragon and still connect to it, how come I never heard the heartbeat before I came to camp?"

Bess slipped her arm underneath her pillow, adjusting it. "You finally got a strong dose of the simulator wavelength and it kick-started your inner eye. Your body knows what it's supposed to be doing now." She sent Tori an apologetic look. "Things will never be the same. It happened to all of us. You'll notice things you automatically blocked out before. Like, you'll be in school trying to focus on a test while in the background your mind is simultaneously scanning the room for movement and calculating the speed of every car that drives past the window."

Rosa rolled on her side and pulled up her covers. "The guys love the added awareness because it makes them better at sports—and okay, it's sort of nice that no one can sneak up on you—but most of the time it's just annoying." She shut her eyes and yawned. "Don't worry, though. You get used to it."

Alyssa turned out the light, and darkness swallowed the room again.

Tori lay wide awake on her bed. Sleep was impossible with the sound of a dragon heartbeat ticking away in her ears. She might as well have tried to doze off with a serial killer breathing down her neck. She kept thinking relaxing thoughts like *It wants to eat me*, and *They're the size of lions when they hatch*.

How was she ever supposed to get used to any of this?

 **CHAPTER 24**

After an hour or so of trying—and failing—to banish both the sound of the heartbeat and the happy thoughts that accompanied it, Tori drifted into a fitful sleep. Her dreams were filled with dragons whose roars sounded like drumbeats. They stretched their scaly wings over her bed, creating a canopy she couldn't escape from. And the next moment she saw Dirk, sitting across the room watching her, his blue eyes serious, deep, brooding. He seemed sad about something, and she wanted to take his hand to comfort him. In her dream, she kept walking toward him, but never reached him. Little creaks from the forest would shoot her back into breathless wakefulness. She had to keep concentrating on the sounds in the cabin to make the heartbeat fade into the background again.

Around 3:00 a.m., voices woke her. A man said, "Look, right there—it's at least two inches."

Tori's eyes flew open. She sat up, trying to figure out who was in the room.

Another fainter voice said, "Check the other one."

The first voice faded, now sounding like it was far away. "I don't see any cracks on this one."

People's voices didn't normally go from loud to faint like that. The voices, she realized, weren't in the room. They were in her mind.

Tori shook her head as though she could shake away the noise. This was bad. She was hearing voices. That was the sort of thing that happened to crazy people.

And then Tori understood why she was hearing the voices. The men were talking next to the dragon eggs. The dragons' ears could pick up the noise, so she could, too.

Tori hugged her pillow to her stomach. She could spy on Overdrake. She was a living wire tap and these men might say something that the Slayers could use to fight the dragons.

Shutting her eyes, she concentrated on their voices to make them grow louder. Part of her wanted to wake up the others and tell them what was happening, but it was the middle of the night, and what did she have to report? Two strangers were talking about something she couldn't understand.

"Are you sure that's a real crack?" a man asked, "It's only a couple inches."

"A two-inch crack is still a crack."

Tori gripped her pillow tighter.

"It might just be an irregularity in the shell."

Sarcasm dripped from the first man's voice. "Let's ignore it, then. When bacteria gets through the crack and gives the dragon an infection, we'll say we thought it was just an 'irregularity.'"

"So what do you want?" The second man said. "You want to try gluing it back together? A few superficial cracks are normal at this stage. Or . . . maybe they're hatching ahead of schedule."

There was a silence in which all Tori could hear was the thump of the heartbeat.

Hatching?

Then the first man's voice grew louder, as though he'd leaned closer to the egg. "We should do a scan to see whether the crack goes all the way through the shell."

The second man scoffed. "We can hardly see the *dragon* through the shell. How are we going to detect whether the crack goes all the way through?"

"We need an MRI. We should take it to Arlington—"

The second man let out an exasperated grunt. "The worst thing we could do to a cracked egg is haul it down the interstate for an hour."

"We'll make sure it's insulated."

"Don't you remember the last time we took an egg to Arlington? That's just asking for trouble."

"But what do we do about the crack?"

Someone sighed. Perhaps both of them. "We'll have to wake up Overdrake and ask what he wants done."

"You can go wake up the king of the cathedral. I still have temperatures to record."

Tori heard footsteps, and then the only sound was the constant thumping of the heartbeat. She dropped her pillow, went to her dresser, and felt along the top for her flashlight. The men hadn't given her a lot of information, but she didn't want to forget anything they'd said. She found the flashlight and flipped it on.

Bess pulled the covers over her face, Alyssa groaned, and Rosa turned over and squinted at her. "What now?"

"I need a pen and paper."

Lilly peered at the clock on the dresser. "Do you mind? We're trying to sleep."

Tori ignored her. She found a pen on her dresser and the report she'd written for dragon class. Tori scribbled the conversation on the back as fast as she could.

Lilly said, "Next meeting, I'm proposing a new rule. Anyone who wakes up other Slayers in the middle of the night gets thrown in the lake."

"I second," Alyssa said.

Tori underlined: "An hour to Arlington on the interstate." Then wrote down the last bit: "Overdrake, king of the cathedral." An address would have been more helpful, but at least they'd given her some information.

"I'm done." She folded the paper and slid into her flip-flops. Dr. B needed to know this information right away. Only a limited number of places in Arlington could do MRIs. If Overdrake decided to move one of the eggs there tonight, perhaps the Slayers could track down the egg's position. Tori headed to the door, the information churning in her mind.

Overdrake couldn't just show up at a hospital and ask someone to scan a huge egg—especially when it contained a dragon. He must have a contact at one of the medical places, someone who was working for him. Tori took three steps out of the door before she realized she had no idea how to get a hold of Dr. B. He wouldn't be at his office.

She walked back into cabin 27. "Can somebody show me where Dr. B's cabin is?"

Lilly squeezed her eyes shut. "I can show you where the bottom of the lake is."

"I'll take you." Bess swung her legs out of bed. "I might as well. I'm awake now anyway. But why do you want to talk to my dad?"

Tori half listened for the men's voices to come back. "I heard some guys talking near the dragon eggs. We might be able to narrow down their location."

"Really?" Bess asked, eyes blinking. "You're sure you weren't dreaming?"

"I was wide awake." Tori held out the paper to Bess. "This is what they said."

Bess read it, shaking her head in amazement. "Wow. You either have an amazing ability or you're completely insane."

Lilly pulled her covers up higher. "Do you want my opinion on that?"

Tori didn't. She walked to the door and Bess followed. Before they'd made it down the porch stairs, Rosa came after them. "Now I'm too curious to sleep. What exactly did you hear?"

As they headed up the trail, Tori told her everything she remembered. The cold night air seeped through her thin flannel pajamas and she couldn't help shivering. She should have grabbed her jacket when she'd gone back inside. That was the problem with being kept up all night—you couldn't think clearly.

Bess and Rosa both wore sweats. The camp literature had failed to tell Tori what the others already knew, that in this camp sometimes you had to go outside in the middle of the night.

When Tori finished her description, Rosa's eyebrows drew together in discontent. "It's not enough information to pinpoint the eggs' location."

Bess was more optimistic. "There can't be that many places an hour away from Arlington that you could hide dragon eggs away from the general population."

"An hour going at what speed?" Rosa asked. "And what if the man meant they had to take back roads for half an hour and then the interstate for a half an hour. Besides, he probably rounded the number. The trip wouldn't take exactly sixty minutes—it might take fifty or seventy. That's a difference of twenty miles."

Tori tried to keep her flashlight beam straight even though her hands were cold. "But if they go to Arlington with a dragon egg, we can tip off the police. It can't be legal to harbor something that dangerous."

Bess grunted. Her long legs ate up the distance on the trail so she hardly had to hurry to keep up. "The way people think about dragons now, if the public found out about an egg, they'd build a zoo for it and coddle the thing until it grew big enough to eat a few tourists."

"It's a shame we have to destroy the dragons," Rosa said. "I mean, people have been fascinated with them for so long."

Bess swept her hand at Rosa as though presenting her as evidence. "You see my point?"

Rosa lifted her chin. "If the dragons were in the right hands, think what science could learn from them."

"But they're in Overdrake's hands," Bess said, "and he wants to use them as weapons. It won't help to feel sorry for them. The dragons aren't going to have any qualms about skewering us."

The thud of Tori's footsteps intermixed with the heartbeat that kept intruding in her mind. It sounded like a stopwatch now, counting down the seconds. "How is Overdrake going to take over the whole nation?" Tori asked. "Even with dragons, he couldn't threaten more than a few cities at a time."

"That's the magic of EMP," Bess said. "Every time the dragons screech, they'll do damage. A few flybys and a city's cars, computers, TVs, refrigerators, and cell phones will stop working. Farmers will have a hard time planting and harvesting their crops without machinery, and even if they do manage to grow a decent amount, they'll need trucks to get it out to people. And you can imagine what EMP would do to a nuclear reactor. How many cities will Overdrake have to cripple before people decide it's better to have him as their ruler than their enemy?" Bess shook her head grimly. "It's one of those subjects we discuss a lot while sitting around the campfire. Most of the A-team thinks that if we don't manage to kill the dragons, the government will fold quickly. When D.C., New York, and a couple West Coast cities are taken down, the country will surrender. Dirk thinks that all

Overdrake will have to say to Arizona is, 'Hey, do you still want air-conditioning?' and they'll not only accept him as America's leader, they'll rename their state in his honor.

"We on Team Magnus believe America is a bit more resilient. People will fight for freedom even if it means losing modern conveniences."

Tori shivered in the night air. "I don't want to find out who's right: A-team or Team Magnus."

"Oh, you won't," Bess said. "If it comes to that point, we'll be long dead. But who knows, maybe one or two of us will survive." Her voice took on a wistful note. "Maybe Leo and Danielle will get their powers back in a real attack."

"Do you think so?" Rosa asked hopefully.

Bess hesitated, then said, "No, I doubt it."

They walked silently for a minute. The trees stood along the path like dark sentinels, their leaves rustling angrily every time a breeze went through them. Tori kept wondering about Brant Overdrake. How did a person become so power hungry, so devoid of decency, that he didn't care about killing innocent people? And how had he gotten other people to help him? Was it all about money like it had been with Dr. B's father?

Tori wished she could talk this over with her own father. He would know what to do. But even as she thought about it, she knew she couldn't share any of what she'd learned in the last forty-eight hours with him. He would yank her out of camp and send her to the best mental hospital money could buy. She'd be sedated, her memory wiped clean.

"I wonder why Overdrake hasn't found and attacked the camp?" Tori asked.

"Maybe he hasn't thought to look for us in the obvious places," Rosa said.

"Or maybe he doesn't think we're a big enough threat to risk murdering us," Bess said.

But Tori supplied her own reason. Maybe he was waiting until the last moment—waiting for all the Slayers to show up at camp so he could wipe them out in one swoop. No sense leaving around people who could fight him.

They didn't speak for the rest of the way to Dr. B's cabin. But with every footstep she took, Tori wondered if Overdrake knew she'd come to camp.

CHAPTER 25

Tori wrapped her arms around herself to keep warm while she waited for Dr. B to answer his door. It didn't take long. He peered out the door at them, his hair sticking up in odd angles and his blue robe hanging crookedly around his shoulder. He glanced at Bess, then surveyed the area behind them. "What's wrong?"

Bess strode inside. "You mean, besides your attachment to that ratty bathrobe?"

Rosa and Tori followed Bess into the cabin and Dr. B shut and locked the door behind them.

"What's wrong?" Dr. B asked again.

Bess gestured toward Tori. "It turns out that sometimes the dragons hear more than just their own heartbeats. Tonight they heard some of Overdrake's men talking."

Tori handed Dr. B the paper. "Their conversation woke me up. They said they're an hour away from Arlington and they might take one of the eggs there."

Dr. B's bushy eyebrows lifted as he took the note. While he read it,

Shirley came out of the hallway, robe on, her curly hair in wild disarray. Really, it was no wonder Bess kept her hair short. With her parents' hair genes, she would probably look like a dandelion that had gone to seed if she didn't keep her curls under strict control.

Shirley put one hand on her hip. She carried a gun in the other. It went slack in her hand and she made tutting noises with her tongue. "Bess Bartholemew, you ought to know better than to burst inside here in the middle of the night without giving me any warning."

"I didn't burst in. Dad opened the door."

Shirley tutted some more and went to put the gun away.

Dr. B lowered the paper and smiled at Tori. "It seems the gift of hearing is a useful skill, after all. Let's see what we can find out about Arlington."

He walked over to the computer on the kitchen table and sat down as he logged on. The girls perched on the chairs around him. After a few moments, he brought up a map of Virginia and zeroed in on Arlington. There were so many places surrounding it. The eggs could be in any direction.

Tori heard the faint sound of voices in the back of her mind and closed her eyes, concentrating. While Dr. B discussed locations of Arlington labs and hospitals, Tori heard clips of a different conversation.

". . . said hairline cracks are normal in this stage. It's part of the shell's stretching and thinning process, and I, of course, should know that."

"Yeah, but if you hadn't woken him, he would have yelled at us in the morning for not reporting it."

The voices grew quieter. The men must be walking away from the eggs. "Next time some issue comes up, it's your turn to wake him. Forget about the dragons; he's the one who's most likely to rip someone's head off."

And then the voices faded completely and all Tori could hear was the steady sound of a heartbeat. She slumped in her chair and opened her eyes. Dr. B, Shirley, Bess, and Rosa all stared at her.

"Are the men talking again?" Dr. B asked.

"They finished checking the eggs and left. But they said they're not going to Arlington. The crack is a normal part of the shell's stretching and thinning."

"Interesting." Dr. B picked up a pen and jotted down the sentence on a piece of scratch paper. "That's not how bird or reptile eggs behave. But I suppose in order to last a hundred and fifty years, dragon eggshells must be made of sturdier material. Now that the eggs are getting ready to hatch, the shell has to change in order for the dragon to break free."

Rosa put her chin into her hand. "But none of that will help us find them or defeat them."

Dr. B sat back in his chair. "I think they've given us a clue to help us find and defeat them. Don't you, Bess? Tori?"

Tori glanced over at Bess to see if she had any insight into what Dr. B was talking about, but Bess's expression was as blank as her own.

"We know the eggs are somewhere near Arlington," Bess said.

Dr. B waved a hand over Tori's notes. "What sticks out to you in all of this?"

"They took an egg out before and had some sort of problem," Rosa said.

Dr. B nodded. "What else?"

"The men don't like Brant Overdrake," Bess offered.

"Tori?" Dr. B asked.

She had no idea what he was getting at. She could only lift her shoulders and let them fall.

Shirley didn't offer any opinions and Dr. B didn't ask her. He kept his gaze on the girls and tapped his pen against Tori's paper. "You need to learn how to analyze this sort of thing. I might not always be around to tell you the answers." He pointed to the phrase "king of the cathedral."

"You don't see anything odd about this?"

The three girls studied the paper. "It should say 'king of the castle,'" Rosa said. "Cathedrals don't have kings, they have priests."

Tori turned the memory over in her mind. "He said 'cathedral.' I didn't write it down wrong."

Dr. B held up a hand, a teacher again, guiding the discussion. "Let's assume he said 'cathedral'; what does that mean?"

"That his men aren't very good with their metaphors?" Bess said.

"That the eggs are actually in a cathedral?" Rosa added. "Are there any cathedrals around Arlington?"

Dr. B pointed to the map on his computer. "You tell me."

The girls leaned closer to the screen. Bess said, "Is there a key that tells you landmarks like churches?"

Tori didn't need one. She saw what Dr. B was talking about: a city called Winchester. There was also a famous cathedral by that name. "Winchester Cathedral," she said. "That's in England, though, not Virginia."

"Yes," he said. "But let's say you built a very large structure in the city of Winchester. What would you nickname it?"

"So you think that's where they are?" Bess said. "Winchester?" She zoomed in on the map until it showed the streets of Winchester. "How will we know where?"

"I'll look at some of the larger structures on the aerial view, maybe take a trip, see what I can turn up." Dr. B ran a hand through his silver hair. "Apparently we have time. The eggs aren't going anywhere, and they're not ready to hatch—although whether we have weeks, months, or years left, I don't know. But the sooner we find them, the better chance we'll have of destroying them."

For one quick moment, Tori was pierced with regret. Rosa's words came back to her: *It's a shame we have to destroy the dragons . . . people have been fascinated with them for so long.*

She thought of them living on a remote island for generations far away from people. "Are they completely evil?" Tori asked. "If we took them away from Overdrake, could they . . . ?" She didn't finish the sentence. She was a Slayer. She knew the answer.

Dr. B didn't roll his eyes the way Bess was. "Are they completely evil?" he repeated as though she was a student who'd asked a theoretical question. "I'm not sure the dragons have the cognizance for that, but I believe what you're really asking is: Could they ever be used for good?"

She nodded, realizing only as he said it that that was exactly what she'd meant.

"Dragons are a wild force like the fire they breathe," he said. "For something to be good, it must be controlled, kept within boundaries. Fire, electricity, and water are like that, too. And if you think about it, so are power and love and procreation. So is society, I suppose." He gestured to the girls, then back at himself. "We have no way to control dragons. Perhaps the dragon lords were fools to ever try—mixing their minds with something so large and dangerous. They might have had good intentions originally, but it was inevitable that eventually a dragon lord would use the dragons as weapons. It was a Pandora's box that never should have been opened. And it's our job to close it. Permanently."

He pulled his attention away from the computer and looked at Tori. "Perhaps you'll hear more later. But it's been a long day and right now, I think the best thing you can do is get some sleep. You'll be less effective if you're tired."

The girls said their good-byes and walked to the door. Shirley gave Bess a hug, then for good measure hugged Rosa and Tori, too. As Dr. B saw them out, he said, "I'm glad you've joined us, Tori. Don't ever think one person can't make a difference. You see the difference you've already made?"

"Thanks," she said. She hoped he was right.

At 7:00 a.m. Tori jolted awake. She was out of bed, her blankets tangled around her feet, before she even opened her eyes. She stepped, tripped, and hit the ground with a slam that should have hurt worse than it did.

Lilly and Alyssa both laughed. Rosa helped her up.

Bess tossed her a glance while grabbing clothes from her dresser. "You get used to it after a few days."

Ten minutes later, Kody came and got them for the morning run. Dirk and Jesse were gone. Dr. B had woken them up early and taken them with him to Winchester. Kody and Shang had no idea why, so while they jogged, Bess filled them in on what had happened during the night. Both guys looked at Tori first with surprise and then respect. Kody laughed and said, "Maybe the odds just turned in our favor."

Shang effortlessly kept pace beside Tori. "Have you heard anything else?"

"Nope. Just my new sound track: the creepy dragon heart." It was a constant thud of background noise in her mind, sort of like Edgar Allan Poe's "The Tell-Tale Heart" come to life.

After breakfast, the group split into twos and went through their rotations. Bess and Tori rode motorcycles through some back trails Booker had set up. Tori zipped around the trees, with only minimal urging on Bess's part that she needed to go faster. When they finished with that, Tori took Bane through the show-jumping range, where he cleared the fences with such grace that Tori told him he should have been named Pegasus. Bane whinnied in agreement.

Then Tori did more target practice. Her accuracy with both arrow and gun improved. She wished Jesse was around to see it, but the morning came and went, and he still hadn't returned.

CHAPTER 26

As the car neared its destination, Dirk slipped on his sunglasses and put on a baseball cap. Even though he wasn't cold, he wore a loose-fitting jacket. This was because Dr. B had insisted that he and Jesse disguise themselves. Dr. B had not only put a temporary brown dye in his own hair, he wore a false beard, a mustache, and his contacts. He kept blinking because they irritated his eyes. All in all, he looked like a cross between a hippie and young Santa Claus who was also squinting in a dust storm.

Dirk didn't like the change. There was something comforting about Dr. B's silver hair and scholarly glasses. Something that made you feel he would always take the time to listen to you and consider what you said. Or maybe it wasn't the hair and glasses. Dr. B was just that way.

He stopped the car on a lookout at the side of the road and he, Jesse, and Dirk climbed out. Dirk got out last. He wouldn't admit it to the others, but his stomach had remained clenched since Dr. B announced they were making this field trip. It was one thing to train and to practice battle games for some distant time in the future; it was another thing to step out into the real world and see those plans through.

Dr. B regarded Jesse and Dirk. "Do you feel any extra strength now that we're close to the building?"

Dirk shook his head. Jesse paused as though hoping he did, then shook his head, as well.

Dr. B took his camera out of a case. "I guess that's to be expected. The building must have some way to prevent the dragon's signal from leaking out. Overdrake wouldn't want that signal coming in contact with any pregnant women who drove by." Dr. B attached a huge telephoto lens to the camera, then looked through the viewfinder, clicking pictures of the property.

They'd also brought two pairs of high-powered binoculars. Jesse put a pair to his eyes. Dirk reluctantly looked through his, as well.

He saw a mile-long cow pasture complete with a barn, a house, and a ridiculously large building, which, according to city records, had been zoned for an office building, but was obviously not an office building. No one put a huge, windowless office building in the middle of a cow pasture.

"Cows to feed to the dragon," Jesse said, and then added, "They wouldn't be grazing so calmly if they knew."

Dirk watched a Holstein standing idly in the grass. "I doubt it matters to them whether they're eaten by people or dragons."

"Do you see the razor wire on top of the fence?" Dr. B asked. "They definitely don't want visitors. How high do you suppose the fence is?"

The Slayers were all good at estimating heights. It came from jumping over things every summer. More specifically, from daring one another to jump over tall things.

Jesse said, "If the cows standing by it are normal size, I'd say twelve feet."

A good guess. Dirk was about to say the same thing.

Dr. B frowned at this number. Most of the Slayers could only leap nine or ten feet. Rosa, who was shorter than the other girls, could only clear eight. Dirk could clear nearly fifteen feet, and Jesse—well, it was hard to tell with him where leaping ended and flying began.

Dr. B moved a bit farther down the road, still clicking pictures. Dirk homed in on the gate and the guard stall that stood there. Instead of paying attention to any of the computer screens around him, the guard's gaze was focused on his laptop. He was probably playing Tetris or something. A pair of binoculars hung unused from his neck. Way to do your job, Dirk thought. You have three people scoping out your facility right now.

Dr. B pointed out details about the property as his shutter snapped away. Jesse joined in, counting the light posts, noting where the trees were positioned. They were both so excited about this discovery. Dirk barely tried to mask the fact that he wasn't.

This wasn't going to end well. It couldn't, and Dr. B and Jesse should both realize that. The Slayers had done a lot of battle simulation over the years and in nearly every round someone had gotten killed. Did Dr. B and Jesse think it would be any different in real life?

It was inevitable that the Slayers would come face-to-face with the dragon lord eventually. Dirk knew that; he did. Every time he came to camp that knowledge pressed into him as insistently as the smell of oak leaves and campfire smoke. But he wasn't going to be happy about it.

He surveyed the length of the property again, and tried to push away calculations, estimates, thoughts about who or how many wouldn't return to camp after a mission out here.

Dr. B moved farther down the street to get pictures at a different angle. He signaled Dirk to keep a lookout.

Dirk nodded and focused on the stall again. The man was still glued to his laptop.

From beside him, Jesse whispered the question Dirk had been avoiding. "Are you picking up a strong connection?"

Dirk didn't want to answer. He kept his binoculars trained on the stall. "The guard has a bulge in his jacket. He's armed. And did you notice that guy trolling around the property on a Segway? That's not a shovel he's carrying. It's a rifle."

"There's nothing here our teams can't handle," Jesse said. "We're trained."

"Tori isn't."

"Agreed. Tori stays at camp."

Good. One less person to worry about. He didn't like the idea of her getting mixed up with the dragon lord's crew. She was too new to all of this.

For a moment her face flashed through Dirk's mind: her large green eyes, honey brown hair, and flawless skin. Everything he'd thought about her had changed last night. Not only because she'd stuck it out at camp, but because she might be his counterpart after all.

He wasn't sure whether to hope for or against the possibility. He also wasn't sure he wanted her to get near enough to figure it out. It would change things to have someone around who could tell things about him, who could maybe even slip into his mind.

Dirk had watched counterparts interact for years, but still didn't know the extent of their connection. They claimed they couldn't read each other's thoughts, but he'd seen evidence otherwise. The way Shang always knew who Lilly's crush would be each summer, practically before he unpacked his bags. Danielle had sometimes finished sentences for Kody. Leo and Bess used to laugh together when nothing seemed funny to the rest of them. And in the tackle hide-and-seek game, the counterparts had to be seekers at the same time, because they could always find each other.

Would that be Tori and him now? She couldn't be more his opposite. She acted like she'd rather be a fashion model than a fighter. And her father was a senator.

Still, he couldn't avoid Tori for the next month. Sooner or later—probably sooner—they'd find out for certain if they were counterparts.

Being able to hear what the unborn dragons heard was such an odd talent. It seemed so pointless, and yet it had brought them here, to this lookout, to all sorts of danger. And this was only Tori's third day of camp. What would happen once she'd figured out how to use all her powers?

Dirk let out a sigh. His father was right. Women complicated everything.

Dirk pushed away thoughts of Tori from his mind. He couldn't let her influence his decisions. Not her, not his friends, not the urgent desire he had to keep them safe—none of that could have sway over him. How many times had Dr. B told him that when it came to a battle, you had to make your decisions objectively?

Dr. B walked back over to Dirk, the camera held loosely in his hands. "If this is Overdrake's compound, it explains why you've always been able to connect to the dragons so easily. It's only a few miles away from where you live."

"Yep, that would explain it," Dirk said slowly.

Dr. B came closer, keeping his voice low. "We can draw all sorts of conclusions about this place, but Dirk, you're our litmus test. Do you feel a strong connection coming from this place?"

What he felt was an end to all their summers together. It was a pain so strong he could barely speak. Still, he nodded and got out, "The dragons are here."

 **CHAPTER 27**

While Tori ate lunch, she heard noises near the dragon eggs—not voices or sounds she could distinguish, just muffled, scraping sounds. What could the eggs be doing? Rolling over? The scraping sounds ended, replaced by a soft humming. The noise seemed vaguely familiar, like she ought to recognize it.

She listened until she grew frustrated. She couldn't pinpoint the sound. Besides, Tori had only understood what she'd been hearing for half a day. She had no idea what constituted normal dragon egg sounds. The hum was probably air-conditioning or something.

After lunch she joined the others in fighting the mechanical dragon. Shang showed her around and gave her weapons: a wooden sword, a rifle that shot plastic pellets, and a compound bow that shot arrows with suction cups on the end. "Be careful shooting," he told her as he motioned to silhouettes of people painted on the walls. "If you inadvertently kill a pedestrian, it's minus a hundred points. If you kill another Slayer, your team loses two hundred."

Well, it was nice to know her life had value.

Shang pointed out the office in the upper corner of the building that housed the mechanical dragon's control center. Then he took her to meet Theo, who ran the controls and was also in charge of all technology-related aspects of camp. He wasn't a Slayer, but was still some sort of techno genius that Dr. B had recruited when he opened camp.

Theo barely looked college-age. He had uncombed brown hair, a nose that looked like it had wandered off of a larger face, and skin so pasty white she wondered if he ever went outside.

"Hey," he said when Shang introduced Tori. "Welcome, new dragon chick. Good luck on your first encounter with the dark side." He laughed as though he was trying to scare little kids on Halloween. "You'd better keep an eye on Bertie, because she'll keep an eye on you."

"Bertie?" Tori asked. "You named the dragon?"

"Had to call her something so I named her after Albert Einstein. You know, because she's so wicked cool."

Theo laughed and put his hands in his pockets. Even his arms were skinny. Or maybe they just looked skinny because she was used to the guys in cabin 26. "Bertie's got a new hydraulic system this year. It's totally sweet. I swear, one of these times, I'm going to have Dr. B run the controls, and I'll sit on Bertie's back and be the dragon lord. That would be awesome."

"Oh," she said, because she didn't know how else to react. He acted like this was fun, like it was some glorified game.

"Well, gotta go to the control room. It's party time." He waggled his eyebrows at her, then turned and ambled up the two-story metal staircase at the end of the building. A few minutes later his face appeared in the window of the control room. The dragon hummed to life, and foot-long beams on the end of its legs twirled menacingly. As it turned, two glowing, yellow eye sockets peered across the room. A white diamond sat on the dragon's forehead, reminding her of a star marking on a horse.

Team Magnus spread out along one wall. The A-team spread out against the opposite wall. Without warning, the dragon swung across the room at high speed. A spray of fire shot from its mouth, leaving a searing streak of smoke. It looked too strong for practice, and Tori wondered if Theo was taking advantage of Dr. B's absence and amping up the flames.

Kody let out a wallop, ran forward with his rifle drawn, and shot the dragon. The bullet made a soft ping as it hit against the dragon's chest. With a metallic grind, the dragon flipped in the air and turned to face him. Kody ran sideways, then jumped into the wall so he could push off from it, narrowly avoiding a burst of flames. "Lilly!" he yelled, "Wake up!"

"Sorry!" She ran around the side of the dragon so she faced it. "I'm getting in position."

"Leo's not here, and Shang can't be everywhere, so pay attention!" Kody called back. It was the sharpest tone Tori had ever heard him use.

Bess shot an arrow into the dragon's neck. The dragon turned on her, swooping downward with a screech as she sprinted out of the way. Shang came up from behind the dragon, trying to get underneath it, but had to leap away before the dragon's swinging tail bludgeoned him.

For the first few minutes of the game, Tori mostly stayed out of the way and watched. Her sword slapped into her leg, unused, but it was easy enough to hit the dragon using her bow or gun. She learned quickly, however, that shooting the dragon didn't do any damage. The dragon's attention just turned to whoever shot it, then lunged toward them at an alarmingly fast rate. So Tori shot the dragon only when it charged someone on her team, and then she made sure she could leap out of the way before it got her.

Every few seconds the dragon blasted out fifteen-foot-long streams of fire. Shang and Lilly generally managed to quench these before they reached anyone. The two tried to stay on opposite ends of the dragon so that one of them could always see its mouth. A few times it swiveled so quickly they didn't have time to position themselves, and then Bess would throw up a shield to protect the others. The Slayers were good at protecting themselves from fire. They had to be, otherwise being in the same room as this mechanical dragon would have been insane.

Once Tori nearly got the full force of the blaze. She could see flames hitting the invisible wall of the shield. Yellow, orange, and red churned in the air inches in front of her. She leaped backward, shaking, and more thankful for Bess's gift than she'd ever been for anything in her life.

She mourned Leo's absence then. He could have been throwing up shields, too. How could he have walked away from his responsibility, knowing what would happen?

Someone hit the dragon and it swung away from her. She tried to get her concentration back, but it took a while until her breathing steadied. The exercise went on.

If the dragon hit someone with its tail or twirling claws, they were considered dead and had to sit out the rest of the round. The other Slayers always yelled out, "Well done!" when someone was killed.

Shang had explained that the phrase was one of Dr. B's favorite compliments, but it also worked as an insult because it described how you were cooked once the dragon was finished with you.

Tori was the first person killed during the first round. And also the first person killed during the second round. She found the humiliation—"Well done!"—hurt worse than the beams slamming into her. But after the third round, she was just happy to be dead. It meant she could go off to the far side of the building and work on leaping without getting burned or pummeled.

The leaps came easier now. She could pick a location and jump right to it. She'd finally gotten her sea legs—or rather, leaping legs. As the air rushed by her, she felt graceful, powerful, like she was skating on the ice with the rink whizzing by. She even tried Kody's move—running and jumping against the wall to push off. It was fun, and after a few practices, she could do it without breaking stride.

Each round took a long time. Without Jesse to fly up and pierce the dragon's heart, the Slayers had to wait for the dragon to come low enough so that someone could manage to leap up underneath it and stab it.

Still, the Slayers were expert with their talents. Lily and Shang doused fire while they were leaping. Bess threw shields up even when she couldn't see the front of the dragon. Kody could not only push away the fire stream with his freezing shocks, he leapt across the dragon's tail and legs as though playing jump rope. Alyssa and Rosa hung back farther than the others, not wanting to risk getting too close. But when Bess got a burn on her arm, Rosa was at her side in seconds, healing the wound while keeping an eye on the dragon.

Then Kody misjudged one of his freezing shocks and was hit by a blast of fire. The entire front of his shirt sizzled off his chest. He fell backward onto the ground, convulsing, gasping in pain. Both Rosa and Alyssa ran to him.

Even from where Tori stood, she could see Kody's skin was bubbled and bleeding—parts of it charred white. It didn't resemble skin anymore. And Kody's face had lost all color. His jaw was clenched in a silent scream.

He's going to die, Tori thought, and wondered if Alyssa and Rosa could heal even half the damage. His wound looked too severe. They should call an ambulance—only an ambulance would take too long to get here. It had been foolish to practice with flames that big. Dr. B shouldn't have left Theo in charge, and he never should have put a bunch of teenagers, including his own daughter, in so much danger.

The dragon still hummed, swinging over them. Lilly had put out the fire, but the dragon made a whooshing sound, as it built up fuel for more flames. This time it would hit Rosa and Alyssa, and then who would be left to heal them?

Tori glanced up at the control room. Did Theo not see what had happened to Kody? He must. He just didn't care. Dr. B wasn't here, and Theo was too much of an idiot to know when to stop the game.

Tori sprinted across the room to the control center. She decided against the stairs. It would take too long to climb them. Instead, she jumped up until she was even with Theo in the glass.

She grabbed hold of the edge of the window, hanging there for a moment. "Turn it off!" she yelled to Theo's startled face. But he didn't. As she fell back to the ground, she could still hear the hum of the dragon behind her, and then the roar of another fire stream. The jerk had tried to fry someone else while Rosa and Alyssa were busy saving Kody's life. And maybe Theo had succeeded.

He had to be some sort of psychopath.

Tori leapt back upward with trampoline height. This time she banged on the window with her fists. It wasn't glass, but some sort of clear plastic that buckled and shattered. Large chunks of it flew into the control room.

She went down, then came back up again, this time at an angle. She sprung through the window and landed on a desk inside the control room. Several of the knobs and levers crunched beneath her feet.

Theo stood at an adjoining desk swearing loudly as he brushed pieces of plastic off the equipment. Feeling more like a cat than a human, Tori leapt to the floor in front of Theo. In two seconds she'd grabbed hold of his shirt and pushed him up against a wall.

Tori had never gotten into a fight in her life, never threatened anyone, yet she didn't hesitate to lift him off the ground. "I told you to stop," she said annunciating every word. "Did you not see what happened to Kody?"

"What's wrong with you?" Theo choked out. He sounded breathless, compressed, so she let go of him. He slid back to the floor.

"What's wrong with *you*?" she yelled. "Kody is hurt!"

Theo smoothed out his shirt from where she'd grabbed him. It was ruined, stretched apart and mangled. "Kody is fine!" he yelled back at her. "Man, look what you did to my shirt—and the window! And I bet you broke something when you landed on the controls."

Tori couldn't muster much concern over his shirt or workspace. She had stopped him from doing more damage. That was the important thing. She turned back to check on Kody and the others.

The dragon had been killed. Its lights were off and it lay limply from its cables. This wasn't a surprise. As soon as she'd distracted Theo from the controls, the others had been able to shut off the dragon.

She expected to see her teammates huddled around Kody. She was afraid Rosa and Alyssa might be on the floor, too, burned and writhing.

But Kody stood up. The color had returned to his face, and he took off what was left of his shirt, revealing perfect, new skin. He high-fived Rosa and Alyssa, then put one burly arm around each of them and pulled them into a hug.

The other campers weren't paying attention to him, though. They were making their way over to the control room, looking up at the window in amazement. And what's more, Jesse, Dirk, and Dr. B were back.

Dr. B peered up at her. "What's going on up there?"

Theo leaned out the window, pointing to Tori. "She tried to kill me!"

Shang called over, "She thought Kody's burn was serious."

Lilly cocked her head and stared up at the control room. "Didn't she see Rosa and Alyssa taking care of him?"

Tori blushed brightly. Apparently it wasn't Theo who had been acting like a psychopath—that part had been Tori's. Yep. Her. The new psycho dragon chick.

She looked at the broken window and sighed heavily. She was never going to figure out this whole Slayer business.

CHAPTER 28

Tori stood outside the building while Dr. B regarded her, pressing his lips together in a tight, unhappy line. He folded his hands neatly in front of his camp polo shirt. "Perhaps no one thoroughly explained the rules of the drill to you, but while fighting the dragon, you're not allowed to break into the control room or threaten the tech support."

"I thought Kody was really hurt." She had already explained this, but perhaps Theo's wailing in the background had distracted Dr. B from hearing it. Or perhaps he'd forgotten it while settling Lilly and Bess's argument over who had won the last round. Lilly maintained the points should go to the A-team since she had been the one to stab the dragon—or rather, push the button that represented the dragon's heart with her sword. Bess said Tori had stopped the dragon when she'd taken out Theo, so the points should go to Team Magnus. And then Lilly said that anything Tori had done didn't count since she'd technically been dead at the time. People weren't allowed to come back from the grave to help out team members.

In the end, the A-team had gotten the points.

Now Dr. B stared at Tori patiently. "I'm glad you were worried over Kody's well-being. That shows loyalty and compassion. However, you must learn to destroy the dragon even if one of your team members falls. When the dragon attacks, we won't be able to stop it from charging every time we need to help one of our own. You have to learn how to deal with these kinds of situations in practice drills so you'll be able to deal with them when they happen in real life."

Tori nodded, even though she didn't imagine she would be much use in a real battle. Being able to hear what the dragon heard wasn't going to help her fight it. She'd probably get killed quickly, like in practice.

And worse still, her parents would never understand why their daughter had died fighting a dragon.

Dr. B must have seen her discouragement. He added, "You managed to leap all the way to the control booth. That was quite well done. None of the others could have managed that height after only a couple days of practice. I dare say you're the only girl who could make that height now."

"It's the ice skating," Tori said. "I've got strong legs."

"And the other girls have practiced jumping for years." He smiled, not letting her brush off the compliment. Then his gaze traveled back to the door. "Well, seeing as Theo needs to fix the control board before you can practice again, and judging by the way he was weeping over it, I imagine it won't be ready today. So I think it's time for an early dinner. I'll ask the cafeteria to bring things down."

He left, taking his cell phone out of his pocket while he walked away. Tori didn't want to go back inside and face the others. She'd messed up again, and this time had ended up breaking the mechanical dragon.

But she couldn't stay out here forever. She trudged back into the Dragon Hall. The Slayers were below the control room, leaping up like supersonic jumping beans. Dr. B was right; none of the girls could get the height she had. Jesse could do it—although Bess kept yelling that he was cheating and flying. Dirk could do it, and Kody and Shang could jump high enough to see in the window, but not high enough to land inside. And Tori had done it three times in row.

"Would you cut it out!" Theo yelled at Dirk as he popped up even with him. "That's getting on my nerves!" When neither Dirk nor Jesse stopped, Theo picked up chunks from the plastic window and pelted the Slayers with them. Kody turned the thing into field goal practice. He jumped up, caught a chunk, then landed and drop-kicked the plastic piece back through the window. After a couple times doing this, Dirk ran interference. He sprang up and caught a football-size plastic chunk before it could go back in the window.

"Interception!" Dirk yelled.

This seemed to be an invitation for every other Slayer to run after him. They tore around the building, laughing while they bounded into and off the walls. Dirk finally passed the plastic chunk to Kody, and instantly the teams formed. The A-team against Team Magnus.

When Shang and Jesse were about to tackle Kody, he tossed the chunk toward Lilly. Before it reached her, Bess threw up a shield in front of her, and the chunk bounced off the forcefield and flew toward Bess. She caught it, then dodged around Alyssa, hurdled over Lilly's head, and sprinted back the way she'd come. Kody sent a shock that flung the plastic out of her hands. Jesse lunged into the air, caught it, and the race was on again.

Tori stood back and watched. It was nice seeing them laughing this way, like they were high school kids instead of commandos preparing for a life-and-death battle. For the first time, she felt the urge to be a part of them and was sad she'd missed all those years when the rest of them had bonded.

Jesse tossed the chunk to Shang, who leapt up and flung it back into the control room.

Theo let out a stream of curses.

"We should stop," Rosa said, slowing to a walk. "We're going to make him cry again."

The group sauntered away from the control room area. Some of them went to the drinking fountains. Dirk looked at Tori, letting his eyes run over her in an appraising manner. She stood there, caught in his gaze, suddenly feeling awkward and expectant.

She hadn't spoken to Dirk since he'd left her cabin the night before, and she had no idea how the whole counterpart thing worked. She ought to ask him for advice on fighting the dragon without much of a usable talent. He obviously didn't get killed first in every battle, or he wouldn't be a team captain.

For a moment, she thought Dirk would come over, but Jesse and Kody walked up beside her and Dirk strolled over to the drinking fountain instead. Kody held up his hand and gave her a high-five. "Hey, thanks for beating up Theo on my behalf. Someday I hope I can return the favor."

"Don't encourage her," Jesse said. "As her team captain, I'm supposed to impress upon her the seriousness of her actions." He turned to Tori and nearly suppressed the smile from his lips. "If you ever do that again, I'm going to make you write 'I will not terrify the tech support guy' a hundred times."

"Sorry," she said.

Jesse nudged one of the broken window chunks with his foot, then looked up at the jagged hole. "How did you manage to jump that high?"

"Adrenaline, I guess. I thought Theo would burn everyone."

Jesse considered the window. "Hmm," he said, as though piecing something together in his mind. "Try it now."

She, Jesse, and Kody walked back over to the corner of the floor underneath the control room. The room grew quiet and she knew the others had stopped chatting and were watching her, too. Tori took a running step and leapt up. It felt like she'd taken a giant jump on a trampoline, all inertia and air. Her head bobbed even with Theo. He was bent over the desk full of knobs and levers, but he glanced up and glared at her when she came into view.

Gravity took effect, and she landed again, but without any of the jarring thunks she'd had two days ago. It was controlled now, as graceful as one of her skating routines.

Jesse didn't speak, just kept watching her.

Theo leaned out of the window. "Tori is not allowed in the control room again. She is hereby *banned* from even jumping up to look inside. *Banned!*" He gave her another glare before spinning around and disappearing from view.

Tori stared back at the window. "He's sort of touchy, isn't he?"

Jesse laughed. Maybe that line sounded funny coming from someone who'd made such a big deal about her hair getting charred off.

But Kody nodded in agreement. "Computer nerds. They're nothing but a bunch of prima donnas."

Jesse hadn't taken his eyes from her. She liked being the center of his attention in a good way. He might have said something about her jump, and it might have even been a compliment, but then the door to the Dragon Hall opened, and Dr. B called out, "Dinner!"

The Slayers sat down at the table, Team Magnus on one side, the A-team on the other. Jesse and Dirk sat at the seats closest to Dr. B, at the head of the table. While everyone ate chicken casserole, Dr. B hooked up a projector to his laptop and focused the image from his screen on a nearby whiteboard.

Finally, he stood in front of them, gathering their gazes. "As you know, this morning I went to investigate places Overdrake might be hiding the eggs. Now we need to discuss the results."

He clicked a remote, and an image came up on the whiteboard—a large, gray building and two smaller buildings surrounded by cow pasture. Several cows grazed in the foreground. "The residence is listed to 'John Smith.'"

The Slayers snickered. "Lame alias," Kody said.

Dr. B advanced the screen to show a closer picture of the property. The building had a huge door on one end. "I'm sure John Smith is an alias," Dr. B agreed. "I'm also sure it's the right place. Armed guards patrol the grounds, and Dirk got a strong connection to the dragons."

Now the group leaned toward the image, their dinner forgotten, several people speaking at once.

"You know where it is?"

"When are we going?"

"Why are we sitting here, then?"

Dr. B held up a hand. "This is an unexpected turn of events—locating the eggs before they've hatched. They'll be easy to destroy if we can get through Overdrake's protections. However, you haven't been trained to get around alarm systems or break into buildings. To be successful, I feel I'm going to have to study this for a while; perhaps bring in professionals—"

The group didn't let him finish. Kody said, "We *are* the professionals. Who are you gonna get who can throw up forcefields or fly?"

Lilly said, "If we wait, Overdrake could move."

"We'll have surprise on our side," Bess added.

Shang said, "We could stop the attack on D.C. before it ever happens. Think of the lives we'd save."

Dr. B raised his hand again. "We've planned on killing the dragons after they attack, but this—" He gestured toward the picture on the wall. "This isn't stopping a twenty-ton carnivore from ripping people apart. This would be breaking, entering, and destroying private property. If we aren't careful, Overdrake could kill you, and the law would count it as self-defense. You would die as criminals. And even if we succeed in our mission, we might be caught, arrested, and sent to jail where we'll spend the remainder of our days reading hate mail from *Eragon* fans."

The group fell silent. Tori pushed some casserole around her plate and wondered how her parents would react to her being hauled off to jail. Probably not very well. Especially since her dad would be campaigning soon. And how would she explain jailtime to her friends?

She tried to read Jesse's expression, to see whether he was for or against the idea, but he stared grim-faced at the projection on the wall. Dirk looked down at his plate, his jaw clenched.

Kody folded his arms. "We'll wear ski masks so they can't identify us and gloves so we don't leave fingerprints."

"What if they capture some of us?" Tori asked.

Lilly waved a dismissive hand at her. "What are you worried about? If you get caught, your daddy will just pull some strings to spring you out of jail. You won't rot in prison like the rest of us."

Shang's gaze flickered to Tori and then back to Dr. B. His voice was almost apologetic. "Tori shouldn't go. She's only had her powers for two days. She doesn't know how to use them, let alone how to work with the group."

Tori bristled. It felt like Shang was saying the same thing Jesse had told her yesterday—that she was undependable, that she wouldn't be there for the group when they needed her.

Bess picked up a carrot stick from her plate and bit into it. "I don't know about that. Theo's afraid of her."

Lilly rolled her eyes. "So Tori will do really well if the eggs are being guarded by defenseless computer nerds."

Dr. B said, "We haven't even decided if we're going, and you're debating who to allow on the teams. We're getting ahead of ourselves, don't you think?"

Kody pushed away his plate, annoyed. "We're going. It's what we've trained for."

Shang nodded. "We need to think of why we've been given our powers."

Dr. B's eyebrows drew together. "Even if you'll be fighting people instead of dragons? You might have to kill someone—a guard who has no inkling of what he's guarding. Could you face a murder sentence? Would you want to see the rest of the Slayers and myself charged as accessories to murder? And the emotional repercussions—I hate to think of you having to carry the burden of taking someone's life." He shook his head. "The more I think about this, the more reasons I have to wait, to let them strike first."

"Even when we know they're fixing to kill innocent people?" Kody asked. "We gotta protect them. We can strike first, so we should."

Rosa fiddled with a celery stick on her plate. "I don't want to kill anyone. Aren't we as bad as Overdrake, then—murderers?"

"The ends don't justify the means," Alyssa agreed. "If we attack first, we're the aggressors. We're the ones in the wrong."

Lilly said, "But we don't have to kill anyone. We could disarm the guards. They won't be strong enough to fight us in hand-to-hand combat. We go in, we destroy the eggs, we get out."

Dr. B examined the picture on the wall, as though hoping to find something he'd missed before. "Of course, we wouldn't *plan* on killing anyone. But things don't often go as planned. Too many variables exist. What would you do if one of your team members was being attacked? Would you kill to save their lives? Your own? Would you kill to avoid capture? These are things we need to think about."

No one spoke. They stared at either the picture or the table.

After a few moments, Dr. B said, "We haven't heard from you, Tori. What do you think?"

She didn't know what she thought. Every time someone spoke she completely agreed with what they said. Yes, they should do a preemptive strike—it was better for society in the long run, but no, the ends didn't justify the means, and how could she kill anyone? It was one thing to theoretically think about it, killing in self-defense or because you had to save society from a greater evil, but to actually do it—to point a gun at someone and pull the trigger, or worse yet, to use her new strength to kill with her bare hands—she wasn't sure she could. And yet, she knew Overdrake wouldn't let anyone near those eggs without a fight. If they went in without being prepared to kill, they could be killed themselves.

"What do the team captains think?" she asked.

"The team captains," Dr. B said carefully, "want you to express your opinions without being influenced by their thoughts."

Bess let out a frustrated groan. "Why do you always want us to come to our own conclusions? Can't you for once just tell us what the right answer is?"

Dr. B put his hands behind his back, the same stance he used to teach class. "I don't know the right answer. I wish I could predict the future and tell you how a preemptive strike would turn out. Although perhaps it's better not to know these things in advance. What if I knew we would succeed in destroying the eggs, but one of you would die in the process—would you still think an attack was the right thing to do?"

There was silence, then Bess said, "It depends on which of us died."

The rest of the Slayers laughed. It was a welcome break from the tension.

Dr. B didn't laugh, though. His tone was soft, but serious. "I'm going to give you an hour to weigh it out in your minds. Then we'll meet back here and discuss it again. If the majority wants to go, we'll go, but I won't force any of you to act against your conscience. If you don't want to come, you can stay at camp."

He snapped his laptop shut, signaling that the meeting was over. The campers stood and stretched, pairing off not with their friends,

Tori noticed, but with their counterparts. Rosa and Alyssa exchanged a knowing look. They had both been against going. They walked out of the room, talking in hushed voices.

As Shang and Lilly stood, their eyes locked, as though checking to see if they were on the same page. They left together, Lilly talking, Shang listening. Kody and Bess walked side by side toward the door. They'd both lost their counterparts. Perhaps as they walked they were thinking about their missing halves. They had spent all that time training together and now had to work alone.

Tori got to her feet. Both Dirk and Jesse were staring at her. Her gaze slid back and forth between them. She could think of only one reason for their interest. She hadn't said which side of the issue she fell on.

If Jesse and Dirk were against a preemptive strike, that would mean she would end up being the tiebreaker. And the one thing she was sure about was that she didn't want the decision to fall to her.

CHAPTER 29

Tori stood up from the table and walked out of the building without stopping to speak to either Jesse or Dirk. She hadn't gone far before she heard footsteps behind her. Leaving the trail, she made her way into the forest and sat down on a fallen log. Then she let her thoughts drift through the layers of green surrounding her while she waited for Dirk to catch up. A few moments later, he did.

When she'd first come to camp, she'd lumped Dirk together with a lot of the guys at her school. Guys with easy good looks and cavalier attitudes. Guys who discarded girls without a second thought.

But maybe Dirk was different. He'd already devoted his life to protecting society. That automatically saved him from being shallow.

He sat down beside her and ran a hand through his hair. In the muted forest light, his blue eyes looked the exact same color as the sky.

"I knew you'd come talk to me," she said.

"Did you?" he asked.

"Because . . . we might be counterparts."

"Oh." He put his hands beside him on the log and looked out into the forest, his usual swagger gone.

She wondered briefly where Jesse was. Alone? Maybe he'd caught up with Bess and Kody.

Dirk kept looking at the forest. His eyes were brooding, a sharp contrast to his flawless face.

She said, "I don't know what we're supposed to say to each other about strategy and all that. I'm too new at this."

"I don't know, either," he said. "I've never had a counterpart. Maybe that's why Dr. B made Jesse and me team captains. There was only one of each of us."

"I doubt he'll demote you just because I've shown up."

Dirk didn't comment on that. "Have you heard anything else from the eggs? Anything unusual?"

"Only some muffled sounds. I don't know what they were."

He nodded, taking in this information.

Tori leaned toward him. "How do you deal with it—always having the dragons there in your mind?"

He looked at her, his eyes finally connecting with hers. "I don't re-member a time when they weren't there, when I didn't have that double vision in my mind."

"Really?" she asked, astonished. "You've always been connected?"

He shrugged like it wasn't a big deal, but she knew it was.

"When did you realize they were dragons?"

"I've always known," he said. "Haven't you?"

She fingered the bark on the log. "I've always suspected dragons existed, and I've always had good hearing. But the heartbeat is new. It's annoying."

He grinned at that, then looked her up and down, studying her. "Do you think we're really counterparts?"

"Our gifts are close enough that we must be. Unless you think there are two more Slayers Dr. B hasn't found yet. Another person with the gift of sight and one with the gift of hearing." She scrunched her nose. "There can't be four of us with such worthless abilities."

He raised his eyebrows and let out a breath of disbelief. "Worthless?"

"Well, we can't do anything cool like fly. We can't even be useful in a fight by putting out fire, healing people, or protecting them with shields."

"It's not worthless," Dirk said, irritation lacing his tone. "You're not . . ." But he didn't finish.

"I'm not what?" she asked.

He surveyed her, tilting his head. "The others can feel when their counterparts are near, even when their eyes are closed. Do you want to try it?"

It sounded cool, sort of like a psychic ability. "Okay," she said.

"Shut your eyes," he told her.

She did. He stood up and took a few steps behind her. "See if you can tell when I come near you."

After a minute, Dirk stepped up behind her. She kept her eyes closed. "I can tell you're there."

"You felt it?"

"I heard your footsteps. I've got good hearing, remember?"

"That's cheating," he said, but his voice was more amused than upset.

"Do you want me to try sneaking up on you?" she asked.

"No, I'll be quieter this time. Keep your eyes closed." His footsteps padded away from her.

She called to him, "I'll talk so I can't hear you over the sound of my voice."

"All right." He stood quite a distance behind her. "Tell me about your boyfriend."

"How do you know I have a boyfriend?"

"Girls as pretty as you always have boyfriends. Let me guess. He's some rich kid who drives a convertible and wears funky leather shoes that cost an arm and a leg."

"He doesn't wear funky leather shoes. They're *normal* leather shoes."

Dirk laughed, probably because he'd been right about the rest. He hadn't moved any closer. "The guy's a jerk."

"You don't even know him," Tori said.

Dirk didn't answer. Apparently, he was ready for her to talk to cover his footsteps. She tried to think of something to say about Roland, but the truth was, she hadn't thought of him today—or much yesterday, for that matter. And sitting here, she had a hard time picturing him. All she could think about was the fact that Dirk stood somewhere behind her, watching her. "Um, Roland and I met in debate club. I'm lousy at debate, by the way. I only tried it because of my dad. Politicians have to know how to argue different sides of an issue, so he wanted me to try it. But most of the time, I didn't see the point in debating. It never changed anyone's minds about anything. Besides, my parents have drilled into me for the last sixteen years that I'm not supposed to publicly give my opinion on anything, so it's sort of hard to undo all that instruction. When your dad's a senator, your parents are always worried you're going to say something idiotic in front of a camera and it will end up going viral on YouTube."

"You're supposed to be talking about Roland," Dirk said. She could tell by his voice that he hadn't come closer.

"Okay, um . . . Roland is nice and he speaks fluent French. He's about as tall as you are, although not as built." She hadn't meant to tell Dirk that she'd noticed his muscles, and she flushed with embarrassment. Thankfully, he was behind her and wouldn't notice. "I mean, he's not as athletic as the guys from cabin twenty-six." That still sounded awkward. Dirk probably thought she ogled all of them.

She wondered, though she didn't want to, if he'd noticed how she was built.

"Roland wants to go into business someday. His grandfather owns a string of hotels, so he'll probably do that." As she took a breath, she listened but couldn't hear anything. "He likes baseball and—" She stopped midsentence because suddenly she felt Dirk was near. And not behind her, as she'd supposed, but right in front of her. In fact, she was almost certain his hand was outstretched near her face.

She kept her eyes closed, but lifted her hand, fingers spread apart, slowly upward until she touched Dirk's hand. Then she opened her eyes and saw that their fingers were perfectly aligned.

Dirk let his fingers slide until they interlaced with hers. He kept hold of her hand while he sat beside her on the log. "I guess this means we're counterparts," he said.

"I guess so." Tori's heart hammered in her chest, but she couldn't tell whether it was because she'd felt Dirk's presence without seeing him, or because he still had hold of her hand.

Her emotions pulsed, came alive. This wasn't supposed to happen. She'd already decided she liked Jesse. She had come back to camp to help Jesse.

But she hadn't expected how this counterpart connection would affect her. Here, with the physical connection of holding Dirk's hand, it seemed as though she'd known him all his life, that she could say anything to him, and he'd understand.

His voice was low. "Can you see into my mind? Do you know things about me now?"

She shook her head. "Can you tell things about me?"

"Yeah, I can tell Roland isn't going to last."

She glanced at her fingers criss-crossing with Dirk's and didn't answer. She should pull her hand away, put some distance between them, but she didn't.

He leaned closer. "Can you tell what I'm going to do next?"

She looked into his eyes and nodded. She could tell, although it probably wasn't due to any connection. It was just the sort of thing you knew when a guy held your hand and leaned close. He was going to kiss her.

He pulled her to him and bent his head down. It was a soft kiss—at least it started out that way. A few seconds later, it grew more insistent, more passionate. She let go of his hand and wrapped her arms around his neck. Thoughts and feelings erupted inside her like hundreds of sparklers going off. She shouldn't be doing this. This wasn't what the counterpart bonds were for.

Besides, she had hardly *talked* to Dirk. She didn't know anything about him. Except that he was good-looking. And a good kisser. And was attracted to her while Jesse probably wasn't. Dirk wouldn't be here kissing her if he knew his friend was interested in her.

It was these thoughts of Jesse, intruding into her mind, that made her pull away.

"Okay," she said, her voice husky, "we probably shouldn't have done that."

He smiled, not in the least bit penitent.

She found it hard to breathe, hard to talk. "I'm not like this usually," she said. "I don't even kiss guys on the first date."

His smile didn't falter. "Poor Roland."

She blushed and hated that fact. "Um, look, let's pretend none of this happened, okay?"

He shrugged, and his eyes glinted wickedly. "You can pretend if you want."

She straightened her shoulders, keeping her posture erect, formal. It was better to bring things around to a more normal topic of conversation. "So are you for or against going to Winchester?"

The humor dropped from his voice and his expression tensed. "Against. It's too risky. There are too many things we can't plan for. If you want to fight a snake, it's best to do it on your turf. You don't go down its hole."

"What does Jesse think?"

Dirk looked off into the forest again. "He thinks we should go."

Tori let out a breath she hadn't realized she'd been holding. She wouldn't be the tiebreaker. The majority wanted to go. Now that she knew how it would be decided, her thoughts automatically grew sharper, more focused—like when she jumped in the control room and pushed Theo up against the wall. Her mind, like her body, had switched into Slayer mode.

She could do this.

Dirk pulled a chunk of bark off the log and broke it between his hands. "I don't blame Jesse for wanting to go. If we fight Overdrake now, our lives are equally at risk. If we wait until the dragons attack, he'll carry the greatest risk because he's the only flyer."

Tori couldn't imagine Jesse using that reasoning. "Did Jesse say that?"

"He didn't have to." Dirk broke another piece of bark. "But it has to influence his opinion." He chucked a piece of bark. It flew farther than was normal, hit dead center into the trunk of a distant tree, and exploded apart. Dirk turned his attention back to Tori. "You don't need to worry about this. The one thing Jesse and I agree on is that you're not going."

"What?" she asked, stung.

"You're too inexperienced, so you don't have a vote. You're staying at camp."

They weren't even going to let her vote? "The two of you just decided that, did you?"

"I was supposed to let Jesse tell you." Dirk leaned back on his hands and smiled. "So you can add that part of our conversation to the list of things you're pretending didn't happen."

She stood up. "I was undecided before, but now I'm going." Then she turned and strode back to the trail. She wanted to find Jesse, to demand an explanation.

She jogged around the forest by their cabins, but didn't see him. Not on the ground, not in the trees. A guy who could fly could be anywhere.

Yesterday she would have been fine with not going. A part of her, the logical part, told her she should be relieved, but she wasn't. Jesse and Dirk both thought she was incompetent. They saw her as a spoiled rich girl who couldn't hold her own.

She ran all the way down by the lake to burn energy. It had built up inside her, just like her frustration.

When nearly an hour had passed, she made her way back to the large building. The others were there already. They'd moved from debating the issue of going to Winchester to planning the attack. Papers and sketches were scattered across the table. Shang and Kody were analyzing pictures of Overdrake's property. Dirk was writing a list of things they'd need for the mission and Jesse was working on a list of questions to be answered. Tori wondered why none of them had called her to join them and then remembered with another twinge of pain that no one cared what she thought.

She sat across from Jesse and Dirk. She glared at Jesse.

He looked up from his list. "What?"

"I have to stay at camp during all this?"

Jesse shot Dirk an angry look, but Dirk brushed off the disapproval with a shrug and a smirk. "That sort of slipped out. Sorry."

"You're not sorry," Tori told Dirk.

"You're right," Dirk said with a slow drawl. "I'm not." But she didn't think he was talking about the voting thing.

She blushed, then looked away from Dirk. She didn't want to get caught up in his intense blue eyes anymore. She turned to Jesse. "I admit I'm not up to speed when it comes to fighting, but I think I can destroy eggs as well as the rest of you."

"It's not the eggs I'm worried about." Jesse made a notation on his paper. "It's the armed men who will be guarding them."

She continued to glare at him.

Jesse regarded her, letting long seconds go by. Finally, he sighed and rubbed at the back of his neck. "All right. You can stay at the van with Dr. B, Booker, and Theo. You can be their bodyguard."

"You're letting Theo go?" She felt insulted all over again.

"We might need him for technical stuff," Jesse said.

Oh. Theo's skills were important enough to matter, but not hers. Wonderful.

She didn't say anything else, because Dr. B came in carrying a large duffle bag. He stood at the front of the table again. "Jesse, Dirk, what have the teams decided?"

Jesse turned away from Tori to address Dr. B. "We've discussed it, and this is what it comes down to: If we attack Overdrake's compound and it turns out to be the wrong decision, we'll bear the consequences. But if we wait until the dragons attack D.C., then the entire city will bear the consequences. We've decided it's better to bear the consequences ourselves. We're going to try to destroy the eggs."

Dr. B's gaze went to Bess, stayed there for a long moment, then returned to Jesse and Dirk. "Part of me doesn't want to let you anywhere near armed men, but the truth is, if you don't destroy the eggs now, you'll have two more dragons to fight later on—as well as whatever armed men Overdrake uses during his attack. So I'll support your decision."

Jesse motioned to the Slayers on the other side of the table. "Dirk, Rosa, and Alyssa voted against a preemptive strike, but they'll go to help us." His gaze fell on Tori. "Tori will be your bodyguard in the van. We're going over ideas for a strategy now."

Dr. B nodded, picked up a marker, and walked to the whiteboard. His earlier reluctance seemed to have been shelved. He was focused now, committed. He wrote the word "strategy," then drew shapes on the whiteboard to represent Overdrake's buildings. Underneath the largest rectangle he wrote "dragon enclosure." In the right-hand corner he drew the house and barn. He drew several balloon-looking lines. "This is the approximate location of the lampposts. My first inclination was to shoot them out to give us the benefit of fighting in the dark, but that would alert anyone in the area that something was wrong. We'd best leave them alone so we don't lose the element of surprise. Surprise will be our biggest asset."

He drew what looked like furry lollypops. "Four trees stand at each corner of the dragon enclosure. Boards are nailed to the trunks of the trees, which tells us they're used for reconnaissance posts." He tapped his marker against one of the trees. "We couldn't spot anyone in them during the day, but we'll need to make sure they're still empty before we raid the enclosure."

He drew a large circle around the buildings. "The fence is twelve feet high, with razor wire on top. It's alarmed and electrified and probably too tricky for us to disarm. What's our plan?"

Jesse said, "I'll fly Bess over the wall. Dirk will jump over. We'll all carry tranquilizer guns. While I take care of the men guarding the enclosure, they'll knock out the guard at the gate. Bess should be able to block any gunfire he gets off before he passes out. Once the gate is open, the others will drive in with the motorcycles."

On the side of the board, Dr. B wrote the word "supplies," and underneath that, "motorcycles," "tranquilizer guns." He paused and then added "rifles." "I can't take you into a dangerous place without real weapons, but use them as a last resort."

Dr. B drew a road going to the dragon enclosure and then a rectangle at the fence. "The front guard is in a bulletproof booth. We'll need to find a way to lure him out so we can dispatch him and open the gate."

"Smoke bomb," Shang suggested. "He won't stay in his booth if he thinks it's on fire."

Dr. B added "smoke bomb" to his list of supplies. "If that fails, what's our alternative?"

"We could tip the thing over," Kody said with evident hope.

"Wouldn't that set off some sort of alarm?" Rosa asked.

"We could really set the thing on fire," Lilly said. "He'd have to leave then."

"Wouldn't that ruin the controls we need to open the gate?" Rosa asked.

Lilly waved a dismissive hand in her direction. "It would be a controlled fire. I can extinguish any flames that get near the electronics."

No one had any arguments for that. Dr. B added "fuel" to his list.

"When the eggs are destroyed, you'll need to get out of there as fast as you can. You might set off alarms, so you don't want to give reinforcements time to show up." He wrote the words "cordless jackhammer," "bolt cutters," and "synchronized watches." "What else do we need to discuss?"

"The door lock," Dirk said.

"Ah, yes," Dr. B said. "I showed the pictures of the enclosure door to Theo, and he said it's triggered by fingerprints. Once the guards are unconscious, you'll be able to hold one of their hands to the control panel to open the door. The jackhammer should be able to cut through the dragon eggs no matter how hard the shells are—and from what Tori told us, it sounds like the shells are becoming thinner anyway."

Dr. B picked up the duffle bag, opened it, and passed out Ziploc bags with an assortment of techno gadgets: wireless radio receivers small enough to wear over their ears, throat microphones, and video cameras to wear on their necks. The bag contained one low-tech item: earplugs. "Any of you who are near the jackhammer will need earplugs."

He handed a set to Tori. "I'm afraid the noise will be especially inva-sive for you."

Dr. B continued, assigning parts, going over contingency plans, and adding to his list of supplies: black clothing, bulletproof jackets, ski masks, helmets. Tori listened to the plans but didn't try and mem-orize them. She knew her part. She was staying by the van.

CHAPTER 30

Brant had read and then reread the text message from his contact. *You have a pest control appointment tonight.* That was code for the dragon Slayers' operation. Although it probably wouldn't have mattered if the message had read: "Your men inadvertently gave away your location. There will be an attack tonight, so get ready."

Dr. B, as far as Brant could tell, had never spied on anyone at camp, not their phone calls or texts. Brant once had his contact steal and send some incriminating texts on a couple of the Slayers' phones just to see what the fallout would be. There hadn't been any.

Still, Brant deleted his text as a precaution. He wouldn't fall into the same trap destined to ruin Dr. B and his followers. Brant didn't blindly trust those around him. A spy could have infiltrated his ranks, too.

Unbidden, one of Dr. B's favorite sayings to the team captains came to Brant's mind: *A leader shouldn't rule like a dictator. A leader should teach correct principles and let the people govern themselves.*

Optimistic drivel—and exactly why dictators would always rule most of the world. Certainly free societies surfaced in history: Rome, Greece, America. But Rome and Greece had fallen. America would, too. It was already imploding—ruled by legislators who represented no one but their own best interests, congressmen who spoon-fed the people anything they wanted to hear. Vote for me and I'll give you everything. If we can't pay for it, no matter. What's a few trillion more in debt?

America would change for the better soon, and then the people would have a leader who told them the truth about life. You don't get everything you want.

Brant sat down in his favorite chair, a recliner that he'd set in front of the fireplace. He always had a fire burning, even on hot summer nights. Fire was everything. It was comforting like an old friend, beautiful and mysterious like a woman, and it was dangerous and powerful like himself.

After a few minutes, he leaned forward, reached into the fireplace, and took out a chunk of log that had broken off from the rest. He held it in his palm, watching the flames flickering up and down. It didn't burn him. That was just one of the benefits he'd inherited from his dragon lord ancestors. When they'd added dragon DNA to their own, their skin had become fire resistant. The heat was nothing more than a tingle against his skin; the soft lick of a pet for its master.

He turned the piece of wood over in his hand as he considered his upcoming guests. He hadn't wanted to fight them yet, and certainly not at his home. It complicated things. If any of the children were killed here, there were bound to be investigations. Questions. People prying into his affairs. It was best to avoid that if he could.

Neutralization, not annihilation had always been his plan for the Slayers. If a few of them died anyway . . . well, sometimes promises had to be broken.

Brant tossed the log chunk back into the fire, and it rejoined the other flames. After a few minutes, he got up and walked outside to his porch, restlessly walking its length while the humid summer air encircled him. The enclosure stood before him, every bit as much of a monument to his life's work as the Great Pyramids were to the pharaohs in Egypt. The vets called it a cathedral when they didn't think he was listening. He wouldn't admit it to them, but he liked the name. He'd taken to calling it that himself lately.

The walls were not only thirty inches thick, they were made with steel-plated, reinforced concrete in order to keep the dragons' signal from leaking out. Otherwise, he'd have to worry about every pregnant woman in the vicinity. Any of them could be a descendant of a dragon knight. He'd be overrun with superheroes before the dragons could fulfill their purpose.

The habitat had taken a year to complete and more than five million dollars to build—and that wasn't including the city regulators he'd had to bribe to get past the building codes. For one tedious year, he had overseen the project. He'd built it three stories above ground and nearly two beneath to give the dragons room to stretch and fly. He'd brought in five thousand tons of dirt to cover the cement floor so the inside of the building could be landscaped with trees and bushes. He'd plumbed the place for ponds, he'd tested and retested the venting, cooling, and heating systems. He'd built a temporary runway so he could fly a private plane from St. Helena right to his property. Before he so much as moved one egg here, he wanted the place to be perfect.

Unfortunately, the flight from St. Helena hadn't been. He'd charted a private plane and packed the eggs with only Styrofoam to protect them from jarring. Putting the eggs in steel-reinforced cement boxes would have made the load too heavy. The plan had been to land on the property and immediately transfer everything into the habitat.

But an unforeseen rainstorm kept them from landing. They'd circled blindly in the air, waiting for the weather to clear. When it hadn't, the pilot had to make a forced landing at BMI to refuel.

For two hours they'd been on the ground—and in range of thousands of women. And at least eleven of them had been both pregnant and descended from the dragon knights.

Soon he would have a reunion with most of those children.

 CHAPTER 31

After the planning session ended, Jesse took Tori to the rifle range and showed her how to use the tranquilizer gun. He was glad for the extra time alone with her. While she impaled targets, he stood next to her, automatically analyzing her shots. Several times he stopped her, stood so that he peered over her shoulder, then put his hand on top of hers to gently correct her aim. It was important she get it right. He wasn't correcting her because he liked holding her hand and standing so close that he could smell her shampoo . . . which was something floral-ish and had probably cost enough to feed a family for a week.

Tori missed two moving long shots in a row, and she glanced over at him. "Why aren't you criticizing me?"

"Because you're doing your best."

She lowered her arm, letting the gun sag in her hand. Her green eyes widened with worry. "You think you're going to die tonight, don't you? You're making sure you don't say anything you'll regret before-hand."

He fought a smile and a twinge of guilt. "I can be nice, you know."

She tilted her head, unconvinced.

"I am frequently a very supportive team captain," he said. "You just haven't been here long enough to realize that."

She turned back to the target and shot the close-range moving target perfectly.

"Good job," he said.

Her gaze slid back to him with a coy arch of her eyebrow. "Now you're making fun of me."

"I'm not," he said. "You happen to be good at close range."

She went back to the targets, but found time between shots to send him sly looks. "Did Dr. B tell you to compliment me?"

Maybe he deserved her skepticism. He'd been hard on her yesterday. But somehow, seeing the hole she'd knocked through the tech office window had changed his opinion of her. She might be untrained, she might have had her doubts about joining them, but her heart was in the right place. And she also had some serious potential as a fighter. She had leaped almost fifteen feet and knocked in a supposedly unbreakable window. Not bad for day three.

Jesse gave her a smile. "You're just easy to compliment."

"Oh, really?" Her voice turned teasing and she took a step closer. "In that case, what do you think of my hair?"

He nearly coughed, because he'd been admiring her hair and he wondered if she knew. Had she caught him sniffing it?

"See?" she said when he didn't answer. "You're still mad I went into town."

He let out a relieved breath. She didn't know. "I think your hair is very pretty. Brandi and her pink salon did a great job."

"Mmm-hmm." She hit the middle of another target. "What do you think of my luggage?"

"Your luggage is very . . . sturdy."

She smiled. "My outfits?"

"Plentiful and flattering."

"Something they have in common with your comments suddenly. My eyes?"

"Gorgeous." He meant it.

"My archery scores?"

"Those still stink."

She laughed and managed to hit the closest moving target dead center. "At least you're being honest about one opinion."

"I'm being honest about them all." *Especially the part about her eyes.* He held up his hand, a conciliatory gesture. "I admit I've been hard on you. When you left camp, I took it personally." He dropped his hand, but kept his eyes on hers. "I found out I was a Slayer when I was eleven years old. Half the time I thought I was the coolest thing since Wolverine. The rest of the time I was scared to death. I guess I forgot about that. I forgot how much we're suddenly asking of you."

He paused, waiting to say the next part right. "When I walked into the Dragon Hall today, and I saw what you'd done—well, you're one of us. I'm glad to have you on my team."

Her eyes warmed. "And I'm glad to be on your team, Jesse."

She turned her attention back to the targets, but there was an ease in her motions now, a happiness.

They went on talking for another half an hour, the conversation flowing effortlessly, until Jesse had to go help pack the van. As he turned to leave, Tori took hold of his hand. "Thanks for this," she said.

He smiled at her. He knew what she meant. "Sure," he said.

She didn't let go of his hand, didn't break their gaze. "Be careful tonight."

"I will."

She still didn't let go of his hand. He could see the worry in her expression.

"I'll be all right." He gave her hand a squeeze. "We're trained. We know what to do."

She sighed reluctantly and let her fingers drop away from his. "Okay."

After he left, and even while he hauled things into the van, he still felt the impression of her hand holding tightly to his.

CHAPTER 32

Tori watched the night scenery flash by while the other Slayers went over contingency plans one more time. By the nonchalant tones of their voices, it sounded more like they were on their way to a school dance instead of a high-security break-in. If it hadn't been for Kody, who kept flexing his arms like he was warming up for a boxing match, she wouldn't have thought anyone's tension was skyrocketing except for hers.

The fifteen-passenger van held not only the Slayers but also their weapons, the surveillance equipment, a computer, and several monitors. The simulator rode in a small trailer hitched to the fender. Booker followed them in another van. He had taken the seats out in order to carry some of the motorcycles and he pulled a trailer that carried the rest.

It was after midnight when they stopped on the street that led to Overdrake's compound. They pulled off the road and parked where the trees hid them from view.

Before climbing out, the Slayers pulled on black ski masks. The change in their appearances was immediate and frightening. The cutouts around their eyes gave everyone a hollow, ugly appearance.

Next, Tori put on her bulletproof jacket and helmet. She and the other girls tucked their hair into their ski masks, which made them nearly indistinguishable from the guys. The thick vests hid anything feminine about their bodies. Then Theo had them test their headsets, making sure the microphones, video feeds, and earpieces worked.

Tori got out of the van with the rest of the group. Booker handed her a .223 rifle and she was surprised that he also handed guns to Theo and Dr. B. Apparently everyone at camp was a trained marksman. She wondered why they needed her as a bodyguard at all, but then reasoned that Theo, Dr. B, and Booker would be busy studying the monitors and keeping track of the Slayers. With her keeping watch, they had one less thing to worry about.

She gingerly put her rifle into the sling on her back. The slings kept the rifles out of the way, but at a moment's notice, the guns could be flipped forward to use. Tori slipped her tranquilizer gun into the holster around her waist, then double-checked her vest pockets for ammo. The other slayers had various contraptions in their pockets to help them break in. She didn't know how to use most of them and wasn't supposed to leave the vicinity of the vans anyway.

Dr. B, she could tell, was nervous about letting her come. Back at camp, he'd made her practice shooting the tranquilizer gun until the group left for Winchester, and she was pretty sure he would have made her practice in the van if he could have.

Now his nervousness was directed toward his daughter. He gave her a pat on her shoulder as she checked her rifle. "Be careful," he said, and left his hand to linger on her shoulder.

"I've got that on my checklist," Bess told him.

He didn't let go of her shoulder. "I'm trying to think about the good of the nation right now, but as a father, I want to order you all back in the van and drive you as far away from this place as I can."

"We'll be okay," she said.

"I don't know how so many parents have done it—sent their children off to battle . . ."

Bess tugged at one of her gloves, adjusting it. "The eggs aren't armed, and Overdrake's men aren't expecting us. This will be easier than most of the drills you've put us through."

Dr. B leaned close and gave her a hug. In a low voice that Tori shouldn't have been able to hear, he said, "Your mother is at home pacing the floor and won't stop until you come back to camp."

Bess gave him a quick hug back. "I'll be fine."

Jesse motioned to Bess and Dirk. "Time to go pay Mr. Smith a visit."

The three of them jogged down the street, keeping their heads low to stay behind the bushes that grew on the side of the road. The rest of the Slayers—except for Tori—followed a few yards behind, pushing the motorcycles so they didn't make any noise.

After Jesse flew over and checked out the defenses, he would come back to fly Bess over the fence while Dirk jumped over. Once the guards were tranquilized and the gate was open, Shang, Kody, Lilly, Alyssa, and Rosa would ride the motorcycles into the compound. They'd pick up Bess and Dirk, take out any other guards in the area, then head to the enclosure.

Alyssa and Rosa would wait at the gate to make sure it stayed open. If Overdrake's men counterattacked and Alyssa and Rosa couldn't keep the gate open, then Jesse would have to fly the Slayers over the fence one by one. Only Dirk could leap over it on his own. Tori didn't like to think about that possibility. It would take Jesse too long. And one of the last things Dr. B had said to the group before they left was that part of any mission was knowing when to cut losses.

Losses. Had he meant lives?

What if you succeeded in destroying the eggs, Dr. B had asked them during the meeting about Overdrake's compound, *but one of you died in the process—would you still think an attack was the right thing to do?*

Now the phrase kept running through Tori's mind like a bad omen.

Eventually Jesse's voice came over the radio in a hushed whisper, "I'm over the property. No one's in any of the trees. Guards are patrolling the fence at the three and nine o'clock position. This shouldn't be too hard." A minute later he whispered, "There's only one guard by the enclosure's door. I'll take care of him, then come back for Bess."

Silence filled the feed for several moments, then Jesse's voice came again. "Direct hit into the neck. He should be out soon."

The radios went quiet.

Tori made a loop around the vans, checking for any unusual motion in the trees around her. Nothing. She made another loop. She couldn't stand still. The knit ski mask itched against her face. She tried to scratch her cheek without jiggling her helmet.

It occurred to her in a detached sort of way that some kids sent postcards from summer camps. She imagined writing one to her friends.

> Camp is a blast. I'll be spending my third night here helping my bunkmates break into a dangerous, high-security compound. I hope we don't suffer any fatalities. How's your summer going?

A hissing sound filled Tori's ear and Dirk said, "Direct hit to the security booth. We'll see if the smoke bomb does the trick."

Tori made another loop around the van. She didn't see anything out of the ordinary, so she peered inside the van's window, trying to catch sight of the monitor screens. One showed smoke billowing from the guard station. A man pushed through it, waving his hands at the clouds of smoke. *C'mon, Dirk*, Tori thought. *Shoot the guy so he can't alert anybody.*

Before she saw if Dirk did, she pulled herself away from the window and made another circular sweep of the area. Guarding the van had to be her first priority. It was an easy job and she would never live it down if she messed up.

A couple minutes later, Kody said, "The gate is open. We're going in." The sounds of their motorcycles purred in her earpiece. She was glad Dr. B had the foresight to buy ones that weren't noisy.

Not long after that, Alyssa added, "We're in place."

Dirk's voice came on the line. "I'll take out the guard positioned at nine o'clock."

Jesse said, "Bess, take Rosa's bike and get the guard at three o'clock. Everybody else, head to the enclosure with me."

No one spoke for a few minutes. Tori fingered her tranquilizer gun and scanned the trees on either side of the road.

Finally, Dirk's voice came over the radio. "I haven't seen the guard who's supposed to be at the three o'clock position and— oh, wait—" His voice broke off, and Tori's stomach clenched.

Was that a *good* "oh, wait," or a *bad* "oh, wait"?

After what seemed like a long time, Dirk said, "I got him. I'm waiting to make sure he goes down, and then I'll head to my guard post."

Jesse's voice came over the radio. "Bess, what's your situation?"

"Same as always—I'm chasing after men who don't know I exist."

"Have you seen your guard?"

"Yeah, and he's way too old for me. Plus, he just went unconscious—those are big turnoffs for me."

"Head toward the enclosure."

"I'm not far away. Don't start the party without me."

The line went quiet for an annoyingly long time. Tori kept making slow circles around the vans. No other cars came by. It was going as they'd planned, and yet Tori was a bundle of nerves.

Tori looked inside the van window to check on Dr. B. He was leaning back in his seat, staring at the monitors calmly. *Calmly.* She had no idea how he managed that. Or for that matter, how any of the Slayers managed it. Bess had been cracking jokes.

Maybe Jesse had been right when he'd yelled at her after she'd gone to Hollings. Maybe she wasn't as brave as the rest of them. Or maybe she was just smarter, because—hello—did the rest of them not realize what could happen when you broke into a place where everyone carried loaded guns?

Dirk's voice came over the radio. "I'm up the tree—there's a very nice platform up here with a swivel telescope in case we forgot our binoculars. A very considerate host, Mr. Smith. The men are still on the ground where we left them. I don't see any new ones approaching. Right now, I'd say my stint at guard duty is uneventful."

"Great," Jesse said. "Kody's got the guard's hand on the door control panel—we're going into the enclosure."

Dr. B chimed in for the first time. "Tell me what you see, especially if there's anything unusual. The quality of the video feed isn't very good in the dark."

Jesse said, "We're in an outer room. There's a circular staircase that leads up to the roof and a huge sliding door ahead. It's wide open, so we don't have to mess with the control panel."

Lilly said, "The walls are superthick, like two feet, and they're made of some weird concrete."

Multiple voices came on the line, most of them saying things like, "Wow," and "Unbelievable."

Kody said, "It's like a park in here. Trees, boulders, and a mess of bushes. There's even some ponds over yonder."

Shang said, "The floor juts down from where we're standing and then slopes down even farther. The bottom is underground and there are no other floors above us. I guess dragons need a lot of room. We're going down the stairs now. It will take a few minutes."

Judging from the pictures Tori had seen of the building, it was three stories high. It must be huge inside.

Bess said, "I caught up with the others. Let the good times roll."

Tori strode around the vans with quick, deliberate steps. *Just do what you have to and get out*, she thought.

"Those must be the eggs," Kody finally said. "They're sitting over there in that cement nest thing."

Another minute passed. "They look like they're made of solid stone," Jesse said, and a tapping noise indicated he hit one.

Which is when Tori realized something was very wrong.

CHAPTER 33

"Jesse," she said into her mouthpiece. "I don't hear you."

"I'm fine," he said, then added, "Theo, check Tori's radio."

"No, Jesse." She tried to push away the panic that clawed at her. "I hear *you*, and I hear a *dragon egg*, but you're not in the same place."

"Do you hear this?" he asked. A smack sounded in her earpiece. He'd hit something, probably the stone eggs, but the dragon's heartbeat went on beating in the silence that surrounded it.

"Those aren't the eggs." Tori's words tumbled over each other in their hurry. "It's some sort of a trap. You have to get out of there."

Kody sounded indignant. "We didn't come all of this way to leave these—"

But Lilly cut him off, "Up there—the doors are closing!"

Someone swore. Tori stopped pacing around the van and looked toward the property as though she could see something if she strained hard enough. After a few moments, someone let out a sound halfway between a grunt and growl. Inside the van, Dr. B stood up. "What's happening?"

"The doors slid shut," Lilly said. "Jesse tried to keep them open until we could get to them and nearly got smashed."

"Break them open," Dr. B said. "You've got the jackhammer with you."

Jesse didn't answer. Another voice came over the line—not one connected to their radios—but one coming from a speaker inside the dragon enclosure.

"Welcome, Slayers," a man said. He had the same sort of almost-British accent that Dr. B had. Only it was thicker, more pronounced. It had to be Overdrake. "Or perhaps I should say, welcome Dirk, Kody, Lilly, Alyssa, Jesse, Shang, Bess, and Rosa."

A cold dread spread through Tori. Overdrake knew who they were. Had he tapped into their radio transmissions? No, that couldn't be it. They hadn't used their names while they were talking. Besides, he hadn't called her name, and Jesse had said it over the radio just a few moments before.

"You wanted to take something away from me tonight," Overdrake said. "Something I care a great deal about. You won't blame me if I return the favor."

"Dirk," Dr. B said, "What's going on outside of the enclosure. Do you see reinforcements?"

"No—wait, yes. A bunch of men on motorcycles came out of the barn—looks like about fifteen. I think they're heading to the gate."

"Take out as many as you can," Dr. B said, "then follow defense procedure two. Alyssa and Rosa, keep the gate open."

Tori didn't know anything about defense procedure two, but she knew the goal of this mission had suddenly and drastically changed. Now they were just trying to get everyone out alive. Her mind raced in that direction. Only Rosa, Alyssa, and Dirk were outside of the enclosure. How could three of them fight off Overdrake's men and free the other Slayers from the enclosure?

They needed Tori's help.

She didn't move.

Without trying to, her mind ran through a list of reasons why rushing into the compound was a bad idea: She hadn't trained with the others. She didn't know how to fight armed men. Jesse and Dr. B had both told her to stay at the van. It was foolish to go in, dangerous.

You're a coward, she told herself. *You care more about protecting yourself than helping others.* Overdrake was right about people. Only heroes and stupid people rushed into hazardous places. Everyone else avoided them.

She sighed and ran to Booker's trailer, where a couple of extra motorcycles waited. She climbed onto one, hoping she was being heroic and not stupid, then spoke into her neck mike. "I'm going to help them."

She turned the ignition, hit the kickstand, and rocketed down the ramp.

Dr. B didn't answer her, perhaps because Overdrake spoke again.

". . . the walls are made to keep full-grown dragons inside, I'm afraid you're not going to be able to break through them, even with your jackhammer. And I've moved the eggs. They're safely out of your reach."

Tori thought of the familiar humming sound she'd heard around the eggs earlier. Now she realized what it was. The sound of a truck driving down the road. Why hadn't she figured it out before? She should have known the eggs had been moved.

Overdrake went on, "Now that you've found me, I'm faced with the choice of relocating everything or getting rid of you. You forced me into this, remember that. It wasn't my choice to destroy you. I don't enjoy doing it." Tori didn't detect any regret in his voice. He sounded chiding, like a teacher who'd caught a student cheating on a test.

"That hissing sound you hear—well, perhaps you can't hear it. If Tori were with you, she'd be able to pinpoint it, but you left her behind, so you'll just have to take my word. It's dimethyl ether coming through one of the air vents."

Tori jolted. How had Overdrake known about her hearing? What else did he know? "I've added a few other drugs for good measure," he went on. "You'll be unconscious soon, and I don't need to tell you what happens to your powers then." He gave a small, chilling laugh. "Of course, your powers will be gone in half an hour anyway. The simulator signal from your van can't penetrate these walls."

Jesse had taken off his mouthpiece, but even though he whispered, Tori still heard his voice through the other radios. "Ether is flammable. We need to find every vent in here. Kody, you shoot fire at them. Bess, throw a forcefield at the one that's not pumping air."

Kody's voice came over the radio, ragged with anger. "How did he know we were coming? Who tipped him off?"

A sharp jab of regret twisted in Tori's stomach. She had told Dr. B about this place. Did everyone think she'd betrayed them? She was the newest Slayer, the unknown. It stood to reason they would suspect her first.

Tori pressed down on the gas pedal. Helping the Slayers escape would prove it wasn't her fault.

She drove past Rosa and Alyssa at the gate and kept on going. Tori was afraid if she stopped and tried to coordinate a plan, they might tell her to go back to the van. So she would head toward Overdrake's men and try to take out as many as she could before they got to the gate. Since her motorcycle hardly made any noise and the headlight was off, Overdrake's men would have a hard time seeing her.

"I wish I could tell you that you'd been worthy opponents," Overdrake droned on, "but you've been pathetically easy to capture." He let out a content sigh. "Now I've got to see to your compatriots outside the cathedral. They're all visible through my cameras."

"If you can see me," Dirk said, "I have something to show you."

Tori imagined but didn't ask if Dirk was giving Overdrake the finger. She didn't have time to talk. Men were coming her way. The buzz of their motorcycles grew louder.

A light pole up ahead was making her an easy target.

That had to go. She swung her rifle into position, aimed, and shot. With an offended crack, the light extinguished. "Dirk, take out any lights you see," she said into her mouthpiece, then drove to the right, out of the motorcycles' path. She made a sharp turn and stopped her bike so she could shoot them from the side.

The motorcycles came into view, their headlight beams bouncing in front of them. Perhaps twelve bikes in all.

On the way up, Dr. B had reminded the group they couldn't shoot moving tires. Something about the physics of spinning objects. Tori aimed for the lead motorcycle's engine block, fired a couple of times, then set two more motorcycles in her sight and did the same.

For a few moments, she thought the bullets hadn't penetrated the engine blocks. All the motorcycles kept going. Then one of the motorcycle spun out, crashing into the bike behind it. The sound of metal clanged angrily, and the bikes thudded to the ground. Another motorcycle skidded right, out of control, and fell spinning on its side. A fourth bike simply slowed to a stop while its rider kicked at the gas pedal. The rest of the motorcycles swerved around the downed bikes and kept heading toward the gate.

Well, she'd given Rosa and Alyssa four less bikes to deal with.

No, make that seven, because three of the bikes had turned around. She was silhouetted in the glare of their headlights and they were coming after her.

She stepped on the gas, zooming away from them. The barn was the best cover around so she headed in that direction. Bullets hissed past her. One, she could tell, hit the back of her Kevlar jacket.

She didn't return fire. Instead, she shot out every lamppost she drove by. The darker it was, the better chance she had of losing her pursuers.

In her mind, she ran through all the possible outcomes of this chase. If she drove to the gate, she would run into more of Overdrake's men, but how long could she drive around the property? The men chasing her would keep shooting, and their bullets might find a place not protected by Kevlar. Or they might disable her bike. With her extra strength, she could beat one, maybe two men in hand-to-hand combat—but three? And they could be radioing to more men right now, setting up an ambush. She needed to disable their motorcycles before any more showed up.

Tori rounded the side of the barn and turned in her seat, aiming the rifle backward over her shoulder. As soon as the men turned the corner, she shot out each of their headlights. With those gone, they wouldn't be able to follow her for long.

She turned back around to see a couple of wooden posts up ahead, one on either side of her. If she had realized what they were, she could have swerved her bike in time, or even tried to jump over them. But she was concentrating on the men behind her so intently that she didn't question why random wooden posts were sticking up from the ground five feet away from one another. She was already making plans to lose the men and double back on them.

By the time she saw the wires stretched between the posts and realized it was part of a fence, it was too late. Her motorcycle slammed into the wires. Metal and wood let out a screech of protest and a section of fence wrapped around her bike, holding it back, while she flew over the top of her handlebars. She tumbled onto the pasture in front of her, gasping.

The sting of hitting the ground didn't hurt nearly as badly as her frustration. She had run into a fence. A fence.

In her earpiece, Dr. B said, "Tori, are you all right?"

She didn't answer. It took her a moment to catch her breath, and by then she saw the three men who'd been chasing her. They'd heard the crash and were off their bikes looking for her. And they weren't that far away. Each held a rifle with the precision of a soldier and each took a flashlight from his belt.

That wasn't good.

Tori's bike was tangled in the remains of wire and posts. The only advantage she had right now was that the men couldn't see her.

She rolled onto her stomach, pulled her rifle into position, and prayed the fall hadn't damaged her weapons. She fired at the closest man's flashlight. The gun worked perfectly and the flashlight exploded out of his hand. She aimed and shot the next and the next, turning them all into plastic shrapnel.

Two men grabbed their hands and let out streams of curse words that were occasionally peppered with the words "sniper," "Slayer," and the phrase "I'll kill you." The other man just shook his hand and kept looking around.

Into her earpiece, Dirk whispered, "Tori, are you okay?"

She didn't answer, couldn't risk speaking. The men were too close and she was crawling as quietly as she could away from her downed motorcycle. The man nearest Tori stopped shaking his hand and held his rifle out again. He took a few tentative steps forward.

"Where are you?" the man asked in a breathless, angry voice.

Tori pulled out her tranquilizer gun.

The men wore helmets that protected their faces, and body armor that protected just about everywhere else. It didn't leave much in the way of an accessible target. A small space on their throats between their collars and helmets was her best bet.

She aimed the tranquilizer at the closest man and shot. He slapped his hand against his throat—a good indication she'd hit her mark—then he let out a yell and riddled the ground to her side with bullets.

Tori flinched at the noise of the bullets, but didn't move away. She was too busy searching for vulnerable spots on the other two men. Unfortunately, both tilted their chins down, guarding the skin on their throats. With their rifles still pointed in front of them, the men turned this way and that, looking for her.

She couldn't let them find her.

 **CHAPTER 34**

Gunshots sounded through Dirk's earpiece and he stopped at the base of the tree he'd just climbed down. "Tori?" he whispered.

No response.

Dirk turned his back on the dragon habitat, scanning the grounds for any sign of her. "Dr. B, do you have video on Tori? I heard gunshots."

"She was behind the barn," Dr. B said. "There was some movement on her camera a minute ago, but her feed is black now."

The pain that had eaten away at Dirk's stomach all day intensified. Things weren't supposed to turn out this way. His dad had promised that none of the Slayers would get hurt during this operation. Apparently his father hadn't emphasized this point to his guards, though, or perhaps he had never meant it to begin with. He'd gotten Dirk's cooperation, and that's what mattered to him.

Dirk briefly wondered if his father had lied about his other promises, too. He had said that when the dragons attacked D.C., he would keep civilian deaths to a minimum. He would only use the dragon's EMP to take out the infrastructure. No ripping through crowds of people. No needless death.

Had his father meant any of it? Dirk wanted to yell, to demand an explanation. His dad would hear. He had been monitoring their communications on a specially tuned earpiece since they'd arrived. But Dirk couldn't say anything, couldn't let the Slayers know he was the dragon lord's son.

Dirk gripped his rifle strap and whispered, "Tori better not be shot."

Dr. B's voice was soft but firm. "She made the choice to go in. Concentrate on defense plan two. We'll get to Tori later if she needs help."

The words, spoken with so much trust, such earnestness, cut through Dirk. Anything that anyone said today had stabbed at him. He could barely function. He gritted his teeth and looked toward the barn, as though he might spot Tori somewhere in the distance.

Only the empty field spread out in front of him.

Dirk had read Dante's Inferno once. It said that in the center-most part of hell, the devil chewed on traitors. But Dante was wrong. A person didn't have to die before hell gnawed away at them.

Dirk climbed onto his bike, hesitating as he turned the ignition. He wanted to head to the barn and look for Tori. He couldn't do it, though. Dr. B could see what he was doing on the video camera.

In the background of his radio feed, Jesse and the Slayers talked to one another—his teammates, his friends. They were trying to figure a way out of the enclosure. There wasn't one, and even though Dirk had known it would happen, had let it happen to them, a piece of him was inside with them, dying.

He never should have let his dad send him to camp all those years ago to infiltrate their numbers. He shouldn't have learned the Slayers' names, seen their faces, grown to care about them. Or found his counterpart.

Each summer at camp he became one of them, and days would pass when he forgot altogether that he was Brant Overdrake's son, that he'd been sent to spy on them.

His father should have never asked Dirk to take part in this trap.

Dirk spent one last moment peering out into the muted gray landscape of the night. Was Tori alive and hiding or was she lying on the ground unconscious and bleeding? He cursed under his breath, then turned his motorcycle toward the habitat.

He told himself she wasn't dead. He would have felt it if she was. His counterpart connection would have told him. He clung to that thought, unsure if it was true, but repeating it in his mind anyway.

The fact that he had a counterpart still amazed him. As much as he tried to figure it out, it made no sense. How had a dragon lord ended up with a Slayer counterpart? It shouldn't have happened, and yet it had.

Was it some unknown variable in her genetics or in his?

The dragon lords had always preserved their records so that their descendants would understand their powers and know how to take care of the dragons. But the Slayers' ancestors hadn't kept many records, which was why Dr. B had needed to study so many different sources to piece together his information. It was why Dr. B's knowledge of dragon lords was spotty at best.

Another jab of guilt pierced into Dirk. It had been too easy to deceive everyone. Dr. B hadn't realized that some of a dragon lord's powers were the same as the Slayers'; that a child who came to camp with night vision and extra strength wasn't necessarily a Slayer. And Dirk's ability to see what a dragon saw was easy enough since he could slip into a dragon's mind.

But hearing what a dragon heard—Dirk hadn't known such an ability existed on either Slayer or dragon lord spectrum.

It had certainly jeopardized his father's location quickly enough, though.

Dirk wanted a chance to figure Tori out, to figure Tori and himself out, and instead here he was, listening to see if she was alive.

Dirk came to the enclosure entrance and turned off his bike. He had to go through the necessary motions so they would be recorded on the video feed. In his earpiece, Bess was reporting to Dr. B about their attempts to break through the enclosure door. Her voice wavered with fear. Bess had always been his willing partner in pranks. And Dirk had done this to her, betrayed her.

"The ends justify the means," his father liked to say. As Dirk got off his bike and rolled it toward the door, he concentrated on the place America would become. A new era. Tighter laws and harsher consequences for criminals. All the nonsense in government dissolved. Like the nation's debts. Other countries wouldn't try to collect once his father ruled. They wouldn't risk provoking an EMP attack. The country could become more prosperous and more powerful than it had ever been.

Dirk leaned his bike against the first doorway, keeping his mind on the future. When people realized society was better off, they'd welcome the change in rulers. His family would be appreciated, honored, and they'd live in a mansion somewhere overlooking the sea. In Dirk's mind, he had seen himself standing on his balcony a thousand times. Every night he would watch the sun set over the waves.

And if he didn't like anything that his father did, well, eventually his father would be too old to rule, and then it would be Dirk's responsibility. He could remake society into anything he liked. How many people in the world ever got that type of opportunity?

All he needed to do was make it through tonight.

And sacrifice his friends' trust in him.

Dirk took hold of the unconscious guard's arm and dragged him to the second door. Once there, he held the guard's hand up to the panel as though checking to see if his fingerprints would unlock the door.

As hard as Dirk tried to concentrate on the new era—on the waves, and the balcony—his mind spun like a severed wheel, lurching, reeling, thinking of the things that wouldn't be after tonight: The long days at camp, jumping through the trees at practice, talking with Jesse like the two of them were brothers.

Into his neck mike, Dirk said, "The guard's fingerprints don't unlock the second door. I'm trying his retina."

With shaking hands, he hauled the guard's head to the panel.

Snap out of it, Dirk told himself. This is the best possible outcome. If his friends' powers were taken away, if their memories were changed, they could go back to their old lives, neutralized, but not hurt. It was so much better than having to fight them later, having to turn the dragons on them.

His father could only mind-link to one dragon at a time, so when it came time to bring down D.C., Dirk would have to control the other dragon. Dirk had always known this. Some of his earliest memories were of his father carrying him into the enclosure and showing him the dragons. Instead of bedtime stories, his father had told him about all the things in society that needed to be fixed, and how he planned to fix them.

When a retinal scan on the guard clearly hadn't worked, Dirk laid him back on the ground.

In half an hour, the only Slayers left with any powers would be Rosa and Alyssa. Two healers. They wouldn't be much of a threat.

And Tori.

He had selfishly been glad she wouldn't be a part of this, wouldn't forget him. It meant they could have more time together. She wouldn't even feel the crushing despair of losing the others. She hardly knew them. Not like he did.

Dirk pulled the control panel lid off the wall with his bare hands and tossed it onto the floor. "Let's see if we can hotwire this thing."

Before he finished speaking, the outside door slammed into the motorcycle he'd left in the doorway. He'd known it would happen. It was a waste of a good motorcycle.

"What happened?" Theo asked, his voice high-pitched with worry.

Dirk didn't answer until he'd squeezed out the door. He barely made it through the space before the force from the wall compressed the motorcycle to the point that the space became unpassable. "Something triggered the first door to close. I made it out, though." He forced some humor into his voice. "That's why you should always prop doors open with bikes, even if it does make them hard to ride afterward."

Over his earpiece he heard the distant sound of men yelling to find the sniper. They hadn't caught Tori yet.

Then he heard more gunfire. The sound of each bullet punctured him. They were trying to kill her, and this after he'd told his father that he liked her, that she was his counterpart, that they'd kissed.

At that moment, something swung around inside his mind. As his anger built, the new era dissolved like frost in the sunlight. His father had broken his side of the bargain, and Dirk wasn't keeping his side, either. At least for tonight, he was fighting his way out of hell.

# CHAPTER 35

Tori lay flat on the ground. The man she'd shot with the tranquilizer gun had already collapsed not far from her. She had heard Dirk call her name and Dr. B report that her video feed was black. It was black because she was lying on her stomach and it was pointed at the dirt. She couldn't answer Dirk, though, not while the men were this near. She wished the Slayers would stop talking. It was hard to concentrate on finding vulnerable spots on the remaining men with so much background noise filling her ears.

Rosa said, "We've got company." Then the buzz of the motorcycles came through her earpiece. Overdrake's men had reached the gate. Gunshots crackled over the feed.

Rosa and Alyssa—they hadn't even wanted to do this and now the two of them had to face armed gunmen. Tori slowly reached for the controls in her pocket so she could turn off her radio feed. She couldn't let any of the sounds from her earpiece alert the gunmen to her position.

One of the men yelled, "I see him!"

Tori braced herself. If they found and killed her, her family would never know the truth about what happened. Should she get up and make a run for it?

But the man didn't point his gun at her. He turned in the opposite direction and sprayed bullets into her motorcycle. It clanged in protest.

Tori finished turning off her radio.

"You idiot!" the second man yelled. "Next you'll be blasting the cows!"

The first man looked at the bike like he'd like to kick it, and while he stared down, a patch on the back of his neck became visible. She shot it with the tranquilizer.

The man grabbed his neck, clawing the dart off. "I'm hit!" He spun around and let off a round of bullets, waist high, sweeping above Tori.

"Stop it!" the second man screamed. "I'll get him." He took a step toward Tori, his hand outstretched, gripping his rifle. Then he took another step. He tugged his jacket collar up and kept his head down so no part of his neck was visible. She couldn't get a clear shot on him—and he was walking right toward her. "Why are you using that dart gun?" he asked. "You ran out of bullets, didn't you?"

She hadn't, but she didn't want to use the rifle. It would change her, she knew, to kill a person. She lay unmoving and tried not to breathe too loudly.

He was nearly on top of her. A few more steps, and he'd kick her.

But with his hand stretched out, the sleeve of his jacket shrank back to expose a layer of skin between his glove and sleeve. She took aim at his wrist and shot. The dart silently pierced its target. In sixty seconds he would be down.

The man jerked his hand back at the sting, yelled, then charged forward. She was just able to sweep her foot around and knock him down before he ran into her. As he crashed to the ground, his grip on his gun loosened. She grabbed hold of it and flung it away. It clattered across the ground far to her right.

Her movement had given away her position. The man plunged into her. For a moment he was on top of her, reeking of old cigarette smoke and sweat. But it was only for a moment. She pushed him off and he tumbled over twice and sprawled out on the grass. She jumped to her feet, hands in defense position, watching him. Before he could pull himself up, a kick to his chest sent him down again.

She moved away, still counting off the seconds in her mind.

Forty-nine . . . fifty . . . fifty-one . . .

"We'll feed your carcass to the dragons!" he shouted.

Fifty-four . . . fifty-five . . . fifty-six . . .

He staggered to his feet, swung one arm out uselessly, and yelled more threats. Dirk wouldn't need her to report her location. He could just listen to this guy and hone in on her position from there.

That was, if Dirk was still alive. Anything could have happened while she'd had her earpiece turned off. What if she was alone now?

The man called for backup, his words slurring until they were un-recognizable. Then he sank to the ground and didn't get up.

Tori turned her earpiece back on. Voices from the enclosure as well as the muted sound of the jackhammer thudded in her ear. She supposed the captains had some sort of protocol for figuring out who to help when two different groups were in need, but she didn't ask. Rosa and Alyssa would have to manage on their own. She was going to the enclosure.

She ran over to the spot where the men had left their motorcycles and climbed on one. It revved to life, noisier than one of Dr. B's motor-cycles, but it would have to do.

As she pointed the bike toward the enclosure, she asked, "What's everybody's status?"

"Rosa and Alyssa were forced off the grounds, but they're with me," Dr. B said. "Overdrake's men have shut the gate. We've moved the vans farther out of range, but no one has come after us yet. We're working on a way to get Rosa and Alyssa back over the fence to help the others."

Tori leaned forward on the bike, urging the motorcycle to go faster.

Jesse's voice came over the radio, still answering her question. "Bess is blocking the vent. We tried digging our way out and hit concrete in three different places. We think the entire floor is concrete with dirt and plants added on top. There's a steel wall in the back of the enclosure. We can't hammer our way through it, though, and we think it's just a partition; a way for Overdrake to separate the dragons. Even if we got through it, we'd probably be trapped on the other side. If that isn't enough bad news for you, we've found some suspicious footprints in here—huge ones with claw marks. They might be a dragon's."

"A dragon?" Tori repeated. "A full-grown one?"

"That's what it looks like. Overdrake has obviously moved it out of here for now. I don't want to think about what he'll do when we're drugged and unconscious." Jesse's voice grew quieter. "We have twelve minutes left until our powers fade and the drugs overcome Bess's force field."

A dragon. An adult one. Maybe somewhere nearby. Tori's hands felt clammy inside her gloves. She passed another lamppost and slowed down to shoot it out. "There's got to be another way out of the enclosure."

"We couldn't find any other doors in this place," Jesse said wearily. "We checked."

But that didn't make sense. "How did Overdrake get a dragon out of there?" she asked. "They don't fit out a normal-size door."

"The enclosure door is big enough," Jesse said to himself, "but you're right. A dragon wouldn't use a door. It would fly out. I'll check the ceiling."

Tori was nearly to the enclosure, but didn't tell Jesse. It was better not to broadcast her location. Dirk hadn't been able to get through the front door, but that didn't mean they couldn't break through the roof.

Since Overdrake used the trees as reconnaissance posts, one grew at each corner of the building. She rode to the nearest one, her gaze bouncing between the branches and the roof. The distance looked like less than fifteen feet, but she wasn't sure how close she could get to the building before the branches stopped holding her weight. Hopefully close enough. She parked her motorcycle underneath the tree, then climbed onto the makeshift ladder nailed to its trunk. As she climbed higher, she saw a pair of black shoes standing on the platform. She froze, unsure whether to hurry down the tree or jump up and fight. Before she could decide, a gloved hand reached down for her.

CHAPTER 36

Tori's heart stopped, her logic racing ahead of her intuition. But the next moment she knew it was Dirk, just like she'd known where he was when they'd talked together in the forest. She looked up at his darkened visor and could almost make out his blue eyes staring at her.

She put her hand in his and he effortlessly pulled her onto the platform. She felt better now that they were together. Safer. Dirk must have had the same idea: to see if he could leap from the tree branches onto the top of the enclosure.

Without saying a word, she climbed from the platform onto a large branch, then edged out toward the building. He followed her. "It's a long way down if you fall," he whispered.

She nodded. "I'll be careful."

Then, in what was clearly not the most careful thing she'd ever done, Tori took three running steps across the limb and leapt onto the roof. Before she could turn around, Dirk landed beside her.

She hadn't realized how big the building was until she stood on it. They could have held a football game up here and had plenty of room for bystanders. She walked along one length, examining it. The roof was made of metal and each step she took made a deep clanking sound. "Look at this seam," she said, following the line with her eyes. It seemed to go around the entire surface of the building. Another seam crossed through the middle. "It's a retractable roof. That's how the dragons get out."

She ran to the short end of the roof, not even caring how much racket her footsteps made. What she'd thought was a row of air-conditioning units were actually gears and motors. Behind them lay a shaft where the roof would slide down when it moved, but she couldn't find any sort of controls. She found a hatch door and tried the knob. It was locked.

Dirk came up behind her. "It won't do any good to break that down. It's the door to the stairs in the outer room."

Jesse said, "I've searched the ceiling. I can only see one seam. It's where the steel wall hits the roof . . ." He let out a grunt of effort. "I can't . . ." another grunt, "budge it."

Over the radio, Theo said, "The roof is probably controlled by remote, but they always make a manual override—either inside or outside the building. Look for a metal box."

Dirk walked to the other side of the gears. "I found it."

He knelt down and opened the box's lid to reveal a keypad and switch. He turned the switch. Nothing happened. "There's a number pad."

"Use your code breaker," Theo said.

With forced calm, Jesse said, "Six minutes."

Dirk took an electronic gadget from his vest, then turned to Tori. "I'll work on this; you patrol the roof for gunmen."

She nodded, and walked toward the long side of the roof. He called out after her, "If anyone starts shooting, get back here and stay behind me, do you understand?"

"I'm not going to use you as a human shield," she said.

His voice was clipped, intense. "Yes, you are. This isn't your fight."

But it was. She knew that now. No one had to convince or coddle her anymore. This fight was intertwined not just with her body but with her soul. "I'm an heir of the dragon knights, too," she said.

He glanced up from the box. "I'm giving you an order, Tori."

"And you're not my captain."

"I'm your counterpart, and I don't plan on losing you after one day. If things go bad, stay behind me." He turned his attention back to the box, his hand gripping the code breaker with fierce determination.

Over her earpiece, Jesse said, "I'm your captain, Tori, and I'm ordering you to do whatever Dirk says. Now if the two of you could get on with it, we have five minutes left until our powers fade and drugs shoot out of the vent at us."

Tori paced along the roof, looking out across the property at the picture-perfect barn and the large brick house that stood behind it. A light shone through one of the windows. Was Brant Overdrake in that room, or had he gone somewhere else? Did anyone live with him? Could such a person have a wife and children?

"Open up," Dirk muttered. Seconds later he called out, "I got the number."

The gears on the side of the building lurched and groaned. One side of the roof stayed put, but the other pulled back, making a slowly widening gap.

Tori stepped onto the stationary lip at the edge of the roof, an area about the size of a sidewalk. She hoped the right side of the roof was opening; if not, they would have to figure out how to open the other side.

As soon as the gap grew large enough to slip through, Jesse emerged. He carried a Slayer in his arms—judging from the size, Lilly—while another Slayer hung onto his back. Jesse deposited them onto the roof, then dived back into the enclosure.

Lilly walked to the corner of the roof, eyeing the distance. "How are we supposed to get down from here?"

Tori didn't answer; she'd spotted four motorcycles zooming away from the gate toward the enclosure. "Incoming," she said.

The other Slayer peered off the roof, and then Shang's voice said, "We've got company from the other side, too."

Tori turned. A jeep roared out of the house's garage. Two men, both clad in black, were coming toward the enclosure. One man drove, the other held a weapon so big it rested on his shoulder. It looked like some sort of rocket launcher.

Dirk took hold of Tori's arm. "We're sitting ducks up here. We'll have to jump the others to the tree." He motioned to Shang, "Get on my back. Lilly, you do the same with Tori. Once you're on the ground, Shang and Tori, you take one bike. Lilly, wait for Kody and take the second. I'll use Tori's motorcycle on the other side of the building."

Without waiting for a response, he squatted down so Shang could get a good grip on his back.

Tori did the same, but Lilly stared at the distance to the nearest branch. "Are you sure you can make it?"

"I made it over here," Tori said, but a lump of uncertainty caught in her throat. It was one thing to leap from a narrow, unstable branch onto a roof. It would be harder to jump from the roof onto a crooked, moving branch.

Dirk took a running jump off the roof and landed on a large tree limb. It swayed and bowed underneath his feet, but he didn't lose his balance. Shang slid from his back and disappeared into the foliage.

Lilly still didn't move. "You've never practiced jumping with another person on your back, so how do you know you can do it?"

"I don't," Tori said. "But we haven't got a lot of choices. The men are almost here."

Dirk jumped back to the roof at the same time Jesse emerged from the opening again. This time he carried Bess in his arms, and Kody held onto his back. It must have been hard to fly with that much weight. Jesse kept sinking over the roof and had to lift himself back into the air. Bess was nearly limp in his arms. "I'm fine," she told Jesse, answering some question Tori hadn't heard. "Or at least I will be now that the simulator signal can reach us again. It's just hard to hold a shield up for that long."

Jesse flew toward the edge of the building by Dirk. "I'll take Kody to the motorcycles, then fly Bess out. Once she's safe, I'll come back to help open the gate." He disappeared over the side of the building without another word.

Dirk strode over to Tori and Lilly, holding his hands out in frustration. "Why are you still here?"

Instead of answering, Lilly climbed on his back. He let out a growl. "Fine, we don't have time to argue about it." To Tori, he said, "Your motorcycle—"

Tori cut him off, because she knew what he was going to say. She needed to run across the roof, jump to the other tree, and take her motorcycle. "I'll see you at the gate," she called and didn't wait for a response. She ran along the narrow edge of the roof as fast as she could manage. The men were close now. The sound of engines reached the building and then stopped. They were getting off their motorcycles.

A bike started up and peeled away from beneath the tree. Probably Shang and Kody. Another followed it. She hoped it was Dirk and Lilly, not enemies pursuing the first motorcycle.

They were leaving, and she was still running across the roof. Why had she left her motorcycle at a different corner of the building than the rest? And why hadn't Lilly trusted her instead of delaying her? Now she was in plain sight where anyone could shoot her. She wore a bulletproof jacket and helmet, but her legs were only partially protected by shin and thigh guards. If they shot her in the knee, would she be able to make it to the motorcycle?

Finally, she reached the end of the building. She leapt toward the tree and landed on one of the inner branches, bending her knees to keep balance.

That's when she saw the gunman climbing up the tree. His flashlight jiggled as he clambered onto the platform. And more flashlights were following him. The gunman saw her and swung his rifle forward.

She was too high to jump to the ground and didn't like her chances fighting men with rifles. She turned and ran back across the branch toward the building. She would go down one of the other trees. The leap came easy and she landed effortlessly on the roof. Unfortunately, the door to the roof wasn't locked anymore. Two figures—the men from the jeep—emerged from it. They wore Kevlar suits, and thick helmets that obscured their faces, making them look like dark astronauts. The tallest of the two stood at least six and a half feet tall, perhaps seven. He strode slowly toward her with the strange rocket launcher-like weapon sitting on his shoulder.

The second man flipped a switch by the stairs, immediately bathing the roof in white light.

Where could she go now? She might be able to get around these two here on the roof—their suits made them slower—but were gunmen climbing all the trees?

She sprinted toward the tree that the other Slayers had gone down. The panic made it hard to speak. "Dirk, were there men near your tree?"

"No," he said. "Why?"

She didn't answer; she had to concentrate. Both men jogged toward her, cutting her off from the corner she'd been heading toward.

Fine, she could beat them to a different corner. She turned, just as the tall man pointed the huge barrel at her. He fired and something gray flew toward her, expanding like an opening mouth. It slammed into her, knocking her off her feet. She crashed into the roof so hard her helmet jammed into her face. She struggled to get back up, pushing against a metallic net that surrounded her. The fibers were strong, and as she moved they tightened around her like strands of a spiderweb closing around its prey. She tried to leap through it, but the mesh wouldn't give. Half a dozen tea cup–size black circles stubbornly held the net to the roof.

"They threw a net at me," she said into her radio. "It won't come off." She grabbed the mesh near her head and pulled at it, using all her strength. Only a small bit ripped apart.

She'd hoped Dr. B would know what to do, would tell her how to escape. Instead, too many voices came over her earpiece simultaneously. Theo asked, "What's the net made of?"

Jesse asked, "Where are you?"

Dirk asked, "How many men are there?"

She couldn't sort out the questions, let alone answer them. The men were upon her.

She tugged at the netting again, this time managing to rip a hole large enough to slip her head through. A little larger, and she'd be able to leap out—

But then the huge man reached inside the hole and grabbed hold of her vest like it was a handle. He kept her in place while the other man leaned toward her.

The curve of the visor distorted his features, making his face look inhuman. Through the smoky glass, his eyes looked too far apart, his nose grotesquely huge. His mouth sneered in rage. "You think you can get away with this?" he roared. She recognized his voice. It was Overdrake. "You think you can cross me and not pay a price?"

Through the radio, Theo said, "This is bad."

Yeah, that was an understatement.

Jesse asked Theo where Tori was, and Theo answered, but Tori couldn't pay attention to them. Overdrake leaned toward her face, still yelling. "Do you know what happens to people who cross me?"

That was probably a rhetorical question. She didn't really want to know. Three more of Overdrake's men had come up the stairs. She tried to shake off the big man's grip on her vest, but couldn't get her arms free of the net.

"Answer me!" Overdrake shouted. "What do you have to say for yourself?"

"Let me go!" she yelled back.

She could tell her words surprised him. Even through the smoky visor, she saw his eyes go wide. He reached over, unsnapped her helmet, then pulled off her ski mask. Her hair fell around her shoulders in messy tendrils.

Overdrake's mouth dropped open, although whether it was because of her age or her looks that he was startled, she couldn't tell. He stood back and examined her. His voice grew calm, studied. "Well, isn't this interesting?" With a flick of his wrist, he tossed her helmet over the side of the building. A few moments later it cracked onto the ground below. "You're quite a jumper, aren't you, Tori?"

How had he known who she was? How had he known she wasn't Bess, or Lilly, or one of the other girls?

"Let me go." Tori tried not to tremble. She clenched her hands into fists so they wouldn't shake. "My father is a senator. If you hurt me—"

"Don't threaten me," he cut her off. "I know who you are." He took a handgun out of his pocket, gripping it in his gloved fingers. "It would be a shame to kill you, so don't move."

He called to one of the men behind him, "Shut the roof until there's a ten-foot gap left." Once the roof was moving, Overdrake leaned toward Tori and unhooked the microphone from her neck. He stepped away from her then, but the huge man had also produced a gun. While one hand curled around the neck of her vest, the other held the gun in her direction. She didn't move.

Overdrake sauntered to the edge of the building until the tips of his black boots hung over. He put his gun back in his pocket and held Tori's microphone to his lips. "Listen up, Slayers. I have Tori. And I know what good friends the lot of you are—so much loyalty and compassion. Well, you have five minutes. If someone doesn't fly up here to take Tori's place, I'm throwing her headfirst into the dragon habitat. If the fall doesn't kill her, the drug will do its work."

It was hard to breathe. Fear washed over Tori like waves pushing her down. Her thoughts came in a staccato rhythm so short and panicked they didn't connect to each other.

Her parents. Her sister. Her friends. Her life. Overdrake could rip them all away. Right now.

She had to stop a moan that tried to escape from her lips. Coming into the compound hadn't been heroic, it had been stupid. But she wasn't going to babble or cry in the face of danger, even though she wanted to do both.

Overdrake lifted the sleeve of his jacket, checking the time on his watch. He was already counting down the time. Five minutes. She might be dead in five minutes.

Jesse hadn't said anything over the earpiece, but she doubted he would agree to trade places with her. He had to know that Overdrake wouldn't keep his word and set her free, even if Jesse came. Besides, Jesse's life was more valuable than hers. He had the best chance of killing the dragons.

He needed to cut his losses, like he'd been trained.

She didn't want to hear him say it, though. She didn't want to hear his apology explaining why he had to think of the people of D.C. instead of her.

She yelled out, "Don't do it, Jesse! Leave!"

The huge man reached over and slapped her across the mouth. On someone without extra strong skin, it would have drawn blood. On Tori it just stung.

The roof was nearly done closing. That would make it easier to escape—if she could come up with a way. She scanned the building, hoping for an idea. Nothing. Nothing. Why couldn't she stop shaking long enough to think straight?

Through her earpiece, she heard the others making plans.

Jesse said, "Dirk, take Bess, and I'll go back for Tori."

"No," Dirk said. "You shouldn't go. I'm dropping Lilly off. I'll get Tori."

Lilly, sounding put out, said, "You can't both go. Someone's got to get us over the fence."

Dr. B's voice came over the radio. His calm tone had worn away, replaced by raw worry. "Coordinate what you're doing. Go off plans, not impulses. Captains?"

Silence filled Tori's earpiece, and then Jesse barked out, "Dirk, get back here! I'm the one he asked for. I'm her captain!"

"Are you going to leave us stranded here?" Lilly demanded.

Jesse didn't answer her. "Tori," he said, "I've got to help the others over the fence. If you're still wearing your earpiece, tell Overdrake I'm coming, but I might not make it in five minutes."

So, he *would* sacrifice himself for her. How sweet. And how utterly foolish. She wasn't about to let him do it. She turned to Overdrake and called out, "He won't come. He's leaving right now."

And if he was smart, he would.

CHAPTER 37

Dirk pressed the gas pedal of the bike, urging it to go faster. Taking Lilly to the fence had delayed him, but it was necessary. He couldn't leave her in the middle of the grounds, and besides, with Lilly and the rest of the Slayers needing help over the fence, Jesse wouldn't fly back to the habitat—at least not until he'd gotten everyone else to safety. Hopefully, Jesse wouldn't come at all.

The Slayers had gone over these types of scenarios in practice. Lilly hadn't spoken to him for three days last year because he'd let her die in a hostage negotiation instead of putting the rest of his team at risk.

But it was different now that it was real. And it was different because Dirk knew he was the one his father really wanted. He'd known it from the instant Tori was captured. His father had heard Dirk say over the radio that he would take the bike on the far side of the building. When his father saw Tori cornered and jumping back onto the roof, of course he'd thought it was Dirk.

Until yesterday, Dirk was the only one who would have made the jump.

So now his father said he wanted someone to fly up and take Tori's place. That, Dirk supposed, was his father's way of punishing him for opening the roof. Dirk had not only punched in the right code, he'd used his voice to deactivate the voice recognition lock.

His father knew Dirk would come for Tori, and knew how Dirk would do it. Yeah, that would be a little hard to explain to the other Slayers later. If his father let him return with them, that is. Perhaps another part of Dirk's punishment was that he had to stay behind. Maybe his father would reveal who Dirk was to everybody.

No, Dirk decided, gripping the handlebars tighter. As long as any of the Slayers were functional, his father wouldn't give up his best tool for spying on them. Dirk was safe in that regard, at least.

The night air whistled by. The grounds were deceptively quiet. Dirk reached around his neck and tore the video feed off. He wasn't about to let Dr. B see what was going to happen next.

Theo's voice came over his earpiece. "Dirk, are you all right? Your video went dark."

"I'm fine," he said. He'd have to come up with an excuse later as to why the camera had come off his neck. Just one more complication to think about.

Man. He'd only met Tori three days ago, only liked her for one of those days, and, talk about your doomed relationships, if she remained a Slayer he'd have to fight her one day. But here he was anyway, ripping up the lawn to make it to her in time.

She was his counterpart. He hadn't expected to feel so strongly about that fact, but then, he'd never expected anyone, anywhere, to *understand him. When she'd touched his hand, he'd realized it might be possible.*

Dirk didn't have a plan, couldn't clear his mind long enough to put one together. There was only anger. Anger at himself, anger at his father. But he knew one thing: He wasn't going to let his father hurt Tori.

CHAPTER 38

Tori watched Overdrake pace back and forth on the edge of the roof, scoping out the grounds.

"Jesse won't come," she said again, loudly enough for her voice to reach the microphone in Overdrake's hand. "But you probably already know that, like you know everything else about us."

Overdrake's gaze slid back to her. "Bartholemew was a fool to let you come here. Untrained, untested—you were bound to blunder about and get caught, weren't you?"

She didn't answer. He was only trying to upset her, even if what he said was true. By getting caught, she was putting both Dirk and Jesse in danger. She hadn't thought of any way to escape and she only had minutes left. Or perhaps by now it was seconds.

"What is your gift, anyway?" Overdrake asked. "Hearing what a dragon hears? Not very useful, that talent. You led your friends right into trouble, didn't you?"

His accusation sent more pain spiraling into her gut. When she heard the men talking near the eggs, she should have considered the possibility that it was a trap. But how could she have guessed that Overdrake knew about her gift? She'd only discovered it yesterday.

Tori turned away and looked out onto the expanse of grass below the building so he wouldn't notice the tears gathering in her eyes. She didn't want to let him see her cry.

Speaking softly into her earpiece, Dirk said, "Don't listen to him, Tori. None of this is your fault. I'm almost there."

"You can't fly, can you?" Overdrake asked mockingly.

She didn't answer. Obviously, she couldn't fly or she wouldn't have been stuck on the top of this building.

Overdrake shook his head at her. "Untrained, untested, *and* pitiful."

The criticism hurt more than it should have. Only Jesse could fly. It wasn't her fault she was Dirk's counterpart instead of Jesse's. Tori slid her foot into one of the black circles to see if she could budge it. It moved, but held fast to the roof.

"They're supermagnets," Overdrake said. "Funny things, aren't they? When they're next to steel or other magnets they have such strength. But by themselves," he said pointedly to her, "they have no power."

She didn't miss the analogy. She was alone and powerless.

She thought of Dr. B's question: *Would the mission be worth it if some-one died in the process?*

It was going to be her. She would die, and they hadn't even de-stroyed the eggs. It was bitterly unfair.

One by one, the mouthpieces went silent. The group was turning them off. Perhaps they thought Overdrake had taken her earpiece so he could listen in on their conversations. It was a logical assumption. Tori wondered why he hadn't.

When the soft hum of Dirk's motorcycle went quiet she felt espe-cially alone. She wondered if Jesse had turned off his mouthpiece, too.

As though Jesse had read her mind, he said, "I'm on my way. Tell Overdrake. That's an order."

Tori remained silent. It was her only hope of protecting Jesse. If Overdrake killed her before he arrived, Jesse would turn around and fly off.

Tori looked out at the grounds below her. It was harder to see in the distance now that the roof lights were on. She wondered where Dirk was and what he planned to do. Shooting either type of gun against these men wouldn't accomplish anything. They were too well protected. He would only put himself in danger by coming anywhere near the building.

Overdrake checked his watch again. "It's been five minutes. Perhaps your friendships aren't as thick as I've been led to believe. Your comrades abandoned you." He walked slowly back to her side. "Just another of life's disappointments, but fortunately you won't be required to deal with it for long." He pointed his gun at her head again.

Every muscle in her body tensed, waiting for the shot.

"My assistant will tie you up," Overdrake said. "If you make any sudden moves, I'll fire. Do you understand?"

She nodded, although she didn't understand the point of tying her up when the net already held her fast.

One of the gunmen brought over a pair of sharp shears. Two others hefted a thick metal chain. It was long, between thirty and forty feet. A large collar connected to one end, the other end had a hook with a latch.

"We planned to use this when we needed to tether the hatchlings," Overdrake said. "It should work to keep hold of you."

The tall man waved over the other men on the roof so that they made a semicircle around Tori. Two of them pointed rifles at her. The other used the shears to widen the hole in the net until it slipped off her shoulders.

The tall man removed her weapons. She itched to leap, to plow into Overdrake and take him hostage, but too many men had guns pointed at her. She couldn't take them all out at once.

Her gaze flickered upward. This would be a good time for Jesse to appear. Or Dirk. She longed to hear one of their voices issuing instructions. If only they had some sort of plan.

But no one spoke. The only sound was the chain scraping against the roof as the henchman took off her bulletproof vest and clamped the collar around her waist. It dug into her ribs, unbending. Her breaths were already coming too fast and too shallow and the collar only made it worse.

Tori's family was miles away, unaware. She wanted another day, another hour with them, a chance to say good-bye.

Overdrake watched her being shackled. "Such a pretty girl," he said into the microphone. "Such a pity." Then he pointed at one of the gunman. "Hook the end of the chain around the gearbox so I can show our guest the work we've done on the habitat." He strode over to her, smiling coldly. "Don't struggle. My men are trained marksmen. It would be a shame to waste their energies cleaning little bits of you off the roof."

She stepped away from him, then kept stepping backward toward the edge of the roof.

"I'm not going to kill you," Overdrake said. "Well, probably not. Assuming you survive the fall, you'll hang in the habitat until you get a good strong dose of the ether. You'll be happier without your powers, without your memories."

The men holding onto her chain yanked it, trying to keep her from going farther back. They needn't have bothered. She'd reached the edge of roof and she had nowhere else to go.

"Before you pass out," Overdrake said, closing the distance between them with deliberate steps, "let me remind you that you failed.

None of you can defeat me. I can outmaneuver you and outfight you at every step."

She heard the soft hum of a motorcycle nearing the building and looked down. Dirk had come. Overdrake saw the motorcycle, too. He grabbed hold of Tori with more strength than she thought possible. She resisted, trying to twist away from his grip, but it proved useless. Overdrake hefted her above his head as though he were the one with extra strength instead of her.

He's one of us, she thought wildly. *The dragons give him powers, too.*

Dirk looked up at her, but she couldn't see his expression through his visor. Before his motorcycle had come to a stop, he jumped off and let it fall to the ground. He took two running steps toward the building, and then she couldn't see him anymore.

Overdrake turned and stepped over to the opening in the roof, still holding her aloft. She grabbed at the only things she could reach, his arms. If she clung on to him, he wouldn't be able to throw her. She caught hold of his watch, but it didn't help. He tossed her into the hole and the watchband simply broke off in her hand. It fell somewhere down below her.

I won't scream, she told herself. *I won't give him the satisfaction.* She gasped in a breath and held it. The walls went racing by in a blur. If the chain slipped, she'd fall to her death.

The chain went tight, and the collar bit into her stomach, punching the air out of her lungs. She didn't dare breathe in, not here where the air was tainted. She bounced, then swung back and forth. Rocks and trees went spinning through her field of vision.

She twisted around until she faced up. Gripping the chain, she pulled herself, hand over hand, toward the opening in the roof. Fresh air would be blowing inside from the hole. She would be able to breathe up there. She might even be able to crawl out of the opening and take the men by surprise.

She could hear Dirk up on the roof shouting at Overdrake. How had he gotten there so quickly?

"Let her go," Dirk yelled. "She doesn't matter to you."

Overdrake's voice held barely controlled rage. "Do you know what matters to me? Destroying my enemies."

She kept pulling herself upward. Without her extra strength, she wouldn't have been able to do it, and she wouldn't be able to do it for long if she didn't get some oxygen.

A scuffling noise sounded up above her and then Overdrake spoke again. "What did you think would happen when you came here? What?"

Dirk yelled, "You wanted someone to take her place? Here I am. Let her go."

"I'll let her go when I'm ready."

Tori hurried, pulled harder, kept her eyes on a patch of starlight above. Her lungs ached; it was getting hard to hear. Her ears buzzed—no, it wasn't her ears—the roof was moving again, closing.

Overdrake had never planned on releasing her if someone came to take her place. When the roof closed, it would most likely cut through the chain, and she'd fall to the ground.

Perhaps that wouldn't have killed her if she hadn't climbed up the chain, but now that she had . . .

She pulled herself up faster. She had to make it to the opening. She couldn't, but she had to keep trying. Up! Up! The word repeated in her mind with such concentration she no longer heard what Dirk and Overdrake yelled at each other. Her body ached. Her gaze zoomed upward, closer to the hole. At first she thought it was a lack of oxygen and this floating feeling meant she was losing consciousness.

She breathed in, letting the air rush into her lungs. And yet, she still soared upward, out of the hole, over the roof, and into the night sky.

She was flying. Flying!

A cry of joy nearly sprang from her lips. *Yes, I can do this.* She pushed up through the air like a bird, the air rushing by her face and fingertips.

Jesse had told her that a Slayer's extra skill manifested itself when one was under attack. She was glad this talent had finally shown up.

The chain rattled, then went tight again, this time pulled upward. It had been looped around a gearbox and hooked onto itself. She was stuck, leashed to the roof.

Dirk and Overdrake stared up at her, their conversation halted. They stood close together, an odd mirror image of each other. They were the same height and build, and both had an arm raised, pointing a finger at the other in accusation. Dirk had no restraint, no net or chain. Perhaps Overdrake knew he didn't have to use them. Dirk had willingly turned himself over.

The tall man saw Tori and lifted his rifle, aiming it at her. She jerked backward, but the motion was clumsy. She didn't know how to control her movements in the air or switch directions. Fear pulsated through her, making everything louder, sharper. At this distance he wouldn't miss, and Overdrake had taken her helmet and bulletproof vest.

Before he could pull the trigger, Dirk rammed into the gunman, pushing him over. The blast discharged somewhere out across the roof.

But the rest of the men had guns, too, and she was floating helplessly above them like a piñata. It was only a matter of time before everyone took a shot at her. She tugged at the collar around her waist. How could she get it off? She didn't see a strap or a buckle. The solid metal sides had fused together.

Something in the air off to her side caught her attention. Jesse swooped down toward the roof like an avenging angel. He plunged into the gunmen first. They fell backward like bowling pins, splayed out on the roof, rifles scattering every which way. Then he flew to the box where the chain was linked, tethering her to the roof. It only took him a moment to unhook. Without it holding her down, she shot up into the sky.

While she wondered how exactly to change direction, Jesse grabbed Dirk and soared off the roof. Jesse looked back over his shoulder at her. "Hurry!" he called. "Get out of their sight!"

He might have told her *how*. She still zoomed upward from inertia. The roof and the men shrank below her. Some of the men stared upward, but thankfully none aimed their guns at her. Perhaps they couldn't see her through the blaze of the roof lights. She wasn't sure if she would be easier to spot when they turned off the lights, but she didn't want to stick around to find out.

She put her hands out in front of her and made swimming motions, which did nothing more than turn her in the air. Jesse and Dirk's dark figures were growing smaller in the distance. She could barely make them out. Her alarm propelled her forward. She picked up speed, although she wasn't sure how. Perhaps fear fueled her. And she had plenty of that.

Jesse checked behind him, saw that she was following, and went faster. He had turned his microphone back on. "We're on our way. Head to coordinate D."

She had no idea where that was, so she soared after Jesse and Dirk while the wind tangled her hair, and the chain trailed out below her like a long metal tail. She flew over the motorcycles she'd shot earlier. They lay deserted on the ground like tiny broken toys. Her gaze somehow pulled her down toward them. She felt herself descending and immediately looked back at Jesse in front of her. She lifted again.

Until she figured out how this worked, she would keep her eyes on him.

She heaved the chain up, looping it over and over her arms as she passed over the fence. The last thing she wanted to do was catch herself on the razor wire.

Jesse checked over his shoulder again, saw she was close, and headed along the road that led away from the grounds. As long as she watched him, her body automatically followed. Beyond that, she had no idea how to steer. After a few minutes, she spotted two dark blue vans moving down the street. She wondered how fast they were going. Certainly not full speed or she and Jesse wouldn't have been able to keep up. Jesse continued flying over the vans, but didn't descend. He seemed to be making sure no one was pursuing them.

At last, he said, "Pull over, Dr. B. We're dropping in."

CHAPTER 39

Dropping in was harder than Tori imagined. She didn't know how to descend gradually. She tried twice and ended zooming headfirst toward the ground at dangerous speeds while the chain swooshed out behind her like an angry whip. Both times, she had to pull back up into the air, and then couldn't slow herself to a stop until she reached about four stories high.

"Point your feet down and sink," Jesse told her. But when she tried to do that, she just hovered in the sky, stuck in the air.

The rest of the Slayers watched her attempts from the van windows, which only made the task harder.

Finally, Jesse flew up to her. "Put your arms around my neck and relax."

She did. She melted into him, which was not quite the same as relaxing, but close enough. She put her head against his shoulder and trembled as they lowered.

He rubbed her back consolingly. "It's okay. You're safe now."

That wasn't why she was trembling. As soon as she had put her arms around him, the emotions, the closeness she'd felt with him the first time they'd flown—it all rushed back. She didn't know why she had two skills, but she did, and that must mean she was Jesse's counterpart, too. Did he realize that? Could he sense it? She wanted to say something to him, but everyone was staring and they didn't have time. Down below them, Dr. B leaned out the driver's side window and motioned for them to hurry. So Tori kept her arms around Jesse and said nothing.

The chain rattled onto the pavement as they lost height. "We'll get that off in the van," Jesse said.

"Thanks for coming for me."

Through the smoky visor, she could see his eyes, looking intently into hers. He nodded and didn't take his gaze from her until their feet touched the ground.

He does know, she thought.

She gathered up the chain as quickly as she could. Jesse took hold of part of it and together they carried it into the van. They had barely stepped inside before Dr. B peeled out down the road again. Booker hadn't stopped at all. His van was long gone.

Tori sat down in an empty seat, and Jesse sat down beside her. The rest of the Slayers still had their battle gear on, so Tori couldn't pick out who was who, although her counterpart sixth sense told her that Dirk sat next to the window in the middle seat. He was wearily resting his head against the window.

He had come back to the enclosure to save her, too. Her heart lurched when she thought about that. She wanted to thank both of them, but the others were talking to her, their words tumbling together in a happy rush.

"You were holding out on us!" Bess leaned over the seat to hug Tori. "Do you have any more talents we should know about? Shields? Shocks? The ability to pick winning Lotto numbers?"

"I'm as surprised as you are," Tori said. "One minute I thought I was going to die, and the next I was bouncing in the air like a beach ball."

"Oh, I wouldn't say you looked like a beach ball while you were flying," Bess said. "You looked more like a kick-butt, fugitive air balloon from the Macy's Thanksgiving Day Parade."

"Or a Goth kite," Rosa said. "I bet they use chains instead of string."

"Personally," Alyssa said, her voice as happy as the others, "I thought you looked like a tightrope walker who didn't quite understand the job description."

"Don't listen to them," Shang said. "I saw you and knew right away you'd stolen the dragon lord's garden hose. Now he'll have to put out all those dragon-induced brush fires with a squirt bottle."

Kody put his arms up like he'd scored a touchdown. "We got two flyers. We're back in business!"

"How did she get two powers?" Lilly asked, who to her credit sounded more curious than jealous.

Theo had left his seat in the front of the van, and now he bent over Tori, examining the collar and chain. He had some sort of meter that he kept prodding at her while he checked the readings. "It's a statistical probability. It stands to reason that someone might have more than one dragon knight ancestor. Tori must have inherited both traits."

"Does that mean she has two counterparts?" Lilly asked.

Even though everyone else still wore their helmets, Tori could still feel their gazes sliding between her and Jesse.

"Who knows," Theo said. "It might be possible, it might not."

"I'm just glad you're a flyer, too," Rosa said, "since that whole hearing thing was a bust. How did Overdrake know we were coming? How did he know our names? That was awful."

"Do you think he knows where we live?" Alyssa asked.

Jesse stared up at the roof of the van, thinking. "He must not, or he would have come after us before now."

Theo stopped probing Tori with his meter and sat back on his heels. "The good news is I can't find any bugs or tracking devices attached to the chain or collar. Unless the rest of you can see someone following us in the dark, we're free and clear."

A general sigh of relief swept around the van. It seemed no one wanted more fighting. The group simultaneously reached up and unbuckled their helmets. Tori's gaze went to Dirk. He looked drained, serious, and still utterly handsome.

"The bad news," Theo went on, "is that the ends of this collar have been sealed together with some sort of polymer I can't break apart." He hefted the chain in his hand, feeling the links. "They built this not to break. Probably titanium. We'll have to wait until we reach camp to cut it off."

Tori shifted her weight, and the collar stopped poking into her back and started smashing into her pelvis. "But we brought shears that can cut through metal, didn't we?"

"Yeah, for fences and locks, but this is too thick . . ." Theo waved a hand over the collar. "Shears will only snip at it and then you'll cut yourself on the edges. Sorry."

"That's okay." Really, having a metal collar stuck around her waist for a few hours was only an inconvenience. A minor thing compared to everything that could have happened tonight.

Jesse looked out the windows into the night. His brows drew together as though trying to figure something out. "Overdrake said he had cameras that could see outside his property. He must have seen which way the vans went. Why didn't he come after us?"

"Maybe he did," Kody said, and he glanced out the windows, too. "Maybe they just haven't caught up with us yet."

Jesse frowned. "Motorcycles could outrun a fifteen-passenger van, and we were stopped for a while."

Dr. B checked the rearview mirror. No other headlights were

visible going either way on the road. "I'm taking a roundabout way to camp. If anyone is trying to follow us, I'll lose them." He pressed down the gas pedal and the van picked up speed. "I'm proud of the way you worked as a team tonight," he said. "Things went wrong quickly and for the most part you handled it well." The restraint in his voice made it clear he wasn't thinking about what they'd done right. "However, several areas needed improvement."

Tori felt a pang of guilt then. Most of what had gone wrong had been her fault. Granted, she'd been able to warn Jesse that he wasn't actually near the eggs, but it hadn't been in time for the Slayers to get out of the enclosure. She had pointed out that there had to be another way for the dragons to get out of the enclosure, but one of the other Slayers would have thought of that eventually. And besides, Dirk was the one who unlocked the door with his code breaker. She had no idea how to use one.

She'd also parked her motorcycle at the opposite end of the building from the other bikes, so while the rest of the Slayers were escaping, she had to go in a different direction and had been captured.

Really, she'd only accomplished two things tonight: she had knocked out some of the gunmen and she'd broken the dragon lord's watch.

The mirror framed Dr. B's eyes as he glanced back at them. "Captains, your thoughts?"

Tori waited for Jesse to enumerate her faults, to tell her she should have stayed at the vans like he'd told her to do, but Dirk spoke first. He turned to Lilly. "I gave you an order, and because you wouldn't trust Tori to jump you over to the tree, she was delayed and then caught."

Lilly's back straightened. "Tori has never jumped anyone anywhere, and you asked her to do it onto a tree limb. What would have happened if she'd missed?"

"Oh, I don't know," Dirk said. "Maybe she would have had to fly you to the ground."

"Nobody knew she could fly then," Lilly countered.

Tori couldn't muster much anger on her own behalf. She'd been worried about jumping with Lilly holding on to her, too.

"Jesse, your thoughts?" Dr. B prodded.

Jesse spoke slowly. "We have an informant. Overdrake knew Tori could hear things. He was waiting for us tonight." Jesse's gaze swept around the van, taking in each one of them. "How many people know about Tori's ability to hear the dragons?"

Dr. B's grip tightened on the steering wheel, but whether it was because he was angry at the accusation or because he agreed with it, Tori couldn't tell. "All the people in this van know about Tori's gift," he said. "Along with Shirley, Booker, and Marylen, the camp nurse. She's the only other staff member who knows what the advanced campers do."

Rosa shook her head, making her long black hair sway around her shoulders. "It wouldn't have been one of us. Overdrake must have figured it out some other way."

"Maybe our cabins are bugged," Shang said.

Theo took off his glasses and used his T-shirt to wipe away a smudge. "That's not it. I do a daily sweep of your cabins and thoroughly go over everything. They're clean—of electronics, anyway."

Tori's mouth dropped open. "You go through our stuff? All of it?" She imagined him pawing through her underwear drawer. "Why didn't someone warn me about that?"

"Even if it were a bug," Jesse said, ignoring her protests, "someone had to put it there. Who is Overdrake using?"

The group fell silent. Tori thought about the things Overdrake had said while they were on the roof, and his comments took on a new light. "Overdrake insulted me because I couldn't fly . . ." It seemed ridiculous to say it, but she went on, "It's like he knew I should have been able to do it. How could he know that before I did?"

Alyssa leaned forward in her seat, her blue eyes wide. "Maybe he's psychic."

"He's not psychic." Jesse rubbed his forehead like he had a headache. "If he was psychic, he would have cut the power to his roof before we came. He didn't think we'd be able to open it."

Tori's gaze went back to Dirk. He'd been the one who managed to unlock it. She tried to catch his eye. She wanted to smile at him, but he didn't look up.

"We have an informant," Jesse said, anger roiling beneath the surface of his words, "and we need to find out who."

Dr. B checked the rearview mirror again. "Until we know how Overdrake is getting his information, we'll need to take more precautions. For example—"

Tori didn't hear his example. A noise filled her ears—a growl like gravel being churned in a pit. She startled, then spun to the window to find the noise. Nothing unusual was there, and Dr. B went on talking, undisturbed.

"Did you hear that?" Tori leaned closer to the window. "That noise . . ."

But she knew as she said it that it wasn't just a noise. It was a living thing. A dragon.

It didn't make sense. Had the eggs hatched? She listened for a heartbeat, but no longer heard the soft thudding in her mind. How long had it been gone? Another sound had taken its place: a rhythmic *wamp, wamp*. The sound of wings?

Her gaze swung to Dirk. His eyes were shut, his face had gone pale.

"What do you see?" she asked.

His eyes snapped open and he stared, trancelike, at something beyond the van. "Everyone needs to put their helmets back on." His voice was even, but firm. "We don't have long before the van stops working."

No one moved. It was as if everyone was holding their breath, waiting for more information. Jesse's expression grew grim. "Are you saying—"

Dr. B didn't wait for an answer. He floored the van. Tori lurched backward with the force of the extra speed. Behind them, the simulator trailer bumped along the road in protest.

Dirk shoved his helmet onto his head. "Helmets on, *now*. We've got to get out."

The Slayers moved quickly, buckling their helmets, checking their equipment. Jesse handed Tori an extra helmet and jacket from underneath the seat. Shang handed her a rifle and sling from the back of the van. Theo fumbled with his own helmet, repeating a blur of swearwords like they were some sort of mantra.

"Is the dragon going toward D.C.?" Lilly asked, slamming a new magazine into her rifle.

Dirk shook his head. "It's headed our way, fast. Overdrake must have told him to find us."

Jesse dumped extra ammo into his vest pocket. It clattered together. "Well, I guess we know what Overdrake keeps on the other side of that steel wall."

Bess rummaged through the supplies in the back of the van, then let out a frustrated groan. "We're in an unpopulated area where we could actually use our heavy artillery, and we don't have it. No grenades. No launchers. We don't even have crossbows or swords."

Jesse picked up the shears, testing the blades for sharpness. "We'll make do."

Dirk stood up, pushed past Rosa and Alyssa, and went to the front of the van. "Where's the remote for the simulator? We need to turn it off. That might be how the dragon is tracking us."

Dr. B gestured to the glove compartment. He was on his cell to Booker, telling him what had happened. "Don't come back," he said. "There's nothing you can do."

Dirk flung open the glove compartment, grabbed the remote, pointed it at the trailer, and pushed the off button. "We won't be able to outrun the EMP. Look for a place to park." He tossed the remote back in the glove compartment.

The van sped down the road so fast the trees they passed were nothing more than blurred silhouettes in a thick, leafy wall. The trees grew too closely together to hide the van in between them. It would have to stay out in the open, but at least the Slayers would have some cover. Was a dragon smart enough that once it saw the empty van, it would know the Slayers were nearby? Was that the sort of information a dragon lord could pass along to the dragon?

Rosa shifted uncomfortably in her seat. "Is this it? Is this the beginning of Overdrake's attack?"

Dirk shoved his rifle into his sling. "Overdrake won't launch a full attack before all of his weapons are hatched and grown." He paused, then gave a shrug. "But who knows? Maybe there's no going back if people see the dragon." He tightened the strap on his helmet, a tense energy in his movements. "Maybe there's no going back."

Out in the darkness, nothing but trees and road spread out as far as Tori could see. There was no one around here to report a dragon attack. And if the dragon had flown high enough over Winchester—or if it had taken out the lights beforehand—the people wouldn't have seen it.

Dr. B glanced at Dirk. "Where's the dragon now? How long do we have?"

Dirk shut his eyes, concentrating. "A couple of minutes."

Dr. B slowed the van and eased it onto the shoulder of the road. It bumped and jiggled as it went toward the trees. "Captains, you're in charge," Dr. B said. "Theo, you'll need to take cover in the trees. Get as far away from the fighting as you can. Jesse, I'll join your formation as backup. Use regroup four when the dragon is dead." He hesitated slightly between the word "when" and "the dragon is dead." Tori gulped. Dr. B wasn't sure they would be able to kill the dragon.

Jesse slipped his sling over his shoulder. "With all due respect, Dr. B, you won't be able to do anything that the teams can't do better, and your chance of getting injured is much greater—"

"I know," Dr. B cut him off. "I'll be there as Bess's father, not as your leader."

A screech like a thousand rusty doors opening filled Tori's mind. Her eyes darted back and forth, scanning the windows for signs of a dragon.

The headlights blinked out, everything around them faded. "Our electronics are gone," Dr. B said. He gripped the steering wheel hard, turning it with extra effort. The van had lost its power steering.

As the van slowed, the Slayers opened the doors. Jesse slid the shears into his belt, so that the handles straddled it. One side awkwardly banged against his leg as he moved. "I'll carry Dr. B," he said. "Tori, you carry Theo and follow me." To the others he said, "Take position fifty yards down the road. Let's put some distance between us and the van."

The Slayers poured out the doors, hit the ground running, and sprinted into the trees.

Dr. B and Theo got out of the van last. Jesse scooped up Dr. B and zipped off into the cold night air. Tori wrapped her arms around Theo, reminding herself that she had the extra strength to carry him. She lifted him from the ground and the two of them skimmed through the air.

Theo was taller than Tori, which made it hard to see around the back of his head. She tilted him sideways a bit. Judging from the way he held onto her arms and gurgled, "Ohhhhaaaahhhhohhh!" he didn't like the angle.

Jesse flew much faster than she could manage. Her chain bumped and spun along the ground behind her, tangling into plants and rocks. She had to move closer to the road so it didn't catch on anything.

Thankfully, the glow of her night vision illuminated the area. She could see Jesse hugging the tree line in front of her.

As she flew, she listened for the dragon. The rhythm of its wings mixed with the wind whistling around her ears and the chorus of crickets chirping in the trees. Fireflies buzzed around her, flashing tiny beacons like hundreds of miniature hazard lights.

When they had gone fifty yards from the van, Jesse cut into the trees and deposited Dr. B, then waited, floating above the ground, for Tori to bring Theo over. The others, went up trees or crouched behind trunks, guns ready.

Tori still didn't know how to lower herself onto the ground. She managed to slow down somewhat, and she'd flown low enough so she could drop Theo without hurting him. Although he still stumbled a few steps when he hit the ground.

Jesse took hold of Tori's arm as she skidded by him, pulling her to a stop. "You should go with Theo," he said. "Make sure he escapes. If the rest of us fail, you and Ryker will be all that stands between the dragons and D.C."

Jesse had said that she should, not that she had to. She tilted her head at him, questioning. "Is that an order?"

"No. It's your choice."

Her choice. She could die here because she was too untrained to fight effectively, or she could die later because she hadn't helped defeat the dragon during its first attack. If eight trained Slayers couldn't kill one dragon, what were the chances that she and Ryker—even with training—could kill several? Assuming, of course, they ever found Ryker.

Jesse didn't wait for her to answer. He soared over toward the others, then perched on a high branch.

Theo walked toward Tori, nervously squinting around at the darkness. "Let's get out of here."

Instead of picking him up, she glanced back at the Slayers. They were completely motionless, waiting, every pair of eyes on the sky. Dr. B had taken a position behind a tree a few feet away. His rifle pointed upward, aiming at the stars. Tori wondered if he could even see in the dark. And yet, he was staying.

"I can't leave," she told Theo.

"Yes, you can," he said. "All you have to do is pick me up and fly that way." He gestured down the road, his hand waving frantically.

Tori floated in the air in front of him, experimenting with making herself rise in small increments. "They need my help."

"You're untrained," Theo said incredulously, "and you're dragging a huge chain behind you. The only way you can help is to fly me out of here."

Tori went up too quickly and had to reach out and grab hold of a branch to stop herself. The chain swayed and rattled beneath her. Tori pulled on it, hanging loops of it from her arm so she could carry it without dragging it on the ground.

"Sorry, Theo," she said. "I'm staying."

Before she'd finished winding up the chain, a low triumphant grumble vibrated through the night, rising into an echoing call. This time, the sound didn't come from her mind. The dragon was near.

# CHAPTER 40

A cold tingle of dread ran down Tori's back. She pulled the chain harder, faster, wrapping the rest into loops around her arm.

Theo turned and fled through the trees in the opposite direction. She couldn't see him anymore, but she heard his clumsy footsteps pushing through the undergrowth.

Once the chain no longer dangled on the ground, Tori slipped the loops around her neck so she'd have her arms free to shoot. It clanged against her chest like an overweight necklace.

Tori floated upward, steadying herself with her hands, until she could peer over the foliage. She swung her gun forward, searched the horizon, and tried to remember every piece of instruction Dr. B had given her.

Think before you act. Your greatest asset isn't your extra powers, it's your brain. Don't get in front of the dragon. Move if he turns on you, and make sure you always have some place to retreat. Don't take unnecessary risks.

At first she could only tell that the dragon was flying toward them. A dark outline contrasted against the backdrop of the star-studded sky. His bat-like wings sliced through the air, and the shape grew bigger. He had an angular head, pointed ears, and a clubbed tail that moved up and down, serpent-like. She couldn't make out his color. Was he black, green, or some other color that had faded in the low light? A strange hump protruded from his back. She squinted at it, but couldn't tell what it was.

Now that the simulator signal was gone, Tori hoped the dragon would fly past them. He might soar away and eventually just return back to Overdrake without finding them. If the Slayers were smart, they would stay hidden and save this fight for a time when they were better prepared.

But even as Tori thought it, she knew it wouldn't happen.

The dragon slid downward through the air, disappearing behind the trees on the opposite side of the highway. A flurry of birds erupted from the vicinity like feathered confetti, scattering away on frantic wings.

Then silence.

Tori watched and waited. What did it mean? What was the dragon doing?

Before she could ask more questions, the dragon bounded upward, flying toward their side of the road. He circled the area, his wings beating out a wind that rushed through the leaves, making the trees hiss. Did he recognize their van?

The dragon drew up to a nearly vertical position, and no hump showed on his back now, just rows of sleek scales that glinted in the moonlight. His tail curled into a C below him as he hovered in front of the trees, surveying the area. Instead of having a white diamond on his forehead, he seemed to have some sort of silver horn there. He was bigger than Tori had imagined. Much bigger. If he had flicked his golden eyes in her direction, he would have seen her, but instead he looked down at something on the ground. She couldn't tell what.

In the space of a blink, the dragon dived out of sight.

What had he gone for? A person? She didn't hear any screams. Tori flew slowly toward the street to get a better view, her rifle gripped firmly in her hand. As she leaned forward, the chain rattled noisily around her neck. Stupid thing. She couldn't be stealthy with it clanking every time she moved. She straightened and with the help of a few tree branches, pulled herself to a stop.

The dragon shot back up into the air with the van clasped in all four talons. His head bent to examine it. When he saw it was empty, he gave an angry shriek, bit into a tire, then dropped the van. It fell to the ground, bounced, crumpled, and lay upside down on the side of the road.

The dragon, as they had expected, wore a large rectangular piece of Kevlar across his underbelly. The straps ran up his sides and connected on his back. Either she or Jesse would have to fly over, cut the straps, and get the Kevlar off in order for their rifles to have any chance of penetrating the dragon's vulnerable underbelly and reaching his heart.

Tori didn't have so much as a pair of nail clippers on her, and Jesse only had the shears. With a sword it might have been possible to cut the straps and fly away, but the shears would take too long.

Their best bet was to hide, retreat, do anything but take on the dragon right now. Jesse had to realize that.

But apparently he didn't.

While the dragon had been busy tire tasting, Jesse flew out of the trees and circled behind him. Jesse looked so small next to the huge figure of the dragon. So unprotected.

She wanted to yell out to him that this was crazy, that he wasn't supposed to take unnecessary risks. And anything but hiding right now was an unnecessary risk.

The dragon spotted Jesse. His head swung toward him, jaws snapping, talons stretched out.

Tori heard the dragon's growl, heard his teeth clench together. It wasn't a sound she wanted to hear. She minimized the noise in her mind as much as she could.

The dragon was gaining on Jesse. Tori rose from her hiding place to get a better shot and fired off a round from her rifle. Some of the Slayers obviously had the same idea—to distract the dragon. Several other gunshots punctured the night, but not the dragon. He turned suddenly, saw Tori, and lunged at her, snarling.

She dived into the cover of the trees, twisting as best she could around trunks and boughs. In her hurry, she scraped into several. The dragon skimmed above the treetops looking for her. Leaves and branches shivered in the wind of his wings. He thrust his head through the foliage, like a heron trying to pluck fish from the water. His teeth clamped together so close to Tori's back that she felt his warm breath, smelled his rancid oil scent.

She dropped lower, tried to move faster.

He didn't come after her again, which was a good thing since the chain tumbled off her neck, caught on some branches, and whipped her backward. She spun out and fell to the ground with a noisy clatter.

It wasn't the best way to get to back to earth, but it worked.

She lay there, breathless, as the sound of the dragon's wings moved away from the trees.

Then Dirk stood over her, holding his hand down to help her up. "I give you a seven-point-five on the evasive maneuvers, and about a two on the landing."

She took his hand and he helped her to her feet. She straightened her helmet, then picked up the chain so she could loop it around her neck again. "Where's Jesse?"

"Out there dancing with the dragon."

"He won't be able to cut through those straps with the shears."

"He might. Don't underestimate him."

She looked around. A few of the Slayers crouched in the branches, others stood on the ground, darting in and out of the trees. Dr. B had moved closer to the tree line, his rifle following every move the dragon made. Kody leapt out into the clearing, wound his arm back like a pitcher, and sent a freezing shock at the dragon's face. The dragon's head reared back in irritation, then sent a stream of fire in Kody's direction. The night lit up with a blaze, illuminating the dragon. He was maroon and each scale was tinged in golds and reds. Kody dodged back into the trees out of the path of the dragon's searing breath. The fire extinguished before it reached him.

Tori scanned the sky behind the dragon for Jesse. She didn't see— No, there he was, right behind the dragon's neck. He had the shears out, but as he went for the nearest strap, the dragon twisted his head. Jesse dashed backward and the dragon went after him, baring his teeth. Jesse dived underneath the dragon's stomach, and the dragon somersaulted in the air, effortlessly following Jesse's path.

Shots rang out as the Slayers tried to draw the dragon's attention with gunfire. It didn't work this time. The bullets plinked uselessly against his scales. The dragon flew, wings pressed back against his body, his glowing golden eyes focused on Jesse. In a moment, the dragon's powerful jaws would be on him.

Bess threw a forcefield up in front of the dragon. Tori could tell because the dragon's head stopped in midair while his body kept moving forward. The momentum pushed his head upward, until his body hit the forcefield. Then it gave way. The shield couldn't hold back his mass. The dragon straightened and pursued again, but it had given Jesse the time he needed to escape.

Jesse shot toward the trees, a human arrow, plunging down into the leafy cover.

The dragon sent a fiery stream after him. Most of the fire vanished before it reached the trees. But Shang or Lilly, or perhaps both, had missed a few flames. A couple of branches glowed yellow, burning, then were extinguished, too.

The dragon glided over the trees, shrieking. Its tail lashed angrily up and down, smacking a tree so bits of branches rained down.

Tori flinched away and put up her hand to block falling pieces of bark. Dirk stood, resolutely watching the dragon pass overhead. Its dark form blackened a section of the sky, snuffing out the stars.

"Overdrake is somewhere nearby," Dirk said.

"How do you know?" Tori glanced around, but only saw the Slayers here and there.

"Someone is controlling the dragon, making him attack us."

Tori remembered the bulge she'd seen on the dragon's back before the dragon had dipped down behind the trees on the other side of the street. It could have been a man. "Is there a way to find him?"

Dirk didn't answer. Before he could, Jesse flew up to him. "Let's do a full assault and see if it buys me enough time. Call your team. Pattern fifteen."

"Agreed," Dirk said. "And if I can get past the dragon, I'll look for Overdrake. Once we take him out, we'll have a better chance."

Jesse shook his head. "This isn't like when Tori knocked Theo away from the controls. It won't make that much of a difference, and I need you to lead your team right now. We'll take care of Overdrake later."

"Agreed," Dirk said, though Tori could tell he didn't like the decision.

Jesse flew toward the others, weaving around trees as naturally as a fish swimming through a stream. Dirk ran toward the others, clapping his gloved hands together. "A-team. Fifteen, on Jesse's call!"

What was she supposed to do now? She didn't know pattern fifteen.

"Now!" Jesse yelled and the Slayers sped out of the trees.

Tori itched to go with them. She found herself hovering off the ground, even though she hadn't consciously meant to fly. It was foolish, and she would most likely just make things worse like she had back at the enclosure, but she had to do something to help.

Dr. B shot at the dragon, trying to draw the beast's attention back to the trees, but it didn't work. The dragon sprang toward one of the Slayers, Tori couldn't tell which. It wasn't Dirk; he led his team on the other side. Whoever it was, the Slayer leapt out of the way. Kody sent a freezing shock that hit the dragon's eye. The dragon jerked its head back and a layer of frost ringed its eye, like a white bruise. The golden iris blinked and seconds later the frost melted.

The dragon bared its teeth and snarled. Fire spouted toward the two Slayers who were sprinting around the dragon's side. Bess threw up a shield and the flames spread against the invisible wall, crackling and lighting up the night with an almost painful orange brilliance.

Jesse flew over to the dragon's shoulder, but as soon as he got close to the Kevlar straps, the dragon turned away from the Slayers on the ground and focused on Jesse. The dragon slashed his tail upward, hitting Jesse so hard he rolled through the air, falling.

Tori zoomed out of the trees, ready to block for him, or catch him, but before she'd gone far, Jesse regained control and shot sideways. The dragon followed, slicing through the sky, wings beating. He sent a stream of fire that nearly reached Jesse before it snuffed out. Jesse changed directions, darting one way and then another. It didn't matter. The dragon blasted after him, ignoring the Slayers on the ground. It was as if he knew Jesse was the real threat.

Of course, the dragon knew—because Overdrake knew, and he was somewhere nearby.

Tori couldn't even fly near Jesse in hopes of confusing the dragon in a shell game of which flyer is the bona fide danger? She was easy to spot. She was the flyer with a chain around her neck.

If only she had come to camp before this year. She could have learned what her powers were and how to use them years ago. She wouldn't have been chained up by Overdrake. She wouldn't be hanging around the treetops uselessly.

Tori let out a deep breath. She didn't want to look for Overdrake. She didn't want to face him again. He had nearly killed her once already, but the Slayers needed help. Jesse needed help. If he died, what chance would any of them have? If she could break Overdrake's link with the dragon, if Overdrake wasn't there in the dragon's mind telling him to attack Jesse, maybe the other Slayers could distract the dragon long enough to allow Jesse to cut the Kevlar straps.

She flew to the woods on the opposite side of the road, dropping into the foliage and winding through tree limbs. It was easier to maneuver around things than to stop, so she glided through the greenery, looking for Overdrake on the ground. Where was he? And more importantly, how could she take him out? He wore Kevlar, so shooting him wouldn't do a lot of good, and he had extra strength so it would be hard, maybe impossible, to defeat him in hand-to-hand combat.

How had Dirk been planning on fighting him?

Her heart was beating too fast. She still wasn't good at flying, but even if she had been able to drop to the ground, she wouldn't have. Walking over plants and dead leaves made too much noise. Gliding through the air was better. She weaved between the trees slowly, scanning the ground. Bushes. Ferns. Rocks. Nothing out of the ordinary.

A bullet zinged into the back of her jacket. Another hit her helmet. Not stray bullets from the Slayers' guns. These had come from the trees behind her.

It was Overdrake's way of tapping her on the shoulder.

If she had been able to maneuver as well as Jesse, she would have flipped over like a swimmer turning in a lane. Instead, her inertia carried her forward and she had to grab hold of a tree branch and clumsily pull herself back in the right direction.

At first she didn't see Overdrake anywhere, then she heard him. Laughing. Not on the ground—he was perched high in a tree. He stood precariously balanced on a branch that didn't seem thick enough to support his weight. With one hand, he held onto a branch above him, with his other hand he pointed his rifle at Tori. "Beautiful form!" he called out. "I'm glad Jesse sent his best Slayer. It wouldn't be sporting if I had to fight with some untrained socialite."

Tori didn't want to keep sliding through the air toward him, so she grabbed hold of a passing branch and pulled herself onto a sturdy-looking bough.

Which only made Overdrake laugh again. He tilted his head back, unconcerned about even keeping tabs on her.

Tori stole a quick glance at the other Slayers. Now that Overdrake was paying attention to her, what was the dragon doing? She located Jesse, swooping so low to the ground he was probably getting grass stains on his jacket. The dragon charged downward, snapping at him, but only managed to get a mouthful of landscape.

Either it took more than a break in concentration to disrupt a dragon lord's link, or Overdrake didn't have to instruct the dragon in every motion. Perhaps Overdrake told the dragon to go after Jesse and it knew how to take things from there.

"It was unwise of you to come here while your rescue committee is busy," Overdrake said. "How do socialites fight, anyway? Were you going to blackball me from all the right parties? Spread ugly rumors? Use your stiletto heels to inflict puncture wounds?"

She ignored his taunting and aimed her rifle at him. "Call off the dragon!" she yelled.

"Or what?"

"Or I'll make your life miserable."

The amusement in his voice gave way to anger. "You already have."

She fired her rifle in quick succession. Not at him, but at the branch he held onto. It dissolved into splinters and he fell backward.

She expected him to drop his rifle. She waited for him to crash through the foliage and hit the ground. He didn't do either. With the gun still clutched in one hand, he turned his backward momentum into a flip. His legs curled and swung around him, then impossibly, he landed on a tree limb a few feet down. He straightened up, tucked his rifle under his arm, and faced her again. His voice took on a scolding tone. "I could call the dragon over here to tear you into pieces," he said. "You fly like a wounded bird. It would take him about two minutes to kill you." Overdrake put his free hand on a branch to his side to steady himself. "The only reason I haven't done it already is that I like you. Don't make me change my mind about that."

He liked her. Sure. She aimed her rifle at him again.

"You can't win," he told her with smug satisfaction. "Not here. Not later. There are nine of you. I have a small army of men to fight for me. Your deaths tonight will be for nothing. I might spare you if you surrender now." He paused. "I might."

She held the rifle steady. "You're wrong. Even if we lose here, people have seen the dragon now. They'll come together to fight you. They'll demand the government takes action."

He laughed deeply, as though he truly thought what she'd said was funny. "What country did you grow up in? You're talking about Americans—the laziest, most self-serving people on earth. They won't fight, they'll run. And if people do catch sight of the dragon tonight, it will only make them surrender."

Tori gripped her gun impatiently. There was no point in arguing with him about human nature. "Who is your source?" she asked. "How do you know things about me?"

"You go to one of those private elitist schools, don't you?" he asked. "Let's see if the tuition is worth it. Do you know what the sign in the Greek temple of Delphi says?"

"No littering. In six languages. I went there last summer. Now answer my question."

"The sign says 'Know thyself.'"

"Okay. I know I don't have a lot of patience." She looked into the site of her rifle. "You might not be so lucky the next time you fall."

"When you understand yourself, you'll be a lot closer to figuring out who my source is."

It made no sense. She didn't reply.

"Who are you, Victoria Hampton?" Although she couldn't see Overdrake's face, she knew he was sneering as he said this. "Where do you come from? What right does your father have to claim any sort of power in the government?"

"He was elected. That's how we do things in this country."

"Not for long," Overdrake said.

She shot again, obliterating the branch in his hand. This time he didn't fall. Instead, he leapt from his branch into a neighboring tree. It was at least a fifteen-foot jump. He wasn't just strong, he could leap, too. What other powers did he have?

Tori swiveled to face him, but was pulled back. She panicked, sure Overdrake's assistant had snuck up on her. Then she realized it was the chain. The back had caught on the branch behind her.

Overdrake saw her flinch backward and he laughed again. "Did I give you two minutes with the dragon? Make that one. You'll probably strangle yourself before he comes."

Tori yanked herself forward. The branch snapped into pieces with a crack. The motion made several twigs wave and slap her.

Stupid chain.

As if it weren't already impossible enough to kill the dragon. Why did Overdrake have to render her useless by sticking her with this . . .

The thought vanished from her mind, replaced by a picture, an idea. She wasn't the only one who could be strangled by this chain.

It would be suicide if it didn't work. But if it *did* work . . .

She glanced back at the Slayers. Jesse was darting around the dragon's head like an angry hornet. He hadn't made any progress with the Kevlar straps. How long could he do this before he got tired, before someone made a mistake and was killed?

Besides, she wasn't doing any good here. She couldn't fight Overdrake.

Tori jumped out of the tree, letting gravity do its work. Right before landing, she willed herself to fly into the clearing, stretching her arms out to lean in that direction. Instead of a jarring thud, she skimmed along the ground, moving faster than she could have run.

She knew Overdrake was watching her, but his attention would turn back to Jesse before long. Because she wasn't a threat. She was a socialite who flew like a wounded bird.

Tori swung her sling so that her rifle rested on her back, then tilted her head down until the chain loops slid from her neck into her outstretched hands. She found the end, then let the rest of the chain tumble to the ground. The links jumped and swished, straightening themselves into one long loop.

Veering toward a group of Slayers, Tori called out, "Block for me!" and hoped at least some of the Slayers who could block fire had heard her.

CHAPTER 41

Tori had no way to explain to Jesse what she wanted to do. Right now she couldn't catch up with him, let alone talk with him. And she didn't want to get too close to where he and the dragon spun around each other.

"Jesse!" she called, hovering as close as she dared.

She couldn't see Jesse's expression through his visor, couldn't tell if he'd heard her or not. He dived downward, leading the dragon toward the ground as though the two of them were connected in a roller coaster ride. The dragon craned forward, wings pressed against his body. His tail whipped so fast it looked like he was convulsing. Just before Jesse hit the ground, he turned and went straight up. The dragon had more mass and couldn't correct his direction as swiftly. He shot off parallel across the grass, then pushed upward against the ground with his feet and tail.

"Tori!" Jesse called.

"Take the other end!" She pointed to the chain, but wasn't sure he saw. With two sleek beats of his wings, the dragon streaked up into the sky, coming after Jesse again.

Did Jesse understand what she wanted to do? Was his counterpart sense letting him know her plan? She hoped it could do that sort of thing.

He hesitated, then yelled, "Throw it!"

Good. He understood.

Her intuition wasn't working as well, though. She had no idea which direction to toss the chain. He wasn't staying in place. She hurled the end in his general area. It rattled noisily, streaming out, then fell like the tail of a shooting star. Jesse swooped downward, caught it, and rocketed by so fast he pulled Tori along with him.

He turned in midair and sped back toward the dragon. Straight on. Tori had no choice but to follow after him. She willed herself to go faster. Faster might get her by the dragon without being barbequed in the process.

When Tori was little, she and Aprilynne used to catch garter snakes in their lawn. Well, Aprilynne found them, and Tori caught them. Each time Tori had reached for snake, an instant of fear had gripped her. If Tori's aim was off and she didn't get the right spot, the snake could turn on her.

And now Tori was doing the same thing on a larger, more dangerous scale. The chain had to connect right below the dragon's head so he couldn't reach her.

The dragon's eyes turned on her, piercing her with their golden gaze. His nostrils flared, breathing inward to fuel his fire stream.

She prayed Shang and Lilly were paying attention. The dragon was so close now, if the fire wasn't snuffed out immediately it would fry someone.

The fire came, but the flames spread out horizontally in an orange wall. Bess had thrown up a forcefield. Heat pulsed at Tori as she went by and the air wavered like liquid.

Tori was instantly thankful that the fire hadn't been extinguished.

The wall of flames blocked the dragon's view for several seconds. He didn't notice Tori sailing by on one side, while Jesse went by on the other. The dragon felt the chain when it hit his neck, though. His head shuddered in surprise and he was pulled backward.

Tori's attempts to change direction to wind the chain around the dragon's head were slow and awkward, but Jesse circled and then lapped her, drawing the chain tight.

The dragon bucked, head lurching, then swiped his tail at Jesse. Jesse zipped out of the way, pulling back on the chain so hard he grunted at the effort.

The dragon let out a strangled growl and jolted his head back and forth. The motion jerked Tori through the air, but every time the dragon yanked her backward, she pushed herself forward again, tightening the chain with all her strength.

In a switchblade-fast motion, the dragon spanned his wings outward, slamming one into Tori full force as he tried to shake her loose.

Tori's breath gushed from her lungs and pain shot through her hip, but she couldn't have let go of the chain if she'd wanted to. It was connected to her middle. The dragon smacking her away had only made the chain go tighter. She scanned the darkness for Jesse. Had he been knocked loose?

No. He'd flown upward out of the way of the wings.

Upward. Good idea. She wished she'd thought of that in time to do it.

She kicked the air, ignoring the pain, and kept heaving to pull the chain tighter. The dragon lurched forward, twisting, thrashing its tail. The action whipped Tori about on the end of her chain, dragging her one way, then another.

Tori had once fallen off a frightened horse. Her foot caught in the stirrup, and after she hit the ground, she'd reached out wildly, grasping for something to hold onto. There had been nothing to grip. She couldn't even see straight. The world had been reduced to flashes of ground and sky and horse hooves.

It felt like that now, only Tori couldn't free herself this time. She had to pull against the dragon, dodging wings and a tail that lashed every which way, while the ground and the sky flashed by her—frictionless, fast paced, jumbled.

What had she been thinking to tie herself to a dragon? Hadn't Dr. B told her not to put herself in a position where she couldn't retreat? That's where she was now. Retreatless. If the dragon killed her, her friends wouldn't even have a way to retrieve her body. She would dangle like a keychain from the dragon's neck until Overdrake saw fit to cut her loose. If he saw fit to cut her loose.

Jesse, don't let go, she thought. This would only work if he kept pulling on the other end of the chain. Her safety depended on him.

A tree spun by her. She reached out and grabbed hold of a thick branch, pulling herself toward it, then embracing the trunk with all of her strength. The world grew less dizzy, lines sharpened.

Over her shoulder, she watched the dragon flailing, sinking. It shuddered and its wings flapped aimlessly. The huge beast was crippled and stumbling.

Where was Jesse? She didn't see him in the sky. She followed his side of the chain. It stretched to the ground in a taut line that led to the overturned van. Jesse must have anchored himself there.

With one last convulsing shudder, the dragon plummeted to the ground. The weight of its fall dragged Tori down the tree trunk. The sharp edges of the collar sliced into the tree, shaving off chunks of bark. Her hands scraped off some, as well, shredding her gloves. Pieces of wood spit everywhere, pinging into her neck and visor. Her palms stung like something had bitten them. Still, she didn't let go of the tree even when she'd reached the ground.

Behind her, the Slayers converged around the dragon. They looked like wolves about to rip apart some downed zebra. Tori tried to erase the image from her mind. This was supposed to happen. The best possible outcome. No one had died. At least she didn't think anyone had died. Nobody was sprawled out on the ground. She tried to count the Slayers, but they kept moving and she was too dizzy.

The dragon's mouth hung open. One golden eye stared at her, the glow growing dimmer and dimmer.

Someone had already taken the shears from Jesse. Judging by his size, it was probably Kody. Part of his jacket had been burned away, exposing his arm and shoulder. He jumped onto the dragon's back and cut off the Kevlar straps.

Tori wanted to yell, "You don't need to do that. The dragon is dead already. Just leave him alone."

Which was a stupid thought. She wasn't so sure the dragon was dead that she was willing to let go of the tree and release the pressure on its neck.

When the straps were cut, a couple of the Slayers pulled off the Kevlar blanket that had protected the dragon's underside. One of the Slayers pointed a gun at the dragon's heart. She didn't know who, only that it wasn't Dirk. He was still standing behind the others, watching the proceedings with his hands clenched at his side.

Was he feeling a lump of sickness in his stomach, or was she projecting her feelings onto him? She couldn't tell and didn't know why she suddenly felt this way. Maybe she'd been flung around too much and had motion sickness. Or a head injury. Or was in shock. Maybe she'd just watched one too many movies with friendly, anthropomorphic dragons.

She shut her eyes so she wouldn't have to see the shots, but she still heard them. Each punctuated the feeling that lay in her stomach. She let go of the tree and another wave of dizziness hit her, which was why she couldn't be certain of what she saw next.

A man—Overdrake—flying over the trees for a few moments, then sinking back and disappearing into their cover.

The next moment, Dr. B threw his arms around one Slayer and then another, shouting joyfully, "Well done, Slayers! Well done!"

It took a group effort to unwind the chain from the dragon's neck in order to free Tori. While Rosa, Alyssa, and Shang did that, the other Slayers combed the trees searching for Overdrake. Dr. B went over to the dragon and examined its scales, claws, and the silver bump on its forehead. He used the blade of the shears to pry the bump off. Underneath was a white diamond-shaped spot. Dr. B ran his fingers over it, then scrutinized the silver covering in his hand. "The records were right," he said to no one in particular. "Overdrake covered the spot so it wouldn't trigger the DNA of any babies the dragon flew over."

The Slayers never found Overdrake.

Tori told the others that Overdrake could leap distances, and that she'd seen him above the treetops, but she stopped short of telling them that she'd seen him flying.

Had it been flying, or had he only leapt up? She couldn't be sure now. If he could fly, why hadn't he come after Jesse and her when they'd gone off his roof?

Finally, Dr. B told them they had better go. Overdrake was gone. They needed to leave and get a hold of Booker.

Jesse flew ahead with Dr. B to find a phone before his powers wore off. The rest of the Slayers ran down the road. Even Tori ran. It was easier to control than flying, and besides, she didn't want to get separated from the rest of the group.

Just before their powers left, they found Theo walking in the same direction. Then they all walked along the road, taking turns telling him what had happened. Kody used hand motions in his descriptions. Bess made a running total of how many points she thought each team had earned. "Should a dragon chokehold be ten thousand points apiece or should Jesse and Tori split that total?" She raised her hands, adding a hip-swinging dance move to her walk. "Either way. Team Magnus cleans up."

"Shang's the one who shot it," Lilly said, sending her counterpart a look of evident pride.

"And he's on Team Magnus, too," Bess pointed out.

"Yeah, next time give the A-team more action," Kody said. "I only got to cut the Kevlar."

"You can't give points for luck," Shang said, his voice a grim contrast to the others. "That's what we were—lucky. If Overdrake hadn't provided us with an unbreakable chain, we'd still be back there fighting, and the dragon would pick us off one by one."

"You're right," Bess said. "I hereby grant Overdrake a hundred honorary points for providing us with the weapon we needed."

"My point is," Shang said, "that's not going to happen again. We need to be better prepared for next time."

"We will be." Lilly motioned back to where Tori brought up the rear of the procession. "We've still got the chain."

Kody waved his hand as though waving Shang's protest away. "Luck is always a part of battle. And so is using your head. That's what Tori did tonight."

Bess chimed in, "A hundred points to Tori because she used her head for something besides displaying those gorgeous extensions."

Tori decided not to comment on that.

Rosa was breathlessly cheerful. Her walk had an extra spring to it. "People must have seen the dragon flying overhead. The government will have to launch an investigation. They'll do things to protect the cities."

Lilly let out a scoff. "The government is just as likely to try and use the dragons for themselves. You know what idiots politicians are."

Tori decided not to comment on that, either.

Shang shook his head. "It will make it harder to keep what we do a secret. When our parents see pictures of a massive dead dragon, they won't want us to have anything to do with dragons."

"Speak for your own parents," Bess said. "Mine are more than willing to shove me in front of huge, flying carnivores. Did my dad even make sure I was okay before he took off with Jesse?"

"Yes," Lilly and Alyssa said at the same time, apparently used to this sort of complaint.

Rosa reached over and patted Bess's arm soothingly. "You were the first person he hugged after we killed the dragon. He wouldn't have known who you were unless he kept track of you the entire time you were fighting."

"And not only that," Theo put in, struggling to keep pace with everyone else. "When you were stuck at the enclosure your dad was getting ready to go after you himself. He was about to go into plan thirty-six mode."

"Okay, he worries." Bess sniffed, still sounding affronted. "But not enough to keep me away from danger like the rest of your parents would."

"Oh come on." Kody playfully swatted her on the shoulder. "You wouldn't let him keep you away if he tried." He sent her a wide grin. "So don't go into Bess thirty-six mode now. We just had our first fight and our first victory. We killed the dragon with Overdrake's own chain. So much for invincibility."

"We still have an informant to worry about," Shang pointed out.

"And we will worry about that," Kody said. "But right now it's time to gloat."

Then some of the Slayers talked about strategies for fighting the next dragon, while some talked about the possibility of government help, and the rest talked about ways to trap the informant. Their enthusiasm should have been contagious. But Tori didn't catch it.

She walked beside Dirk at the back and neither one of them spoke. Now that their powers had gone, she felt everything more keenly. The cold humid air, the strain of running around all night, and especially the ache in her hip where the dragon had hit her. It made her limp a little. The heartbeat of the embryonic dragons, she noticed, had returned to the back of her mind.

"I can hear the heartbeats again," she told Dirk.

He only nodded.

"Why weren't you and I tuned into the adult dragon all along? Why did we only connect with it when it attacked?"

He shrugged, unbothered by this fact. "Maybe because it was the signal from the eggs that triggered our DNA in the first place."

She walked silently for a few more steps, not sure she wanted to voice her feelings, but then figured Dirk would understand, even if he didn't know the answer to her next question. "Why did I feel so sick when Shang shot the dragon?"

"He was still alive until then, and you'd made a connection with him. You were inside his mind in order to hear what he heard. That affects you whether you want it to or not."

She knew the connection had affected him, too, and wondered how long it would last and why no one had mentioned it would happen. She wished she'd been better prepared. She could still see, in a way that twisted her insides, the dragon's eyes staring blankly at her, their glow fading.

About an hour later, Booker's van pulled up to the group. Dr. B and Jesse were already inside. Tori hadn't meant to leave Dirk and go sit by Jesse. It happened because she had trouble climbing into the van. Stepping up sent a sharp pain through her injured hip. As Dirk helped her up, Jesse reached down and half pulled, half lifted her inside. He guided her to the seat next to his.

Once they were all inside, Booker headed down the road, still driving toward the dragon instead of turning around. Tori stared past Jesse to the window. "Why are we going in this direction?"

"To take pictures of the dragon," Jesse said.

Tori blinked at him. "What?"

"Booker was far enough away that the EMP didn't affect his equipment," Jesse explained as though that's where her confusion came from. "His camera still works."

Tori watched the trees flash into and out of the van's headlights. Everything else was dark. "Why do we need pictures of a dead dragon?" Her voice came out high-pitched, but she didn't care. She wanted to get as far away from this place as possible. "We already know what it looks like."

Jesse leaned back against his seat, and rubbed his hand across his forehead tiredly. "The pictures aren't for us. They're to send to the news outlets and the government."

Rosa twisted around in her seat so she could join the conversation. "Once everyone sees proof that dragons exist and people realize they're connected to the power outage, the government will have to do something. They'll form some sort of task force to fight them."

Tori had supposed that somebody else had already gotten pictures. So many people had cell phones with cameras, and who wouldn't take a picture if they saw a dragon flying overhead? But then again, it was in the middle of the night in a remote place. The dragon had flown over quickly and in the dark. Only cameras that were set up for low light and distant action shots would have been able to capture a picture of the dragon—and even if someone had been outside with one of those cameras, poised and ready, chances were the EMP would have destroyed the camera anyway.

In other words, there probably weren't any pictures of the dragon.

Tori leaned her head back and stifled a groan. A person should only be required to be brave for so long and she'd reached her limit. She wanted to go somewhere safe and curl up and sleep. "I thought you didn't want to tell the government about the dragons," she said.

"We want the government to know about the dragons," Jesse said. "We just don't want them to know about *us*. There wasn't a way to do one without the other before. But now we can submit the pictures anonymously. That way, the government will work on ways to fight the dragons without endangering us in the process."

He and Rosa seemed so happy about this that Tori couldn't complain anymore about their return trip, but she watched the passing trees with a growing dread. Hadn't anyone else in this van ever watched a horror film? You always thought the monster was dead and then somehow it managed to get back up one last time to tear someone's head off.

And okay, those were just movies, but still. The sanest thing would be to drive as fast as they could back to camp.

When the van got close to the area where they'd fought the dragon, Booker slowed down and cut the headlights. Since the traffic lights had been destroyed by the EMP, the van was plunged into darkness. Booker put his infrared glasses on and kept driving. He may have been able to see, but no one else could, and Tori found herself gripping the edge of her seat. It was no use telling herself that the dragon obviously wasn't alive or she would have her powers back. It wasn't the dragon she was worrying about now. It was Overdrake. He wouldn't leave the dragon sitting there for people to find. He would come back for it. In all likelihood he was already there. And they were driving right to him.

# CHAPTER 42

Dirk's head was throbbing even before Booker stopped the van and threw it into reverse. No one asked why. They didn't need infrared glasses to see what Booker had seen. Down the road, a truck was stopped and shining its headlights on the lifeless form of the dragon. Two large cranes and a flatbed semi completed the semicircle in the road.

Some of his father's men were getting the cranes in position to lift the dragon onto the flatbed.

"I don't think anyone saw us," Booker said as he guided the van backward, out of sight of any headlights.

"Pull off on the side of the road." Dr. B twisted in his seat, checking the windows. "We don't want to be hit from behind."

Dirk knew what Dr. B would say next. He and Jesse were the fastest runners of the group and Jesse was already worn out. That meant the job would fall to him.

Sure enough, Dr. B handed Dirk Booker's night-vision goggles and the camera. The long telephoto lens was already attached. "Get as close as you can without being seen."

Dirk nodded. As he made his way to the door, he thought about handing the equipment to Kody and asking him to do it instead. But that sort of request would raise questions, and Dirk wanted to answer questions even less than he wanted to take pictures. So he said nothing and got out for the third time that night.

He jogged into the cover of the trees until he was hidden from sight of the van, then took off the infrared glasses and let them hang around his neck. He stepped into the air and glided, flying just a few inches off the ground, so his footsteps wouldn't make noises that his father's men might hear.

Dragon lords could fly longer than Slayers, and his powers hadn't worn off yet.

He'd always kept his ability to fly a secret. He didn't want to draw attention to himself by having two powers, and he didn't want people wondering why he could fly and yet wasn't Jesse's counterpart. But now that Tori knew she could fly, would she put the pieces together? She must have wondered how he got on the roof so quickly.

He shook his head. He was still trying to figure out just what her power of flight meant.

He would have thought that she came from a dragon lord line and wasn't a Slayer at all—the dragon lords' powers were close enough to the Slayers' that Dirk had been able to masquerade as one for years.

But that didn't make sense, either. Women hardly ever inherited the gene that allowed them access to a dragon lord's powers. His own sister hadn't inherited it. His aunts hadn't either. You had to look a long ways back in the records to find any women dragon lords. And besides, Tori was the same age as the Slayers, and her powers faded at the same time. If they'd remained longer, she certainly would have mentioned it.

He didn't think about the mystery for long. The dragon came into view. His dragon. Tamerlane. Named for the medieval conqueror of Western, South, and Central Asia.

Dirk's stomach lurched, clenching with anger and sadness all over again.

His father had undoubtedly thought it was a fitting punishment to attack the Slayers with Tamerlane—the dragon Dirk took care of, connected with, and rode. Dirk had had to choose whether to help kill his own dragon or see it destroy his friends.

Once a dragon lord established a mind link with a dragon, it was nearly impossible to sever, even by another dragon lord. Dirk had only managed it one time tonight—when Tamerlane chased Tori into the foliage. The dragon would have killed her if Dirk hadn't turned it away. And Dirk had probably only managed to do it then because the dragon had been his, because he'd slipped into Tamerlane's mind so many times before.

Dirk focused the camera lens on the limp form sprawled across the road. The car headlights spotlighted the dragon's neck and back so that his face was half-hidden in shadows. Dirk didn't need the light to see Tamerlane clearly, though. Every line and curve had been etched into his memory long ago.

Dirk would never experience the raw power of Tamerlane's mind again, the feeling that he had bridled a lightning bolt. Dirk already felt the emptiness of that fact.

He took several pictures, then moved farther down the tree line and took some more. It was ironic, because he had wanted to take pictures of the dragons since he was old enough to know what a camera did, but his father had never allowed it. Now Dirk was being forced to do it when he didn't want to.

Dirk switched the camera to video and slowly moved farther along the road. If he didn't bring back good footage, Dr. B would probably come out here himself, making enough noise in the process that he'd end up getting shot.

As hard as this was, Dirk had chosen his side tonight. He had to see it through.

The men had finished attaching chains to the dragon. One of the men signaled to the cranes and the machines let out a grinding protest. Thirty tons fought against the chains, but slowly the dragon was dragged, lifted upward toward the semi's open bed. Tamerlane's head flopped. The lifeless eyes seemed to stare in Dirk's direction.

Dirk looked away and turned off the camera.

It didn't matter that, had his father commanded it, Tamerlane would have attacked and killed Dirk without a second thought. It didn't matter that loyalty between a dragon lord and dragon could only be one-sided. Dragons didn't form attachments for other dragons, let alone people. Still, Dirk wished he could have connected to Tamerlane one last time, to try to explain, to apologize.

It was a stupid thought. He might as well try to explain the years of intrigue and divided loyalty to his horse. Animals couldn't understand because only people did this sort of thing to themselves.

Dirk hoped the video was long enough to satisfy Dr. B. He turned away from his father's men and headed to the van.

# CHAPTER 43

It seemed to Tori that the trip back to camp took forever. This was partially because they drove to D.C. first. Booker got out at an all-night Internet cafe. He was going to download the video and send it to as many news sources as possible, along with the address of Overdrake's compound. Booker would also send the files to several departments in the Pentagon, and offer to give them information, as well.

The trip also took longer because Dr. B drove in a roundabout way, making sure no one had followed them. Before Booker had gotten out, he and Dr. B had talked in hushed voices about whether it was even safe to go back to camp. Did the fact that Overdrake knew so much about them also mean he knew where the camp was? Could he already be planning an attack there?

A call to Shirley reassured them that nothing strange had turned up on any of the camp monitors. With the Slayers' weapons and equipment already there, and with cameras set up to warn them of incoming danger, Dr. B and Booker finally decided camp was still one of the safest places to be.

About half an hour after they'd left D.C. Tori fell asleep sitting up. The jostling of the van made her head slide sideways onto Jesse's shoulder. She jerked awake, said a groggy, "Sorry," and sat back up.

He gave her a smile. "It's okay. I don't mind. You need some sleep." He had taken off his jacket to use as a pillow against the window, and he leaned back into it, shutting his eyes. Her head probably didn't bother him that much. Besides, she wasn't the only one using a guy as a headrest. In the seat behind them, Lilly was nestled into Shang's side. Her blonde hair cascaded down his arm as she slept.

Tori leaned against Jesse's shoulder, relaxing into him and inhaling the smoky scent of his clothes. She enjoyed the warmth from his body underneath her cheek so much that it made her feel a little bit wicked. He had most likely only offered his shoulder to be polite, and she was memorizing the smell of his clothes like some stalker.

A moment later she opened her eyes, positive Dirk was staring at her.

He rolled his eyes at her, then turned away.

She blushed, hating how transparent the whole counterpart thing made her. Then she wondered if Jesse could sense that she liked snuggling up against him. Probably. And he probably thought she was an idiot, too, but was too nice to show it.

She didn't think about it for long. She drifted back to sleep and the next thing she knew, the van had stopped and Jesse was shaking her awake. They were in the camp parking lot. The sun was up, infusing the world with color again, and the clock on the dashboard read 6:35.

Dr. B took the keys from the ignition and slipped them into his pocket. Dirt smudged his sleeves and face. "Leave any equipment you have in the van. You can go to your cabins and get some sleep. We'll meet at one o'clock in the Dragon Hall for lunch."

Tori climbed out of the van, the chain rattling with every step she took. As she walked across the parking lot, Theo came up beside her. "I can get that collar off in my shop now."

She nodded and followed him toward the main office where the carts waited. It felt odd to be walking through camp in the daylight—the group of them dressed in black and Tori dragging a huge chain connected to her waist. She wound some of the chain around one arm. It wasn't much less conspicuous. Fortunately, it was early enough in the morning that no one would be around to see them.

Dirk walked a little ways ahead of her. When she caught sight of his back, she quickened her pace to catch up with him. The sick feeling she'd had last night had gone, like a memory that didn't quite make sense. She assumed Dirk's connection to the dragon had stopped bothering him, too, but when she reached him she could tell by the set of his jaw and the tenseness in his eyes that he was in a dark mood about something.

"Are you all right?" she asked.

He nodded, looking at the trees, not at her.

"I never thanked you for saving my life back on the enclosure roof."

He momentarily glanced at her. "No problem."

"I would say I hope to return the favor someday, but that seems like wishing something bad on you."

He let out a grunt. "Heaven knows, I don't need that." His dark mood flickered and a smile lifted the corner of his lips. "I guess you'll just have to be in my debt."

Before she came up with an answer to that, Dr. B called out, "I need to talk to the captains."

Dirk said, "Later," then walked over to where Dr. B stood. Jesse was already there waiting.

Tori slowed her pace and let her gaze linger on them. Dr. B spoke in a hushed tone, his eyes on Dirk. Judging by the stern line of Dirk's brow, he didn't like what Dr. B said. She was watching them so intently she didn't notice Cole and David—the guys she'd met on her first day of camp—until she went right by them. They stood by the trail in shorts and T-shirts, warming up for a run.

"Hey," Cole said, eyeing her from head to toe. "You're up early."

"Yeah, you are, too." She considered trying to hide the chain, but he'd already seen it, and besides, she had nowhere to put it.

"What are you guys doing?" David asked, looking directly at the dragon collar around her waist.

"We were . . . um . . . doing some camp stuff. Metal working. Making chains. I thought this was a nice fashion statement . . . that doubles as a philosophical statement. Because we're all chained to something."

David stared at her, unconvinced. "Uh-huh."

The Slayers had passed by and she knew she'd have to hurry to catch up. "So, uh, I'll see you later."

Cole raised one eyebrow. "Hey, you remember when you asked me if I thought anything weird was going on in this camp and I told you no?"

"Yeah," she said.

"I've changed my mind."

She laughed like he was joking, even though he probably wasn't, and then hurried to catch up with Theo.

At lunchtime, Tori sat beside Bess, Rosa, and Jesse. As they ate, everyone at the table either talked about the events of last night or made guesses as to what the news had reported. Rosa was nearly beside herself with curiosity. She asserted that every news show and Internet blog must be talking about the dragon, and she wanted to know whether people were more afraid, fascinated, or—hopefully not—sad.

Wouldn't it just be their luck if the government tried to find and prosecute them for killing a dragon.

Dirk sat on the opposite end of the table with Kody and Shang. Although Tori tried to talk to him a couple of times, he hardly looked at her. She wanted to tell him, "Hey, I figured out another counterpart ability. I can tell when you're purposely ignoring me." But it wasn't the time for those sorts of observations.

While Jesse was busy talking with the others, Tori stared at him, concentrating to see what her counterpart sense could reveal about him. As it turned out, not much. Probably because she couldn't untangle her emotions for him. All she really learned was that he could tell when she stared at him. He kept glancing at her and then she had to pretend she was actually staring at something over his shoulder. Like, hey, what a cool cinderblock wall.

Before long, Dr. B came in. His hair was a wild mess of gray and his clothes were rumpled. If he'd slept, it must not have been for long.

He set a pile of paper on the end of the table. "Let's do a quick review of last night's mission, and then I'll give you the update."

More than one impatient moan went up from the Slayers. Rosa put her chin in her hand. "Can't you tell us about the news stories first?"

"We won't improve," Dr. B said, "unless we know where we need to improve."

Grudgingly, the group talked about what they had done, hadn't done, and should have done.

Tori felt awkward through most of the analysis since a lot of it related to her. When Overdrake captured her, she'd inadvertently put both Dirk and Jesse in jeopardy. But she had also came up with the solution to kill the dragon, a solution that hadn't been in any of the Slayers' drills or strategies.

She wondered how often life was like that, how often chance events decided the outcome.

The discussion changed to what Overdrake had done, hadn't done, and where he could be getting his information from. The group threw out the same sort of theories they'd discussed in the van last night, but nothing explained the inconsistencies. If Overdrake had an informant in camp, why hadn't he attacked before now? And if he did have an informant, who was it? Could one of the regular campers have come down to the Slayer camp without being seen by the cameras and planted bugs in the cabins that were so sophisticated Theo's sensors hadn't detected them?

Tori told them everything Overdrake had said to her, including his "Know thyself" remark. She hoped somebody would shed some light on his comment, but it didn't make sense to anyone else, either.

"It was just another one of his insults," Bess said, fluttering her hand to erase the subject. "I mean, seriously, Overdrake wouldn't tell you anything about his source."

Bess was right, but Tori still knew the phrase would rattle around her brain for an annoying long time. *Know thyself.* She *did* know herself and *she* wasn't the informant.

When they'd finished with that subject, Dr. B gave them the first piece of bad news. "Booker went back to Winchester this morning to scope out the compound. The entire thing has been abandoned. We have no idea where Overdrake is or where he took the dragon eggs and the remaining dragon."

Kody put his sandwich down long enough to speak up. "If he had another dragon, wouldn't he have used it last night? We never would have won against two."

"I doubt," Dr. B said wryly, "that Overdrake thought you had a chance against one. And he can only connect with one dragon at a time. He probably didn't want the liability of having an uncontrolled dragon around while he's still trying to keep their existence a secret."

Dr. B paused as though even he wasn't sure this explained the lack of the second dragon. "Although, quite frankly, I always assumed Overdrake had children who would help him when he attacked." Dr. B tapped his fingers against the table, mentally sifting through possibilities. "But Overdrake might be childless, or his children might be too young to help him, or perhaps they just didn't inherit the right genes. Whatever the case, until we know differently, we have to assume he not only has the eggs, but another dragon, as well."

Dr. B picked up the stack of papers he'd put at the end of the table. "As far as the news stories go . . ." He flipped through the papers, grimacing. "The local station reported the power outages and damage to electronics in certain parts of Winchester, but the major news outlets are ignoring the dragon story. Booker didn't even get any calls requesting more information. Not from the news, not from the government."

"What?" Bess asked. Her mouth remained open in disbelief.

"That can't be right," Rosa said. "Some people must have seen the dragon. They must have called to report it, too."

Dr. B nodded. "A few dragon sightings were reported on the radio and we uploaded our video onto YouTube. The general consensus is that it's some sort of publicity stunt or hoax and that people who believe in dragons are . . ." He looked down at one of the papers and read, "either a few boxcars short of a full train, or pathetic individuals who'll claim anything in order to have five minutes of attention."

"Who said that?" Kody asked. "I want to show them what five minutes of my attention feels like."

Bess crossed her arms. "And I want to show them where they can put their boxcars."

Dr. B raised a hand to silence the group. "The tabloids, at least, realize something strange went on." He held up printouts from websites. Two proclaimed UFOs had flown over Virginia. A third stated that a terrorist group had done a test run of an EMP weapon. He dropped those onto the table and held up the last printout. "Only one tabloid used our pictures."

Underneath the headline "Medieval Beast Discovered!" a picture showed the dragon, head down, sprawled out on the ground. It looked indistinct, as though the image was made out of imagination and Photoshop.

Dr. B dropped the paper onto the table with the others. "They ran the story, but since they're also currently reporting on a horse boy and psychic vampires, I doubt anyone will pay much attention to it."

Lilly put her drink down with a forceful thud. "How stupid can people be? They saw a dragon flying overhead and thought it was a UFO? How many UFOs flap their wings?"

Dr. B tapped the pile of printouts. "According to the *Weekly Globe News*, one. That's part of their article. 'New alien technology.'" He let out a tired sigh and ran a hand through his hair. "It's amazing how people see only what they believe is possible."

Rosa blinked, her brown eyes nearly wilting. "So the government still won't help us. No one will."

"Our objective," Dr. B said softly, "has always been to see how many people we can help, not to see how many will help us."

Lilly pushed her plate away. "Yeah, because we already know how many people will help us. None. Overdrake is right. People only care about themselves. Why in the world are we risking our lives for them?"

For a moment, no one said anything and Tori wondered if a lot of the Slayers felt the same way. They had all risked their lives last night. Any one of them could have died. In fact, it was only by a stroke of luck that they hadn't all been killed. Was it too much to ask that someone out there at least care?

Dr. B rested his hands against the table. "Do you think you're the only selfless people around? Would you say those sorts of things to foster parents, firefighters, or soldiers?"

"No," Lilly said sullenly, "but at least they get paid every month."

Dr. B straightened. "The reason we live in a free country is because enough people thought freedom was worth fighting for. The day we lose that selflessness is the day this country will fall."

Lilly picked at a potato chip on her plate. "I'm not going to pull a Leo and Danielle. I just wish for once someone else out there would be selfless and give me a break."

"One thing that last night taught us," Dr. B said, "is that this fight will be harder than we realized." His gaze swept slowly over them. "In order to succeed, we need every single one of you. And . . ." His voice dropped. "We need Ryker, too." He looked past the group off into the distance and shook his head. "I thought for certain he would have contacted me by now, but, well, hopefully we'll hear from him before the dragons hatch."

No one commented on the likelihood of that. It seemed like a faint hope. Anything could have happened to Ryker. He could have died in infancy. But then again, that didn't mean there wasn't another Slayer out there. Tori had found her way to camp. Someone else might, too.

Ryker. Ryker. The name repeated in her mind like a prayer.

Dr. B glanced at his watch. "On to the next item of business. As you know, our location may be compromised. I have staff monitoring the surveillance cameras, but it isn't a long-term solution. After we're through here, I want you to pack up your things and take them to the van. I'm moving you to a backup location for the rest of the month. We'll set up our spare simulator there so you can finish your camp training."

Several people asked, "Where?" and "How far away is it?"

But Dr. B shook his head to indicate he wasn't answering. "You'll see when we get there." He picked up his computer printouts, tucked them under his arm, and as he turned to go, he said, "Tori, can I see you for a minute?"

She stood up and followed him, feeling everyone's eyes on her. He didn't speak until they got outside. By then she was convinced he was either going to give her some sort of talk about how she needed to get up to speed fast, or he was going to tell her the van didn't have room for all of her stuff and she'd have to leave some behind.

Instead of stopping outside and delivering a speech, Dr. B walked along the trail that led to the stables. "I'm going to see Leo's and Danielle's horses before we load them onto the trailers. They've both grown listless since their riders didn't come this summer." He reached into his pocket and pulled out a couple of carrots for her to see. "I try to give them extra attention when I can."

Tori walked beside him, waiting for him to say more.

"Bane is much happier since you've come," he said. "He was the despondent one in summers past."

A wave of guilt hit Tori. She hadn't even known the horse existed, and it had been pining for her. "He's a great horse. I'll give him lots of attention this summer. And I'll ride Leo's and Danielle's horses, too, if you think it will help."

He smiled at her approvingly. "You're very thoughtful."

She didn't answer him. He was only being nice.

"Thoughtfulness is a necessary trait for a captain," he said.

Oh, no. He couldn't want that from her. "I'm not a captain," she said.

His pace slowed. "But once you're trained, you will be. You're a flyer. The flyers have to go after the dragon, so they're best able to direct the battle. The A-team needs you."

"No," she said, a feeling of horror rushing over her. "Dirk is the captain. It's his job."

"And he'll continue to do it until you're ready. I imagine that will take a while. For now, you'll stay on Team Magnus and Jesse will train you."

She relaxed, but only a little. She still had time to convince Dr. B that she wasn't suited for the job. Lilly and Alyssa weren't going to want her as their captain. Ditto for Dirk. "Does Dirk know?" she asked, but even as she said the words, she knew he did. That was why he'd barely talked to her since they got back to camp, why he hadn't looked at her during lunch.

She realized with relief, and also with a surprising amount of disappointment, that her ability to fly had ended their very short romance. Dirk wouldn't have romantic feelings for the girl who was forcing him out of his place as captain. He was the type who didn't like taking orders; he wouldn't want to take them from her.

"Dirk has always known flyers were best suited for captains," Dr. B said. "His team just didn't have that option before now. He'll step aside graciously when it's time."

Right. Tori had no idea how to be a Slayer, let alone a captain, and Dirk was supposed to turn his team over to her? He wouldn't want to do it. Not this summer, not any summer.

CHAPTER 44

The Slayers rode an hour through bumpy back roads to the new location. The cabins didn't look much different from the ones they'd left, except these had bars across the windows. The new Dragon Hall was just a covered pavilion with a generator where a mechanical dragon could be hooked up. There was no shooting range, and the stables were so close to the rest of camp that Tori was sure the smell of manure would waft over. But at least they didn't have to worry about Overdrake finding them. Not even the Slayers knew where they were.

The cabins were full of dust, cobwebs, and rodent droppings. A couple of bats had taken up residence in the shower stalls, and the guys seemed downright happy to find a snake lounging in one of their dressers. They threatened to keep the thing as a pet until Rosa launched into a speech about the dangers of venom and Bess swore she would personally kill anyone who lost any powers because they'd messed around with a snake.

When Booker arrived with the first horse trailer, Tori went to help him get the horses situated. Bane nipped at any horse that got too close, but he settled down when Tori took his reins and obediently followed her to a stall.

As she walked out of the stable door, she came face-to-face with Dirk leading his horse in. It was the first time they'd been alone together all day and for an awkward moment they just stared at each other. Then Tori blurted out, "I don't want to be captain."

He nodded and gave her a wry smile. "I'm glad you told me. I was wondering what you wanted."

She ignored the innuendo. "You should be captain. We'll just have to make Dr. B see reason."

"Yeah, good luck with that. You might not have noticed this yet, but reason doesn't change that many things in life."

"We can still try. You'll always be better for the job."

He fixed her with a serious gaze. His mouth opened to speak, but then he shut it again, changing his mind about whatever he had been about to say. Instead, he reached out and put his hand on her arm. "I don't blame you for this, Tori. You and I—we're counterparts."

It felt too intimate standing here with him like this. Their automatic familiarity could be a bad thing, she realized. His gaze could suck her right into its blue depths without much thought or effort on his part. "We're counterparts," she agreed, "but I can fly, so I must be Jesse's counterpart too, right?"

Dirk dropped his hand from her arm and tugged on his horse's reins. "I'll see you later." Without another word, he walked past her. She watched him go and had to stifle the urge to call him back. She wished she had been able to say something that made him happier.

When they ate dinner under the cool, wall-less shade of the pavilion, Dirk talked and laughed with the others, but not her. He only looked at her once. His eyes held onto hers with an intensity that made it hard to breathe. She could only stare back at him, trying to read the emotion in his eyes. Was it a challenge, a longing, or something else? He turned away before she could tell.

Jesse looked at her a lot, measuring her responses to everyone else. She wasn't sure why, but it didn't surprise her that he waited for her to finish eating even after everyone else had left. When she was finally done with her dinner, he walked beside her along the trail that led to the cabins.

"Can I talk to you?" he asked.

"Sure," she said.

"Not here." He took her hand and pulled her upward. At first she stayed on the ground, not sure how to transition into flying, but he pulled her harder and she moved upward, following him like the tail of a kite.

"Dr. B told me to help you practice flying," he said, and led her off the trail into the curtain of the forest.

The sailed lazily around the trees, floating higher into the scent of fresh leaves. The wind tingled through her hair, streaming it out behind her. She reached out her free hand, caressing the air.

A rush of happiness hit Tori. She could enjoy flying now. She wasn't fleeing from Overdrake's compound or avoiding a dragon's jaws, she was just soaring, like the times she flew in her dreams—but it was better, because Jesse held her hand. The world was lush and growing, peaceful.

Jesse made a sharp turn downward and then shot up. Tori laughed because it felt like she'd just come off a waterslide.

Next he somersaulted, switching direction and flew face-upward. After a few moments, he spun back onto his stomach and let go of her hand. "Okay, now let's see you do a somersault by yourself."

She weaved around the trees in front of her and tried to slow down. "I already have a huge bruise on my hip. Do I really need a matching concussion?"

He followed her, floating a few feet above her. "You can do it. Come on, try."

"I don't know how to stop yet and you want me to do tricks?"

"Try," he urged.

She bent into a turn and ended up heading straight to the ground.

He dived after her, grabbed her hand, and led her through a flip so she flew upward again. Then he pulled her to a stop. They hovered in the air, and he led her over to a sturdy tree branch. In one graceful movement, he swung himself onto the bough, then motioned for her to follow. She pulled herself to the branch, much less gracefully, and sat between him and the tree trunk. The bark was rough and poked into her legs.

"You'll get the hang of it soon," he said.

She gripped the trunk and peered down at the ground below them. It looked so far away. "How did you manage to learn to fly by yourself?" she asked.

"It's innate. Your problem is you're overthinking it right now." He reached out and took her hand from the trunk. "You don't have to worry about falling, you know."

"Right," she said. She forced herself to stop looking down. It was better to look into Jesse's brown eyes anyway.

Of course, as soon as she did, she couldn't think of anything to say.

"So," he said, drawing the word out, "is something going on between you and Dirk?"

Her cheeks flushed. It wasn't a question she wanted to answer. She had expected Jesse to talk about flying. "Why do you ask?"

Jesse hesitated. "He's acting strange."

"He doesn't like the idea of me replacing him as captain." Tori let out a sigh. "Which makes two of us, because I don't want to be captain." But the answer didn't feel like the truth. She fiddled with the bark underneath her fingertips. "And well, okay, he did kiss me yesterday, but I don't think it meant anything to him."

Jesse arched his eyebrows, processing this piece of information. He shifted on the tree limb so he could see her better. "Why do you think it didn't mean anything to him?"

She felt herself blushing. "Because it was a spur of the moment thing. He was trying to see if I could read his mind . . ." On second thought, she didn't want to go into the details. "Dirk just seems like the kind of guy who kisses girls without thinking much about it; somebody who rotates through girls quickly." She paused. "Am I right about that?"

Jesse shrugged. "He's had a lot of girlfriends."

"You're not like that. I mean, about kissing girls without thinking about it." Tori suddenly felt as though she'd said too much. She flicked a nearby leaf to give her hands something to do.

"I'm not like that," he agreed.

Neither of them said anything for a moment. Out in the forest, a pair of birds chased each other around the trees. The sun had gone down far enough that a pattern of mottled shadows spread out across the forest floor.

Jesse's gaze didn't leave her face. "Dirk came after you when Overdrake captured you. He wouldn't have done that if he didn't like you."

"He was helping out a fellow Slayer," Tori said. "You came after me, too. That doesn't mean you like me." She turned to see his expression, to see him agree.

Instead, Jesse stared back at her. "That might not be the best example to prove your point."

"What do you mean?"

He regarded her without speaking. His eyes were warm. "I didn't come after you just to help out a fellow Slayer."

Her heart made several short, frantic beats. She *hadn't* imagined everything between her and Jesse. After a moment's hesitation, she reached out and put her hand over his. The feel of his skin made her fingertips tingle.

He looked at her hand and didn't move. "Dr. B has always said we shouldn't get romantically involved with one another. It could lead to problems on the team. Favoritism. Clouded judgment."

"Oh." She removed her hand and tried to pretend his sentence hadn't sliced her to the core. "I guess that makes sense."

"Plus, we're only going to be together one month out of the year. We're not supposed to keep in contact with each other outside of camp."

"Okay," she said, stung again.

"And we're from completely different social spheres."

How many reasons did he plan on giving her? "Okay," she said. "I get it."

"And political spheres. You're dad's a Republican senator, my parents are Democrats."

Tori folded her arms, angry enough that she forgot she was perched high in a tree. "Do you really need to keep listing reasons why I'm not right for you?"

"Yeah," he said. "If I keep going, maybe I'll convince myself."

His answer instantly dissolved her anger. She smiled and put her hand over his again, this time tracing the length of his fingers with one of her own.

"You're not making this easier," he said.

"Good." After she made lazy circles on the back of his hand, she twined her fingers through his.

He let out a sigh that was almost a groan, then took her hand and pulled her closer. Time slowed. The wind whipped a strand of hair across her face, and he brushed it away, letting his fingers linger on her cheek. Then he leaned over and kissed her.

It felt like victory.

She melted into him, forgetting they were in a tree, forgetting about the work ahead of them, forgetting everything except the fact that his lips were on hers. She wound her arms around his neck and leaned closer, letting her fingers brush against the back of his hair. She wished this moment could go on forever. Jesse holding her. The soft caress of his lips.

Finally, he lifted his head. "You should be glad you can fly."

She smiled back at him. "Why?"

"Because if you couldn't, you would have fallen out of this tree."

She looked down. She wasn't sitting on the branch anymore. Sometime during their kiss, she'd slid off and was hovering in front of him, unsupported. She reached out, grabbed hold of the branch, and pulled herself back over. "Yeah, that would have been awkward to fall to my death while you kissed me."

He took hold of her hand and gave it a squeeze. "I'm going to have a great time teaching you how to fly."

"Good," she said. "I liked my first lesson."

He pushed off the branch, pulling her with him. They glided hand in hand around trees and through patches of sunlight. *This is wonderful,* she thought, and the next moment she heard a voice in her head, near the dragon's heartbeat. She enlarged the sound while she threaded through a maze of branches.

"Hello, Tori," Overdrake murmured. "I know you can hear me. Isn't that convenient? I can chat with you whenever I want. I can make you listen to whatever I want. So many possibilities. I'm deciding which is better—my CD of fingernails scraping blackboards, or the Bee Gees' greatest hits. Maybe I'll play them both.

"But here's the thing I want to say first. You killed one of my dragons. I'm not going to forget that. Granted, in the long run you did me a service. You showed me that the dragons have a weakness I didn't know about." He let out a laugh that held no amusement. "If there's one thing I can't abide, it's weakness. So rest assured, I'll fix that problem. You won't be able to choke any more of my dragons. And here's a message to pass on to all of your little friends: Stay out of my way from now on, or I'll crush every single one of you."

Then the beginning verse of the song "Staying Alive" jolted into her ears.

Wow, a bunch of guys singing falsetto badly. She could see Overdrake's point about that CD.

She minimized the sound, but Jesse must have seen the effect Overdrake's speech had on her. He slowed down, waiting for her.

"What's wrong?"

She was not about to let Overdrake's threats ruin this outing with Jesse. There would be time to pass on Overdrake's message later. "Nothing," Tori said, and let go of Jesse's hand. She was getting the hang of flying now. She didn't need to propel herself through motions. It worked through vision and a part of her heart wanting to go a certain direction; that's what steered her. She grinned over at him. "I bet you can't catch me," she said, and darted off into the forest.

Jesse followed after her, and proved her wrong.

CHAPTER 45

Ryker Davis was finishing up work on the simulator when his cousin, Willow, walked into the basement. She had been at his house since the start of summer, but he still wasn't used to having her pop in and talk to him. Most of the time she stayed holed up in her room reading, and he forgot she was around. Then she would finish a book and be there, a flurry of chattiness, until she started a new novel and disappeared again.

Even now, she carried her Kindle in one hand, absently fingering it while she walked toward him. She was tall and graceful—willowy— which was a good thing, because it would be hard to live down a name like Willow if you were short and dumpy. She sat down on the stepstool next to him.

"Just so you know, you need a better password on your Web site."

He attached a transmitter circuit on the simulator's bread board, barely looking at her. "I don't have a Web site."

"What you mean is, you don't want your parents to know you have a Web site. You're going to be in trouble when they find this." She flashed her Kindle screen at him, showing the Internet home page for RykerDavis.com. The title proclaimed: All You Ever Wanted to Know About Ryker Davis.

Oh. That Web site. He should have known that was what she was talking about.

Ryker's dog, Griffin, trotted over to Willow and nudged her hand, a clear request to be petted. Griffin—named because he was a mixture of who knew what—hated most people, but adored Willow. Probably because she couldn't resist cooing and petting him anytime he was around. She scratched his ears as she scanned RykerDavis.com.

"So, do you have any juicy secrets you reveal on your not-so-well-hidden Web site?"

"It's not my Web site," he said, checking the simulator's power output. He needed more power, better batteries, and made a mental note to buy some the next time he went out. "There's more than one Ryker Davis in the world, you know."

"Yeah, and your parents might buy that story if you had a better password." She tilted her chin down patronizingly, making her dark blond hair spill over her shoulder. "I mean, come on. The hint is: What animal does Ryker dream about?" She let out a disparaging grunt. "It took me two tries. Once 'hot women' didn't work, I knew it had to be dragons."

He placed the circuit board inside the simulator's chassis, centering it perfectly. "For your information, I mostly dream about snowboarding, or if it's summer—hang gliding." He shot Willow a grin. "Okay—I confess—sometimes I dream of hang gliding with hot women."

Willow nodded philosophically. "Well, that's all I ever wanted to know about Ryker Davis." She scrolled down the page and paused to read some of the entry titles. "Although you're unaware of it, you belong to an elite group called the Slayers. . . ." She stopped petting Griffin and looked up at Ryker. "Dang. I was hoping it would tell me your secret to acing math tests."

"My secret is I'm smart."

She silently read for another minute, then said, "What is this anyway? Some kind of interactive novel?"

He looked around for his toolbox. "Seriously, Will. I didn't write any of it. I've read it, but I didn't write it." He spotted the box next to the step stool and held his hand out to Willow. "Can you give me the Phillips screwdriver?"

She gazed down at the tools. "You named one of your screwdrivers Phillip? That's a clear sign you've been working on that thing for too long."

"Phillips is a type of screwdriver." Instead of explaining what kind it was, he walked over to the toolbox himself. Really, how could a girl reach the age of sixteen and not know what a Phillips screwdriver was? Granted, her parents weren't handy, but neither were his, and he'd been taking things apart all his life. "If I was going to name a screwdriver," Ryker said, "I wouldn't call it Phillips. That sounds like a butler. I would name it something manly, like Rodrigo." He picked up two screwdrivers from his toolbox and showed her the difference. "This is a flat one and this is Rodrigo, the screwdriver of doom."

"Hmm," she said. "Wouldn't it be easier to just make one kind of screw?"

He didn't have an answer for that, so he said, "Come, Rodrigo. It's time to make some screws do your bidding." Then he began attaching the circuit board to the card slot.

Willow went back to reading the Web site. He knew what she would find. He had read it enough times himself. He'd discovered the Web site two years ago when he'd Googled his name, and since then it had become a secret hobby of his to check and see what the mysterious Dr. B had posted. Dr. B updated it the first Sunday of every month, usually with some sort of message for Ryker. Well, not really for him. For a magical Ryker Davis that this Dr. B had invented. Still, it was pretty cool having a superhero named after him. Where else could you get personalized entertainment like that?

"Dr. B," Willow said, testing the name in her mouth. "I wonder what the B stands for. Batty? Bonkers? Bored beyond belief?"

Ryker didn't answer. He'd finished attaching the circuit board and was now screwing the panel in place.

"On second thought," Willow went on, "he probably used the letter B because X and Z had already been taken by the cool supervillains."

"Dr. B isn't the villain," Ryker said. "He's the good guy. Overdrake is the bad guy."

Griffin nudged Willow's hand, reminding her that he was still in need of a dog massage. She stroked his fur again. "There's a 'contact me' link after every single entry. What's that about? Does he ask for money to tell you how the story ends or something?"

"I don't know," Ryker said. "I've never contacted him. You know how my parents are about that kind of stuff. They think everybody is out to commit identity theft or worse."

Willow went back to surfing the Web site. When she drew in a sharp breath, he could guess which page she'd landed on. Her gaze ricocheted between the simulator and the specs on the Web site. "Are you actually building this guy's machine?"

"Maybe." Ryker hooked up the patch antenna, suddenly wishing he had gone with a cavity-back antenna instead. The specs said either would work and the patch antenna was cheaper, but maybe the cavity-back worked better.

Willow stood up to get a better look at the simulator. "Okay, I thought I was the ultimate dragon geek because I've written fan fiction for so many fantasy novels, but this . . ." She nodded at the machine. "This means you win."

Ryker straightened, pointing the screwdriver at his chest. "Excuse me, I'm not any sort of geek, dragon or otherwise."

"Says the guy who names his screwdrivers and is building a superhero machine."

"I was just curious to see if I could follow the specs on the site and actually build the thing." He couldn't bring himself to tell her the real reason he'd spent the last few weeks buying and constructing parts for the machine. As farfetched as it seemed, Ryker had begun to believe—well, maybe not believe, but at least entertain the possibility—that the Slayer and dragon stuff was true. He was the same age as the Ryker on the Web site. His parents had lived in Virginia when his mother was pregnant with him, just like the Web site said. It didn't add up to coincidence.

Who Dr. B was, what he wanted, and his level of sanity was another matter. Building this machine would at least rule out, or possibly confirm, the sanity issue.

With the antenna secure, Ryker stepped back and surveyed his creation. It was done. A simulator following the instructions that Dr. B had put on the Web site. "Are you ready to see what this thing does?" he asked. He hadn't expected to feel nervous about it and yet found that he was fidgeting with the screwdriver.

"Turn on the switch," Willow said.

Ryker did. Nothing noticeable happened. He couldn't even be sure it was actually running.

Willow pursed her lips. "I was expecting a little more magic."

Ryker turned it off, turned it on again, then picked up the printout of the specs and reread them. When he finally looked up at Willow, she was typing something into her Kindle. "There," she said.

"There what?" he asked.

"I just e-mailed Dr. B and told him that if he was going to save the country from the clutches of the dragon lord, he needed a better superhero machine."

Ryker nearly dropped the specs. "You e-mailed him?"

"Yeah. I told him I was the real Ryker Davis's cousin, and if he wanted you for a Slayer, you needed equipment that was more along the lines of the Batmobile."

She smiled at him, but he didn't return it.

"What's wrong?" she asked. "I'm sure the guy has a sense of humor." She motioned to her Kindle's screen. "I mean, look at the stuff he writes."

"Exactly," Ryker said. "He could be anybody. He could be some psycho." *He could be Overdrake, and the whole Web site is a trap to find me.*

It wasn't the most comforting thought. Even his subconscious was beginning to believe the Slayer stuff.

Willow tipped her head to the side. "It's not like I told him where I lived, or what my Social Security number is. I didn't even tell him my name."

"Yeah, you told him my name."

His words came out too sharply and she fluttered her eyelashes at him, hurt. "Well, he kind of already knew your name."

Ryker didn't say anything. He didn't know how to explain.

She shrugged and her voice was soothing, the same tone she used to calm Griffin down. "It's not like anyone is going to grab you off the street and shove you into a van. You're what? Seven feet tall? They don't make vans with that much headroom."

"I'm six-four," he said.

"Close enough. Besides, we'll probably never even hear back from Dr. Alphabet Letters." She looked down at her Kindle screen, her eyes suddenly wide. "Hey, look. He already emailed back."

"What?" Ryker asked. In two strides he had grabbed Willow's Kindle from her hands. Sure enough, there was a new e-mail with the subject line: Re: the simulator.

That had been fast.

He opened the e-mail and saw two sentences. Please tell Ryker it's imperative that he call me. We need to talk. *A phone number was listed next.*

When Ryker built the simulator he had wondered if he would feel anything. Now, he did. He felt like everything was about to change.

Thank you for reading
this **Feiwel and Friends** book.

the friends who made

SLAYERS

possible are:

JEAN FEIWEL, *publisher*

LIZ SZABLA, *editor-in-chief*

RICH DEAS, *creative director*

ELIZABETH FITHIAN, *marketing director*

HOLLY WEST, *assistant to the publisher*

DAVE BARRETT, *managing editor*

NICOLE LIEBOWITZ MOULAISON, *production manager*

KSENIA WINNICKI, *publishing associate*

ANNA ROBERTO, *editorial assistant*

FIND OUT MORE ABOUT OUR AUTHORS AND ARTISTS
AND OUR FUTURE PUBLISHING AT
MACTEENBOOKS.COM.

OUR BOOKS ARE FRIENDS FOR LIFE